— EXIT GRETCHEN —

also by G. Henry Hofer

THE EBOLA FACTOR

•

PASSING THE REINS
Volume I of The Sunhorses of Time

G. HENRY HOFER

Exit Gretchen

THE SUNHORSES OF TIME

VOLUME II

FITHIAN PRESS, SANTA BARBARA, CALIFORNIA, A.D. MM

Copyright © 2000 by G. Henry Hofer
All rights reserved
Printed in the United States of America

Published by Fithian Press
A division of Daniel and Daniel, Publishers, Inc.
Post Office Box 1525
Santa Barbara, CA 93102
www.danielpublishing.com

Cover painting: "Interior," by A. Moore,
collection of Mr. and Mrs. G. Henry Hofer

LIBRARY OF CONGRESS CATALOGING-IN-PUBLICATION DATA
Hofer, G. Henry (Gunter Henry), (date)
    Exit Gretchen / by G. Henry Hofer.
        p.   cm. — (The sunhorses of time ; vol. 2)
    ISBN 1-56474-321-7 (alk. paper)
    I. Title. II. Series: Hofer, G. Henry (Gunter Henry), (date)
Sunhorses of time ; v. 2.
PS3558.O34394E95   2000
813'.54—dc21   99-36032
                                             CIP

For Vera

ACKNOWLEDGMENTS

This story takes the reader around the Pacific Rim, from California to Hong Kong, to Indonesia, Singapore, and Australia. Our own travel experiences, Vera's and mine, were augmented by maps and literature generously provided by the host governments. Striving for authenticity, we drew from the expert knowledge of our friends, notably the travel writer and photographer couple of Eva and Bill Fremont, who were unstinting in sharing their own impressions with us.

This is also a story about art, the business thereof. Here authenticity had to share the spotlight with conjecture, because much of what really goes on in that field is cloaked in, shall we say, confidentiality. Still I had generous help when I asked for it, and I am indebted to the J. Paul Getty Museum for allowing me access to their research library, and to art dealer Suzanne W. Zada for vetting an important point in my manuscript.

The final responsibility is all mine, and for any mistakes and errors, however unintentional, the proverbial buck stops at my desk: Peccavi.

Contents

Part One: In America, Both Coasts
 The Gathering : 13
 The Divorce : 31
 The Getty Job : 48
 Making Ready : 64

Part Two: In Asia
 M.O. Riley : 83
 Hong Kong : 91
 Flight : 138

Part Three: In Australia
 Passage to Darwin : 165
 Magnetic Island : 192
 Neutral Bay : 217
 Road's End : 230
 Fiona : 253
 The Birthday : 273

PART ONE
In America, Both Coasts

― CHAPTER ONE ―

The Gathering

It was James Frazer, as the de facto head of the family, who had called the meeting. In his written invitation, faxed to all members of what he defined as "Gretchen's immediate family," and in his follow-up telephone calls, he stressed that the gathering not be tagged a *wake*. "For one thing," he said, "we are none of us Irish enough to hold a proper one, and in any case, this is not her funeral, but her birthday we want to observe. Her fiftieth, no less. She will be with us in spirit, and we all know she wouldn't like long faces and keening and rending and carrying on like that. Don't we? So please, clear your schedules. You have a month to plan for it: Friday the thirtieth of January. We'll meet at our house in Connecticut. Try to be here on the day before: we'll put you up, we have enough room. After all, we won't be a large crowd. Although probably a noisy one, what with four small kids keeping us busy."

James Frazer, member of the one hundred and fifth Congress of the United States from Connecticut, made these arrangements in the first week of January. He instructed his staff to clear his schedule for the weekend in question, as it would follow the president's State of the Union address and nothing much would be going on the rest of that week in the way of legislating. "Taking the long weekend off would not be a problem," in the words of his secretary.

It would indeed not be a large crowd that he and Nora would welcome to their Southport home. Their own family would make up the largest contingent: Jim and Nora plus their three small children, the five-year-old twins, Lillie and Helen and a boy, two-year-old Ian Malcolm, nicknamed Scot (with one "t," to stress his grandpaternal origins). The only other couple with a small child was the Winthrops, Reg and Dagmar, with their daughter, Inga, a pretty and precocious four-year-old. They flew up from Dallas, Texas, but opted to stay at the Westport Inn, down the road a way from the Frazer home. Dagmar and Reginald Winthrop were not related by blood to the Frazers, being in-laws of sorts by way of Jim Frazer's father, Ian, having married Charlotte, whose daughter, Dagmar, was from a prior marriage. This made Dagmar a step-sister of James and the lamented Gretchen. A lively and artistic woman, Dagmar had met her husband, Reg, through James after she was rescued some years back from a dangerous escapade while on a visit to St. Petersburg. James had been the rescuer—with a timely assist from his young brother, Duncan. Reg Winthrop had been the facilitator, if that is a fitting description of what a CIA station chief can do to help from the U.S. embassy in Paris. Afterwards the two couples had become close friends. Reg had resigned from government service after a brief but unsatisfying stint at Langley, and been hired by a Dallas firm specializing in security. He had become a senior analyst since then, with a salary several times what he had drawn as a civil servant. And even though Texas was far from the clamor and glamor, such as it was, of Washington, D.C., the money was good. And so was the Texas living.

James, in going over his list of invitees, shook his head; what a bunch.

Except for Gretchen, and of course his children, James had no direct blood relatives; everyone was step- or half-brother, or sister, or an in-law. It had all begun when their mother died back in 1975. Gretchen, the elder child, was already married and the mother of two small boys, and James was in graduate school. Their father, Ian, soon after—too soon, some felt—had met and married Charlotte, a divorcée with a daughter, and they had a son together. Dagmar and Duncan, half-brother and -sister. Step-sister and half-brother to James.

James ticked them off his list. They would show for the meeting.

Dagmar's mother, Charlotte, now Ian's widow, had married again: An old friend of the family, Stuart Rosenberg, who had been Ian Frazer's business partner and whose wife, Sonia, had died of cancer. It was a most agreeable match, two grieving friends slowly becoming close to one another and starting afresh one more time. They lived in Manhattan, where, they liked to explain, they enjoyed the many cultural advantages of New York without having to commute from their former Connecticut homes. When they agreed to come to the meeting they said that there would be no need for them to stay overnight; they'd take the train on Friday morning and return that way in the evening, unless it became too late for some reason. However, they had invited the Winthrops to come to Manhattan and spend the weekend after the meeting with them before returning to Texas. It was Charlotte's great desire to spend time with little Inga as often as possible; she doted on her only grandchild.

Grandchildren to be visited was also the main reason that Nora's mother, Clem Patullo, and her longtime friend Trummy Trumbull were eager to come around from their home on Long Island, and why Nora had thought to invite them. The honoree, Gretchen Goodridge, lived in Southern California, but being Jim's sister she had been at all the christenings and at some of the holidays in recent years. Clementine Patullo was Jim's mother-in-law; where Gretchen Goodridge had a right to be with the Frazers, Clem had the right as well, only more so, she thought. So Clem and her near-husband Trummy—who would have been her real husband were it not for certain Trumbull trust provisions—would drive over to attend. They'd make the most of the opportunity to visit and would stay in their accustomed digs, the converted coachmen's quarters above the former stables, now the garage of the Southport house.

Also staying at the house would be Gretchen's two sons. George Goodridge would be flying in from Frankfurt, where he was currently on a General Motors fellowship at the Opel works in Rüsselsheim. His younger brother, Frederick, would fly in from Southern California, where he was finishing up his B.Sc. degree at U.C. San Diego. Their father, Wilfred Goodridge, who had divorced his wife abruptly three years ago, had not been invited, a decision that James had made after conferring with the three people closest to his sister: Gretchen's two sons and her half-brother, Duncan, who was living at the Goodridge house while a student at U.C. Los Angeles. Duncan and Fred would be flying in together to arrive on Thursday. James would pick them up at JFK airport, after meeting George's plane from Germany a few hours earlier.

That, in essence, was Gretchen Goodridge *née* Frazer's family, sons, brother, half-brother, nieces and nephew, step-mother, and the motley crew of assorted in-laws. They would be the ones who would gather to mourn her, if that meeting were a real wake, which it wasn't—according to James.

They—plus one more: Gwen Harleman, M.D., from Pasadena, California, Gretchen's lifelong friend and, lately, her doctor. Duncan took it upon himself, when he received the invitation, to inform Gwen Harleman of it. He thought it only fair: Hadn't Doctor Gwen, as she was referred to by all her patients, been genuinely distraught about the whole mess that had surrounded Gretchen's demise? Had she not blamed herself for not having been more forceful in treating Gretchen after her divorce? Over and over again she had said, "I am a gynecologist, not a shrink. I sent her to a psychiatrist, but it did not do her any good. She thought it was a sign of weakness to go to a shrink. I knew that about her, that damnable sense of self-reliance that she had. I should have assumed some responsibility myself."

Duncan, a senior at UCLA, had tried to console her. "It's beyond your power, Doctor Gwen. You could not have prevented what happened to her. Nobody could. You know that. As a matter of fact, you did her a lot of good. Gretchen told me more than once that without you she couldn't have weathered the storm. You were not just her doctor and her friend but, as she put it, her anchor."

"Anchor? Really, did she say that?" But Gwen Harleman remained doubtful.

Uninvited, except that she had asked Duncan to inform his brother she would put in an appearance at the meeting, Dr. Gwen bought a ticket on the red-eye to New York, rented a car, and drove out to Connecticut.

Halfway along on Interstate 95 she had some second thoughts about her arrival at such an early hour. Would it not be an imposition to show up as an outsider and seat herself at the family breakfast table? Not that she wouldn't be seated, surely; James was all courtesy and gentlemanliness, former diplomat that he was. She had met James only a few times, the last time when he came out to California on some legal business having to do with his and Gretchen's father's estate, for which Wilfred Goodridge had been a trustee. James had stayed at his sister's newly acquired condo in the Los Angeles suburb of Pacific Palisades. Gretchen had cooked dinner, inviting Gwen and her husband, Eric, to join them. There had been tension in the air the moment the four sat down at the dinner table. Gretchen had been palpably nervous, to the point of forgetting to remove the Yorkshire puddings from the warmer-oven, then dashing out to fetch them and dropping one off the serving plate as she ladled them out. "Oh my!" she cried.

James bent down and picked it up, putting the pastry on his plate. "No harm done," he smiled. "Relax, Greta. It's okay." He called her Greta rather than Gretchen; Gwen learned later that it dated back to their childhood, when the older and taller sister wouldn't let her little brother use the diminutive. That evening, though, it sounded vaguely patronizing.

Patronizing was also the attitude James displayed toward Eric, Gwen's artistic liberal-Canadian husband. It was spring of the year in which James had decided to run for re-election to the Congressional seat from his home district. It was impossible not to have the table conversation turn to politics. Predictably, James championed what Eric at one point called a "motherfuckin' tough take-no-prisoners" conservative line, to which James took no visible umbrage. Instead, he calmly lectured "our Canadian friend" on the timelessness of the American Constitution and how it was in danger of being diluted by an onslaught of demands for rights without concomitant responsibilities. That cut no ice; neither did his remark that "character" would be an issue in the fall campaign, Bob Dole having plenty of it and Clinton apparently none.

It was a farcical exchange, each man eyeing the other as the enemy along party lines and becoming increasingly more irascible, until Eric remarked, "If you are practicing your stump speech here, Jim, remember it'll work only when you are preaching to the choir. Outside, it'll fall flat, because you people are still in the minority."

The women shushed the men quiet, Gretchen brought out her dessert of caramel custard soufflés—which miraculously had not fallen, neither in the oven nor off the tray—and peace was restored with a good California port.

Gwen sighed remembering this not-so-long-ago episode, a little less than two years ago, to be exact. Much had happened since, not to mention that James Frazer was elected to Congress with the Republican majority, and was now poised to do it again. She shook her head: It wasn't politics or any such mundane thing that had caused Gretchen to be so tense and ill-humored then; there was a deeper sense of being out of sorts, out of kilter, that Gwen the doctor thought she detected in her friend the patient. There was never really any chance to touch on that, though, for her patient resisted all attempts at what she disdainfully called "therapy." Just once Gwen had had her ear when she mentioned that she had heard from Eric that the Getty Trust was looking for art-oriented people, volunteers not employees, who would travel for them researching possible acquisitions. "Really?" Gretchen had said, without the slightest ironic undertone. Perk up she did, mentally and physically. "I'll go and see them about it." That she did, and she got the job. Alas.

Gwen sighed again. What if she had kept her mouth shut? Would Gretchen now be here with them? Gwen had to dismiss any guilty feelings there; Gretchen had been a longtime docent/volunteer at the Getty Museum in Malibu, and her connections to the Getty people were solid and of proven worth. Sooner or later someone would have mentioned the acquisitions project to her. Right?

Taking a Norwalk turn-off, Gwen steered herself to a roadside café and ordered toast and coffee. She bought *The New York Times* and got lost in the pages of the newspaper. Pages and pages of Clinton trouble; cartoon of kid watching T.V.: *"Oral oval office sex and the President,"* mother rushing in to pick up kid, kid asking *"Mommy, what's a president?"* Gwen shuddered. What's the matter with that man? She had voted for him, twice...what's the matter with us? Better to delve into the weekend section, see what time the museums were open. Ah, the Met: 9:30—special exhibit of Indian watercolors. Perfect. She was staying over in Manhattan, taking the Sunday evening flight back to Los Angeles.

When she looked up, an hour or so and more coffee and a piece of apple pie later, she saw that the weather had turned. What had been a bright, if cloudy, day had become what looked like the forerunner of a storm. She could see people across the street bending against the gusts. Except for a couple of Connecticut State policemen seated at the counter, she was the only customer left in the restaurant at that pre-noon hour. She became fearful. The temperature outside was well above freezing; if there were a drop to below thirty-two degrees, and if those clouds being driven in would bring rain, would this become another one of those ice storms that had paralyzed New England earlier in the month? If she left now, would she find her way to the Frazer house, still some ten or more miles away in the secluded Southport section? This was not like Los Angeles, where the streets ran at right angles to each other and the numbers told you what block you were on.

She got up and walked to the counter, asking the young girl who had served her, "Could you tell me how to get to Southport without getting lost in traffic?" She gave a little laugh, as if that were a silly question.

The girl, a buxom blonde, shrugged: "You can take the Post Road—"

"Ma'am," one of the troopers turned to her, "she's right. Take this highway you're on right here, the Boston Post Road, until you reach Fairfield. Then turn right. Piece o' cake." He pointed to his pie, looked up at her, and smiled kindly, like a good son to his mother.

It irritated Gwen to be thought of as old enough to be his mother. Did she really look the part? Granted, her hair was graying, but she had had it cut short in a youthful—her hairdresser's word—bob, and her hands were still firm and smooth and her face had nary a wrinkle. "Well," she said a bit testily, "I'm a doctor, and I'm used to being careful, getting the right information." She realized it was a silly remark, telling them that she was a doctor; as if doctors were masters of everything. So she added, returning his smile, "Like surgery—it's best to know beforehand what you are doing."

Now the older of the two policemen spoke up. He was stubbing out his cigarette and swiveled to face her: "Southport is right by the Sound, as you know, and that's where a storm may be coming from. Where exactly do you want to go in Southport?"

"North Hill Road." Gwen fumbled in her coat pocket for a piece of paper and read, "Number fifty-five."

"That's a very exclusive area, large properties, two-lane roads." He shook his head. "Are you seeing a patient?"

"Not a patient. Friends. The Frazers."

"Jim Frazer? Congressman Frazer?"

"Congressperson," the younger man grinned.

"Okay." The trooper got up. "Ma'am, Doctor...?"

"Harleman. Gwen Harleman."

"Doctor Harleman, we'll get you there safely. You just follow us, real close, and we'll keep an eye on you, too." He motioned to his partner, "Come on, Mark." Gwen was going to protest, but he waved her off. "It'll be a pleasure. Let's go."

Gwen put ten dollars on the counter and told the waitress to keep the change. She followed the troopers out, got into her car, and started the engine. The wipers cleared the windshield. The sky had turned solidly gray. Gusts of wind blew leaves and paper up the parking lot driveway. When the police car moved in front of her she was very glad to have the escort. State troopers! Jim Frazer must be a popular man, she thought, at least among peace officers.

It was slow going because the traffic on the busy Boston Post Road was crawling in spurts from light to light, so crawl along they did through Norwalk, through Westport, and into Fairfield, until the police car blinked the right-turn signal. She followed, carefully duplicating every move of the car ahead. The side street was less crowded but narrower, and it seemed to head straight south toward the shore of Long Island Sound. Their little caravan passed through a picturebook New England scene: a solid stone church here, a schoolyard there, a park, a library, all well set back from the roadway, and all under tall, leafless trees. Gwen had flashbacks to her student days "back East," and thought about how often she had found it cozy to stay indoors during such weather, a blanket across her knees, a mug of tea warming her hands, looking out the dormer window at the rain pelting the panes.

They had reached a parking lot at the shoreline, water and sky forming one gray wall beyond. A yacht club was to the left, but the patrol car turned right onto a narrow road. The younger man's arm came out the window, motioning her to follow east along the water's edge. A short distance, and now the officer's arm came out again, pointing to a lane that his car began to turn into. When both cars had moved up a few yards, the police car stopped and the young officer got out and came to the passenger side of her car.

Gwen let down the window. "Is this it?" she shouted across the passenger seat.

"Not quite yet." The officer let himself in. "This is North Hill Road, but it's a bit up a hill, true to its name, and there are no numbers on the property. So we thought I'd ride with you."

Gwen smiled. "Thank you," she said and let him in.

"Yes ma'am. Put it in low." He fastened his seatbelt. Gwen kept smiling and did as she was told. The police car had started up again too.

"So, what's the occasion?" he asked. "You coming all the way out here."

"The occasion," she looked at his name tag, "Officer Marklow, is a birthday." So that's what this was: Checking her out....

"A birthday, huh? Whose—the congressman's?"

"His sister's. We're old friends, went to school and college together."

"No kiddin'. Yeah. It pays to come out for that." He nodded. "You're expected. We called ahead." After a while he said, "Now, you watch for a gate that comes up on your left. We'll pull to the side and let you face the gate. Okay?"

The gate was a wooden one, six feet high, with an arrow sign pointing to a squawk box on the side. Officer Marklow got out, went to the box and, having pressed a button, announced Gwen's arrival. Or so Gwen presumed, for by the time she had lowered her window he had stopped talking and was now listening. The answer came—a man's voice. "Okay, come on up." And the gate moved open, sliding sideways into the right side of the wall.

Gwen nodded to the officer, waved at the older one sitting in the patrol car, and shouted, "Thanks, thanks for your help. You're great!" She put the car in gear and slowly moved up the slightly curving driveway.

It was an impressive entry, with tall trees spreading their leafless branches over the macadam lane. She peered through the windshield for the house, but no, not yet, she laughed to herself. On her right she passed a building she almost mistook for the main house, but it was just a four-door garage with a story on top that, by the looks of the windows, held living quarters. She drove on, to her left a spacious lawn bordered by trees and hedges, until she came to what had to be the actual residence. She gave off a whistle: wow. A New England mansion, too big to be just a house, sitting on a slight rise overlooking the grounds before it, with large windows, a porticoed entrance in the middle, second-story balconies protruding on either side. The gabled roof showed more windows, small ones, that she imagined belonged to rooms with slanted ceilings, pegged wooden floors, a view, and curtains billowing in the summer breeze.

Ah, the privileges of wealth.

Gwen pulled up, shut off the motor, gathered up her coat and handbag, and climbed out of the car. Before she reached the portico she saw the house door open, and a man—not James—in a business suit came toward her. He held an open umbrella. Heavy drops of rain were beginning to fall.

"Doctor Harleman? Welcome to the Frazers." He extended the umbrella over her. "I'm Jeff Johnston. The house manager."

"Oh, hi...." Gwen shook his hand.

"Your luggage? In the trunk?" He pointed to the car.

"Thank you, but I don't have any. Just a carry-on bag. I'm not staying long." She made a dismissive gesture.

The house manager—butler?—smiled: "As you wish." He preceded her inside once they had reached the portico and held the door for her. He took her coat and cap and hung them in the closet. Gwen was wearing fur-lined boots, jeans, and a turtleneck pullover, all in navy blue, and a salt-and-pepper tweed jacket. California assumptions: It's winter, so it has to be cold. She wondered briefly if she was dressed wrongly and decided she wouldn't care. She'd only spend the afternoon. By evening she'd want to be in New York.

There were some voices and laughter coming from the back of the hallway. Laughter....

"They're all in there," the house manager nodded toward the back of the house. "May I lead the way?" Without waiting for her answer he walked ahead, and Gwen followed. They crossed the dining room and passed through wide doors into an obvious addition to the back of the house, a bright space that looked like—and was indeed—a winterized patio that ran the length of the building, with windows high to the ceiling and vertical shades now pulled to the sides. And yes, pegged wooden floors. Gwen smiled inwardly as she walked toward the people assembled along oaken trestle tables, chatting, holding plates and glasses. The food was served buffet style: salads, breads, fruits, cheeses, meats, including hot dishes and a carving board for roast beef under a heat lamp. A separate, smaller table with rattan chairs around it occupied a corner of the room; at it sat a woman minding four small children who wouldn't sit still.

James looked up, recognized Gwen and, putting his plate down, strode toward her, hand outstretched. "Gwen! There you are! I'm glad you could come. Did you have trouble finding us?"

They were pumping hands. "No, thanks to Connecticut's finest. They escorted me to your gate. And—uh...Mister Johnston, is it?—took me in."

"Thank you, Jeff," James nodded.

"Troopers," Jeff told him. "They called from en route."

"I'm glad," James smiled, and let go of her hand. "Come meet everyone." They walked to the middle of the room, toward a tall blond woman who was conversing with a gray-haired man. "Nora," he said, "Gwen Harleman has arrived. Gwen—my wife, Nora. And this gentleman is Delbert Trumbull."

They shook hands. Nora said she'd want to take Gwen around to introduce her to everyone, but before she could do that a lean, angular young man strode over, hand waving. "Doctor Gwen! You made it!" He gave her a bear hug.

She laughed. "And whose fault is that, Duncan?" She patted him on the back. "I decided at the last minute I should be here."

"Absolutely!" Duncan beamed.

"We agree," Nora smiled, taking charge. "Come meet the rest of the family, Gwen. Mind if I call you Gwen?"

The woman who had been standing with her back to the group turned around and introduced herself: Clementine Patullo, Nora's mother. Gwen guessed she was pushing sixty, but she surely could pass for a woman closer to her own age—passing fifty. How did she keep her skin so radiant, her hair so naturally full and dark blond, her figure so firm? Gwen was envious. Then she noticed that the hand that held a drink showed veins and a bit of mottle. "Hello, nice to meet you," Gwen said, and smiled.

Youthful looks could not be attributed to Charlotte, Duncan's mother and Gretchen's not-so-adored stepmother. She and her new husband, Stuart Rosenberg ("Call me Stu, please!"), gave the impression of the kind of Manhattanite seniors who could be found at every opening, from Lincoln Center to the Met to the Guggenheim: he spare and a bit bent, with trimmed white hair and rimless glasses; she somewhat faded but well coiffed and bejeweled and dressed with that careless elegance that bespoke cultured good taste. They conversed warmly with Gwen until they could introduce her to Charlotte's daughter Dagmar and her husband, Reg, who were pointed out by Nora. Duncan poked his head into the group and said, "If you want to say hello to

George and Fred, they're at the chow table, Doctor Gwen. You could do with some refreshment yourself, I bet!"

"Now that you mention it, I think I could. Thank you, Duncan. Lead me to the trough? Excuse us," she said, and she followed him to the table.

She had known Gretchen's sons since the boys were in their teens. Her own son, Guy, was the same age as Freddie; and since George was only two years older, the three boys had spent some school years and summer camps together. It was old home week as they hugged and exchanged greetings. Duncan, several years younger than either of his "nephews," stood by, grinning benevolently.

Gwen felt good in the company of these young men who were busy filling a plate for her and fetching a glass of punch. There was a surfeit of females in her professional life, and besides, she always ached for the presence of her son, who was at U.C. Davis finishing medical school. Too soon grown, too early gone....

Nora came over. "Come sit with us, Gwen. Before you do, let me show you the kids, okay? Before they have to go up to the playroom." Gwen said she'd love to and was led to the far end of the room, where a woman was busy keeping four lively youngsters, two of them toddlers, occupied spooning some ice cream into their mouths—with mixed results, evidently. The woman, about Gwen's age, she guessed, looked up and said, "Oomph! What a mess!" and laughed.

Nora said, "Gwen, this is Judy Johnston, Jeff's wife. Judy, meet Gwen Harleman, one of Gretchen's friends. Gwen is a doctor." The women shook hands. "Judy is a nurse by training, Gwen. We are very fortunate to have 'Jay and Jay,' as we call them, with us. Indispensable. Jeff was on the White House detail when Bush was president. He and Jim knew each other when Jim was still with State. When Jeff had to retire—they put them out to pasture at a relatively young age at that job, believe me—Jim persuaded him and Judy to come live and work with us. We are friends, really, aren't we, Judy?"

"I don't do windows," Judy replied, a smile still on her lips. "That helps." Then she added hastily, "We are friends in that we like and respect each other. Sometimes I feel like Nora's older sister."

"Exactly!" Nora beamed.

The children were introduced: Lillian and Helene, called Lillie and Lenie, looking so much alike that Gwen knew she could not tell them apart. Five-year-olds, they had started kindergarten in the fall. Their brother was three, a sturdy little fellow with curly dark locks and a serious, almost pouty mien. He was called Scot, with one "t" because of his grandfathers Ian and Malcom, Nora explained, whatever that meant. Then there was a pretty little four-year-old who didn't want to put out her hand from behind her back: Inga. Nora pointed to her parents, "Dagmar and Reg Winthrop, from Texas. Have you met them yet? You've got to meet them. Dagmar is a former ballet dancer. Come with me!" And she took Gwen across the floor to a couple who stood in conversation with Jeff Johnston. Introductions were made, smiles and small talk exchanged.

Just when Gwen was going to become concerned that she was out of place here, what with everyone being close and cozy with one another and she the obvious outsider, James turned up. "Nora, I thought I should give Gwen the tour." He was carrying Scot, who had his thumb in his mouth.

"Of course!" Nora asked Gwen, "Would you like to see the house? It was a really old rundown place when we bought it five years ago, but we loved the grounds and the view, and over time we've fixed it up to be really comfortable."

"I'd love to see it," said Gwen.

"Perfect!" said Nora. "Jim, you do the tour, and let me have Scotty."

James laughed. "I have just rescued him from three girls who were teasing him mercilessly. Now it's time for father-son bonding. Eh, Scot?" He bounced the boy on his arm. It did not dislodge the thumb, but it caused a wee smile. Nora laughed and patted her son on the diapered behind. "Off you go!"

The tour was instructive. There was a basement with a sauna and what James said was the beginning of a bowling alley—suppose they skipped that? Okay by Gwen. The ground floor was all living space, dining room, kitchen, pantry, sitting room, library, and offices for both James and Nora. Nora taped her radio commentary for WABC there. One day, when the kids were bigger, Nora would go back to a television job. And of course Gwen had seen the sun room, where they had just been. Right? Okay. The second floor was all bedrooms and bathrooms and the children's play room. Gwen said, "Let's skip that, too. What's in the attic?"

"Ah," James exclaimed, "glad you asked. Let's take the elevator. Scot loves riding the elevator. Don't you, boy?"

So they rode up to the top floor. What Gwen had surmised was a number of rooms with pegged floors and billowing curtains turned out to be a vast open space interspersed only with bearing columns and traverse beams. No hardwood parquet, but a sort of linoleum that looked like tiles. There were tricycles and kiddie cars and a jungle gym. even a sandbox in the far corner.

"The outdoors brought indoors, for when it rains or snows." James put his son down, and the boy raced over to the plastic-domed, red-and-yellow car, yanked the door open, and placed himself in the driver's seat. "He loves that car," James said, "particularly now that he knows how the pedals work. Come on, let's you and I walk over there and sit down." He pointed to the far wall on the other side, where a seating area was arranged in front of wall cabinets and counters. They sat down. James offered soft drinks, and when Gwen declined helped himself to a Coke from the little refrigerator under the countertop.

"I got your note, thank you," he said. "Now we can discuss it. What did you mean, exactly, about the DNA? And that you could help out with it?"

"Well, of course, as her doctor I may have some tissue information from her. And I was wondering what kind of genetic ID of hers you have received. A sort of positive identification, even if it's just a scrap of tissue?"

"I thought that's what you meant. The point is, we have received nothing of the sort. The whole thing is such a mess, I don't know if it'll ever be resolved to anyone's scientific satisfaction. It puts quite a strain on us."

"I can imagine. With all the resources you have at your disposal as a congressman and with your former State Department background, I figure you'd have put some pressure on people to get results. Use the media, even."

"Horrors! Not the media. All you get is hot air. There were no survivors. What am I supposed to say—Yes, there must have been one, my sister? Who'd believe that? So I'm the troublemaker, claiming one of mine was the exception? On what basis? That I'm a rich man and can afford the extra effort, futile though it would surely be?"

Gwen smiled. "Well, you certainly are not poor, Jim." She made a sweeping gesture with her hand. "I read about you in *Time* magazine, how you are among those who can afford the cost of getting elected these days."

"The article was mainly about Senator Kerry and Governor Weld of Massachusetts and Steve Forbes. It went on to mention recent elections to the House and Senate, how candidates draw on private wealth to run."

"I didn't mean to sass you about it, Jim. I'm sorry."

"Let me tell you something, Gwen." He leaned forward, his arms on his knees, looking at her earnestly. "Having a lot of money, and I mean plenty of millions of it, is becoming almost the rule for a lot of people. Our stockbroker is a case in point: he has more and makes more than we can ever have. No envy there, just a statement of fact. In our case, Nora is the one who has the money. Her rather substantial inheritance. We made a deal: We live off what she and I make from our professions, and she decides what and where we use funds from her estate. There are trust funds for the children. I was able, with Nora's help, to run for Congress and not care about raising money for it. Those are the plusses. Then there are the minuses, foremost among them the possible threats against my family. We were made aware that certain adversarial factors existed, even after we thought we had neutralized one of them, the main and only player we thought, back in the days before we got married. We are vulnerable, especially with the kids. So we take precautions, as most people would. We hire competent help, we live in a protected environment, we do not draw attention to ourselves, we avoid making ourselves extra visible.

"Being in politics, however, brings forth its own visibility factor. But I am a neophyte Republican, unknown and seldom seen at photo ops. I take good care of my constituents; I am available to them, and I respond to them. They seem to like that. We are the Constitution State, and we take the Constitution seriously. I am a back-bencher in the House. My committee assignments are Armed Forces and Intelligence. I cast my votes, I keep my mouth shut, I am a team player. I sat on my hands during Clinton's State of the Union address on Tuesday, but I'm sure nobody noticed. In my own party I don't cater to Newt, because Newt knows nothing about what I am specialized in, and I don't need to kiss his ass for RNC money. All that spells low profile, and Nora and I want to keep it that way."

"Good heavens, Jim. I didn't mean to stir up a hornet's nest of trouble here. I was just thinking of poor Gretchen." She sighed. "Let me just ask you one more time: Are you absolutely sure she's dead? Is there any proof of that you have been given?"

James drew his hands over his face and groaned. "Don't you think I've asked myself that over and over again? There is no proof. There is also no Gretchen. What am I supposed to think, huh? You tell me!"

"I don't know." Gwen shook her head. "What actual facts do you have?"

"With my brother-in-law Reg's help I sent a special investigator down there. He uncovered, and we identified, pieces of her personal belongings from her luggage and her flightbag, and there was also her boarding pass stub. We knew that she had left Hong Kong for Indonesia, and that she was leaving Jakarta to fly to Thailand, then board a plane to Europe, where she was going to visit with George. Owing to the time difference, the call she made to George in Frankfurt was just a message on his answering machine. That was the day before she left. Her voice was normal, her message routine. There was no sign of hysteria or illness. The morning of her flight she checked out of her hotel, caught the airline bus to the airport, checked her bags—two of them—passed customs and passport control, and boarded, with the airline gate portion of her boarding pass the last item she left behind. The rest is silence. So what are we to think—that she somehow, miraculously, is still alive? Just because we couldn't find her DNA in that mud at the crash site?"

They both sat silently for a while. A noise came from somewhere, a whir, and the elevator door was pushed open. Nora emerged. Scot saw his mother and came pedaling up to her. Nora spoke to him, and kissed the crown of his head. Then she walked over to the seating area. "Hi, you two. We are going to have a piano recital by Duncan in the library soon. Coffee and cake, too. How're you doing?"

James sighed. "Not too well. We haven't solved the puzzle."

"No, we haven't," said Gwen. She looked at her watch. "I think I would like to be excused. I want to be in New York before it gets dark."

"Couldn't you wait till morning? We have plenty of room, and you are most cordially welcome. Please?" Nora said.

"I have reservations at the Plaza. A long-cherished experience. You are very kind, really, but I hope you understand. It's a weekend treat for me." Gwen got up slowly, straightening her jeans.

"Oh, of course." James rose too. "We understand. You deserve a break. And we are so very grateful to you for coming all the way out here. It means a lot. Gretchen would be pleased." Nora nodded as he said this.

They stood, but nobody moved because Gwen seemed to be hesitant about something. "There is one more thing I should tell you," she said.

Glancing from one to the other, she continued, "Did you know that Gretchen was writing a book? Anyway, she was and she finished it. Before she left she gave me the manuscript to read."

"Did she?" Nora sounded astonished, but James said yes, he knew.

Gwen said, "It's a biography of Queen Sophie Dorothea, but it reads like a novel. About the wife George I left behind and locked up for twenty years while he went off to become king of England. And she was the mother of a future King George II and the future queen of Prussia. A terrific story. She really got all the plots and characters right. I brought it with me, in my bag in the car. I was thinking perhaps you know of an agent and could get it published? It would be a fitting epitaph for Gretchen. I saw that monstrous husband of hers, every time she described George I. He really did her wrong, you know, Wilfred did."

"Oh, my gosh, yes, we would love to have it!" said Nora.

"Yes, please," said James. "And I appreciate that you did not mention it downstairs. After all, Wilfred is still the father of George and Fred."

"She dedicated the book to you, James," Gwen said.

"Did she!" James exclaimed. He seemed genuinely surprised. He took off his glasses and pressed his fingers over his eyes. "Did she really?"

Nora hugged Gwen. "You are a wonderful friend, Gwen. I do wish you could stay. We must find a way to get together sometime soon."

Gwen hugged her back. "Come see us in California. And thanks for the tour, Jim. You have a wonderful house, Nora."

"How'd you like my kitchen?" asked Nora. Gwen smiled and looked at James. Nora looked at him too. "Don't tell me. You didn't show her the kitchen? Our great, liveable, modern kitchen? Just like a man! Come, I will show it to you, Gwen. You can't leave without seeing it!" She took Gwen by the arm and led her to the elevator. James picked up Scot, and followed.

It was Duncan who saw Gwen to her car after the goodbyes had been said. He held an umbrella, and as he took the manuscript from her he said, "You know, I still can't accept that she's dead. Is it just me, or what?"

"You just haven't had proper closure. It'll come, in time."

"There is something…I don't know…eerie or unreal about it. Gretchen's been like my second mother, we were that close. I took her to the airport the day she left. We sat and talked. Now—gone, without a trace."

She stroked his cheek. "I know. It's tough. We all miss her."

Duncan nodded and swallowed hard. "When did you see her last, Gwen?"

"That same week. Thursday. She came to my office for a tetanus booster. She brought this book she'd been writing, and asked me to read it." She shook her head. "I did. It's very good. I hope Jim can get it published."

Duncan held the car door open for her. "Thank you. See you in L.A., huh?"

― CHAPTER TWO ―

The Divorce

Gretchen Goodridge was divorced by her husband Wilfred Goodridge IV in their twenty-fifth year of marriage, a few months short of their silver anniversary. It was done by him telling her so as they returned from a trip to Hawaii. The event occurred so swiftly, and the announcement came so unexpectedly, that it left her stunned, incredulous. Having spoken, Wilf turned from her, threw his bags into the cab, climbed in, and told the driver "Los Angeles."

Los Angeles was not their home; San Marino was, near Pasadena.

It happened at six o'clock on a cold Monday morning at LAX. They had just returned from Honolulu, where Wilf had been attending a weekend confab of the Trial Lawyers Association, of which he was the immediate past president; wives had been in attendance at the social functions. They had barely talked during the three-day, two-night stay at the Hotel Halekulani, Wilf having been busy chairing panels and whatnot. Gretchen had found her own fun in the sun at the beach with other wives. There had been no spouses of the male gender, come to think of it; she wondered if the few female trial lawyers had come solo. Otherwise she had sat in the shade of the lanai, perusing the research she had done on her book. On the flight home, a night flight, the cabin darkened, Wilf sat back in his seat with his shades on, sleeping all the way—or pretending to. Gretchen knew that if he were really asleep, his face would have been slack and his mouth drooling spittle. At home she would change the pillow case every morning.

Gretchen took the next cab. The driver told her that a trip to San Marino would cost her extra, as he could not be sure of a return fare. She said sure, okay.

On the hour-long ride she drew back into the corner of the cab, her mind racing, her heart beating over what had just happened to her. Was this a joke? Big Wilf Goodridge was capable of being a practical joker at times, but only if he could observe the dupe's consternation and guffaw over it. And he had never—well, hardly ever—made his wife his victim. Of course, she would never give him any reason to. She strove to be submissive, pliant, and always loyal to a fault. She saw that as her proper role as wife and mother; in the latter she was often the peacemaker when the boys bucked up against their father's one-man rule.

The boys—ohmygod, the boys! What would she tell them? Georgie, at Johns Hopkins in Maryland, Freddie at U.C. San Diego…what was she to say?

A fear crept up in her: Was Wilf all right? She had read recently that a person can have a stroke and not really know it, that there were some minor symptoms—what were they called? TIA—transitory internal accidents, or something like that. A person would change his or her character, blow up at the slightest provocation, until one day—kapow!—the whole enchilada. Was that what was wrong with Wilf? Maybe he needed help! After all, he was fifty-nine now, more easily upset than he used to be. Or was it the other thing—you know, sex? Men fear nothing so much as loss of their potency. You hear that everywhere, and the bedroom stuff, his to hers—oh, dammit, intercourse, okay?—for a couple of years it hadn't been the greatest, truth be told. Or was it the prostate? Their friend Jay had been diagnosed with cancer of the prostate at around that age. Dead and gone now!

She shook her head. Even given all that, it would not excuse what had just happened at the airport taxi stand. Wilf had turned to her and said, with an indifferent voice and a vacant stare, "I'm not going home with you, Gret. I have an apartment downtown. I am divorcing you. You'll hear from Bob Wall." Then, he had turned without a further word or gesture and gotten into that cab. Bob Wall was a partner of Wilf's;

he made a living suing people. Divorce a specialty, expertly handled; low-decibel, big-ticket divorces.

Slowly, something was dawning on her, and it made her catch her breath. This was for real. She had just been given notice that her walking papers would be handed her by that squat, bald little shyster Bobby Wall, whose real name was Walensky, and whose wife—his second, much younger wife—was a head taller than her "Bobby." Wall called her "Helen-dear," holding her hand as she smiled back at him oh-so-sweetly despite the pre-nup he had made her sign! Helen-dear was a fellow docent at the Getty Malibu where Gretchen had actually sponsored her and taken her under her wing, all for the sake of the partnership. And now that crummy Wall was Wilf's point man?

She groaned and half slid off her seat in agony.

"You all right, lady?" The cabbie looked at her in his rearview mirror. "You wish to stop somewhere, perhaps?" He had the peculiarly modulated speech of the African in his English. He was coppery black. Nigerian, she guessed. She had been there once, in Togo actually, with her parents, when she was eight years old. They had stayed at an old plantation-like hotel, and there had been a swimming pool where her dad had coaxed her into learning the crawl, and everybody around had been black except all the guests at the hotel, who were "European."

She sat up straight. "I am fine, thank you. I must have been dozing off. Mind the Pasadena Freeway up ahead. Keep to the right." She wished she could read his name off his license on the dashboard; she always liked to address people by their names.

"Oh, yes, madam." The driver grinned broadly. A friendly grin. Like that of the hotel porter back then, who always referred to her in the third person, as "the young miss."

Why was she remembering something that had happened forty years ago? Was her mind throwing up a defense, a shield from the reality that was looming, dark and menacing, up ahead?

The thought made her furious. What was she, some kind of helpless wifey who lived only as a creature of her husband, or was she a woman of this day and age—of the nineties, if you please—who had accomplishments of her own, and not only that but who had dreams of her own, too, and plans, and a future chock-full of new experiences, of life! And who wasn't even fifty yet!

She slammed her fist on the plastic seat cover. So Wilf wanted a divorce? He was going to get a divorce. She was picking up the gauntlet. She, the original Margaret Cosima Herter, commonly known as Gretchen Goodridge, was not going to be a pushover. She hit the seat again. The plastic cover made it sound like a slap.

The driver looked at her.

"Take the Fair Oaks exit," she told him, forcing a smile.

When the cab pulled up at the curb in front of her house, Gretchen saw a young man come out the front door, a satchel slung over his shoulder and a laptop computer in his hand. Duncan. He waved when he saw her and came loping toward her as she climbed out of the taxi.

Duncan was a houseguest. More than that, he was her brother—half-brother to be exact, from her father's second marriage. The difference between their ages was so great, and the explanations so tiresome, that all and sundry presumed Duncan to be her nephew, and the matter was left at that except for close friends. Gretchen hadn't known him very well during his growing-up years, for several reasons. One, the distance; Duncan lived in Connecticut. Another, she had her hands full bringing up her own sons, who technically were Duncan's nephews, three to five years older than their uncle. Third, Wilf's dislike of her side of the family, which did not make for particularly cordial relations. Duncan Frazer was thirteen when his father died (her father, too). When it came time for him to choose a college he opted for UCLA, where Professor Ian Frazer Herter had been teaching anthropology before Duncan was born. With her own sons having gone their ways, Gretchen was delighted to offer her home as a base for Duncan ("good for your empty-nest syndrome," Wilf had harumphed), and it had all worked out. He was a treasure to have around, polite, caring not just with words but with practical things, matters around the house that needed attention, like taking the dog to the vet's or hanging up the curtains when they came back from the cleaners—anything. She loved Duncan. And could he play the piano!

Too bad that from Mondays to Fridays, sometimes Saturdays as well, he roomed at his frat house off campus. She actually missed him on those days. He would call, though, often, and he would be back for most weekends.

This being a Monday, he was on his way to school, taking the bus to downtown Los Angeles and then the Freeway Flyer to Westwood and the UCLA campus. Gretchen felt quietly relieved. How could she explain what had just happened?

Duncan put down his briefcase and gave her a hug. "Had a good time in Hawaii?" She hugged him back. "You know—Hawaii. How can you not have a good time?" He held her at arm's length and gave her a searching look. "Tiring, though, huh? I bet it was the night flight."

Gretchen felt some unease. Could people already tell? Did she look a wreck already? She laughed a little. "It was kind of rough." Then she turned and paid the driver. "Hey, Duncan? I'm paying him for the return trip—why not let him take you to UCLA?"

The driver said, "That'll be a detour for me, it'll cost extra."

She took out another twenty and gave it to him. "Okay, Duncan, get in. You are late, anyway."

Duncan hesitated a moment. "Where is Uncle Wilf?"

"Oh, he had to go downtown. We took separate cabs. Come on, git!"

"Thanks." Duncan picked up his briefcase and eased his long frame into the back seat. Looking at his sister, he said before closing the door, "I guess it wasn't such a good trip, huh?" He had eyes that could see right through you.

Gretchen shook her head as the cab pulled away. Why had he said that? Was he just guessing? She waved. She waited to wipe away the tears until the cab had turned the corner.

Gretchen had a friend, Gwen Harleman, who was also her gynecologist, whom she called right after her talk with Wilf.

The talk with Wilf? A disaster, a hand-wringing emotional mess? No.

Not really. It took place in the law offices of Goodridge and Wall on the day after the return from Hawaii. A Tuesday. Gretchen had spent all day that Monday doing the practical thing—checking all her papers, the banks where they had accounts, the investments, the safety deposit box, the floor safe at home, her jewelry case, the artwork in the house. Nothing was missing, no changes had been made, no withdrawals had occurred. Everything was held in community property; wills and trusts were in Bob Wall's custody. The next step was to go to see Wilf. No appointment necessary. She was still the boss's wife.

Wilf came out and ushered her into his office right away. In the anteroom sat the new secretary—Vivian had retired the past December at the age of sixty-five. The new secretary was faceless and disinterested, barely nodding from behind her computer screen. Wilf didn't bother to introduce her. He walked Gretchen in, closed the door behind them, and pulled out a chair for her, being very solicitous, asking if he could get her anything.

Gretchen shook her head, restraining an impulse to blurt out, "Yes, get me my marriage back." Instead she pulled her skirt over her knees and clutched her purse to herself. She knew she looked vulnerable that way, but she let it be, saying nothing and hoping she could hold back her tears; she had been "close to the water," as her mother used to call it, when she was driving down here.

Wilf showed no sign of any discomfort. He took his place behind his desk, fussed a bit as he sorted out the space in front of him, cleared his throat, and said, "Now, then. Thank you for coming. I know how hard this must be for you." He took off his glasses and pinched the bridge of his nose. "It isn't easy for me, either, I assure you."

Gretchen kept looking at him.

"Well, there comes a time, probably in the majority of marriages, if not in all of them," here he gave a fleeting smile, a world-weary kind of smile, "when there is a divergence of life goals that puts a strain on the man or the woman. Sometimes that strain can be healed. Oftentimes not."

Gretchen hated the word "oftentimes." As a writer she always avoided it. She said, "Oftentimes applies to us?" She knew she sounded sarcastic, and she shouldn't be; her image of what she would say or do in her husband's office, under these circumstances was to be cool—not cool as the kids used the word, but as in cool and collected. Then, when she had confronted him, she would express her outrage, and if the occasion warranted, throw something at him, his desk clock or his bar association trophy, being careful not to hit his person but breaking something, the vitrine behind him, for instance.

Wilf droned on in a mournful voice, lamenting the turn of events as if it were an act of nature, an earthquake or a flood, against which they were helpless both in terms of how it began and how it ended. It was pure malarkey, that would be found to have nothing to do with their marriage if one peeled away the heavy layer of words. Gretchen realized that Wilf was addressing her not as a wife, but as though she were a juror who, in concord with eleven others, was to bring in a verdict of "not guilty."

She sat there and listened, incredulous that such verbosity should be directed at her by the pompous fool across from her who was her husband! The man who had been her man for nearly all of her adult years, to whom she had been faithful and obedient, for better or for worse, in sickness and in health—but not, as the nuptial vows promised, until death did them part, but....

But until what? Until inconvenience set in? Boredom?

Suddenly it dawned on her that the man behind the desk was a stranger. Yes, she had married him and taken his name; yes, she had borne him two sons, and she had shared his bed and board for a quarter of a century. She had always thought she loved him, that the way they lived together was typical of marriage, any marriage, with its "ups and downs," as people were apt to say when there was trouble. No, it wasn't like that at all. There had been darkness and light, a few bright spots while they were plodding through the murkiness of their coexistence. An arrangement, intuitively taken, in which they each held up signs that read invisibly, "Please do not disturb! Think of the children, and the dog, and the mortgage!" Now the children were grown up and gone, the mortgage paid off (almost), and never mind the dog.

It was over.

She was free.

"Wilfred!" She held up her hand to stop his flow of rhetoric.

"Gretchen?"

"Stop talking. I understand."

"You do? Actually, I knew you would, or rather I was hoping—"

"Shut up, Wilf." She flung her purse to the floor and leaned forward. An emotion was welling up in her that she sensed was not fear, not sadness, but a much stronger force: anger, a cold, heart-numbing wrath such as she had not experienced before. She spoke through clenched teeth.

"I heard you, yesterday and today. I was totally unprepared for it, and that may have been your intention; cowards always strike the unwary. You win. There will be no battle, in case you are wondering—"

"Of course not, Gretchen! You are my wife, for God's sake!" He leaned forward in a pleading mode that had served him well in many a client interview. "We shall part as friends!"

"Two things, Wilf. One, leave God out of it, now and evermore. It has nothing to do with Him. Two, as of yesterday, I am not your wife anymore. Cut the possessive crap. A former wife of twenty-five years? Yes. A separated wife, a soon to be divorced wife? Oh, yes. But not y*our* wife. Got that?"

He leaned back again: "Gretchen—"

"Listen, Wilf. I'll hire a lawyer. There are plenty at the country club who'd be only too anxious to take me on. I'll want every penny that is mine. I want you to move your things out of the house pronto. The house will be sold. As will everything else that we own. What exactly that everything else might be, will be determined by discovery. Is that the right term, Wilfred? Discovery? Well, I'll let my lawyers worry about that. Meantime, don't move anything, don't cut me off, don't shut me out. Okay?"

Wilfred just waved a hand weakly.

"Third, and most important, the boys. Have you talked to them about this? Do they know?"

He harumphed. "Only Fred. He called me yesterday. He needs a fee paid for the whale-watching excursion to Baja. It's part of his marine mammals class. They're leaving tomorrow. I thought it best to tell him, as he'll be gone a week."

Why hadn't Fred called her at home, when he knew it yesterday already? In his big, blustery way, shouting into the phone, "Mom, what's going on with you and Dad? Are you guys crazy?" He hadn't called. What, or rather *how* had his father told him?"

She said, "I take it George doesn't know?"

A nod. "He doesn't."

"I'll call him. This afternoon, when it's evening in Maryland. *I'll* tell him to call *you* after. Did you tell Freddie to call me? His *mother?*"

"Uh…it was just a brief converstion…he was busy…no, I didn't—"

"I will call him." She bent down to retrieve her purse and got up. "I have no idea where your apartment is downtown. I need the address. Presumably you have a private phone number. Don't bother writing it down. Call the answering machine at home and leave it on the tape." She walked to the door, and Wilfred jumped up to see her out. She paused in mid-step.

"One more thing. Is there another woman? I don't want the name. A yes or no will do."

Wilfred hesitated, cast his eyes to the ceiling for strength from above. "Yes." He sighed and looked at her. "You know her. Vivian."

She was thunderstruck. It couldn't be! "Vivian? Vivian? The mother superior? Your former secretary, the iron virgin? Who just retired to her bed-and-breakfast place in Napa? Who is ten years older than you?"

"Not ten. Six and a half." Wilfred looked pained.

She gaped. "Wilf! Wilf! What's come over you?"

He strode to the door and opened it. "Thank you for coming."

The urge to say something nasty was very strong, but she held her tongue. It was the wrong time, the wrong place. Besides, she was unaccustomed to swearing. Or, for that matter, to throwing things.

She phoned Gwen Harleman at her office from her car while she was on the freeway. Fortunately, Gwen was in and could take her call. And yes, Gretchen should drop by even if it wasn't urgent. Was she all right?

Gretchen assured her she was, "Physically. I may need a shrink, though. You won't believe what happened to me, Gwen. Wilf is divorcing me!"

"Oh, my. I am with a patient right now, but I'll see you when you get here. Drive carefully!" Gwen's voice sounded concerned.

The office was on Green Street in Pasadena, in a one-story California ranch-style edifice flanking a flagstone patio surrounded by jacaranda trees. This was March; in a few weeks, those trees would burst into an abundance of flowers, every branch laden with blossoms, lavender, against a light blue sky. It was Gretchen's favorite season. There were jacarandas on her property, too, and she didn't mind the mess they made when the petals fell off onto the lawns. Wilf always grumbled about it: Cut them down. Kids tramp the blue stuff all over the house. Gretchen used to smile. Same thing with the bougainvilleas, and the oleander. Would he cut those down too?

She sighed. She wouldn't be saying that anymore.

Gwen received her right away, and led her into an examination room and closed the door. Then she embraced her. "Gretchen, you poor thing!"

Gretchen hugged her back, then disengaged herself. "I'm all right, Gwen. Just don't make me cry." As she said that she felt tears brimming in her eyes.

"Here, sit down." Gwen patted the paper on the examining table.

"Gwen! I'm not sick! I came here to talk with you! You're my oldest friend!" They had been at Westdale Girls School together and at UCLA, although they had different majors—biology for Gwen, art and history for Gretchen. They had often been taken for sisters, both being the same height and having wavy blond hair, although Gwen's was more curly and had a tinge of red, and her eyes were green. After graduation their paths had diverged, Gwen's taking her to medical school at Stanford, Gretchen's to marriage, motherhood, and volunteering. They had lost sight of one another until about ten years ago, when they attended the same Los Angeles Philharmonic fundraiser, where they fell into each other's arms, hugging and exclaiming and dancing around "like a couple of damn fools," as Wilfred remarked afterward. The "damn fools" met again and again as time permitted (Gwen had opened her practice just then, in Pasadena of all places!), and eventually their husbands met, too. The men did not hit it off too well. Gwen's Eric, a laconic Canadian who was trying to establish a career as an architect, had given up a partnership in Vancouver to follow Gwen south to California. They had one child, a boy now in his teens, and no more, as Gwen decided she was becoming too old for childrearing. As for Gretchen's and Gwen's friendship, it was strictly that, and only gradually, as Gretchen's ob-gyn man retired, had she sought Gwen's medical advice. The ob was over, they agreed, and the gyn that Gwen championed was the modern, all-woman kind that allowed her to treat her patients as more than carriers of reproductive organs. Gretchen liked that idea; with menopause just over the horizon, she felt a woman doctor would be more intuitive.

Gwen said: "Let me explain something here. I am your friend, of course, as you said, your oldest friend. I can be supportive, hold your hand, take care of some things for you. But I am also your doctor. You have just been traumatized by the sudden rupture of your marriage. Soon, very soon, the whole extent of that trauma will make itself felt. You could go into the mental equivalent of shock. Believe me, I have seen it happen. I took a residency in psychiatry before I switched to gynecology. The body and the mind have a yin-yang relationship to each other. There can be illness resulting from such an upset of the equilibrium. The mind can make the body sick, and vice-versa. Do you see what I am getting at?"

"Oh, Jesus," Gretchen sighed, and put her hand over her eyes. "You're telling me I'm going mad, or I'll mess up my body." She dropped her hand and glared at Gwen. "I'll have you know I'm not made of sugar and spice! And just because I don't have a professional degree doesn't mean I don't know which end is up!"

"Good!" Gwen smiled. "Your fighting spirit. We'll need all of it."

Gretchen got off the table. "Okay. Fine. Can I go now?"

"Of course. Tell me, though, what did you come here for?"

"To…uh…talk to you. Share my trouble, as friends do. I didn't think a pap smear would help."

"You did the right thing, sharing your trouble with a friend. As a bonus, I am also in the position to help smooth things out for you medically."

"Gwen! I don't get it! Why did you want me on the table?"

"To take your blood pressure, draw some blood, look at your eyes, listen to your heart and lungs, give you a general examination. Repeat the tests tomorrow on a fasting stomach, and do a urinalysis. Why? To establish a base line, determine how well you are. That alone might come in handy someday, if there is a lawsuit. Remember, your soon-to-be ex is a lawyer. Also, I want to refer you to a psychiatrist simultaneously, to determine your mental base line as well. Together we would fortify you against what lies ahead."

"Fortify me!" A groan. "You think it'll be that bad?"

"It could be. But it can be helped. I mean, we can counteract. It's important that you know your strengths and weaknesses. After twenty-five years of marriage, two kids? An unsuspecting wife gets kicked out by her husband? You told me on the phone I wouldn't believe what had just happened. You were right, I didn't at first. You also mentioned a shrink, in a jocular way, but still you said the word. So I gave it some thought. And I realized you'd need all the help you could get. Now here I am, enlisting on your side."

Gretchen shook her head as she took off her jacket, skirt, and blouse and climbed back onto the examination table. Gwen took her blood pressure, which was well within the normal range, and drew a syringe of blood. She looked into Gretchen's eyes, ears, and mouth; palpated her neck, her armpits, her breasts, and her abdomen; listened to her heart and her lungs; and did her bit with the little rubber hammer, all the while entering the results into Gretchen's file.

Finally she said, "You are checking out fine. Can you come to the hospital lab early in the morning? Would eight be all right? I'll meet you there. Eat only a light meal tonight, and nothing tomorrow morning."

"Yes, doctor," Gretchen grimaced as she put her clothes back on. Gwen smiled at that.

Gretchen asked, "I've had my annual physical with you only this past December. Do you see anything different in your findings?"

"No."

"Then I'm okay, right? I've already been traumatized—your word. Where's the wound? Where am I bleeding?"

Gwen pointed to her head. "Up there. We can't see it, and there is no blood, but that's where you got hurt. At the very core of your being. It was a very sudden, cruel blow." She stepped forward and held Gretchen in an embrace. "We're going to keep your body well, and your mind too. But you need to help! It's like giving birth: You've got to push!"

Gretchen's head sank onto her friend's shoulder. A sob escaped her. The two women held each other tight, Gwen stroking Gretchen's back. Then, abruptly, Gretchen freed herself, grabbed her purse, and fled the room without a backward glance.

That evening Gretchen made some calls, the first one to her son George at his rented digs in College Town, Maryland. It was at that point that the finality of her situation sank in: She'd be on her own from now on. And everyone she knew would react to the news in essentially the same way: First, incredulity; then sympathy tinged with pity. Poor Mom, poor Sis, poor Gretchen.

Dammit, pity was the last thing she needed! Support, moral backing—yes, of curse. Sympathy (not the maudlin kind)—okay, within reason. But no mawkish sentimentality, if you please! And no condemnation of Wilfred! In fact, no mention of him at all in her presence, from now on!

"Mother!" George, always the sensitive, thoughtful child, broke in. "You are talking about my father! How can I leave him unmentioned in the presence of my mother? I am the son of both of you, and I'm not the one who is doing the divorcing! I'm sorry, I don't mean it the way it sounds—"

"Oh, it's all right, Georgie." She fought back a lump in her throat. "I have to hang up now. I've got a lot more calls to make. Jim—would he be in his office, at this hour? It's close to nine o'clock in the evening there."

"Mom, this is Tuesday, and you know Jim bunks down at his office in the Sam Rayburn building when the House is in session. Do you have his private line? You do? Okay. Just try him, or leave a message on his machine. And, Mom? This changes nothing between us, you know that, don't you. I'm here for you."

"I know, Georgie. Thanks for saying that, though. Bye for now." She hung up quickly and let out a bellow of a sob, and when she blew her nose it came out as such a honk she had to laugh as tears rolled down her cheek.

Next she called Duncan at his fraternity house in Westwood. A man answered the phone—the pay phone in the entrance hall, she knew—and she asked for Duncan Frazer; tell him it's his aunt.

A moment later Duncan came on. "Hey, what's up?" His voice was bright.

"Am I taking you from something important? Want to call me back?"

"Uh-uh. Nada. I was just noodling on the piano."

"Okay. Look, there's something I have to tell you."

"Oh?" A sudden change of voice; concerned. "Did something happen?"

"Yes, something happened. No, it's not what you think. Nobody's died or anything." Gretchen took a deep breath. "Wilf and I are getting a divorce."

A few seconds of silence. "Uh...so that's what it was when I saw you yesterday morning. I thought there was something wrong. Geez, Aunt Gret, I'm sorry to hear that. Damn. Damn, damn, damn. Pardon me." A sigh. "I guess it's too early to ask how and why. But tell me, who's divorcing whom?"

"Wilf is, me. He surprised me with it at the airport when we arrived in L.A. yesterday morning. I had no idea. Shows you how naive I am."

"Trusting is the word that comes to my mind. Wow. This is awful, Gret. How are George and Fred taking it? And what's next for you now. Are you moving out? D'you need any help? I have some important lab classes this week, but I think I can be excused and make up the work later."

"No, no, no. Thanks for offering, Duncan, but at the moment nothing has changed except that Wilf has moved into a downtown apartment. Next come the lawyers and all that business, and then, some way down the pike, the house will be put up for sale, and so on. That's months away. At this point, I just wanted you to know. And yes, the boys know. I just talked to Georgie. Freddie is on a field trip to Baja; Wilf talked to him yesterday. So I'm okay, in a manner of speaking. But thanks for asking. It means a lot to me." She felt her voice breaking. "I'm hanging up now. Okay? Bye."

Duncan stared at the receiver before putting it back. He shook his head. This was bad news. He wondered what was going on there in the seemingly solid Goodridge marriage. Wilfred divorcing his wife? And the wife not knowing until it happened? Was Wilf playing around? Hard to imagine, considering his general comportment—the vestryman, the respected lawyer and leader in his profession, the devoted father and provider for his family. Never mind that he was sometimes overbearing and loutish. Was it Gretchen's fault? He hadn't asked her, but he doubted it. His sister was so decent a woman, so obviously honest and moral a person, that the mere hint of suspicion of unfaithfulness on her part was preposterous. What makes two such decent people suddenly renege on their commitment and break up a union that had lasted for a quarter of a century?

The phone rang again before Duncan had left the hall. He picked it up. House rules: the brother closest to the phone answers it.

It was George Goodridge, calling from Maryland. Duncan recognized the voice instantly, a little nasal, with a sharp edge, almost military in the way it sounded, although George had never served a hitch unless you counted the Santa Barbara prep school he had attended that stressed Spartan ways and values. George came right to the point after Duncan told him what he had just heard.

"What do you make of it? You are on the scene, close to both my mother and my father. Did you notice anything that in retrospect is unusual? What's your take on the whole thing?"

"Nothing. I knew nothing, noticed nothing. Your mother looked and sounded a little stressed when she came back from Hawaii, but I thought it was from the night flight. My take on the whole thing? It's a big mess."

"Look, I'm coming home this weekend. Don't tell them yet. They'll probably say it isn't necessary, blah-blah-blah, but I'll just be there. How's my Jag? Still in the garage?"

George was a car nut, and his Jaguar was a graduation gift from his parents, a seven-year-old Vandenplas that a client of Wilfred's had shed in disgust when the engine quit on him once again. Wilfred's lowball offer was accepted, and George became the ecstatic owner of a silver-metallic English body with sunroof, leather upholstery, and a cell phone. No stranger to the workings of the internal combustion engine, George contacted Ford, which has just bought the Jaguar company, and wrangled an invitation to have a new Jaguar engine installed by a local dealer. He would be present as a "summer intern" (read "grease monkey") who did all the dirty work and deferred eagerly to the mechanics, who gradually got used to him. Thus George learned a lot. By the time he flew to Baltimore in the fall to enroll at Johns Hopkins School of International Studies he knew that his career would not be in the world of striped pants but of overalls, not in diplomacy but in automobiles. However, he wisely kept that to himself for the moment.

Yes, Duncan assured him, his precious car was safe from bird droppings and other befoulments.

"Do me a favor?" George asked.

"Sure, Georgie."

"Bring the car down to the airport for me? I'll call you about the exact time when I have booked my flight. I'll drive you back to your frat house and go on without you, if you don't mind. I want to be there, unannounced, on the spot, first with my mother then with my father, unencumbered by a third presence. You understand, don't you?"

Duncan said he did, indeed, but the unannounced bit might not work, because Gret would notice him moving the car out of the garage. George had obviously thought of that too. Tell her the Jag needed service, which it did; then he, Duncan, would take the car to the dealer in West Los Angeles, have it ready by Friday, and come to the airport on Saturday morning. Okay? Thanks.

Okay. They hung up. Duncan lingered for a moment, his hand still on the receiver, until he let go and turned away. As he walked back to the piano, where he had left music on the stand that he needed to gather up, he was struck by the thought that this...uh...event that had just happened, although not to him but to his sister Gretchen, would have the makings of a major upheaval in his own life, too. Perhaps upheaval was the wrong word; turning point, more likely. He wished he had someone he could talk to, someone close he could go to for hashing things over, a bosom pal, a confidante. He realized that he had no one who would qualify for that. Not here in the frat house, "brothers" though they were, all for one and one for all as the bullshit went. He was a very recent member, pledged just last fall, totally beholden to the hierarchy. No, he hadn't made any real friends yet.

Nor on campus. This was easy to explain: He had arrived last summer, a seventeen-year-old kid from "back East," too smart and too young for his own good. He was viewed, when at all, with a shade of suspicion: Who was this tall thin boy who barely shaved yet, with a certain smart-ass attitude he showed in class, especially physics and chemistry—inorganic chemistry at that—and who was not making an effort to be one of the inner circle, no sucking up and therefore no putting him in his place?

Duncan tried; God knows he tried. But there were too many divisions on campus. There was the obvious one of black versus white—separate tables at the lunch places. He felt uncomfortable with that because there had been black boys in Fairfield Prep who had been known not as "African-American" but as Jeff or Bob or Ed, some of whom were his friends. You liked one another or you didn't. No sucking up needed.

Then there were the Latinos. There hadn't been any to speak of at Fairfield, an Episcopalian school, except for the son of the Argentinean ambassador. But he was half English, and his name was Harry. Here at UCLA? Latino, *La Raza*, la everything, with a log of *machismo* and *hermanidad*. Forget it, kid.

The Asians—now there was a good group he could be *sympático* with, smart as they all seem to be, well dressed, polite, sharing many of his interests. But he was an outsider among them. All the sucking up in the world wouldn't have let him in.

His own kind was stratified in political and sports layers, with no prospect as yet of making even one close friend, even though he went to Pauley Pavilion with the bunch to cheer and groan on command, depending on which basket the ball fell through. And even though he joined in a hatred for the Trojans he hardly knew, it was not enough.

Politically, there were the campus Republicans, instantly recognizable in their jackets and ties. They were nice, congenial guys (there were hardly any girls), but he stayed away from them; one day it would come out that he was the brother of a Republican congressman, and that would be the end of it. No girl would ever go out with him.

There was one light, though, at the end of the tunnel: Schoenberg Hall, where he was taking a class in composition. Nobody in his family knew about this. He was a declared science major, with the end goal of going to medical school, something that had all been agreed to and fixed up in his admission application and for which his family, his widowed mother in particular, was shelling out mega bucks in tuition and allowances. He wished he had been more truthful and said outright that he wasn't interested in mucking about in other people's bodies, dead or alive. It wasn't too late yet to change his major, but he felt it was too early to spring it on the folks. Now that this divorce thing of Gretchen's had hit, his own plans would have to be put even further on the back burner.

Man, oh, man, what a mess. Would Gretchen keep the house? Most likely not; it was far too big for her alone. She would move, the house would be sold, and with it would go his use of their piano, a very good grand that he had come to like. Duncan realized he was being selfish here, but where would he practice? The frat house Yamaha was constantly out of tune and already had some keys out of whack, making him wince when he hit a dead key where he should hear a live one. Then he remembered: There were practice rooms at Schoenberg.

He raced upstairs and got his windbreaker and helmet, came down and pulled his bike out of the backyard shed. He put the lights on, on his legs and at the front of his mountain bike, ready to go out into the darkening evening. It was downhill to Gayley Avenue. A nice melody went through his head every time he saw the street sign, "Gay-ley, Gay-ley, U—C-L—A-ley." But before he could lay claim to it he remembered he had heard it in one of those German romantic operas of which his father had left a stack of L.Ps; *Freischuetz* he thought; darn it. Besides, even if he could use the tune in some way, the text with the connotation "gay" was a non-starter.

A mega non-starter. Not only did he not have a girlfriend, but going with the artsy crowd at Schoenberg put you dangerously close to being, as his father used to put it, "from the other bank of the river." It scared him. The only antidote to being thought of as gay, particularly when you were of the piano-player crowd, was a woman—not just a girl, but a real live woman, with long fragrant hair, hot lips, big boobs, round hips, and long legs. He had wet dreams about that, which made his eyes dart constantly for the real thing whenever he was in mixed company.

To no avail, so far.

But, hey, maybe with the turning point his life would become less structured, and new as yet unknowable opportunities would open up!

— CHAPTER THREE —
The Getty Job

Gwen Harleman's idea that Gretchen should make herself useful at the new Getty Museum took root, although not right away. Gretchen knew that the museum complex under construction on a Brentwood hilltop would not be open to the public until late in 1997, a year or more down the line.

That was fine with her. She was in no position to do anything for them at this point in her life anyhow, while her divorce occupied most of her waking hours. She, like the museum, was a work in progress. But unlike the museum she felt she had no master plan, no vision of where she was headed once the final decree was issued.

It made her feel uneasy and restless inside, almost as if she were waiting for an aftershock. The when, where, and how of it were beyond her ken.

Divorce, she was told, was indeed a major event like an earthquake. The one who told her that most often was Gwen.

They were having lunch at the sun-dappled patio of the Bel Air Hotel one warm but breezy September day. Gwen had some seminar to attend at UCLA Medical Center, and as Gretchen was living nearby, so to speak, in her condo in Pacific Palisades, the Bel Air venue just above the UCLA campus recommended itself. Change was in the air, Gwen had said when she called Gretchen. She was preparing to move her practice from obstetrics—too expensive, too exhausting at her age—to "gynecic oncology," a field crying for specialist attention in view of the increasing incidence of ovarian cancer.

The patio was busy. All tables were taken soon after the noon hour, and waiters were moving swiftly. Chatter was rising, but the noise was absorbed by the awning over the vine-ranked trellis. Down below in the canyon swans could be glimpsed hovering on their pond, now and then gliding gracefully this way and that. There was a scent of jasmine in the air, its sweet aroma belying the world outside, especially the raucous world of election politics. James was running again. She had sent some money—a hundred dollars, as that was the maximum contribution James allowed for his campaigns—although she couldn't vote for him here in California. Which reminded her, she hadn't yet re-registered to vote since her move to the Palisades. Should she bother? She sighed.

"What are you thinking?" Gwen snapped her fingers.

"I love coming here." Gretchen turned to her. "I wish I could be like Tony Curtis, renting a suite here, no worry in the world, getting everything done for me...not that he is idle, mind you. He paints, and rather well, too." She took a sip from her drink.

"Is that what you see yourself doing, retreating behind your easel and having all the mundane things taken care of?" Gwen smiled.

"No, of course not. It's just a dream. Besides, I'm not that talented."

"Oh, I don't know. You're still writing, aren't you? You're good at that! How's your book coming?"

"There's been a sort of hiatus...." Her gaze wandered.

"But you're getting back at it, aren't you? Gretchen?"

"Yes." She had caught herself. "I'm working on it. Going to the research library at UCLA. And at night twice a week there are the docent training lectures for the Getty."

"Keeping busy, in other words? Enjoying your new home?"

"The place is gorgeous, really, despite the noise from Sunset Boulevard. In the back it looks out over the ocean. And the mountains to your right. And the blue sky above. And all the stores in walking distance. Yes, I have that, and more. Quite a change from my previous life."

"I'll say."

Their order was served, and they began eating in silence, looking around to see who was there that they might know. Nancy Reagan's alcove table was empty; she hadn't shown yet.

"What about Duncan?" Gwen asked. "How's he doing?"

"Oh, fine. There's a guest bedroom in my condo; I told him he can have that, and he comes by on occasion but rarely stays overnight. I think he comes more for the piano. It's an upright, but a Steinway. He says it's as good as the grand we had, but I feel sometimes that he is just being polite. I miss him. But I suspect he'd rather bunk with his buddies at the frat house. Freddie is doing that at San Diego. The guys love it, I'm told. Not that I can understand why. You should see the mess!"

Gwen nodded. She concentrated on her whitefish. "Have you heard from the Getty?" she asked. "Anything in the offing for you?"

Gretchen shook her head. "I don't expect to, just yet. Another year, I am told, before the docent operations can start up again. We are still in the preliminary, organizational stages."

"I meant about this business of acquisitions. That has nothing to do with the actual building. And the Getty has money to burn. They are buying where and when they can. That's what I see you doing, once you are settled. Flying off to London, Paris, Rome, negotiating purchases."

Gretchen gave a small laugh. "You wish! The actual purchases are done by the top brass. I'd be more like a gal Friday, running errands."

"Running errands to the fleshpots of Europe? Sign me up for that, too!"

"Gwen! Get serious! That's not how it works! I'd be a small cog in a big wheel, the way acquisitions are handled. Mostly I'd be keeping my nose to the grindstone, or rather in the books, doing research about what art has surfaced in Europe, for instance, after the fall of the Soviet Union, what the provenance is, who owns it now or holds it without owning it, and so on. It's a form of sleuthing, really. Not that I mind. Interesting work. And work is what I need. Except that all this is at least a year off."

"Meantime, I hope you're beginning to go back on the social circuit. Don't you think it is time you did? With you here on the Westside and us in Pasadena, the casual, quick get-togethers are becoming harder to schedule. All we do is lunches, it seems. That's not enough, Gretchen. Although I admit, this—" she made a sweeping gesture, "—is certainly worth the effort."

"By social circuit," Gretchen smiled at her friend, "you obviously mean dating, don't you? Right now that, too, is a long way off. I want to find my balance first and foremost. Do something for myself for a change. Then, maybe. Or maybe not. If I make an odd number around your dinner table, don't invite me to dinner parties."

"Now, don't be silly." Gwen reached out with her hand to Gretchen's. "The day will never come that you are not entirely welcome at our dinner table!"

Gretchen smiled, "I knew you'd say that." She clasped Gwen's hand.

The massive Getty complex on its hilltop perch above the freeway in Brentwood was essentially finished by the summer of 1997, with the planting of the gardens remaining as the last major task. Long before, the museum's director had turned his curators' labors away from antiquities—which was to become the Malibu Getty's emphasis—and toward enlarging the stock of paintings from the seventeenth through nineteenth centuries. The results were spectacular. Major works began arriving—Rembrandts, Van Goghs, Cézannes, Poussins. Famous and not-so-well-known works of Impressionists were uncovered and generously paid for. Still, the director was not satisfied. When it became known that watercolors and oils by Camille Pissaro that had previously been misattributed to a minor Danish artist had been uncovered in the 1980s, the Getty was busy wresting away as many of them as possible. Gretchen was involved in some of the research. Pissaro had done these sketches as a young man on St. Thomas, his birthplace in the Virgin Islands, where he had befriended Fritz Melbye, the Dane, whose country was the overlord of the islands in those days. Pissaro had not given serious thought to art as his calling, but was expected to join his father in business. Melbye and Pissaro traveled together for a while until Pissaro moved to Paris to do what he needed to do, paint and study with the masters. His old friend Fritz, upon removing himself to China, deposited his works with another painter friend, Frederick E. Church, in the Hudson Valley of New York. There, all the sketches, drawings, oils, and watercolors were signed *Melbye*, including dozens by Pissaro, whose signature was ignored. Conversely, several of the pictures thought to have been by Pissaro may well have been Melbye's.

This search for authenticity and provenance was a searcher's delight, and Gretchen threw herself into it with renewed vigor and enthusiasm, even though her role was minor, being part of a team where most were more expert than she would ever be.

Gretchen didn't mind. This was interesting work that challenged her, made her want to get up and going in the morning and put a sparkle in her eye. She even thought she saw an improvement in her golf game, or so she told Duncan, with whom she played once a week on Wednesday afternoons. Duncan smiled benignly, and with his careless and unselfconscious swing did a drive straight down the fairway that landed inches away from the green.

Though not an expert, Gretchen had other qualities that the Getty liked, in the opinion of the assistant curator George Natalian, who supervised her. He was a squat man with a bald pate and a thin-lipped grin who often waved his arms when he spoke. His voice rose in pitch when he was excited, which was nearly always. Gretchen laughed out loud when she met him for the first time, at the beginning of the Pissaro project. This man looked a dead ringer for a character on the "Seinfeld" sitcom that she had come to enjoy, a show "about nothing." To make matters even funnier, the character was named George and also wore wire-rim glasses. George Natalian took no umbrage.

"Whatsamatter, is it my tie?" He wasn't wearing one.

"No." She hadn't caught herself yet.

"What, my baldness. You think bald is funny?" He rubbed his pate.

"I'm sorry, it's just, uh, nothing. My oldest son's name is George, too."

"George Two? Who's George One?" He didn't wait for an answer. "And what kind of a name is Gretchen? I'll call you Gretel. Okay? Now we're even."

They became good friends. There was a free and easy exchange between them, often kidding. She told him about the Seinfeld character. He said, "Oh, yeah? Maybe because Jason Alexander is my twin?"

"The actor? Your twin?" She looked at him in total surprise.

"You think Alexander is his real name?" His voice rose, his smile widened.

"It isn't?"

"Whatta you know? Wasp." He made as if to spit the word. Then he smiled at her over his glasses.

George Natalian had a Ph.D. in art history from Dartmouth. Gretchen was a volunteer, and eager to learn. For every question she asked, George made sure she understood his answer, explaining, demonstrating, referring her to sources. She sopped it all up. It occurred to her that, if he were older and not married and asked her out, she'd consider the distant possibility of getting hitched again, even in an Armenian Orthodox church. Such was the state of her self-imposed equanimity that she toyed with such thoughts on occasion, although she kept them to herself. George was a total hypothetical, anyway.

At the new Getty, plans were being made for an official opening of the center on Sunday, December 14, 1997. The contractors departed, except those involved in landscaping and interior work. The tramway was running, a four-minute ride from the parking area up to the mountaintop. Pre-opening schedules were laid out for leaders of government and the arts, for the press foreign and domestic, and especially for the neighbors in Bel Air and Brentwood, who for over ten years had been put upon by an army of bulldozers and trucks, their serenity disturbed, their streets clogged, their views altered. All along, the Getty people had been considerate, anxious to be good neighbors. This was not like the edifices of certain showbiz moguls that had also sprung up in the vicinity, grossly tasteless mansions resembling resort hotels. No, the Getty was all good taste and style and grace, a crowning glory, a diadem upon the brow of the Queen of the Angels.

Gretchen was proud to be part of such a glorious enterprise, however small her contribution might seem. She felt good when passing people on the site, and glances would be exchanged, or nods or smiles—the camaraderie of a shared experience. It made her want to do better, to go back to school, get a master's degree in fine arts, and then go back to the Getty ready to make a real contribution.

Yes, she would do that, after the opening. She'd go back to her good ol' UCLA. Keep Duncan company (what would he think?), honor the memory of their father, who had taught there. Then, with some effort, by the turn of the century—or rather the millennium—she could have her master's. Too old? Never. She'd only be—what—fifty-two, -three?

A dream worth dreaming....

On a hot Monday morning in August George Natalian came to her cubicle carrying an armful of books. "These are for you, Gretel. Right down your alley." He plunked the books on her desk with a thump.

"And a good morning to you, too, George," she smiled. "And what might these be?"

"Caspar David Friedrich, 1774, Greifswald, to 1840, Dresden. Ring a bell?"

"Sorry?"

"Am I mangling the German? Treading on your sensitive half-German toes?"

"George!"

"Get familiar with the guy, real quick. Browse, read up on him. Then come see me. Before five o'clock?" He turned and walked away.

She called after him. "Five o'clock of what day, George?"

He looked back, smiled and gave the thumbs-up sign.

Gretchen laughed to herself. She was at the Getty Mondays, Tuesdays, and Thursdays. She'd report to him on Tuesday. After all, she was busy with other things—cataloging, for instance.

The books were hefty tomes. One was the "F" volume of the Grove. Another the one-volume Janson *History of Art*, with a sliver of paper placed between the pages following Turner where, *voila*, C.D. Friedrich was located. Next, she opened a book much thinner than the others, titled simply *Friedrich*; its cover bore a striking picture of large shards of ice piling up against each other in brilliant sunshine against a deep-blue wind-driven sky. She was immediately captivated by what her eyes beheld as she riffled the pages. On the color plates the dominant theme was fog, mist, murkiness, dark browns and greens, pale or orange skies. If the term "Romanticism" had any meaning, if "moon" teamed with "swoon," this was it. She sighed. Not her cup of tea; Impressionism was. This was not the exuberance of Impressionists, Friedrich seemed—well, a dreamer, a storyteller like E.T.A. Hoffmann, a bit on the bizarre side.

But on with it, she commanded herself. Get this stuff back to George.

She started with the Grove: five pages, four illustrations, plenty of bibliography. Hmm, perhaps there was something to it. Caspar David, born in the university town of Greifswald, in a part of Pomerania that was then still Swedish, being a holdover from the spoils of the Thirty Years War. Educated at the art academy in Copenhagen. Later professor at Dresden Academy. Excellent draftsman, emerging painter especially of land- or seascapes invariably set in the dawn or dusk of day, if not in moonlit nights, with human figures clad in capes and wide-brimmed hats that would submerge their facial expressions, the figures positioned at the side, their backs half turned, as observers of the scenes before them—gloom pairing doom.

Or was it? Why did she feel an attraction creeping up on her?

She read the much shorter entry on Friedrich in the art book, where he was ranked with Turner and Delacroix as one of the most incisive artists of their time, when Europe and the New World began to transform themselves into new societies, when feudalism and slavery were swept away by revolutions and liberty and human rights were arising. Seen in that light, in that dawn of a new day, perhaps the Romantics could be perceived as the keepers of the true flame, the preservers of beauty.

Her interest piqued, Gretchen delved into the monograph on Friedrich. The provocative cover, with those huge shards of ice colliding and apparently having crushed a sailing vessel in the background, was from the painting "The Polar Sea," now at home in the *Kunsthalle* museum in Hamburg. As she read through the book—over her lunch hour, so engrossed that she didn't take a break—she felt great sympathy and admiration for the artist and his work. This was wonderful!

She grabbed all the volumes and trooped over to Natalian's office.

Her supervisor looked at his watch, took off his glasses and leaned back in his chair: "Three-thirty. You are returning the library books already? Thank you." He pulled up another chair. "Sit down, Gretel, sit down."

Gretchen put the books on the floor—George's desk was a mess, with not an inch free for more—and sat down, brushing some stray hair off her forehead. She knew her cheeks were red.

"Hard work, huh?" said George.

"Very interesting, this guy Friedrich," said Gretchen, nodding. More hair came loose. She tried to brush it back over her ears.

"You like him? He's saying something to you?"

"I don't know what you mean by that, George, what he is *saying* to me. He grows on you, once you overcome his weirdness. He *is* weird, you know. All of his human figures are looking away from the viewer. Even his wife, standing at the window. And all those ruins! And dark forests! And masted ships! It's a bit much, at times. But I like his colors, his contrasts, his…I don't know. Do we have any of his works?"

"Just one. A small oil titled 'A Walk at Dusk.' It'll be hung in nineteenth-century European paintings. His work was kind of forgotten after his death. As you mush have read, there was a rediscovery in the early 1900s. All of a sudden Caspar David Friedrich was all the rage." George took a sip from a water bottle he kept under his chair. "Then came the war, two wars actually, and a lot of turmoil and commotion. Old Caspar did another disappearing act. A couple of his paintings went up in flames in Berlin and Dresden. Things got worse with the partition of Germany. Each half had some of his works."

Gretchen nodded. They sat in silence. "So," she said at last.

"So, if one turned up somewhere, we'd be very interested," said George.

"Did one? Turn up, I mean?"

"Funny you should ask." George swiveled his chair and pulled a folder from his desk. "I have some homework for you, if you are interested."

"You're asking? Sure I'm interested. What's involved, a report?"

"At this point, I just want you to read it." George opened the folder. It contained some brochures and a number of xeroxed pages that were stapled together. "Let me tell you what we have here. These brochures are from art galleries, one in New York, one in Santa Barbara. We have done business with the dealer in New York, a very reputable firm, good on provenance. Not cheap, but you get what you pay for. The one in Santa Barbara is run by an old friend. I want you to study both catalogs closely, as if you were dealing with them from your own purse. Then we have these pages here that I copied from an exhibition program by Colnaghi, that famed and venerable art dealership on London's Old Bond Street. Perhaps you have heard of them."

Gretchen shook her head.

George continued. "There are two articles in particular that I want you to study: this one, titled 'Art, Commerce, Scholarship,' and this one, 'Museums and Dealers.' We, the Getty, are mentioned several times, always with reference to our money. And therein lies a tale." He looked expectantly at her.

"What tale?" Gretchen asked.

"Ah. That we'll discuss after you've done your homework." He closed the folder and handed it to her.

Gretchen took it. "When do you want it back?"

"We are a bit pressed for time. Would tomorrow afternoon be too much of a burden?"

"It would, if I were a social butterfly. As it happens, I have time, ample time, a commodity you seem to be pressed for. See you tomorrow, George." She rose.

George reached down and pulled up one of the books she had deposited on the floor. It was the Friedrich art book. "Here, you take this with you. It's not a library book, it's my own." He pointed to the cover. "Pay special attention to the 'The Polar Sea.' There'll be a test." He smiled and gave it to her.

"A test, and a tale. How fascinating."

"You're not kidding." He waved at her, his back already turned.

As she trundled down on the tram to the parking garage, Gretchen took a quick look at the folder. Wow. A dozen pages, small print, each page about a thousand words, she guessed, so roughly thirty normal book pages. This would be a good hour's reading. She looked forward to that. It would kill another dull and lonely evening. Monday evening. Mondays were the worst; the beginning of a whole new week alone. Duncan had left to go to New York and Connecticut, and wouldn't be back until after Labor Day. Her own sons? Well, George was in Germany working for General Motors. Freddie was with his father up in the Napa Valley for the summer. He had made noises lately that he wanted to learn the wine business. Gwen and her husband were in Vancouver, visiting his family. They wouldn't be back until early September, either. Her golfing buddies were only for that, golf. Twice a week. Friends? Not too many, as yet. Her own fault, probably.

When she got into her car she turned on the air conditioning full blast. It was hot outside. There'd be a sea breeze in her Palisades home. Come to think of it, she might go down to the beach and walk, watch the sun sink red-hot on the far horizon. Then grab some takeout food on the way back. She wished she had a dog again. Her old Lab had died before she moved out of the house. Every year since she had said to herself that she needed a dog again, but in a condo the situation was different. She couldn't have a dog that weighed more than twenty-five pounds, according to the bylaws. She hated small toy dogs. Lately she had thought of having a terrier, Jack Russell maybe. Lively and intelligent. A breeder had been recommended to her. She was on his list for a male from the next litter, in September sometime. That'd be good.

The next morning she reported back to George Natalian. "Here.

I've read it. Interesting, in a general sort of way, this stuff about the art business and museums and such. Now give me the test, tell me the tale."

George said: "Keep the folder, it's yours."

"Okay. You were kidding about the test, right?"

"First the tale, then the test." He rose from his chair. He hadn't even asked her to sit down. The chair that had been free yesterday now had stacks of magazines piled on it. "Let's go to the cafeteria for some latte. You like latte?"

"I do. I call it milk, and I use it in my coffee. No sugar, in case you are ordering."

They sat down at a table near the back wall where there were no immediate neighbors. George put sweetener in his coffee and pushed some her way. She declined. They sat quietly for a while, sipping their brews.

Then George said, "Let's start this way: Would you be free to travel?"

"It depends. Sure. Yeah, I would." Gretchen suddenly had visions of Rome, Paris, London....

"Everything hinges on that point. It might be for a week or two, or three. We are talking soon, probably September. Still think you're free?"

"Yes." She nodded vigorously. Sure she was. She'd talk to the breeder; a couple of weeks later wouldn't make any difference in getting that pooch.

He cast a sideways glance at her to see if she was serious. Satisfied, he said, "From here on, everything I tell you is confidential. Okay?" He leaned back in his chair. "That Friedrich guy—you must have been wondering why I gave you all that reading material. Maybe you guessed that there's an interest on our part in his works. And you'd be right."

"It crossed my mind," she smiled.

"Regarding 'The Polar Sea:' You have read in the book that there was an earlier painting on the theme of ice floes in the Arctic, commissioned by a wealthy Saxon art patron, a Baron von Quandt. It preceded the one that he did as 'The Polar Sea,' and it also contained a shipwreck, this one supposedly connected to Peary's search across the Arctic for a northwest passage. Another player at the time was the Russian art emissary of the grand duke, later tsar, Nicholas I. Vasily Shukovski; I know you have read all that. I'm just trying to connect the dots here, because that first painting is generally described as and presumed to be 'disappeared.' Now, word has come to us that it—let's call it 'Number One Polar Sea,' or 'One P.S. for short—is about to resurface. Pay close attention, Gretel, because this is the test: How much of what I'm going to tell you can you put into your memory bank without notes, huh?" He pointed to his forehead. "Because there ain't gonna be no notes."

"Fine with me." She mimicked his gesture.

"Good." George was serious now. "Look, this whole thing has to do with provenance. And with money—meaning Getty money. Let's talk provenance first. It goes back to that guy Shukovski. There is some evidence that he obtained the painting—remember, we're talking 'One P.S.' here, exclusively—for his boss, the future tsar. Quandt was probably the middleman, his stated desire to have a 'north' and a 'south' painting for his collection is okay as far as it goes, his selection of Friedrich for the 'north' one logical in that the painter, in his middle years, was good yet still cheap to buy. But Friedrich was beginning to have a name; Quandt had made a good investment. Now came Shukovski, who had a nose for such things, as we have reason to believe based on what he has said about Friedrich at the time. He saw Friedrich as a typical Nordic artist, brooding, strange, mirthless, just as the Danes and the Swedes were thought of then. The grand duke, his boss, was all that and more, almost entirely descended from German and Danish ducal houses, married to a Prussian princess. He lived in St. Petersburg, another Baltic location. So Shukovski, ever the toadying courtier, acquired 'One P.S.' for the duke, Quandt remaining prudently silent. The painting was wrapped and transported by coach to the northeast, but it never made it to the Hermitage or to the tsar's private quarters. We lose track of it in Riga, en route so to speak, and there the story ends: 'The Wreck of the *Hoffnung*,' as it was called when it was first exhibited at Dresden in 1822, had *disappeared*."

George paused and sipped from his coffee. Gretchen said, "Hmm-hmm?" He continued.

"The reason I gave you the articles from the Colnaghi catalogue is to make you aware of the way this art business operates. Major dealers have major clients, and major sources. They deal both ways. They also have minor dealers interjected into the processes of acquisition and sale, who in turn may have the actual buyer. Look at it this way: You go and buy an appliance, say a toaster, from a store down the street. The store has bought it from the distributor or wholesaler, who in turn has bought it from the manufacturer. Roughly put, we in the museum business—unlike those auction houses that rely on bidding frenzies—do it the reverse way. We go to the major dealer, who may have a contact to a minor dealer, who may have a client who wishes to sell what we want to buy. We are loathe to cut out the middle levels because we don't want to be known as direct buyers, and also because the dealerships set realistic prices, ones that the market will bear. This is particularly true when the Getty name becomes involved; people think we have money like water. It would tend to raise prices, and the whole art market would suffer the consequences."

Gretchen said, "I've become acquainted with that since working here."

George looked up, surprised. "You have? How and where?"

"I was involved in the Pissarro research, remember? There was a lecture at the County Museum of Art on the subject of provenance. It had to do with the '*fake*' Van Goghs; about the 'Sunflowers' bought by that Japanese insurance company for forty million dollars ten years ago that may have been a fake painted not by Van Gogh but by one of his friends, and so on."

"Yes. Oh, yes. Eternal vigilance is the price of art, too. Very good. Now we can go to our current scenario. One of our major art dealers in New York, by name of Schlesinger and Baldwin, S. and B. for short, specialists in nineteenth-century European paintings, have been approached by a party I shall describe later with a proposition: The early Friedrich of the Arctic Sea, our 'One P.S.,' has turned up and is for sale. Not here in America, but abroad. Our ears perked up. We made some skeptical inquiries: How could that be, that a painting arises that was buried, so to speak, for a hundred fifty years? Well, it seems that the painting was not of interest to the soon-to-be Tsar Nicholas, a dour man with plenty of troubles at home, so it never left Riga but was kept by a secret society, a brotherhood or guild of Riga's leading businessmen dating back to the arrival of the Hanseatic League and the Teutonic Knights in the thirteenth century. The guild was like a lodge, housed in a handsome building in the center of Riga, accessible only to members. However, visiting Russian royalty would show up for tours and sign the guest book. The house held many valuable works of art, especially silver chalices and such dating back to the Middle Ages, and all the rooms had paintings on the walls, portraits and such. Miraculously, the building and its contents survived all wars and turmoil until the Russian takeover in World War II. The Iron Curtain came down, and the building ceased to exist. What happened to the painting and other valuable artworks since then is anybody's guess. We are only too well aware of the havoc wreaked in the art world by the Nazis and the Soviets. The Riga house was just one more victim. Now, here's the kicker: The new Latvian government is interested in rebuilding the landmark guild hall, an undertaking for which, as always, money of the hard-currency kind is needed. What would you do if you were a Lett and you had an old oil nobody ever really liked but that could bring plenty of Yankee dollars?"

"A rhetorical question, George. Go on." New visions of a trip to Europe began forming in Gretchen's mind. George was going, and he wanted her along.

"Right. Our friend S. and B. were contacted. They in turn contacted us. The ball started falling. We are very cautious. A hundred and fifty years of un-checkable provenance; should we buy it? We had the dealer ask for the usual, you know, authentication of the work from the ground up. It all came back positive. It could have been painted by Friedrich. We asked for a direct view. Then boom, the game changed. The party involved changed the venue, sent out feelers through the art grapevine, in essence put the work on the open market. We immediately bowed out. Our presence would have jacked up the price unconscionably."

"You bowed out!" Gretchen exclaimed. There went the trip to Europe.

George nodded, then winked. "In favor of a wealthy private collector."

"Who?"

George leaned back and folded his hands behind his head. "You."

"Me? George I don't have that kind of money. In fact, I have no money."

Still looking amused, Geroge said: "How would you like to fly to Hong Kong, all expenses paid? Visit an art gallery, maybe make a purchase?"

Gretchen stared at him, speechless.

"Look." George came forward, put his arms on the table. "Remember the retailer-wholesaler analogy? An old friend of ours who used to be at the Malibu Getty has opened a gallery in Santa Barbara. He has connections to S. and B. in New York, who, in turn, reciprocate with one of Hong Kong's finest, the Watson Elementary Art, Limited. Dear Watson has been approached by the Letts, who obviously want to plumb the riches of the Orient. What do they have? Among other things, such as silver and amber antiquities, they happen to have a Friedrich. Word went out to several galleries in the U.S. as to what's available here. Your old friend Charles Lamb, up in Santa Barbara, thought of you immediately, as you had intimated to him that you have divorce funds—or is it fungibles?—for a solid investment with growth prospects. He'd like you to come up and talk to him. We agree. We think you should go, take a little time off. You deserve it."

Gretchen held back an immediate answer, searching in his face, his eyes, for the truth. George did not flinch.

She said, "Tell me about this Hong Kong trip, in plain English, George."

He nodded. "Remember, we started out asking if you had time for a trip? Well, this is the trip: First class to Hong Kong, a stay at the Regent Hotel, plenty of cash and a charge account. All we ask in return is that you act the lady you are, not necessarily born to wealth but comfortable with it. Go to Watson, have them show you the painting, let the aura of it sink in on you, get the feel of it—a fake or not? Stuff like that. Keep in touch with Charles by phone, consult him regarding price and competition if any, and make a deal if it all comes out right. Charles will deal on through S. and B. to get his cut. That's the way it works. In the end, we deal with S. and B."

"And I carry the painting home in the overhead compartment of the plane? And what if there is no deal?"

"Ha-ha. The overhead compartment. I like that. No, dummy, you take it out of the fame, roll it up, and put it in your carry-on."

"What?"

"Smuggle it through customs." He took her hand. "Hey, I'm kidding. Of course you carry nothing. The dealers arrange all that. You just sign the papers, write the check. We'll give you an account to do that on. Then you'll stay as long as you like, enjoy yourself. No hurry. It's all on the house."

"Good lord. My head is reeling. And what about the other possibility, that I don't get the deal?"

"You mean someone else will get it? Sure. Could happen. Then you just tell that to Charles, maybe try to find out who the other party is if you can. No skin off your nose."

Gretchen shook her head. "It puts a big burden on my shoulders, George. Failure looms large, as much as or perhaps more than success. Here you are, the Getty people, sending me on a first-class trip to Hong Kong. How am I supposed to feel, using up all that money for nothing?"

"Gretchen! Gretel! How much are we paying you now?"

"Now? Nothing, I'm a volunteer."

"And how much work have you been doing for us? Huh? Care to guess what it's worth? Put a price tag on it?"

"Well...."

"Besides, the commission we'd pay to Charles, not to mention S. and B., is in multiples of your expense account. Don't be a fool, kiddo. Take the trip."

Gretchen put her hands over her face and groaned. When she lowered them, she had tears in her eyes. "I want to go, George, really I do!"

"Atta girl! Let's shake on it." He held out his hand. She gripped it hard, and he felt the wetness of her tears on his palm. "Thank you, Gretel. You're doing the right thing."

— CHAPTER FOUR —
Making Ready

Gretchen kept herself in seclusion during the Labor Day weekend, the Monday holiday falling on the first of September this year and everyone she knew still being away on their August vacations. She was rather glad of the solitude, the weekend having begun with the horrendous news that Princess Diana had died in a car crash in Paris. Press and television coverage was full of the weepy, maudlin, melodramatic aspect of the event, and to her surprise Gretchen found herself bawling along with each new report, blowing into countless tissues and running to the bathroom during commercial pauses—oh yes, there were those—to splash cold water onto her face. She grimaced at her red-eyed, red-nosed countenance in the mirror and chided herself for being a sentimental fool. Then she rushed back to the living room because she could hear that so-and-so was about to report from London.

There was nothing new; the flower tributes were mounting at the gates of the royal palaces, people were weeping openly—reserved, stiff-upper-lip British people—and there was talk of bringing Diana home to a state funeral. The queen would be heard from; Prince Charles and his two sons—Diana's children—would emerge from self-imposed privacy at last, and Earl Spencer, Diana's brother, was making voluble, plummy pronouncements already. The two other people who had died in the crash and the severely wounded bodyguard were...well, incidental, mere victims.

Disgusted, Gretchen turned off the T.V. She had done her own research on the royals for her book, from all the Georges on up, and it had not served to make her a monarchist. Nor the opposite: She found them all profoundly common, in the sense of sharing in all the human frailties. In the back of her mind she wondered how she would have fared if she had been one of the many princesses who had come and gone in that family. Would she have done better? Worse? It was just fantasizing, of course. Still, having read as much as she had, she was keenly aware of the vagaries of noble blood lines. Were they all really as noble as they seemed? Where did all the bastards go? She wondered about that.

Early on, when she was a small child and even later as a young girl before she reached her teens, there had been times when she would crawl at night into her mother's bed when her father was away on one of his trips and little Jimmy was sleeping his angelic deep sleep in his room down the hall. "Tell me a story, Mummy, please!" And her mother would pull her to herself. "What kind of a story, sweet?" "A real story, not a made-up one!" "Well...." And off she would go, spinning tales of fair maidens and chivalrous men, of witches and sorcerers, of dukes and princesses, Gypsies and soldiers, wondrous tales of men and women in faraway places, long-ago times. Now and then she would hum a melody or breathe a song, with words the child could not understand, and it would put the little girl to sleep.

Gradually as she grew up, Gretchen recognized that the stories her mother told her were the plots of operas, the songs arias, the languages Italian and German and French. They were also prudently edited, eliminating the last acts: Othello did not strangle Desdemona, Tosca did not fling herself from the prison wall, Madame Butterfly did not commit hara-kiri. Her mother had been an opera singer, so she learned, in her native Germany. Or was Germany her native land? Had she not stated, upon renewing her passport, that she was born in Hengelo, Holland, a fact ten-year-old Gretchen could clearly read on the copy her mother had left on her desk? Mothers are not to be asked about something that a curious child would discover about them. Instead, Gretchen went to the encyclopedic dictionary she had been given for her tenth birthday, and there it was: "Hengelo, a city in E. Netherlands."

Next, she went to her father to ask with knitted brow and serious eyes, "Dad, tell me, where does Mummy come from? Is she really a princess?"

Her father threw back his head with his deep-throated laugh. "Has she been telling you tales again, this time about her princely family?" He took his gangly daughter by the arm and led her to the library shelves. "Look, all these books are about history, stories about events that occurred in the past, here in America and in England and France and Germany and Italy. I hope eventually you will make use of these—" he made a sweeping gesture up and down the library shelves "—as you become more interested in what went on before. You will like it, you'll see. You have an inquisitive mind." He looked down fondly at his bright and earnest daughter.

"What about the princess, Dad?" she insisted.

"Okay, yes. One of the ancestors she has—and you have, through her—was a d'Este. Here is how it's spelled." He wrote it down on a writing pad from the nearby desk. "They were from Italy originally, and some of the branches of that family went to Bavaria and then to the north, to Brunswick."

"So it's true, Mummy is a princess?"

That deep throaty laugh again. "Gretchen, that was a long time ago in faraway lands. Her mother's mother came from the d'Este line. Your great-grandmother. You know how many sets of parents that is? Let's count them: You have two, Mummy and me. Mummy and I each also had two, that makes four." He took another sheet of paper from the writing pad. "Look: Each of our grandparents had two parents, who all had two, and so on." The diagram now held sixteen mums and dads in one line. "And this one, she is the d'Este, one out of thirty—adding two plus four plus eight plus sixteen. Right? Do you see that?"

The girl nodded gravely. Then she took the pencil and, putting the tip on the one marked d'Este, drew a line straight up the page to the spot where her name was circled. "It's not so many stops, Dad, I'm the fourth down. Right?" She smiled mischievously.

Gretchen smiled now, thinking back on that day nearly forty years ago. She shook the cobwebs of memory out of her head. Time to think of what lay ahead. It had been a busy two weeks preparing for it. George Natalian was keeping close tabs on her.

There was first a quick visit with the art dealer in Santa Barbara. She'd take her car and go along the coast to avoid the hated Ventura

Freeway. She was quite familiar with the area from many a visit with her—dare she say it?—husband, Wilf, during happier days, or perhaps more innocent days. "Ignorant" and "naïve" were probably better words, *dammit*. No way she'd ever be that way again....

Charles Lamb, the dealer, had called her on the prearranged ruse of inviting her to see some of the items in his collection that might conceivably be good investments of a portion of her "funds," as he called it. As she drove up State Street, which was thronging with summer visitors, she looked out for Carrillo Street, made a quick right, and there it was across the street in a handsome old adobe: Charles Lamb Fine Arts. Parking was not a problem: Charles had told her he would put red traffic cones out in front of his store, which he would remove when she arrived so she could park her car safely. There was an arrangement with the local police for a temporary allowance that would give local merchants a break.

Gretchen had no idea what Lamb looked like; George had described him as a retired art restorer, so naturally a gray-haired, bookish little man came to Gretchen's mind, and when he told her over the phone about the traffic cones, in a raspy voice, now and then clearing his throat, the picture was complete. She was not prepared for the tall, lanky New Englander-type gentleman who came dashing out of the store and waved at her, picking up the cones one-two, three-four, throwing them over the small gate at the front entrance to his store and, job done, wiped his hands and motioned her to pull into the space. The only guess she had right was the gray hair, and even that was a bit off, as he had close-cropped white hair over a tanned, ruddy face. Well.

She parked the car and got out. "Hi!" Lamb spread his hands: "Dirty. Come on in." He led her across the tiled forecourt to the entrance to his gallery, which was on the ground floor of the Spanish-style building. Inside, he said, "Nice to meet you, Mrs. Goodridge. Need to freshen up? Follow me to the washrooms." The show space was surprisingly modern, extending to a back patio visible at the end of the showroom. A woman was sitting at a desk, answering the phone. The washrooms, at least the one Gretchen used, were Spanish tiled. Very pretty, all of it, she thought as she sat down to relieve herself none too soon.

Lamb was waiting for her outside. "D'you mind if we use the back patio? It's a lovely day." He smiled at her, with perfect teeth. Probably capped, Gretchen thought; he's got to be well over sixty.

"That'll be fine," she smiled back, and she followed him.

"Well, then...." He pulled back a chair for her. It was wrought-iron, but padded on the seat and back. "Ready for a little espresso? I got that handy machine over in that corner. How do you take it?"

"Milk and sugar, please." She felt a bit tired and in need of a rush.

He brought the steaming little cups and sat down next to her. She took the business card he handed her. It was embossed with a lamb icon.

"Very impressive," she said, just to say something.

"What—the lamb?" He laughed. "Many illustrious namesakes, English and American. No relation, though. What about you, Mrs. Goodridge? Any non-relation to famous people?"

"Plenty," she laughed. She began to warm to this man.

"Good. Then let's be like common folk. I'm Bud." He held out his hand. "How do you do?"

She shook his hand. "And I am Gretchen. Nice to meet you, Bud."

The woman from the telephone came out, bearing a plate. Hot scones and little jars of jam. Paper napkins and small knives. Lamb made the introduction. "This is Evelyn, my wife. Gretchen Goodridge, from Los Angeles." Evelyn Lamb was not much younger than her husband, now that Gretchen could see her in broad daylight. A faded blonde. Tasteful jewelry. A whiff of perfume. Evelyn Lamb smiled and withdrew.

"Just a quick bite." Lamb sounded apologetic. "Hope you don't mind. We'll have lunch later. Please, help yourself."

They ate in silence for a few minutes, Gretchen looking around. She liked what she saw. Fine-ranked trellises, rose beds, red tiles atop the low walls around the garden. The morning sun filtered through the slightly swaying leaves of a eucalyptus tree, dappling the lawn. Beyond the back wall, over the bougainvillea, she could see another red-tiled roof.

Lamb had followed her gaze. "That's quiet old Santa Barbara for you. He smiled. "A real nice place. Good neighbors."

"Nice to be close to the ocean, too," Gretchen smiled back.

"Paradise," Lamb said. Then he began, "For the record, we are having this meeting because you asked for it. As a collector, you have heard through the art grapevine that an early Caspar David Friedrich has surfaced from behind the fallen Iron Curtain, and you have asked me, a previous acquaintance, to look into it. I, in turn, used my connection to the old and well-regarded New York art firm of Schlesinger and Baldwin to research this for me. They did, and we are here today to discuss the results."

Gretchen nodded. The script, as written by George.

Lamb nodded also. "They tell me that a painting by Friedrich titled 'The Polar Sea, Version One', previously thought lost, has turned up in Hong Kong, where it was offered for sale to the well-regarded art dealership Watson, Limited, by parties unknown but with apparent claim to ownership. The owner is a lodge or fraternity of sorts in the city of Riga, Latvia. The lodge was outlawed during the Soviet occupation of the country for over fifty years. Prior to that, the painting hung in plain view in one of the common rooms, although the view was plain only to those who had access to the lodge, which was limited to members—all male—and occasional invited guests. With me so far?"

"Yes. What George hasn't been able to tell me, though, is where the painting has been kept for half a century. I understand that in the end the building was destroyed, what with all the warfare going on. Did your sources tell you anything about that, Bud?"

"Good question. They didn't tell me about that in particular, either, but the sellers claim that the painting was preserved by being hidden behind the back of another painting, a mediocre work of the same size in a simple frame, and that it was kept in one of the members' homes out in the country. Until now. The lodge wants to raise funds to rebuild the house. The Latvian government's funds are not sufficient."

"The removal of the painting during wartime, saving an apparently mediocre work—that would indicate that the lodge brothers were well aware they had a valuable piece of art in their hands, would it not?"

"Yes, or—let's not be naive here, there is an alternative—it is all part of an elaborate ruse to create a credible provenance. Or perhaps the whole thing is a scam, the painting a fake. Worse things have happened in the hallowed halls of the art trade."

Gretchen gave a short laugh. "I hope it is not up to me to decide which is which!"

"I doubt it. In fact, I don't think it's up to you at all. All the experts at S. and B. seem to be sure it's the real thing. And the Getty people believe them, which is really what it all comes down to. You go to Hong Kong, play your role, and make a deal before more customers turn up and drive up the price."

"Speaking of price, Bud, can you tell me, as my trusted dealer, how much I should offer? Is there an upper limit?"

Lamb laughed. "If it were my money, there sure would be! But with Papa Getty involved, you have a pretty free hand. You tell Watson what you want to pay for the painting—after you have seen it and been convinced that it is the true article, of course. It will require some show of skepticism, some repeat visits, before you make your first bid."

"How much should that be, do you think?"

"I would guess I would start at two-fifty."

"Two hundred fifty thousand dollars?"

"Yes. American."

"And you think it will not be accepted?"

"I'd be very suspicious if it were; you might then be dealing with some small-time thieves. No, I think they'll make a show of indignant response. And remember, they'll have to pay a hefty commission to Watson. I would give a smiling apology and go up to five hundred."

"Which would also be rejected?"

"Probably. Move up in increments of fifty, then of a hundred. Be sure you keep the ball; don't let the initiative be taken away from you. It works pretty much like an auction, particularly if there is another party involved. Remember, the other party or parties ought to be verified by Watson as legitimate. No sham bidders allowed in the game."

"Where is my limit? You still haven't told me."

Lamb shrugged. "You have the deeper pocket behind you. I doubt the others will be as deep. This is not a world-class work of art we are after. It is valuable; and it is desirable for the Getty collection, which is lacking in certain areas. But it is not that valuable to others. I think it will stop short of the magic million."

"From which you will get your commission?"

"Indirectly. Getty pays S. and B., they in turn pay me. Twenty percent of twenty percent. Nice change. It'll keep the doors open a while longer." He gestured towards the gallery behind him.

Gretchen finished her coffee. She thought about what her trip might cost the Getty—first-class airfare, top hotels for two weeks, plus the spending money on the credit card George had mentioned. It could easily come to almost as much as what Bud here would be getting.

Bud said, "When you've finished, let me show you around. Okay?"

They went to the showroom. The front part, near the window

aimed at tourists, was crammed with big, splashy, colorful paintings in gilded frames. Bad imitations of Impressionists, untrue colors.

Gretchen crinkled her nose. Lamb said, "It keeps the wolf from the door." The back room was better, much better: there was quality, there was art. Gretchen's senses were honed to a fine point by her daily exposure to good art. She complimented Lamb, and he seemed pleased.

"There is one more thing we have to do." He went to his desk and pulled out a file. "I have taken the liberty of creating a paper trail of communication between us over the past few weeks, copies of faxes to you, message slips of phone calls from you, letters from our gallery to you, and so on. All fictional, of course, but designed to bolster your legitimacy in Hong Kong. After all, you'll be asking me to wire as much as a million dollars to old Watson—or rather cause them to be wired, because S. and B. will be the actual disbursers. We should have a past." He said that in mock confidentiality, with a wink and arched brows. "Here is a duplicate file for you, Gretchen. Read it, carry it home with you." He put the file in an envelope for her.

Mrs. Lamb came up. "It is almost two o'clock. We should go now, or we won't be seated for lunch anymore."

"Actually," Gretchen looked at her watch, "I think I'd rather skip lunch, if you don't mind. If I leave now I'll make it home by evening. Lots of things still to do. I'm supposed to fly to Hong Kong by the first week of September."

"Of course," Lamb said.

"We understand," said Mrs. Lamb. "It would be nice to chat and get acquainted. Perhaps when you get back? You have a standing invitation."

Gretchen thanked them. She told them it was so nice to have met them, and she really meant it. Yes, they'd do it when she got back. For sure.

George called her up a day or so later and wanted to know how it had gone with Lamb. Gretchen said fine, and gave him a brief report. Was she confident she could handle the transaction? Oh, yes, she was, she replied. George grunted his satisfaction. "Listen," he said, "there is one more thing for you to do: get a medical checkup. You don't mind, do you?"

Gretchen said she didn't; her doctor would be back right after Labor Day.

George said that would be too late; anyway, it would be a Getty doctor who'd have to do the checkup. You know, for the record, and just in case there was any reason she couldn't or shouldn't undertake a long journey.

Gretchen became indignant. She was perfectly healthy, and she did not, repeat not, have any illnesses or disabilities!

George hastened to tell her that he was aware of that. However, for reasons of liability or what have you, the powers that be insisted that one of their doctors do the checkup. Hey, he said, it wasn't a big deal! Besides, it was time to make airline and hotel reservations, and the doctor's report had to be in before that. So get with it!

George was right, it wasn't a big deal. She wrote down the number he gave her and promised him she'd call for her appointment as soon as they hung up. She did. The number was for a Century City medical group. The appointment she got was for eight o'clock Monday morning, August 25. Please have only a light meal the night before, and eat or drink nothing before coming to the office in the morning. Was she menstruating? No. All set, then. Gretchen wrote down the time and place.

The exam was routine. It included blood and urine tests—both of which were later reported to her as normal—and an EKG. The kindly doctor, an elderly man, pronounced her in good health. He would, however, recommend that she be vaccinated for hepatitis A, and he suggested that she contact her own doctor for a booster shot against tetanus. Good advice. Gretchen agreed to the hepatitis shot right away, and for tetanus she said she'd talk to her doctor when she was back after Labor Day.

George was delighted by the news. He told her he had already anticipated it and that he had made the reservations for both the airline and the hotel, in her name. All she'd have to do was to go to the Beverly Hills United Airlines office and pay for the tickets, with the new platinum card he would give her when they met at the Beverly Hilton—say, tomorrow morning?

They agreed to meet for breakfast at the hotel coffee shop. Old George was there ahead of her, waiting, grinning broadly. "Hi, toots!"

"And a good morning to you, too, George." Gretchen slid into the booth. "Does your wife know where you are?"

George kept grinning. This whole thing is like a game to him, thought Gretchen. Now he was waving a small leather wallet. "Lookee here," he said, "a card with your name on it, backed by the full power and resources of the Trust. Use it wisely." He handed it to her.

She took it and pulled out the card. It was a silvery platinum color, and it had her name embossed on it. Valid until August 1999.

She looked at George. "Unlimited funds?"

"Within reason."

"You trust me with it?"

"Explicitly."

"Well, then, let's go see if it works." She slid out of her seat. "You stay here, George. I should be back in a little while, flaunting my first-class ticket."

Gretchen came back twenty minutes later with her ticket envelope. "Flight One, leaving September 5 at noon, arriving in Hong Kong at seven-thirty P.M. the next day. Row 3, seat B. Worked like a charm, George. The Trust is some kilo-bucks poorer." She sat down again and poured herself some more coffee. "All I have to bring is my passport."

George hit his forehead: "Passport! I forgot to ask! You have one, and it is valid beyond six months from now?"

"Not to worry. It's valid until 1999. I used it last spring to fly to Germany to visit my son George. He's there on a General Motors grant to study automotive engineering with Opel."

"Hey—I have an idea. We Georges have to stick together. Why not visit your son again? If things go smoothly, you could return from Hong Kong via Germany. Let the airline rewrite your ticket!"

"And charge the Trust the difference? More kilo-bucks?"

"Why not? Consider it a bonus, for a job well done."

She searched his eyes. "You're not kidding, are you?"

He reached for her hand. "Listen, Gretel. We can't pay you a salary, but we can pay in kind. Don't skimp when you are over there. The Regent Hotel already has an open account for you. I, your business manager, ahem, have called ahead and had them credit your account with a full week's stay, by way of this card you are still clutching in your hands. And you'll be picked up at the airport in a limo. All part of the deal. So don't be shy. Live the image we want you to portray. Quiet wealth, simple elegance, pleasant manners. Suit you to a tee." He pulled a brochure from his jacket pocket. "This is the hotel. Nice, huh? You're on the Kowloon side, with a fabulous view. I've written the confirmation number right there, on the front. If you need me, if you have trouble with anything, call me under my real name but at my home number. On the back cover. See? You can tell people I'm your financial advisor."

"Oh, George." She held his hand with both of hers. "This sounds so exciting! I hope I can do the job for you!"

"I know you can." He looked at his watch. "Now, if you'll excuse me, I've got to call my wife. Tell her where I am." He winked at her.

On that eventful weekend that ended with Labor Day, Gretchen started to do her packing. Partly to test the card at a merchant's and partly because she really didn't have any luggage suitable for a lady of means, she bought two designer bags, one for checking through and one for carrying onboard. While in the shop, she saw a display of wear-on-your-person waterproof document holders that had compartments for cash and passport, and she bought one on impulse. George had said she should draw a cash advance from the card in the amount of several thousand dollars, and she went ahead and did that, filling both compartments with hundred-dollar bills. She put that aside until the morning she'd dress for the flight.

Speaking of dress: It would be hot in Hong Kong, not unlike the way it was in Los Angeles right now, except more humid. Light clothing would be the order of the day. If, on the other hand, she went on to Germany afterwards, it would be considerably cooler there, but even then a raincoat would do. Putting out all the dresses and blouses and skirts that she had that were suitable to the climate, she was dismayed to find that she owned nothing that was really chic and stylish. It shocked her to discover that she had neglected her appearance so much since the divorce. That would have to change! First thing Tuesday morning, she'd go to Neiman Marcus and Saks Fifth and buy several outfits, hang the expense, although there would be post-Labor Day sales on, and of course she'd not use the George plastic, as she had begun to call it. And while there she'd make an appointment to have her hair styled, and her nails done, and maybe even a facial.

The phone rang. A familiar voice said, "Hello, we're back!" It was Gwen. "How've you been?"

Gretchen was instantly suffused with pleasure. "Gwen! I've been fine. So glad to have you back! I have loads to tell you."

Not over the phone, of course, except for the barest of facts. The two friends made a date to get together the very next morning at the stores.

Gwen said Gretchen would need a second opinion on her purchases.

When they hung up, Gretchen felt an urgent need to talk to her sons. Freddie should be back in his San Diego digs by now; classes started again the next day. He was in. Mother and son had a warm and satisfying half-hour over the phone together. Freddie wished her well and asked if she would bring him a certain diver's watch—he named the brand for her—if it would cost less in Hong Kong. Gretchen promised she would, regardless of the cost. Afterwards she realized that in all their talk the name of her sons' father, her former husband, had not come up even once.

It was now going on ten o'clock at night, and Gretchen decided to dial Georgie's number in Frankfurt; he was nine hours ahead of her in Germany, so it would just be getting-up time for him. She was lucky again: With a sleepy voice, George answered the phone. Gretchen told him pretty much the same thing she had told Fred about her forthcoming trip to Hong Kong. Unlike his brother, though, George was curious: What was the purpose of her trip, just fun? Was she going with a friend? A group? Gretchen said it was an art-related trip; and yes, it would be fun. When she said that on the way back she could stop in Frankfurt, he said she should do that, definitely, for sure, as he'd found a girlfriend he'd like her to meet. "Georgie!" Gretchen exclaimed, laughing. "I'd be delighted. I'll call you from Hong Kong."

Tuesday was a shopping day. Gwen dragged Gretchen from one store to the next to another, creating, as she put it, "…a new you, Gret, from the ground up." They bought summer dresses and cocktail attire, casual clothes and sport outfits (Gretchen said she'd try to get in a game or two of golf), shoes for every occasion, a coat, a hat, shawls and handbags (two of each, for day and evening wear), panties, bras and slips, and a satin negligée with matching dressing gown. They broke for lunch in between and stowed bags in the trunk of the car, then resumed in the afternoon, after Gwen had called her service and been told there was nothing urgent. By evening there were more bags in the trunk, and the two friends bade each other an exhausted goodbye.

There was a message from Duncan on her phone when Gretchen came home. It was brief, in his normal, pleasant baritone that sounded the way she remembered her father's voice when they spoke on the phone. She found it uncanny that they should be so much alike, even in their looks sometimes, or in a gesture. But of course her father was his father, too. James was not nearly so reminiscent of their father; he was more earthy, more solid, more Dutch, like their mother. Duncan had this unmistakable Frazer way about him, more lithe than lanky, his dark blond hair often falling over his right eye before it was combed back with splayed fingers, and when he sat on the piano, his head tilted back, his long-fingered hands flying over the keyboard—Mendelssohn, Schubert, Brahms—there were times when she worried about him: Was he a closet queer? Weren't all such artistic types? Until she found out, quite by accident when she visited his new apartment near campus, that he was living with a young woman who was divorced and had a child. Living with her not just as a tenant, but as her lover. The woman was a nurse doing night duty at the UCLA Medical Center emergency room. They had met when Duncan worked there as an orderly the previous summer, Duncan being a pre-med major. He was home with her child, a bouncing two-year-old boy named Dicky, when she was at work, he doing his studying, dozing off, and watching the kid until she came home around three in the morning. Kathy was her name, a dark-haired Irish quicksilver some five or more years older than Duncan, Gretchen guessed. It seemed a happy arrangement, but one that was kept discreetly quiet.

Gretchen was relieved and pleased in equal parts, that that's how it was, and kept her knowledge to herself.

In his message Duncan asked if they were playing golf on Wednesday, the next day. They always met when possible on the day the country club gave women members their priority tee-offs.

Gretchen remembered that she had a standing eight A.M. tee-off, which she would have to cancel for the next couple of weeks. She called him back—he had his own line at the house—and said, yes, let's do it. She was glad to hear his voice again; had he had a good time back east?

He said marvellous, really, interesting, they'd talk tomorrow.

Duncan came on his mountain bike and parked it at the pro shop. He brought only two clubs, his favorite driver and putter, tied to the frame of the bike, their handles sticking out behind the seat.

He did wear a cycling helmet, but was otherwise in shorts and golf shirt. His shoes were regulation, but without spikes. Gretchen disapproved of all of that, from the new-fangled non-spikes to his riding the bike through busy Westwood, always worrying he would get hit by a car. Duncan laughed it off. "I use the bike to go to classes, Gretchen. I take mostly residential streets. And besides, in the morning rush hour I'm here faster than if I took my car." Probably true; the country club was a couple of miles away down traffic-choked Wilshire Boulevard. They embraced warmly.

Today, as most of the times they played, Duncan had time for only nine holes, which suited Gretchen fine. She still had lots to do at home. If they could play through they'd be out in two hours.

Duncan's tee shots were, as usual, unworried, unhurried, and dead on. Gretchen decided not to fuss, either, and was rewarded with longer, arcing drives. That made her happy, in addition to the good feelings she always had in the company of her younger brother. When they had to wait for a foursome to clear a green, she decided she'd tell him more than she would otherwise about her forthcoming trip to Hong Kong. She said she was going over there for the Getty, checking out the particulars of a painting that was being offered by some eastern European party, although officially she'd be like a wealthy tourist who had been tipped off to this find by her dealer.

"That so?" Duncan raised his eyebrows. "Who's the dealer?"

"You won't know them. In Santa Barbara, Lamb Fine Arts."

"Lamb, as in Mary-had-a-little?"

"Yes. But it's all just pro forma. The Getty has it set up."

"Then why doesn't the Getty act directly? Wait, let me guess: It would drive up the price?"

"Exactly. As an individual, I am supposed to have only limited funds. For me it's a fun trip, all expenses paid. First class, no less! I just got through buying a new wardrobe."

"Well, it does sound like fun. When will you be back?"

"Two, three weeks. Maybe more. I'm planning to return via Frankfurt, to see George. He's got a new girlfriend he wants to introduce me to. You know anything about that?"

Duncan grinned. "Nope. Good for Georgie, though. When are you leaving?"

"Day after tomorrow."

"Wow! What time of day?"

"Noon."

"I'll take you to the airport."

"Oh, I'd love that! Won't you miss an important class, Dunc?"

"Don't worry about it. I'm doing fine."

"I'm not worried about you," Gretchen smiled.

At another hole they talked about Duncan's trip to the east. He had seen Jim in Washington. Spent a week with him—weekdays only, actually, as Jim always went home on weekends. Duncan said he was a bit worried about Jim, he seemed to be quietly fuming about everything that went on in Washington, at both the Capitol and the White House, and frustrated that he and his like-minded pals were unable to exert any influence.

"Is Jim right-wing?" Gretchen asked.

"Of course, but to the left of right wing, which is to the right of center, only more so." Duncan guffawed. "He's the embodiment of the Republican dilemma: too liberal for the true conservatives, too conservative for the true liberals. There ought to be a center party."

"Is that your opinion, or his?"

"His, I think. Not that he's ever said so."

"Well, don't you put any bees in his bonnet. If he really thinks that, he'll go nowhere fast. The Republicans and the Democrats are two sides of the same coin. There's no room for a third choice. Never has been." Duncan grimaced and lined up his tee shot.

On Friday he was at her door at nine-thirty sharp. Gretchen was ready. She had spent a restless night; now that she had nothing more to prepare for her trip, worries and vague fears began crowding in on her. Before dawn she got up and drew herself a bath, pouring the last of her bath oil into the steaming water. Aah, fragrance. Too much fragrance; it kept clinging to her skin even after she had dressed.

Duncan noticed it. "Hmm," he said after he had hugged her, "you smell good. What is it?" He was thinking of a new perfume.

Gretchen waved him off and rolled out her big suitcase. She said this was her only luggage and she'd check it through; her purse and a leather satchel she would take with her onboard.

First class had its rewards: a fast check-in, and a pass to the airline lounge until the flight was called. Duncan insisted he'd stay with her until then. "Always a sucker for freebie," he grinned as he helped himself to some goodies from the breakfast—or was it lunch?—bar. Gretchen just sipped some coffee.

"You may not want to take the time to write to me," he mumphed, "but you should call occasionally. Did you take my number with you?"

Gretchen said she had it right there, on her person. She patted her stomach area. They both laughed about that. She had told him about her special compartments.

Then Gretchen became serious again, looking into the distance. After a while Duncan spoke, wiping his mouth. "Are you all right? You are so quiet!"

She turned to him. "I'm all right. I've been thinking...."

"Yes?"

"It's nothing, really. Never mind."

"Look, I'm your brother! Talk to me!"

"And I am your sister. Do I need to know everything about *you*?"

"I'm sorry. I didn't mean to pry. I was just...concerned."

She reached over and touched his cheek. "And I didn't mean to be secretive." Leaning back, she said, "Yes, there is something. It kind of hit me last night, woke me up out of deepest sleep."

"Go on."

"I know you'll think this is very silly, and it is silly, but I can't get it out of my mind." She shook her head. "Today, you know, is the fifth of September. Every once in a while, Labor Day falls on Monday, September first."

"Yes, probably once every seven years or so, stands to reason."

"Not quite. You forget leap years. The gap between years when September first falls on a Monday goes alike: six-five-six-eleven."

"Tell me more. I'm listening."

Gretchen smiled. "Thank you. I appreciate it." Then she sighed. "I'm having trouble verbalizing it. But here goes: On Friday, September fifth, 1975, my mother was killed in a plane crash at around five in the afternoon. It was a scheduled commuter flight from San Francisco to Los Angeles. Near Santa Barbara, a small plane hit the big one. Both crashed, no survivors."

Duncan looked at her quizzically. "I know that, Gret. It's part of the family lore. Surely you're not—oh, come on! There's no connection between that event and your flight today!"

"Of course not—"

"There isn't, Gretchen! The odds are infinitesimal that your plane would crash on the way to Hong Kong just because on the same day twenty-two years ago your mother's plane crashed. Mega-millions to one, if any. Get it out of your head!"

She said calmly, "There were two other Fridays, September fifth, since then, in 1980 and in 1986. I checked them in my diaries; nothing happened on those dates. This one is eleven years after the last one, and I've wondered about that long hiatus, being the sum of the two previous gaps of five and six years, if that meant anything." Now she had to laugh. "At that point I decided to have a long bath, and I overdid the bath oil."

"I hope you washed those cobwebs right out of your brain, too. Let me predict, right here and right now, with near-total certainty, that you will have a wonderful flight, and that you will return hale and hearty, relaxed and happy, into the bosom of your loving family. There; how's that sound?"

"Your word in God's ear," she tousled his hair. "I'm ready to leave. It's time, passport control and whatnot."

They rose. Outside, like rocks parting a stream, travelers passing them on either side, they hugged and kissed on both cheeks.

Duncan stayed and watched her walk away until he could no longer make her out in the throng of people down that long, straight passage to the departure gates. He turned and headed back across the overpass to the parking garage. He shook his head: gosh, he missed her already.

At the passport control counter Gretchen handed in her passport, which she had already shown at the airline check-in counter. It listed her as Gretchen Goodridge, as did the airline ticket and George's credit card. She was fully prepared to be challenged by the passport officer, however: In 1996 it struck her as unacceptable that she should still be known by her divorced husband's name. She consulted her attorney; could she not have her maiden name back? The answer was yes, but it would require a court petition. She told him to go ahead and file one. He did. It took a year, but she became again Margaret Cosima Herter, the name she put on the new passport application. Just a week ago she had received it in the mail, and when it arrived she realized with surprise that her attorney must have forgotten to send in her old passport with the name Goodrich to be canceled. So now she had two passports—but which should she use? Her tickets said Goodrich, but her heart said Herter, so she had decided to take both; let the authorities challenge her as they may. But despite her concerns, the immigration officer made no comment other than, "Have a good trip, ma'am," as he handed the Goodrich passport back to her. She thanked him. Yes, she would have a fine trip.

PART TWO

In Asia

— CHAPTER FIVE —
M.O. Riley

The message he had expected was waiting for him when he downloaded his e-mail shortly after seven in the morning. He didn't bother to read it but printed it out right away because translations would be necessary before he would be able to make sense of the gobbledegook that was beginning to pour into his printer. The message had originated in London less than an hour before, when it was eight o'clock GMT the previous evening. It was addressed to "fanyson"—his e-mail moniker—and the sender was his only source of mail from this network.

Martin O'Patterson Riley was honorably retired from Her Britannic Majesty's service, living a life of frugal contentment in his native Sydney, an Aussie with a "Pommie" accent owing to his decades of living in the mother country. Truth be told, he had heard nothing but the Queen's English from his blessed mother, who to her dying day had never adapted to what she politely called "that beastly accent" with a sweep of her hand that included the whole continent of Australia.

Although not yet fifty years old, he had asked for and received an early retirement package. That was not such an unusual move; where most employers, government or private, would frown on allowing their employees to drop out during their productive years, his service, rightly called "Secret" at times, made it generously available to its people. It was said that their work, highly stressful and often dangerous, made every year count double. By that reckoning, Pat Riley had fifty years under his belt. Not that he couldn't have stayed on if he had wanted to; but there had been such a confluence of bad luck, beginning with the death of his wife from cancer, that the thought of calling it quits and crawling into a hole somewhere in the megalopolis of Sydney was the only attractive choice left for him. Their only daughter, Fiona, was graduated from London University and eager to begin her own life. Pat vowed he would see her often. So far, it had been Fiona who had flown down to Sydney, for Christmas or for his fiftieth birthday last June. He was overdue to return the courtesy.

Easier said than done. Riley lived in constrained circumstances. He had a house, yes, on the North Shore at Neutral Bay, but the title was held by Fiona, and it was a mere cottage, with three rooms and a kitchen and a bath. He found it perfectly sufficient for his needs, and the company of Winnie, his border collie, was his sustenance. He did not want for more, he told himself.

Except, perhaps, a little excitement now and then. His old service had put him on retainer, to make himself available if and when something came up in his neck of the woods where his experience and proven discretion could be put to use. It was not a retainer in the usual sense of the word, however. Pat received no salary, no remuneration except for expenses on a *per diem* basis and the use of a company credit card that would allow him to charge such big-ticket items as airfares and hotels.

The arrangement worked fine. He had made one trip to neighboring New Zealand to check out an ongoing problem with nuclear-powered submarines not being allowed into that country's ports. Another trip took him to newly opened Myanmar, formerly Burma, for a field report that the home office wanted. In each case Riley appeared as a tourist, an academic sort of fellow with a friendly smile and keen eyes who minded his own business. What was his business? Well, engineering, for one. Or tourism, for another. He appeared to be a well-spoken, obviously well-to-do Englishman who wore suit and tie and polished shoes, who disdained crowds and preferred to dine alone, and who would sit for hours in the hotel lobby perusing newspapers and having coffee or a sherry, depending on the time of day. And who tipped well.

Riley sighed with impatience. The printer was still running, an eighth page by now. It would take him hours to put all that verbiage into plain English. Better to leave it until after breakfast and take Winnie on his morning walk.

The dog was ready for it. Following Riley as if Riley were Winnie's charge, not the other way around, traipsing from room to room, from house to yard, from yard to tiny one-car garage and back into the house again, the dog never let his master out of sight, except at night when he took up his post in the kitchen hallway like the sentry that he was in the canine order of things. For the time that the printer had been humming he had sat on his haunches, head cocked this way and that, his intelligent eyes observing every move.

Finally the printer whirred to a stop.

"That's it, Winnie. Let's go out for a bit. What do you say?" Riley took the leash down, although he didn't really need it; Winnie would heel as long as they were in the residential area. When they had reached the stand of eucalyptus trees near the golf course, the dog was free to roam. No need to worry; he always kept within sight and smell of his master.

Riley was excited, he had to admit to himself. Ten pages, close-spaced as usual, would mean a rather large assignment. That, in turn, would mean a hefty deposit into his dollar account, U.S. dollars with a U.S. bank in Sydney, where his money would earn a small amount of interest. Fiona had arranged it for him. Her name was on the account, but Pat had check-signing rights, provided the checks were co-signed by her. Fiona Riley knew about such things. She worked for a British-Belgian bank consortium in the Euro advance section. Very clever girl. At her last visit Fiona had left her father a stack of numbered checks already signed by her. So as not to forfeit interest, Riley would not draw against the account more than three times a month.

Slowly but surely, it seemed Riley would work himself out of that rut he was in—never to recover completely, of course, but at least to provide some margin of comfort. He was often in a tight squeeze at month's end before his pension check was deposited into his Australian bank. He had joked to Winnie that his dog food morsels looked mighty tasty, pretending to eat one while Winnie gave him a sideways glance and wagged his bushy black tail.

Back at the house, the dog content to lie on the stoop and let the cool air from the bay ruffle his thick winter coat, Riley took the bunch of pages from the printer and sat down to breakfast with it. Halfway through his orange juice he noticed there were some Cyrillic letters on the pages. That would mean a simple translating, as Russian was not encrypted by the home office. Next he looked for a geographic place name, indicating where he was to travel. The name would be spelled backwards, and he would have to consult the current list of where that place really was: "Sirap" for Paris, and Paris being, say, Vienna on that month's list. He guessed that "Emanirus," which appeared several times, could be Suriname, and it was a safe bet that they were not sending him to South America. But where, then?

He quickly finished his toast and took his coffee with him to the room he called his studio, where the computer and printer were.

Suriname, for the month of August 1997, was—surprise!—Hong Kong. That pleased him, as he had not been to the former British colony since he served a tour of duty there some twenty years earlier.

Now to deciphering the text. At the home office this was done on the computer, taking only seconds. He did not have that software at his disposal, for security reasons, so it would take laborious translating, first letter by letter, then word by word, until he had a clear text, written on paper that he would turn soon after, along with the computer printed pages.

Riley set to work. It would be hours before he had it done.

He cursed through clenched teeth as he went along when something that turned out to be very obvious had defied his understanding at first try. He cursed loudly at some of the redundancies the encrypter had chosen to explain, for instance the meaning of "provenance," or when the Russian words were translated for him; did the fellow not know that he was a trained Russian expert, fluent in the language?

But much of the text was actually very interesting. The Russian thing, for instance, "Golovnyi tcherniya," meant "Black heads," its meaning stretched further as in *heads* of an organization and "black" having an illicit connotation, as in "black market." The text then went on to elaborate that there had been, in Riga, Latvia, a guild dating back to the Middle Ages of merchants and freemen who called themselves "Schwarze Häupter" in the German spoken by the Teutonic knights. It was, the report explained, not unlike Masonic lodges giving themselves fancy names. With the fall of communism and the restoration of

Latvian nationhood—that, too, painstakingly explained!—the old guild had been revived, but on two tracks, the Latvian one seemingly legitimate, and another, illicit one run by what the report called "former Soviet functionaries."

The latter group knew of the former, but the former was unaware of the latter. Or so it seemed; Riley should make the determination. The point being, a delegation from Riga was en route to Hong Kong carrying a valuable painting ("presume high six figures, in U.S. dollars") that they were anxious to sell to a wealthy American buyer. To whose benefit? And why not just give it to Christie's to auction it off?

The report wasted—in Riley's opinion—reams of print on the person of the painter, "a German Romantic, contemporary of Turner, by name of Caspar David Friedrich," as if Riley could not have culled that information from the *Britannica* right there on his shelf. Then it said precious little about the painting itself, which was titled "The Wreck of the *Hoffnung*," an Arctic shipwreck, hitherto "presumed lost." Lost by whom? Where? Not said.

Here, at last, came the point of the mission: Riley should give the impression of being a scout for a potential rich buyer and show up at the Hong Kong dealership of "Watson Elementary Art, Ltd.," run by Geoff Watson, a longtime Hong Kong resident and now expatriate Britisher. Good old Geoffrey, as it happened, had at one time or another done a favor to the service, and Pat should use his discretionary judgment to let him assume that the service was interested in information, not in the actual purchase of the work of art.

To sum up: Who were the sellers, group A or group B? Where had they gotten the painting? Was it authentic? How much were they asking—and getting—for it? Of lesser interest was the identity of the buyer, whoever that might be, who would arrive during the second week of September.

The report closed by stating that the matter was not as trivial as it might seem ("Hear-hear!" Pat exclaimed), but tied in with a larger picture that the service was putting together.

Riley cared not a farthing whether or for whom "the matter" was of importance. He had long adopted the cynical view that much of what the service did was bureaucratic wheel-spinning. On the other hand, this assignment was his trade now, and he had better let the home office know that he was ready and able to take it.

All that was needed to accept was to reply on the electronic mailer, with a pre-set phrase that meant he understood "the matter" and would comply with all terms. That would trigger a wire transfer to his bank account of his *per diem* expenses, one week's advance his minimum requirement even if the assignment was completed in less time than that. At the completion of his mission he would file for the rest of the days on the job. He would not use up the *per diem* allowance, he made sure of that. The unused portion was his "profit," and the past two trips had been on a fifty percent "plus side," as he called it.

The second week of September was less than two weeks away. He would want to leave on a Saturday, to arrive in Hong Kong on Sunday and be ready for business on Monday. He would call Quantas to make a reservation. The airfare would be charged to a credit card with his name on it, but in fact the card was owned by the service and usable only when he was on assignment. For longer trips he was allowed to book business class for appearances' sake as well as for reasons of better attention if his routing had to be changed unexpectedly.

The same card would allow him to charge his hotel stay. Quantas, as it happened, had a "business special" on offer for one of the better hotels, the prices having slipped somewhat since the British relinquished sovereignty. He took it. He was all set the day after he had received the letter. He had a week to prepare himself and put his personal affairs in order.

There were, he knew, three concerns that needed to be satisfied: his dog, his cottage, and his daughter. The first two had been taken care of quite well on his two previous trips: Winnie would stay in the house, and his neighbor, an elderly woman called Adelaide Moore, would gladly feed the dog and let him use the yard by day, locking him up in his accustomed place at night. Miss Adelaide, as she was called, was a painter of some renown. Riley had bought one of her oils that she let him have for a pittance. It hung over the fireplace.

A no-nonsense woman, Miss Adelaide was once again helpful. "Where're you off to this time, Pat? Nowhere to come home from with a bad tummy, eh?"

He had had the trots after the trip to Myanmar. "I'd ruddy well better not have a repeat, now, had I?" Riley replied, and left it at that.

He called Fiona on his cell phone from the pub after he had his dinner there. It was still morning in London, and she was in her office.

"Where are you calling from, Father?" She always called him Father, the old "Dad" appellation having been left behind with her other childhood things when she went off to university and a place of her own. "I'm hearing a lot of background noise!"

"The pub. I've just had my dinner here. How are you, sweetheart?"

"I'm fine, thank you. Is Winnie there with you?"

"He is, right under the table."

"You didn't feed him any scraps, did you?"

"Just the bone from my chop, Fi. It's good for him."

"It is not, Father, and you know it!" Fiona was betrothed, or whatever they called it these days, to a veterinarian who was teaching animal husbandry at Truro Veterinary College. She had no pet of her own, but that did not stop her from having strong views on pet care, no doubt enforced by her…what, friend? They were not officially engaged yet.

"I'll let Winnie decide that. Fi, I'm off again on another jaunt. It's Hong Kong this time."

"Hong Kong! Whatever for? And for how long?"

"Art theft, it seems. Some Eastern European buggers. I'm to have a look-see. It's probably no more than a week, but I'll try to stretch it to ten days, if possible."

"It's not the Russians, is it?" She didn't wait for his answer. "We hear so much of Mafia-like behavior on their part, especially in banking. Be careful, Father!"

"Oh, I will be. It's not Russians, but Latvians, actually."

"Good. Hope the job works out for you. One of these days you'll have to think of something more permanent to do."

"You know I can't do that, Fi!"

"Not yet, no. But with time, things may change. You can't go on flitting to the four corners of the world forever, Father."

"Nothing is forever, Fi. I'm taking it one day at a time. Like old Winnie, here."

"Give him a pat on the head for me. Call me from Hong Kong?"

"I will, sweetheart."

"Be well, Father. Bye!" Fiona had hung up before he could say, "And you, too." He knew she was close to tears again. The loss of her mother, soon to be followed by her father's demise, had left scars that had not healed yet.

• • •

On Saturday, September 6, Pat Riley boarded the daily Quantas flight to Beijing with stopover at his destination, Hong Kong. He wore a lightweight, light-colored suit, with shirt and tie. He hefted his carry-on bag into the overhead bin and put his briefcase with the laptop computer under the seat. His business card, recently printed, bore a North Sydney post office box address, and under "M. O'Patterson Riley," it said "Arts & Antiquities." When he was stationed in Paris, the abbreviation M. was often mistaken to stand for Monsieur. It was Martin, his mother's favorite name for him. Hardly anyone else had ever called him Martin, though. It was always Pat—at school, in college, in the service. Pat Riley, a good old Irish chap.

CHAPTER SIX
Hong Kong

Gretchen's airplane ride across the northern rim of the Pacific was "smooth and uneventful"—that was how she put it in the postcard she wrote hastily when the plane had made it safely into Kai Tak airport and was taxiing to the terminal. The postcard was addressed to Duncan. He would know that there was a hidden meaning behind those routine words, and perhaps he would smile remembering her sense of dread and his flat-out, amused dismissal of her fear. No, the fateful fifth of September did not repeat itself for her, as Gretchen had rationalized well enough herself; but all through the long fifteen hours, way down in her unconscious there had sat that gnome of horror of her mother's demise, unperturbed, smirking. It was always there, she felt, even when she managed to damp it down. It still lurked below, mute and glowering.

Throughout the long day, when the sun would not set until they were approaching Hong Kong, Gretchen lay in the darkened cabin, stretched out on the "ergonomic" seat that had more controls than her car, rousing herself only for meals and trips to the toilet, watching two movies in a row on the pop-out video screen, dozing to the strains of music classical and country, staring at sitcoms that she was astonished to learn played to popular acclaim. Until at last came the descent to Hong Kong.

Another successful white-knuckle landing amidst the tenements and skyscrapers of Kowloon. Soon—next year, the brochures said—the new airport would open on a distant island and even this last thrill of what used to be British Hong Kong would face into memory. Gretchen shrugged mentally: No concern of hers. She would be long returned home by then.

Passport control, customs, baggage retrieval—with personnel in neat, trim uniforms, looking astonishingly like they must have under British rule, passing her into the outside world.

A car was waiting for her—not a "limo," but a plain black Mercedes. It was air-conditioned, quiet, and driven by a chauffeur in a white tunic and cap. A short ride on busy streets past stores and buildings that would not have looked out of place if transplanted to Manhattan gave Gretchen a first inkling of what kind of city was taking her to its bosom. She felt a tingle of excitement; maybe this trip would be fun!

Check-in at the hotel was smooth, courteous, and swift. An elevator ride to the fourteenth floor—the highest of the non-smoking floors, it was explained to her—with a petite front-desk lady, her black hair tied into a neat bun, who led her to the room.

The door opened, and Gretchen knew instantly that she would be happy here. The wide picture window revealed a view of nighttime Hong Kong that was breathtaking. She rushed forward, stifling a cry of joy as she beheld the glitter and grandeur of tall buildings, each one different from the next, lining the waterfront from right to left and beyond, with dark mountains in the back topped by heavy clouds. Water traffic crisscrossed the bay.

"This is wonderful!," she exclaimed.

"Yes, madam," replied the lady, with a slight bow, and went on smilingly to explain, pointing this way and that: the television, inside the cabinet; the bathroom, all marble, with jet-faucets in the tub, separate shower, and closed toilet; free newspaper in the morning; breakfast included in the room price. The bellboy came to deliver her bags. Gretchen tipped generously, but not the lady, who withdrew waving off the gratuity.

Alone at last. Gretchen threw herself on the bed, folding her hands in prayer for her safe delivery, until her eyes were drawn to the view again. She would keep the curtains open. A quick bath, and then to bed.

She dreamed—or was it her imagination—that she was free, a blithe spirit arising from the broken shell of her former life. To be reborn. To live. It gave her such an inner glow, such serenity, that she let it linger as her dream gave way to wakefulness. She opened her eyes and saw the first rays of the sun strike the sides and the roofs of the tall buildings across the water, bathing them in bright orange, glowing red, and blinding white. The waters still lay dark, and a few boats pushing across from shore to shore left silvery wakes. She had not closed the curtains overnight, and this was her reward, seeing her first day in Asia dawn over Hong Kong. She threw back the covers and rushed to the window to see more, to take it all in. How lucky she was. How beautiful the world. This was Sunday; she would make it a holiday, not think about her "mission"—hadn't George in fact said to do so?—but go out and see the sights.

But wait. She had better call George Natalian to let him know that she had arrived. She had promised him that. Besides, she was curious how their communications "link-up," as he had dubbed it, would work, what with the time difference and all. George had given her his special number and said for her to call "...anytime. I've got a pager, call forwarding, call waiting, the works," and Gretchen had said she would.

She picked up the phone, studied the dialing instructions, and punched in her numbers. George was there on the third ring.

"Gretel—that you?" His rough, nasal voice that in the beginning had grated on her was music to her ears now.

"Yes!" She was not alone. The link-up worked! "How'd you know it was me?"

"Been expecting your call. It's four in the afternoon here. Saturday. How're you doin'? They treatin' you right over there?"

"Oh, George, it's wonderful! You should see the view I have of Hong Kong across the bay! And everything's so luxurious!"

"Now, don't get carried away. You're supposed to be used to luxury. A woman of means out to make a major purchase. Remember?"

Gretchen laughed and said she'd try. They chatted another minute and agreed that she would call at this hour every other day unless there was a need to check with him about something urgent. He wished her a nice weekend, and she replied that she was already halfway through one. George cackled and hung up. Gretchen decided she'd go to the sauna and the pool, then have a leisurely brunch. After all, she had to make up for her lost Saturday.

Pat Riley arrived at Kai Tak the same Saturday after a long flight that would have been exhausting had he not had three seats across to stretch out on and catch a few winks. Riley had a chum at Quantas; after having booked business class and charged the fare to the company's credit card, his mate had told him confidentially that cabin class was only half booked and he could have room to lie down if he cancelled the one and rebooked the other, pocketing the difference in hotel vouchers. At the same time, he had a deal for Riley in a city-view room at the hotel, a room that would have fax modem facilities and separate phone lines. The kicker was the exchange rate: For the less desirable room the Hong Kong dollars per night would cost the home office a pound sterling amount low enough not to raise an auditor's eyebrows. Riley, however, would reap an off-the-books benefit of about eight thousand Hong Kong dollars from his ticket exchange, a boon to his somewhat threadbare wardrobe. The hotel vouchers were useable at the hotel shops. Buying a suit and a couple of shirts, for instance, could be justified in terms of "looking the part" if the pencil-pushers came upon it. So went Riley's reasoning. He had learned to cover his backside.

Riley had also done his homework: He would have two anchors in Hong Kong, one his base at his hotel in Central, and the other Geoff Watson's art shop on Hollywood Road. His map told him that the two were a short walk apart. That was good, not only because it would save cab fare (which would nonetheless be payable to him under his daily cash allowance—a pound retained was a pound earned) but also because he expected to pop in at Watson's quite regularly. The Letts—or the Russkis as the case may be—were going to show up there, too, according to the latest intelligence he had received. The closer he was, the easier his job would be.

It was early evening when he emerged from the airport, carrying his one suitcase and his laptop shoulder bag. He saw a double-decker bus to Tsimshutsui, the tip of the Kowloon peninsula, and climbed aboard. He got off near the waterfront clock tower and walked over to the star ferry terminal. Crossing Victoria Harbor on the ferry boat put him in the right mood; the view of both Hong Kong Island ahead and

Kowloon behind was simply spectacular. Deeply he drew in the air that rose from the water, rich, warm, softly humid, with that salty, almost fetid smell of tropical harbors. He had relished that when he was in the navy. Harbors were ports, destinations arrived at, new experiences awaiting. Then and now.

Pat Riley was ready. He gripped his suitcase when the ferry had docked and walked through the underpass to Connaught Road. His hotel was a block away to the right. Hong Kong, here we are.

The room he was given was adequate to his purpose, even though it looked out on busy Chater Road. Riley drew the curtain. Unpacking was done in a few minutes. For his stomach it was going on midnight, Sydney time, so he decided to just help himself to one of those little bottles of Scotch he found in the minibar, and to a bag of chips. Drink in hand, he searched for and found the modem outlet near the desk. He unzipped the computer bag and put the laptop out on the desk. Time to let London know he had arrived. He connected the printer that came with the laptop, marvelling again at its small size; it would fit in one of the tins his favorite single malt came in. He had bought the equipment only recently. This was the first time he would put it to use from a location abroad.

Tap-tap-tap—he transmitted his room number and phone connection, the local time, and signed off "fanyson." As always when he used that nickname, he wondered what people would think it meant if they came across it—not that that was likely, outside of channels. Simple enough, really: "Son of Fany," Fany being the acronym for the women's auxiliary to the British Secret Service in World War II, of which his mother had been a member. It had originated in the Anglo-Boer War, the letters standing for "First Aid Nursing Yeomanry." The unit had never been officially decommissioned, so it came in handy half a century later when the need arose to have women join the service. Later on, of course, the acronym had been dropped, along with the second-tier status of women; so when his mother went back to England in the seventies to work for what was then MI6, she did so as a fully vetted member of the organization. Riley had gone there just ahead of her, after completing his navy tour of duty. It was a job, and a good one with a pension.

He had been stationed outside of London in a country house setting in picturesque Wiltshire. It was there that he had met and fallen in love with a lively blond who was guiding tours at Salisbury Cathedral. He had been so smitten, enchanted by her voice and demeanor, that he had stayed around for another tour, and another, crowding ever closer to her at the tombs, the nave, the apses, until at last she had noticed him. She smiled. He blushed, felt awkward, shy, and bemoaned that inwardly. His first words, therefore, had not been suave, not even self-assured. A mumble. As the sightseers dispersed, he had managed to say something about having a pint. Did she have a favorite pub? To his great astonishment, she had said yes. Her name was Ellen Dobson-Smithe, and she taught at the Wilts grammar school for girls. Ellie. Sir Christopher, her father, was a Q.C. of some renown in London legal circles. They had married at Christmastime. Their daughter Fiona—their only child, she would be—had been born in October.

Fiona—he had to call her. London was eight hours behind, early afternoon, but this being Saturday she might not be home. She wasn't, as it turned out. He left a message: Name of the hotel, room number, telephone number. Love you, Fi. Call you again tomorrow.

He briefly thought of calling Miss Adelaide, but of course she'd be in bed. He'd call her tomorrow, too. Hoped old Winnie was all right.

One more thing to do: the books. A set of two, one from which he filed his expense reports, and one he used to figure his daily "profits." He could not afford to run a deficit, not from his only source of "income."

Not to worry: he had a "plus" day.

Gretchen spent all day Monday acquainting herself with Hong Kong—a trip to Victoria Peak in the morning, a harbor tour on a modern junk in the afternoon. She ate on the run and fell into bed, pleasantly spent, at eight in the evening. The next morning she awoke refreshed, no trace of jet lag anymore.

According to plan, she went to the concierge desk and asked for a list of art galleries specializing not only in Oriental but also Western art. A list of five such establishments, two in Kowloon and three in Hong Kong, was delivered to her room by the time she returned from breakfast. To her private glee, Watson Elementary Art, Ltd., was on the list. She called the concierge and asked to have appointments made for her to visit the ones in Hong Kong. A car was ready to take her.

As Gretchen emerged from the cross-harbor tunnel, the first gallery was at the Art Center. Gretchen knew her visit there would be perfunctory, but she drew it out so as to appear seriously, albeit casually, interested in what was exhibited there. Next stop was at the Connaught Center, in the huge shopping complex full of French and Italian fashion boutiques. The art gallery there was of equal artistic merit—every wall full of mostly pretentious modern works she almost hated to spend her time on. She asked her driver where they could stop for lunch and he suggested a "very good dim sum restaurant" in the Center. She asked him to join her, and he accepted with a dignified bow, leaving his cap in the car.

It was early afternoon when the car took her uphill, past Government House into an area of narrow, winding roads and streets that had the unmistakable look of Chelsea, Soho, and Montmartre blended into a kind of Chinese mélange of shops, stores, and trendy restaurants. There was no parking. Her driver turned into a public structure and told her he'd wait for her to return; she should just walk down Old Bailey Street to Hollywood Road, and not fail to come back up the same way, as streets were very small and crooked, and it would be easy to miss one's way. She thanked him and set off, traffic whizzing past her on the narrow footpath at what she thought was reckless speed.

Gretchen almost missed Watson's Elementary Art. She had expected a store with a street entrance, wide showcase windows, and a large sign over it all. Checking and rechecking the street address, she finally saw a small sign saying "Watson's," with an arrow pointing to the side of the building, and another sign over a simple door that led to a hallway with a steep staircase. At the top was another door, which, finally, spelled out the establishment's full name. There was a bell to be rung. She pressed it. Waiting for something to happen, she noticed a security camera above the door. At last she heard footsteps on the other side. A peep door in the door was pulled back, and a Chinese woman's face asked curtly, "You have an appointment?"

"Yes," Gretchen answered. She gave her name, and the hotel's as well.

The peep door closed, the big door opened. Gretchen stepped inside and found herself in a reception area furnished with a couple of chairs and a table with a red-tasseled lamp that gave off a low-watt illumination of art magazines on the tabletop.

The Chinese woman, youngish but severe in dress and manner, told her to wait and disappeared behind another door. Presently the door opened again and revealed a man who at first sight could not be other than an Englishman, an impression confirmed when he spoke in a ripe, round voice: "Mrs. Goodridge. How do you do? I am Geoffrey Watson. Won't you come in, please?" He swung his arm wide like a showman, and as she rose he brought it back to grab her hand. "Very glad to meet you, madam," he said, ushering her inside with a flourish before he released her hand.

A surprised Gretchen, still feeling his firm grip, finally spoke: "I am pleased to meet you, too, Mr. Watson."

"Indeed, indeed." Watson brought himself up erect like a military man before his queen, and all that was missing, an amused Gretchen thought, was a swagger stick clamped under his arm, and for her a hat and gloves.

He stood silent for the moment, as if awaiting orders. His grayish-blond hair, wavy and a bit too long over the ears to make the Cold Stream Guards, fell partly over his forehead and somehow matched the color of his shirt and tie. He wore no jacket, nor trendy suspenders, but a belt with a buckle that pointed slightly downward below the peak of his belly bulge. His blue eyes were attentive, if a bit watery.

Gretchen realized it was time for her to take the initiative.

"Mr. Watson, I've come here on the recommendation of my art dealer, Lamb Fine Arts, of Santa Barbara, California. You may have received an advance notice from him? Charles Lamb?"

"Ah!" he said, as if lightning had suddenly struck. "Yes. Yes, of course. Shall we go to my office?" Again his arm swung and he followed it, marching off. Gretchen came close behind, taking in the scene. They passed through the gallery space hung with paintings. Gretchen caught only a fleeting glimpse, but enough to assure her that the artwork was not all bad. Against one wall were shelves stacked deep with prints and posters, she guessed. Now they came to a workshop where several people were busy, with frames on long tables and at computers. The establishment was obviously more sizeable than her first impression had led her to believe. That, too, was reassuring.

The march ended at a half-timbered wall that had windows with potted geraniums in boxes in front and a Dutch door with its upper half open. The whole thing looked like a set from Hansel and Gretel.

"Here we are," Watson exclaimed, pushing the lower half of the door open.

Gretchen stood for a moment. "How absolutely marvelous!"

"Really? You like it?" Watson seemed genuinely flattered.

"My dear Mr. Watson, this is the last thing I would have expected in the midst of bustling Hong Kong."

"Yes," Watson said. "Penny's idea to wall it in, and all that." He made a sweeping gesture. "Used to be a gambling den, you know, this place. Don't know that you couldn't say it is still." He gave her a half smile. "*L'art pour l'art,* eh?"

They sat down on a bright red corner sofa. The Chinese woman came in and brought tea, Chinese tea, with small white porcelain cups and a teapot. Then she left. Watson said, "May I?" and poured.

Gretchen asked, "Mr. Watson, do you know why I am here? What did Charles tell you in his letter?"

He leaned back, balancing the cup with both hands on his stomach. "It's a bit of a delicate matter, I should say, wouldn't you?"

"Hmm," she said, slurping softly from her cup. If he wanted to dance around a bit, she wouldn't mind.

"Hmm." He seemed deep in thought. Then he spoke. "Ours is a peculiar business, you know. Much of what we deal in is quite valuable, but the value is chimerical, not real. Is a painting of a bunch of flowers, no matter how well done, really worth tens of millions of dollars? Quite so, obviously, to some. So money enters into the equation, lots of it, to the point where it becomes a power game. Look here, it says, my position in life is such that I can spend the equivalent of a whole town's annual budget on a whim, and you shall come and worship me for it. But why, you ask, quivering in your boots, is this one bit of art so valuable? Is it because the artist is dead, the art is great, the piece is one of a kind? Because if that is so, then I can show you right here…" Watson swung his arm wide "…several works of art to which those criteria apply; yet you can have those for a pittance. He will glare at you, our fellow will, and if you are very lucky he will ban you from his sight. If you persist, woe betide you. He will set his hounds upon you, and you shall perish." His arm came back, and his head was raised heavenward as if pleading for mercy.

It was an impressive performance. Gretchen nodded her understanding. She said, "I presume you are referring to that famous Van Gogh. My aspirations are very modest by comparison, a fraction of one percent of the other fellow's ambition. So I assure you, Mr. Watson, there are no hounds on my side, if I may borrow your metaphor. Not even a pack of chihuahuas."

Watson let out a bellow of a laugh. "Splendid! Well put." In one agile move he jumped up and went to his desk to reach for a letter that he must have put there in anticipation of her visit. He held it up. "Charles Lamb Fine Arts, as you say. Yes, I've got it. He has connections to a major house in New York, Schlesinger and Baldwin, as do I. They are the ones who were approached by the selling party first. Then that party abruptly changed venue to Hong Kong, where for obvious reasons there are supposed to be wealthy buyers. Well, the handover of the crown colony to China occurred—and nothing much changed, don't you know. The truly rich people had already taken their portable riches abroad. The selling party was distressed. Here he is, sitting on his painting, so to speak. Time is money, especially in expensive Hong Kong. What he needs is a new buyer. Mr. Lamb tells me that you are one such, Mrs. Goodridge. Not that there couldn't be others."

"Yes, I could be. It's what I came out here for. Of course, I would have to see it, and see the papers that come with it. Do you have it, Mr. Watson?"

"Do you mean, do I keep it on the premises? Certainly not. It's in a vault at a bank. Neither the selling party nor I have a key to the vault. That is kept in the safe hands of a firm of solicitors not previously acquainted with either of us."

Gretchen nodded. "Good. You may consider me a serious prospect. Will you arrange a showing?"

Watson's eyes narrowed. "Mr. Lamb informs me that you have a special interest in that painting, but he is not forthcoming with details."

Gretchen nodded again. "My mother comes from the part of Europe where Friedrich painted. We are talking about Caspar David Friedrich, are we not?"

"Oh, yes, indeed. One that was thought lost, as a matter of fact. Now miraculously resurfaced."

"'Miraculously,'" you say. "You doubt the provenance?"

"My dear lady, I wash my hands of that. As long as my sources are credible, and the parties to a deal are competent, I am satisfied. I run a business here; it is not just for my aesthetic pleasure."

"I see." Gretchen stood up. "Thank you, Mr. Watson. Please let me know when a showing can be arranged. I am staying at the Regent in

Kowloon. Now I must go. I am keeping my driver waiting."

Watson held the door open, then walked out with her.

"I shall make phone calls tomorrow," he said. "I hope we can arrange something for Thursday or Friday."

"Why would it take that long? Why not meet tomorrow?"

"The bank, the solicitors—plus the other party. And us. Busy schedules all around."

"Well, I'm not that busy. And I'm the one with the checkbook. Let's bear that in mind, Mr. Watson."

"Ha! Delightful. What directness. How American. I shall do my best."

"You flatter me, Mr. Watson." They had reached the outer door. Gretchen smiled her goodbye.

Pat Riley had been listening in on the conversation. He was in the framing room, where Watson's people were busy putting prints onto mattes and into frames. Watson ran a profitable side business in pictures suitable for businesses and hotels. With earphones barely visible, Riley was tuned in to a microphone in Watson's office. It was Penny Watson's job to do that kind of eavesdropping now and again, when it was important enough; Geoff Watson's mind tended to wander a bit, not a good thing when exact terms and information were needed in a business transaction. The clients weren't told of it. Some of them were probably wired themselves. Penny—the second Mrs. Watson—had worked in hotel security; she had no illusions.

An arrangement was made for Riley to take Penny's place when Mrs. Goodrich's visit was called in from the Regent Hotel. He had seen the American lady enter and leave. The word "class" sprang to mind, from a template that he had acquired in his years of service in England and elsewhere when certain kinds of people had crossed his path. They were well dressed but never ostentatiously so, and they had a natural bearing that was at once relaxed and alert, in keeping with their status in this world. Moneyed, educated, well brought up. Most of them, but by no means all, were American. As was this one.

Watson came by Riley's desk after Gretchen had left. "Pat, a word, please." Riley got up and followed him into the office. Watson motioned him to sit down on the red sofa.

"Turn the thing off, will you?" Riley asked.

Watson reached under his desk and said, "Done. What do you think?"

"Interesting, Geoff. First impression—she is a serious buyer. We could be wrong on that score, but that will come out one way or the other when the actual negotiations begin."

Watson nodded. "About the two Letts—what have you heard?"

"Too early. I expect to hear from London by tomorrow morning. The one with the Swedish passport, that Arvid von Vietinghoff fellow, seems to be the genuine article. If you were on a secret mission, would you run around with a name like that?"

"Cor! I can't even spell it!"

"There you are, then. Let's keep our eyes and ears open, but I would guess that the party you are dealing with is the genuine one. Which would lend greater credence to the genuineness of the painting."

"I suppose I should set up the meeting for Thursday afternoon. What do you think?"

"The first meeting, yes. Then comes a weekend. The next meeting perhaps on Tuesday? That's when you should start talking serious money. What are your price parameters?"

"That's my business, isn't it, Pat, old chum?"

"Good heavens, Geoff, I wasn't prying. You earn your money, you certainly do. I'm just curious what the inducement would be for foul play."

"Well." Watson grunted. "I'll tell you this much: Last October Christie's in London had a Friedrich, an oil about the same size as our object, for three hundred forty thousand pounds. A known painting; one of two of the same subject. Now, ours here is supposed to be a 'lost' one. Use your imagination—what would that bring?"

"I see. You had better watch your rear, then, hadn't you, Geoff?"

"I thought you were here to watch it for me, Pat, old boy."

"Indeed I am." Riley grinned. "And all for free, too."

Gretchen took the next day off. She didn't think Watson would call, and if he did it would be just as well to be unavailable, so as not to appear too eager. She booked an all-day trip to Canton, leaving from the hotel at seven in the morning. When she returned in the evening there had been no calls. She was relieved; it had been a very interesting if strenuous day, much to see, more to think about. Now she was tired, jet lag making itself felt. She went up to her room and straight to bed, the glorious nighttime sight of Hong Kong in her picture window.

The next morning she had two messages, the first before she had left her room. It was from the young woman who had been yesterday's guide on the Hong Kong side: she had stayed on through the China side of the trip even as the new guide was taking over. All the tourists on the bus had been western, and had come in groups of two or more. Gretchen had been the only single person, so it was natural that from the Chinese border on she would sit next to the young woman guide, who was now silent. It proved to be a bonus. Terry Zhu, the young woman, was a student at Hong Kong University, fluent in both Mandarin and English. Gretchen asked question after question, and received a private tutorial in the bargain. By the end of the trip, as they sat in the express train that whisked them back to Hong Kong, Gretchen asked her if she would find the time during the coming days and weeks, to be her personal guide around Hong Kong for a couple of hours a day as her schedule permitted. Miss Zhu, a wisp of a girl looking younger than her age, somberly thought it over before she declared that yes, that might work, provided Mrs. Goodridge was flexible enough on short notice. That was agreeable, and they shook on it. Gretchen was pleased.

"How do I contact you? May I have your address and phone number?" asked Gretchen.

"No. That is too complicated for you. I have your hotel number. I will call you when I am free."

"Thank you, Terry. May I call you Terry?"

"Yes. And you are Mrs. Goodridge. That is how it shall be."

So here she was, Terry Zhu, on the phone at eight-thirty in the morning. Would Mrs. Goodridge have time to take a walking tour of Hong Kong, starting with Central? Yes, was the reply. Perhaps around ten, at the Star Ferry terminal at Connaught, which meant she would have to cross Victoria Harbor from where she was now? Yes, again. They agreed to look for one another just before the underpass in the terminal, never mind the exact time.

Gretchen smiled to herself as she hung up. The one thing she was uneasy about was traveling as a single woman. She had no desire to become an adjunct to a friendly couple or, worse yet, another single woman traveler; not to mention a middle-aged businessman ten thousand kilometers away from home. Having young Terry around for a couple of hours now and again was the perfect solution. She had a lot of empty hours to fill before the art deal was done.

Besides, there had been no word from Watson.

It was a surprise to see Terry, and if it hadn't been for her intelligent eyes picking Gretchen out of the crowd streaming from the ferry terminal, Gretchen might well not have found her. The schoolgirl of yesterday, in jeans, running shoes, and a tee shirt, had been transformed into a sophisticated young woman in a well-tailored pink suit, her hair done up, clutching a purse and an umbrella. Medium-high heels in her walking pumps made her look even more grown up. Gretchen was wearing a summer dress and a sea-green linen jacket, casual shoes, and a sun hat. It was already hot, with humidity to match. They greeted one another.

Terry handed her a city map. "I get one hundred dollars Hong Kong per hour. Lunch is extra. That is okay?"

"That is okay. Thank you for the map. Where do we start?"

"The underpass, to Statue Square. Then you tell me what you want."

It would turn out to be a very demanding foot march. They passed through the Landmark shopping center, welcome to Gretchen primarily for its air conditioning. Through traffic that rivaled Fifth Avenue they wound their way to Alexandra House, Connaught Center, and Jardine House. Terry pointed out that if one compared the skyline to the new emblem of Hong Kong, one would see that the Jardine House skyscraper had been left out. Why? Because the Jardines were the bad guys in the Opium Wars. China wanted nothing to do with them.

They used walkways that connected the downtown buildings, passing from one air conditioned haven to another. By noon they found themselves in the Mandarin Oriental Hotel.

"People will soon be queuing up," Terry said as they passed the ground-floor restaurant. "If we want to eat here, we should go in now."

An amused Gretchen hailed that as a good idea, and they were seated at a window table, a plate glass thickness away from the passersby outside.

It was western food that dominated the menu. Gretchen ordered a salad and ice tea, Terry a cheeseburger and coffee. When the food came it was heaped high on large plates, the Caesar filling a large bowl, the saucer-sized burger dwarfed by the pile of french fries and salad leaves. Gretchen exclaimed "Oh, my!" but Terry quietly attacked her mountain with determined gusto. Before long she was clearly on a winning course.

The restaurant was filling up rapidly, mostly with well-dressed business people and a sprinkling of obvious tourists. There was talk all around, and the decibel level was rising. Gretchen watched with interest; if this was China, it was the equal of New York or London. Terry agreed with a chuckle when she said that.

The table next to them was taken by a lady who was fussed over by the maitre d' as she was seated. A valued customer, apparently, and one who had a standing reservation for the window table that had been given to Gretchen and Terry. Gretchen apologized, and offered to switch tables.

"No, no, please, stay where you are," the lady said. By her accent she seemed to be American. "It is not important. Are you enjoying the view? The street, the people—that's why I prefer that table. There's a whole world out there." Her speech sounded a bit slow and slurred. Gretchen wondered if she had been drinking. She didn't look like a lush; was she on medication? The lady was middle-aged, tall, and thin; her long hands were nervous, with a slight tremor.

Turning away, Gretchen made small talk with Terry. It was difficult, however, to mind their own business when their bench neighbor was such a presence, ordering Chinese food and, when served, using her chopsticks to shove rice clumps and noodles into her mouth directly from the plate. A snuffling half cough with nearly every breath was an unpleasant accompaniment.

Gretchen gestured to Terry with her eyes: Shall we leave? Terry nodded yes, pushing her nearly finished plate away. Gretchen summoned the waitress. In the interval before the check was brought, the lady addressed Gretchen once more: Would she mind refilling her teacup? Gretchen obliged, wondering to herself what this woman would want next.

The check came, and Gretchen paid with her credit card. The waitress picked it up, and before Gretchen received it back, something happened, trivial though it was, that would change the course of her life profoundly.

The woman, silently labeled "my lady" by now, dropped her teacup with a loud clatter onto her plate, splattering chow mein onto the tablecloth and environs. Obviously distressed, the woman leaned back, fighting for breath. Was she choking? Gretchen touched her on the shoulder to see if she should do the Heimlich maneuver, which Duncan had taught her when he was taking a first aid course. But how could she do that when the woman was sitting down, her back against the bench? Wouldn't she have to make her get up first? And how would she do that? Yank her from the seat?

While these thoughts were flitting through her mind, the woman spoke. "I'm sorry." It was in a low croaking voice that she labored to continue. "I...I...am not well. Would you mind, you two, taking me to my room?" With a fluttering hand she revealed a card key next to her small purse on the table. "I'd be much obliged." Gretchen said yes, of course they would take her.

The waitress came back with the credit card slip for Gretchen to sign. "Mrs. Tait had a mishap? You wish to go to room?" The waitress was addressing the woman. "I will get the bellboy. He will take you up."

Gretchen said "That won't be necessary," as she signed the check with an extra tip. "We'll do that. Won't we, Terry?"

With Terry nodding agreement, they helped the woman off her seat, making her stand. "Can you walk?" Gretchen asked with some concern. She had seen her come in under her own power. When the woman nodded, she motioned Terry to lend support on her side, and so they left the dining room slowly, the woman's head bobbing a bit, spittle drying on her lips.

It was an arduous trip to the elevator and a silent ascent to a top floor. The woman told them her room number, and Gretchen followed the directional signs. At last they reached the door, pushed in the key, and led the woman to a wing chair she indicated by the window. Gently they put her down.

"There," Gretchen said. She took a tissue from her purse to wipe off the spittle. "May I?" she asked, doing it.

The woman looked at her with deep, dark eyes. "I'm so grateful." She had found her voice again. "I have a nurse. She is off until four."

That was more than two hours away. "Will you be all right alone until then?" Gretchen asked. In a flash of compassion, she said, "I could stay, if you like. It wouldn't be a bother."

The woman's head inclined downwards, bobbing a bit but not coming back up. Gretchen repeated her suggestion. The answer came:

"Yes, please," with a groping for a kerchief tucked in the side of her chair. The woman, with both hands trembling, dabbed her eyes and her nose. Still her head was downcast.

Gretchen was touched. Here was someone, a stranger but a fellow human being, alone and in some misery, a woman about her own age probably as far away from home as she herself was, who needed help. It was out of the question to say goodbye and leave.

Turning to Terry, who stood observing the spectacle without comment, Gretchen said, "Let's step outside for a moment." In the corridor she pulled her wallet from her purse and, thanking her, gave Terry five hundred-dollar bills. Terry gave a hundred back. "Lunch hour does not count," she said. Gretchen took the note without argument, sensing that this was an important gesture. She asked Terry to call her again when she had free time. Terry said she would, and left.

Gretchen let herself back into the room. This time she noticed that it was a suite, with a bedroom beyond a half-open door. The woman's head was up now, resting against the right wing of the chair. Her eyes were open.

"You are very kind," she said, seemingly in control again. "May I know your name?"

"Gretchen Goodridge. I hope you're feeling better?"

"How do you do, Gretchen Goodrich. You are certainly both, good and rich in sentiment. I am Anthea Tait. Tait, as in that gallery." Her speech was coherent but still had a strained quality.

"Nice to meet you, Mrs. Tait—as in that London Tate, I presume. Tell me, you're American?"

"Was, before I met Mr. Tait, who's Australian." She held out her hand. When Gretchen took it she felt how cold and bony it was. It troubled her. How sick was this woman? She had said she wasn't well.

Forcing some cheer, Gretchen said, "I'm American too, as no doubt you have noticed. From California. Los Angeles, to be exact." When there was no visible response, she said, "Speaking of galleries, I am here to check out the local art scene. I'm interested in art, as a collector."

The woman smiled wanly. "Fancy that. I own a gallery. Not here, but in Townsville. That's in Australia. Now I'm doubly pleased to meet you."

"So am I! You're a gallery owner! We'll have something to talk about. But first I must ask: Are you a little more comfortable now?"

The bony hand was raised in a resigned gesture. "I have a sickness that our doctors cannot cure. I've come here to see if the Chinese can do better. So far, no luck."

"Oh! Still trying, I hope? What is your sickness?"

The hand came up again, wagging a finger. "You are getting too close for *your* comfort, Gretchen of that Faustian name. Most people say 'I'm sorry' and change the subject, anxious to leave. Go ahead, say you're sorry."

Gretchen looked at her watch. "Almost two hours yet before your nurse returns. Plenty of time to say sorry later. Tell me what ails you!"

Mrs. Tait's eyes moved to gaze out the window. "I can tell you what it is not. It's not infectious. It's not inherited. It's not cancer." She paused. The words did not come easily and were at times swallowed, as if Mrs. Tait had her mouth full. "There is not much point in going on."

"Am I supposed to guess? All right. Is it neurological?"

The eyes darted back to bore into her: "What are you, a doctor?"

Gretchen shook her head. "My mother was a neurologist. There was much talk about odd and gruesome cases she had come across. She wished I'd go to medical school. But I got married right after college."

"Do you have children?"

"Two sons, both in college now. None in med school. But I have a young half-brother who wants to become a doctor. He's like a son to me, in a way." Gretchen knew she was talking just for the sake of talking. "I don't know why I'm going into such detail. And I didn't mean you when I said gruesome."

"No matter. Your mother—past tense?"

"Yes. She died in eighty-five. Look—what was your first name again?"

"Anthea. My father taught Greek. It means 'the flowery one.'" Again she swallowed hard. "As for myself, I have no children. You are the lucky one. I thought I had so much time. Then I married a younger man. Alas, too late."

Gretchen said, "We are getting away from the question. What ails you?"

"What *ails* me?" A flaming look. "Leave out the 'i.'"

"Leave out the 'i?' From what? Ails? A word game? All right: A, drop the I,—L, S. ALS. Alzheimer's? No, that's with a Z. A-L-S—oh my God!—is that it? Lou Gehrig's Disease! Amyo-something lateral sclerosis!" Gretchen stared at her in unabashed horror. "How dreadful!"

"*Gruesome* was your word."

"I'm so sorry!" Gretchen was so overcome she dropped to her knees and clasped the woman's hand.

"Now you've said it. Now you may leave, Gretchen Good-rich."

"Anthea Tait! I will leave only if you insist. But I want to stay. I want to help. We are both far away from home. I'm not all that busy. Please!"

"I have a nurse."

"I'm not a nurse. What I mean is keeping you company, talking. Today, tomorrow, whenever you need diversion. Maybe talking is not good for you, but I'm a talker. I talk a blue streak. You be the listener. You can always stop me when it gets on your nerves. Nerves! I'm sorry, I didn't mean it that way!" Gretchen's hand flew to her lips.

"You have to stop saying you're sorry. That's the first condition."

"All right." Gretchen got up and sat down in a chair opposite Mrs. Tait. She smiled. "That's better. First condition. What's the second?"

"Don't do nursery things, like wiping my lips. And I'm not incontinent. But companion? Yes, I would like that, very much. If you can spare the time."

"Done! What's next?"

"If I find we don't get along, it's over. I have no time for politeness. If miraculously we do match up, I want total honesty. No maudlin sentiments. No weeping. That cuts both ways. You must tell me when you've had enough."

"Done, done, and done." Gretchen gave her a radiant smile. "Using first names—that all right with you?" When Anthea gestured her agreement, Gretchen continued, "Now, how about Scrabble. Do you play scrabble?"

"Don't have one. Lovely game, though."

"I'll bring one next time."

"Next time." Anthea's eyes closed. "I need to rest now. You may go, Gretchen. Leave me your hotel telephone number on this pad." She indicated the note pad next to her on a side table. "I'll call you."

Gretchen groped for the hotel brochure in her handbag, pulled it out, and wrote down the number. "You're sure you want to be alone now?"

Mrs. Tait opened her eyes. "My friend, I'm alone most of the time. You mustn't worry about me. It spoils the fun. Just do as I tell you."

"Fair enough." She snapped her handbag shut. "I'm taking one of your hotel brochures with me, just in case you forget to ring me!"

On her way across Victoria Harbor Gretchen sat on the right side of the ferry, her hair fluttering in the breeze, her thoughts still very much on the episode just behind her. Had she been too rash in her response? So often people act impulsively in the presence of suffering of another human being, in essence offering no more than a noble gesture. After that they go back to their own ordered lives, feeling good about themselves for having done "the right thing." Her mother had told her that; being a doctor was not just about compassion, but mostly about helping. Compassion by itself got nothing done, her mother had said. Was this what it had been about with Anthea? Empty emotion? Would she really want to spend her own precious time with—let's call a spade a spade—that wretch suffering an incurable, horribly worsening ailment?

Yes, she would. Her mother would have wanted her to.

A fine rain was falling as she walked back to her hotel; she didn't notice. She felt at peace.

Pat Riley was standing in line for a seat at the restaurant when the Anthea Tait commotion occurred, just a few tables away from where he was. The queue extended into the outside hall, and Riley stood at the door waiting patiently, reading a day-old edition of *The Australian*. The clatter of the teacup dropped onto the plate was not so remarkable amid all the noise, and he would have not done more than glance up and go back to his paper had it not been for the woman fussing over the noise maker. He recognized her immediately from having observed her at Watson's gallery.

Mrs. Gretchen Goodridge. What an extraordinary coincidence.

Just last night, in his room upstairs, he had received a fax from London describing the "personage in question," and it had been quite a surprise. The woman was known to the service as "the daughter of Ian Frazer Herter, a.k.a. Ian Frazer, British-born (South African, 1923), naturalized U.S. citizen, now deceased (1990), formerly professor of anthropology, adjunct lecturer at the Farm Academy, dually vetted. Subject herself is without pertinent record, U.S. citizen, divorced, resident of Los Angeles, California. End of search."

Pat knew what "dually vetted" stood for: A person who has mid-level security clearance for both the British and the American intelligence agencies. It usually applied to academics or journalists who were in a position to supply special information or who were given access to the same; not spies, not agents, but persons whose knowledge was helpful, whose judgment could be trusted, and whose discretion could be relied upon. He also knew that the number of such persons was small, and growing smaller by attrition. The services were no longer inclined to make use of their citizens' voluntary input. Too much oversight, too little mutual trust.

So this was our Gretchen Goodridge, Riley had whistled. A bit of kinship there, wasn't it. And her age about his own, judging by her father's birth year. He liked the personal touch that revealed itself here. His previous assignments had dealt with more generalized matters, involving no persons. This one would be different.

The clattering noise had apparently originated with a woman who was now being helped up and out by that Mrs. Goodridge and a young Chinese woman who held her by each arm as they wound their way past the queue. Riley tried not to be obvious as he glanced sideways over the edge of his paper. Good-looking, that "personage in question," now that he could see her close up. Full-bodied, ripe, well tended—like a vintage wine. If one were to put a label on her....

Riley caught himself. Where were they going? Hadn't that Goodridge woman told Geoff she was staying at the Regent, in Kowloon? He peeled out of the line and kept his distance as he followed the trio down the hallway, past the lobby, and into the elevator bay. Keeping out of their line of sight, he dashed into the same elevator car that they had entered. He waited until they had pressed their floor, then nodded as if that were his also, and buried his nose in his paper. When they got out he got out, turning in the opposite direction with brisk steps, like a man who knew where he was going.

The three women were not walking very fast; he could afford to disappear down the opposite corridor, then turn around and catch up with them at a safe distance. His instinct told him that it would be prudent to know what was going on here with this Mrs. Goodridge. Had she moved from the other hotel? Perhaps. All he needed was the room number; he had the floor already. Further information could be elicited from a desk clerk.

Now the women were opening a door. Riley waited until they had entered and the door had closed before he ventured past it and took note of the number. As he hurried back to the elevator he tried to put the puzzle together: His "subject," as he labeled her, was probably an acquaintance of the middle woman, whose room this must be. He couldn't imagine why Mrs. Goodridge would leave a Regent telephone number with Geoff if she were staying here, at the Oriental.

As for the Chinese girl, she could be Mrs. Goodridge's local secretary or interpreter. He had heard Mrs. Goodridge address her in a low voice during the elevator ride. Well, all that would explain itself when one or the other or both emerged from the elevator again. He would be down there, sitting in the lobby, watching the doors.

The Chinese girl came down fairly soon and headed for the exit. Check one.

For the reappearance of Mrs. Goodridge Riley's patience was tried. It did not happen until nearly an hour later. He saw her leave the hotel without delay. Rising, he saw her walk in the direction of the Star Ferry terminal. Back to Kowloon, no doubt.

Check two.

The identity of the third woman, who was a registered guest here, he figured he could get from the waitress in the restaurant, where he was now headed for a late lunch. He used his indirect questioning, friendly, conversational, as he signed the bill and put down his room number: About the lady who had that sickness spell earlier—had it happened before?

Yes; she was not well. It's not the food, is it? he joked as he left a good tip. Oh, no; Mrs. Tait would get those spells....

Check three.

He decided he might as well take a jaunt across to Kowloon himself. Walk around a bit, Nathan Road and so on. Have a drink in that famous Peninsula Hotel rooftop bar.

It was a pretty stupid touristy thing to do, actually. The crowds were pushing out of the buildings at the end of their work day, and diesel exhaust from all those buses mixed with the hot and humid air made his lungs feel assaulted. He rushed into the Peninsula, took the fast lift up to the "Felix" bar—and when he saw how small and crowded the place was, with no view to be had except the backs and bellies of the chatting and smoking drinkers, he fled down again. Try the Regent; why not?

What a relief. In the vast lobby bar the piano player was just limbering up with *My Fair Lady* melodies. The skyline of Hong Kong was a marvellous sight to behold. Riley sat at a single table, ordered his favorite scotch and, when it was brought, leaned back and savored it. This was good.

To his quiet surprise, a tall, good-looking woman walked directly past him, ushered along by the head waiter. Mrs. Goodridge, herself.

Riley drew a whiff of her perfume. It matched her appearance. He watched her being seated about ten tables away, tables that would soon be filled by other guests, blocking the sight of her.

He raised his glass in a silent toast: Cheers, Mrs. Goodridge. Here's lookin' at you. "I've grown accustomed to her face…" the piano sounded just then. Indeed.

A half hour later Riley left the bar. It had been a good day, after all.

As for Gretchen, when she went back up to her room she found a message blinking on her phone. It was from Geoff Watson: Could she come to his gallery by, say, ten the next morning? An eleven o'clock meeting had been arranged at the bank. He would take her there. No need to call back unless the day and time were inconvenient. Ta-ta.

The next morning Gretchen was once again awakened by a telephone call. She knew who it was. "Good morning, Terry!" she said cheerfully, lifting the receiver.

A raspy voice answered. "Terry? Who is Terry?" More throat clearing. "This is Anthea Tait. Is that you, Gretchen Good 'n'rich?"

Ah. The woman from yesterday. "Yes. By the way, it is Good-ri*dge*," she spelled it out. "The *rich* part is a bit off the mark. How are you, Anthea? Feeling better?" Her cheerfulness was forced now.

"Never, *never* ask me that again. I'm on a downhill slope." A deep intake of breath. "Were you serious about being my companion? Be honest!"

"Yes, I was. I don't know why, exactly, but I was, and I am. That's honest. I'll come and see you again today if you like, but it will have to be in the afternoon. I have a commitment that may stretch into lunch."

"That'll be fine. You know my room number. Just come on up." The throat-clearing sounded more like a fight for breath. There was an explosive cough. "Sorry. Thank you, Gretchen." The line went dead.

Gretchen held the receiver away from her with an expression of disgust, as if phlegm were oozing out of it. Lordy, what had she let herself in for?

A call from Terry had not come by the time Gretchen came back up from breakfast. It vaguely disquieted her; she needed that young woman to guide her around, because Hong Kong somehow overwhelmed her. She left a message with the front desk that if a Miss Terry Zhu should call to tell her that she should call again in the evening or early the next morning, or else leave a number where she could be reached. Then she changed into a light summer dress with a colorful silk shawl and called down for a taxi.

She arrived a bit early at the Watson gallery, traffic having lightened up. Geoffrey Watson made delighted exclamations upon seeing her. Once again he shouted for Penny, but once again Penny was absent. Never mind; they might as well go. Better to be early than late, eh what?

Where are we going, Gretchen asked? She was told that the bank involved was in the Bank of America tower, very fitting, don't you know. He gave her a wink when it came to "America." And the solicitors were at Hutchinson House, right next to it. All in Central, walking distance were it not for the winding hillside streets and the traffic. Much better to take the car. Besides, there'd be four of them going, two people from his office to fetch and carry, as it were.

The car was brought around, and it had to be by split-second timing that they climbed in as it pulled up: Hollywood Road had no stopping allowed. The car was an old Austin and looked as if it had seen better days as a London taxi. There was even a partition between the front and the back seats. The driver and the woman next to him were from Watson's gallery. Gretchen recognized the woman as the Chinese lady she had met on her first visit. Seated to the left of the driver, the woman was clearly in charge, telling him when to stop, where to turn, to slow down or to speed up. The driver was a stoic; he never so much as turned to her or said anything. With the partition up it was like watching a silent movie.

"You've met Mrs. Giles," Watson said, pointing to the woman. "Married to an Englishman, now divorced. Runs my office." He gave Gretchen a knowing smile. "Very efficient. Like my mother, in absentia."

The driver dropped them off in front of Hutchinson House and then drove on down busy Connaught Road to find parking. Watson and the two women trouped to the elevators. "Mrs. Giles, Mrs. Goodridge," he said by way of belated introduction, nodding in either direction.

They went up to the eleventh floor. The office they entered had a long brass plaque, highly polished, with the names so small Gretchen had to get close to read it. "Bing and Stothers, Barristers and Solicitors," and underneath a line of Chinese characters.

The interior of the office was a surprise. Chinese imperial red and British royal blue were the dominant colors for the eclectic mixture of furniture and wall treatments. Hunting scenes from merry old Regency England alternated with Chinese scrolls and drawings. Tall vases and planters were placed cheek by jowl with heavy club-style tables and easy chairs. No interior decorator could have had a hand in the arrangement, Gretchen mused.

From an open door a plummy voice called, "Do come in. Come in, won't you?" as the secretary announced the visitors. Crossing the threshhold Gretchen and Watson found themselves facing a huge mahogany desk, behind it a round-faced, bald gentleman wearing a perfectly tailored blue suit, a white shirt with French cuffs sticking out from the sleeves a fashionable one inch, and a red silk tie matched by a kerchief drooping from the breast pocket. The wearer grinned broadly. A Buddha of Bond Street.

"Mr. Bing!" Watson rushed forward, hand outstretched. "Good of you to see us. I trust you are well?"

"Quite well, thank you, Mr. Watson." The outstretched hand was met by a fleshy one that had a large diamond on the pinkie. "And you are well, too, I take it? And Mrs. Watson?"

"Quite so, yes, both of us, thank you. May I introduce Mrs. Goodridge, who has come from America to see that painting. And you know Mrs. Giles."

More how-do-you-do, bowing, handshaking, and then Bing ushered them to a seating area just as the secretary brought in a tea tray. English tea in one pot, green tea in another, and small delicate rice cookies. Tea was poured, milk in first for the Earl Gray. One lump? Two? Try the sweets, do. Such ritual. It was necessary to observe the good graces.

Gradually the talk took on substance. In Mr. Stothers's office down the hall, Mr. Bing revealed, there were at this moment two gentlemen from Eastern Europe—Riga, Latvia to be exact. One was a baron of

Swedish nationality, the other a commoner. Both were emissaries of the newly free government of Latvia, which, alas, had no mission to the PRC. Nor to Hong Kong. Pity.

Mrs. Giles had unfolded a notebook and began writing.

However, Mr. Bing continued volubly, using ten words where one would do, the Swedish gentleman had been vouched for by the Swedish embassy in Beijing, and by extension so had the Latvian. It would appear, therefore, that they were dealing with credible, if not accredited (a small chuckle here), emissaries. Bing looked at Gretchen to share his amusement. Gretchen acknowledged it with a slight smile. Mr. Bing's hands formed an arch, the pinkie blinking in the sun.

Taking advantage of a temporary lull in the conversation, Gretchen said, "I presume the painting is in the room next door, Mr. Bing?"

It was the cue Bing needed to explain some more. The painting was in a safe at the Manufacturers Bank in the Bank of America building, but was at this moment being brought in by one of Mr. Watson's assistants and one of the firm's junior solicitors. When he saw Gretchen's raised eyebrows, Bing, hands now unfolded, hastened to explain that there was no problem of security, none at all. The two men had it safely between them for the short trip from one building to the next, the men acting natural while quite alert. The painting was of course not framed, and being of moderate size was carried in a leather portfolio not unlike a briefcase. Not to worry.

Gretchen decided to say nothing. She could envision a situation in which the two men were in cahoots and would abscond with the valuable piece of art, jump into a junk at the pier and have it handed over to a speedboat that would take it to one of the numerous islands hereabouts and from there to god knows where. Taiwan, probably.

She had seen too many abscond-with-the-loot chase movies, probably, starting with *The Maltese Falcon* and all the way up to *The Pink Panther*. After her divorce she hadn't been much into the genre anymore, her taste running more to Jane Austen and Daphne du Maurier adaptations.

"Ah," Bing interrupted himself. "I hear them coming. Excuse me." He hurried out of the room. Several male voices were heard. Presently Bing returned. "There we are. All done. Shall we go to the conference room?"

The party from Mr. Stothers's room was already there when the

Watson group entered. Bing made the introductions: Mr. Von Vietinghoff, Mr. Albert Baludis, both names spoken so quickly that Gretchen did not make sense of them until she saw them printed on paper later on in the proceedings. These gentlemen from Latvia represented the painting's owners. Stothers was known to Mr. Watson and Mrs. Giles but not to Gretchen. They all shook hands. The two Balts bowed over her hand. Stothers was thin and tall where his partner, Bing, was stout all around, and he seemed to be a Scot or a northern Irish, Gretchen couldn't be sure; but he was definitely not Chinese. The Swedish Von Vietinghoff was even taller and thinner than Stothers, whereas the Lett made a better match with Bing.

The two groups took seats around the conference table. The junior solicitor was excused, the other man, Mr. Watson's assistant, positioned himself at the door like a guard—which perhaps he was in addition to being the driver. All heads were turned to the bookshelf near the window, where space had been cleared to place the painting, now covered with a black cloth.

Von Vietinghoff rose to stand before it. "The painting we have is a genuine Caspar David Friedrich. There are papers to prove its authenticity. We have them in a separate portfolio in a deposit box in the office safe here of Bing and Stothers." His English was correct but had a strange lilt to it. "Will the gentlemen confirm that?"

Both lawyers somberly declared that that was so, and moreover that they had the authenticity not only of the papers but of the painting itself, examined and verified by art experts at the university. Those verifications, too, were contained in the portfolio in the safe.

It was now time to unveil the painting. Von Vietinghoff reached over to switch on a light bar and remove the black cloth. There it was: He made a dramatic gesture. "I present to you—'Das Wrack der Hoffnung,' 1822, Caspar David Friedrich." He stepped aside.

Gretchen sat unmoved and unmoving. She looked at Watson, who nodded at her. She said: "May I see it?"

"Yes, please, madame." The Swede bowed.

"I'd like to have it here, at the table."

After a moment's hesitation, Von Vietinghoff took the painting down and brought it to her, placing it upright in front of her, holding it by the top with his fingertips. The painting was contained in a thin temporary wood frame.

Gretchen took it from him. She had to spread her arms, as if she were reading a newspaper. Even so, the painting was considerably smaller than Friedrich's *Polar Sea*, of which she had seen a life-size reproduction at the Getty.

Von Vietinghoff said, "Seventy by fifty-five centimeters. Oil on canvas. Very well preserved, as you can see."

Gretchen said, "I am very fond of Friedrich. I have studied his work in detail." She turned the painting to the natural light and looked closer. "With the shipwreck much bigger, it is different from *The Polar Sea*."

"Quite so, yes," Von Vietinghoff said, his long face brightened by a smile revealing teeth as long and as yellow as a horse's. A baron, indeed. Horses and hounds. Gretchen noticed that he smelled slightly of leather. She wondered if it was natural, from a lifelong proximity to horse saddles and bridles. Or could it be his after-shave?

"Well," she turned the painting to Watson. "Have you seen it?"

"When it was brought here, yes. Do you like it?"

"It looks like a Friedrich. Based on the authentication you have, it appears to be a Friedrich." She gave a radiantly happy smile. "How wonderful!"

Indeed. Yes. Absolutely. Nodding consent from everyone around the table.

"A lovely work of art. It would be a desirable painting to possess." Gretchen heaved a sigh. "If the terms are right." She released the painting back to Von Vietinghoff, who handled it with exaggerated care.

Watson reacted as if on cue. "Thank you, gentlemen. My client and I would like to entertain a proposal of sale in writing, to which we can reply with an offer in like manner. Do you suppose we could hear from you by, say, Monday noon?"

The Lett went over to Von Vietinghoff and took him aside. He spoke to him audibly, presumably in Latvian, which nobody else could understand anyway.

Von Vietinghoff replied in a soothing voice. Then he turned around and spoke in English. "We have had offers already, madame and sir, from other interested parties. We look forward to having yours. We shall take the best, of course."

"My dear fellow," Watson said, "we shan't sit below the salt. Nor shall we strive to be to the right of the Queen."

"Yes, yes," Von Vietinghoff said, puzzled until he caught the meaning. "I understand." Quaintly, he added: "*In medio tutissime ibis.*"

Watson rose and expressed his thanks to all. Gretchen got up also, and together they walked out of the conference room, Mrs. Giles with her notebook bringing up the rear. The chauffeur held the door open for them but stayed behind. He and the young solicitor were to return the painting to the vault.

Outside on the street, Watson suggested they have a quick lunch. The car would be at least forty-five minutes or so before it could pick them up. The invitation sounded half-hearted. He seemed relieved when Gretchen said that she had a luncheon schedule. Could he point her in the direction of the Mandarin Oriental? Ah, yes, straight back this way. Can't miss it. Call you Monday, then? For a good chat? With all the facts? Splendid. Cheerio.

It was really not far to walk, although the noise and the speed of the traffic were deafening. Gretchen felt a sudden pang of hunger when she entered the cool and quiet ambience of the hotel. She would love to have a bite to eat before calling Anthea. She half hoped Anthea was out for lunch herself.

Eat first? Or call first? Call first won. The phone rang several times, and she was about to hang up when it was answered. On the other end was a high-pitched voice with a foreign accent, the nurse's presumably. Gretchen was ready to suggest a visit in about an hour or so when, to her chagrin, the nurse handed the phone to Anthea, who invited her up to the room. She was insistent: The lunch table was just being set; Gretchen could order what she liked. Just come on up. She wouldn't mind, would she, eating with her? The nurse was there, taking care of things.

No, no, Gretchen said. Not mind at all. She'd be up in a minute. As she hung up she felt a little angry. Where was the quiet delicious lunch she had envisioned for herself?

Perhaps, she thought as she rode up in the elevator, this would be a good time to let Anthea know that she had limits to her availability. After all, she was here on business.

It was no use. When she saw Anthea sit in her wing chair, propped up by pillows everywhere yet dressed in a stylish suit that surely had a Parisian label, her face finely made up, her hair styled, greeting her with a wide smile that looked strangely lopsided but with eyes that shone with genuine joy, Gretchen was moved. How could she have thought even vaguely of deserting this brave woman?

She rushed over and gave her a hug. "You look wonderful, Anthea!"

"You think so?" Her eyes were rimmed with tears.

The nurse cut in, reprovingly, "We spent all morning getting her dolled up." The nurse spoke American English. She was in charge and not amused.

"You did the right thing, Anthea. Good for you!" Gretchen ignored the nurse and sat down at the table that room service had placed near the window. It was set for two. A wine cooler stood nearby.

"I was hoping you would come," Anthea said. "I ordered cold poached salmon. You don't mind fish, do you? You must tell me. We can order something else."

"No, no, I love salmon."

"I'm glad. So do I." She signalled for the nurse to uncover the serving dishes and place the plates before them. Then, in a surprise move, she dismissed the nurse, telling her to eat downstairs and to come back in a couple of hours but not to leave the hotel. Connie, the name by which Anthea addressed her, didn't seem to mind. Before Connie left she showed Gretchen some contraption on wheels that she called an aspirator and how it worked.

Anthea made a face after her. "Connie is a good girl but very bossy. Her name is Concepción. She has a work permit here. If she loses her job she has to return home. I keep telling her she should get more patients. I won't need her much longer."

Gretchen ignored the last reference to the nurse and cheerfully began ladling out the fish and the side dishes—cucumber salad and a spicy vegetable purée. She put small bite-size portions on Anthea's plate. The wine, a sauterne, was already uncorked, and when they drank she helped Anthea lift her wine glass. They made small talk as they ate. Anthea labored at swallowing; each bite was an effort. There was a view of Victoria Harbor, but it was not as wide and spectacular as the one from Gretchen's room. The busy ship and boat traffic proved a welcome diversion, and Gretchen made much reference to it.

At last, with the plates put away and a flan-like dessert with fresh strawberries before them, Anthea began to talk. She wondered if Gretchen would have the time to accompany her on an excursion. But she told Gretchen she must not hesitate to decline if she felt it to be an imposition. Gretchen told Anthea to go ahead and tell her about the excursion.

Anthea nodded, but her head drooped forward and she had difficulty bringing it back up. She declined help saying that there was a trick to it. She threw her head back with her thin hands and then held it in an upright position until it "took," as she explained. "It wasn't like this when I arrived here a month ago," she said. "And it'll be worse a month from now." She gave a smile. "Time works against me."

Gretchen was silently aghast. "Excursion to where, Anthea?" she asked.

Anthea spoke in her asthmatic way, struggling with every breath. "All I can look for is relief. Less suffering. Not relief from pain so much as from helplessness and from fear of suddenly choking to death. And relief will come, unless—I seek—Nirvana." Pleadingly, her eyes locked on to Gretchen's. "I wish to go to Macau, where there is a Chinese practitioner recommended to me. This man has herbs and potions that will calm the mind and temper the ills of the body." She paused, swallowing. "Can you take me there? You and your Chinese girl?"

Gretchen said immediately, "Yes, Anthea. I can, and I will. But I don't know about 'my Chinese girl,' as you call her. Terry Zhu is a student and works part-time as a tour guide. I have an arrangement with her to take me around, but only when she has time. She has not called me today. This weekend I expect she will be especially busy. Why would we need her? How about your nurse?"

"Connie is Filipino. She is here on a work visa. Going to Portuguese Macau means leaving Chinese Hong Kong and she fears that she might not be let back in. Silly, of course, but real to her. Besides, she does not speak Mandarin. I need an interpreter. And I need two people to prop me up, as you two did in the restaurant. Above all, I very much need you, Gretchen. I need your presence, your sincerity. That is, if you will let me lean on your goodness."

Gretchen, touched, came over and planted a tender kiss on Anthea's forehead. Anthea, whose voice had started to quaver, burst into tears, with deep hawking sobs. It made Gretchen kneel down beside her chair, putting her arms around the frail body, making soothing noises until her voice became thick and her tears, too, began to roll. There they were, holding on to each other.

Gretchen freed herself. "I'm ruining your beautiful suit, Anthea.

My mascara is running." She tried to be resolute. "Let's get a grip on ourselves. Where exactly is that wonder doctor in Macau?"

Anthea pointed to a file that was lying on the table. From it Gretchen learned that Anthea had seen another Chinese specialist in herbal medicine who told her that a Doctor Shi Chen practicing in Macau had knowledge far exceeding his own and that she should go see him. He would make a phone call to advise of Mrs. Tait's coming. There was a notation to the effect that such a call had been made and that it was up to Mrs. Tait to obtain an appointment. A Macau phone number was given. In the notes the handwriting appeared strong, if strangely round and simple; the nurse had been taking the notes, Anthea explained.

Gretchen said she'd be glad to call and make arrangements for a visit to the Macau doctor. For what day should those arrangements be made? "Soon," Anthea said. "Tomorrow. Sunday. Soon!"

Gretchen went to the phone. To her surprise, the call was not much different from calls she had made for herself to doctors' or dentists' offices. There was a secretary who sounded just as businesslike as secretaries in the U.S. as she searched her appointment book. Weekends were out, of course. Monday was fully booked and so, it appeared, was Tuesday. Gretchen relayed that information to Anthea, who became agitated. "Tell her it's urgent. I have a referral! Tell her!" Mentioning Tait's name did it; the receptionist found an open slot for Tuesday afternoon at two o'clock. Done. Tuesday it was.

"You know, Anthea," Gretchen said as she hung up, "that is probably the earliest time we could make it, anyway. I'm sure Terry will have called me by then. And my Monday is taken for my own business."

Anthea sighed. "Time. It is so precious. We all think we have so much of it." Then she said, "What is your own business?"

Gretchen began to answer the question, vaguely at first until she realized that she would have to lie to Anthea if she wanted to disguise the true nature of her business here in Hong Kong. Somehow, she could not bring herself to do that, nor could she just stop and leave the generalities in place. She knew that Anthea would sense that she was not being told the truth and feel hurt. Adding more hurt to her suffering was impossible for Gretchen to do. It would hurt herself to do that.

By the time Connie came back up and started to hustle and bustle about, alluding to her schedules that Mrs. Tait had to observe now,

Gretchen had told Anthea everything, from her divorce to the Getty to the Friedrich. The lot.

Anthea motioned her to come close, took Gretchen's hand and placed it on her own chest. "I have you in my heart now," she whispered. "Thank you."

Gretchen hugged her. Both women wept again. Then Gretchen straightened up, pressed Anthea's hand, and left the room.

Geoffrey Watson wanted a word with Pat Riley when they returned to his gallery. What had he thought of how the meeting had gone? Without waiting for an answer, he urged Riley to get in touch with London and have them find out what they could about the financial condition of that Mrs. Goodridge. No point in beating a dead horse, if that's what it was, was there? Furthermore, he ordered Riley to get in touch with those Balts, take them out for a pint, bend an elbow fellow to fellow, and see what they had up their sleeves.

Riley, if for no other reason than to stop Watson's blimpish figures of speech, said he'd do it. This being Friday, though, he could not promise that London would reply in time for the Monday meeting. At any rate, would Mrs. Goodridge have made that long journey just to back out on a deal?

"Ah," Watson exclaimed. "That's where you just don't have it, old chum. There was something about that Mrs. Goodridge. She had no zest, no fire in the belly about that painting. It's the feel one gets in this business, for just how badly someone wants to buy a work of art. Art being intrinsically worthless, as we all know. It is not gold nor diamonds. Just some paint on any old canvas. Dreadful stuff, often enough. Not even pleasant to look at, just drips and dabs splashed on haphazardly. That Jackson Pollock fellow."

"Okay okay," Riley said. "I got the picture. I'll see you Monday."

Terry Zhu had called at the hotel and left a phone number for Gretchen. Overjoyed, Gretchen returned the call right away. Yes, Terry would like to work with her again but not this weekend. She was too busy giving tours from morning to night. Monday was okay, so was most of the rest of the week. Tourism was slowing down since the handover. They arranged to meet Monday afternoon at the Mandarin Hotel lobby. Gretchen mentioned Mrs. Tait's wishes to Terry and that a trip to

Macau was in the offing. Terry said she would bring all the necessary information, including maps and brochures. They could have their own private water taxi, hydrofoil-fast, if Mrs. Tait would like. Gretchen said that was a good idea, and she looked forward to seeing her on Monday.

Anthea Tait was glad to hear the news, too, when Gretchen phoned her. She said that she had physical therapy and massages planned for Saturday; she'd probably be too tired to see her that day. How about Sunday? And would Gretchen bring the Scrabble game? Yes and yes.

It was just as well that Saturday would not work out for a visit. At the crack of dawn, or about late afternoon on Friday, Los Angeles time, Gretchen was awakened by a call from George Natalian. The ensuing conversation took so long that at one time Gretchen had to ask him to hold because she needed to go to the bathroom. George wanted to know everything that had transpired in the meetings with Watson and the Balts. No detail was too minor to be left unmentioned. He was interested particularly in Gretchen's "gut feeling" about the painting; did it "ring true?" If so, why? Natalian pressed Gretchen for a description.

Gretchen sounded generally upbeat. Yes, she thought the painting was the genuine article. No, she didn't think the Balts had made a deal yet.

George instructed her to get in touch with Watson right away and tell him that she was ready to make a deal on Monday for five hundred thousand dollars American. There'd be some upward leeway as she saw fit to use in her own good judgment. But he instructed her not to exceed, say, twenty-five percent of the sales price.

Gretchen was listening so intently she was getting a headache. How was this all going to work, in practicality?

George said never mind the details, they would be taken care of by the Lamb gallery and Watson. She was just a rich lady letting others worry about that. Electronic fund transfers, shipping, customs, etcetera, etcetera. Okay?

"I guess so," said Gretchen.

George sounded pleased. Just tell Watson to prepare to close the deal on Monday. He'll find a fax from the Lambs to that effect by then. Tell him.

If you say so, George.

Good girl, Keep in touch. Call me Monday. Click. End of call.

Replacing the receiver, Gretchen glanced out the window. The morning sun was breaking through the cloud layer, casting a golden sheen on the high tops of the Hong Kong skyline. Beautiful. She stretched and yawned. This would be a day just for herself. She would call the butler, and have him bring up coffee and orange juice. Then she would go down to the fitness center, get a massage, relax in the sauna, and swim in the pool. Sipping a cool drink, she'd call Watson from poolside and tell him the deal is on. "See you Monday morning. Ten o'clock all right? Or is eleven better?"

She would have a lazy day. In another week she'd be in Frankfurt, meeting with *her* George.

All this, including poor Anthea, would be behind her.

Riley found the reply from London on his e-mail on Sunday morning. He had asked if there was any way Mrs. Goodridge's financial liquidity could be ascertained. A simple question: Did she appear to have the money to purchase the painting?

The answer was surprising; then again, perhaps not. There was no direct evidence of the lady's personal wealth, nor did she seem in constrained circumstances. However, she was the sister of U.S. Congressman James Frazer, Republican of Connecticut, who was married to the former Aleanora Patullo, daughter and heir of Malcolm Patullo, declared one of the wealthier men in the United Kingdom. London made the assumption that Mrs. Goodridge could be fronting for her brother, who as a simple congressman would be ill-disposed to make such a frivolous purchase. The report ended by stating that if the Balts were genuine, with no adverse parties involved in the completed art deal, Riley should consider filing his conclusions and return to base.

Well, Riley said to himself. Well, well, well. So that's where it's at, is it? The Patullo name was not unknown to him. Patullos were Scots, Tory supporters, friends of Maggie Thatcher's, yet "European." Quoted now and again in the papers. This was an interesting bit of news—useless, though, in the current proceedings. Old Watson wouldn't care a farthing for it. Best to keep it to himself.

The "art deal," said London, was almost anticlimactic when it came to fruition on Monday morning in Watson's Hansel-and-Gretel house. Geoffrey Watson had submitted through "Sting and Bothers," as he called the solicitors when he dictated the terms to Mrs. Giles, a final, a binding proposal on Saturday. He had also suggested that the parties meet as soon as possible; Mrs. Goodridge's patience should not be tried further, lest her desire wane and the deal be off.

He had an answer from Mr. Bing almost immediately. The other party was agreeable to the terms, and would appear, with Mr. Stothers, on Monday at the Watson gallery at ten in the morning. Would Mr. Watson please confirm, and ask his client to appear perhaps an hour later, when the papers would be drawn up and ready for her signature, for the agreed-upon price of $500,000.

Shouting a gleeful "Aha!," Geoffrey Watson picked up the phone and made all the arrangements. There would be, of course, an extra twenty percent as his commission, paid by Mrs. Goodridge directly to him. Well—fifteen percent, if she quibbled. Ten, at the least. Ten would almost be an insult, wouldn't it?

Gretchen had given her role a good deal of thought over the weekend. She would have to act like the kind of woman she had grown to dislike thoroughly, a child-woman who had married well, who did lunch, whose golf game was a fashion exposition, and who had easy enthusiasms, especially when impressive dollar figures were attached to them.

Now that Anthea was her confidante, she discussed it with her over the Scrabble board. She wondered aloud if her insincerity would show.

Anthea listened attentively, her eyes glistening with curiosity. "What do you think of the painting, regardless of the circumstances?"

"Well, it's in the Friedrich style, and I am partial to that."

"The money aside, would you hang it in your living room?"

Gretchen wagged her head. "It's a shipwreck, amid ice floe. Stark in colors. No living soul to be seen. Artistically, it's a strong statement."

"But it's not you. It doesn't speak to you. Is that it?"

"Yes. That's it, exactly. Why would I want to buy it?"

"So, you're afraid that when it comes to forking over the money, a lot of money, you will look insincere."

Gretchen nodded.

"My dear girl, let me put you at ease. Paintings like that aren't bought because people want them on their living room walls. They are investments. What you buy today at half a million you'll sell for twice that a few years hence. That's the idea. The enthusiasm lies in the profit, not in the aesthetic pleasure. The less emotional you are, the more credible you will appear. Go to it tomorrow. They'll love your money."

Gretchen laughed and said she'd remember that.

Later, when tea was brought up to the room and Gretchen observed how Anthea wanted hers served in the English manner, albeit with a glass straw, she asked, "Anthea, I don't know where you are from in America. Do you mind my asking?"

"Not at all. My horrible affliction has taken center stage too long. I do have a past. I am from Boston. My father was a Harvard classicist, my mother a teacher also. I was their only child. They sent me to Cambridge, first to the one, then to the other. I spent most of my adult years, before I married Jerome, in England. When my parents died within a year of each other, I inherited all they had. It turned out to be a lot, at least by my standards. Jerome swept me off my feet, and my money went along. He said that the Australian hinterland was a gold mine for the likes of us." She stopped, suddenly having to cough violently.

Gretchen helped her through it. When some calm was restored, she said, "I hope I didn't upset you, asking that question."

Anthea shook her head, clutching a tissue to her mouth.

Some time later, Anthea asked, "Are we all set for Macau on Tuesday?"

Gretchen said they were, explaining again that she and Terry would pick her up in mid-morning, and they'd depart from the Macau ferry terminal by private water taxi. She would do all the passport and customs papers for the two of them—Terry had different regulations. They'd be back here by late afternoon or early evening. Anthea's hotel bill would be charged with the costs of the trip. It wouldn't be cheap. And the doctor's fee would add to the cost.

Anthea said, "I have more money than I have breath left. I can't tell you how grateful I am to you, Gretchen."

Gretchen just patted her hand.

Anthea said, "When your deal closes tomorrow, how long will you stay before going home?"

"I'm not going home directly. I'm planning to fly to Germany to visit my son George, who works there for General Motors. I may spend some time with him. Maybe go to England, too." She shrugged her shoulders. "It's open ended."

"If it's open ended, could you spend a couple more days with me?"

Gretchen had seen that question coming. "A few, yes. Not too many."

"Over the next weekend? I'd reimburse your costs...."

"Costs are not the issue, Anthea."

"Will you? Just yes or no."

"Yes. Over the next weekend."

Anthea let her head drop back. Her eyes closed. A smile crept across her lips. "Thank you, my friend."

The whole deal with Geoffrey Watson was anticlimactic. Gretchen had worried for nothing. It was a signing ceremony, plain and simple. Von Vietinghoff, solo, represented the Balts; Mr. Stothers, the solicitors. Charles Lamb was on the phone—it was Sunday evening for him in California—asking Gretchen to let him do the work with Watson. From the way he talked, Gretchen could tell that he had been primed by George Natalian. She gladly handed the phone back to Watson.

When it came to signing the papers, two money drafts were presented to Gretchen for her signature. One was for $500,000 made out to the Balts in care of a Swedish bank. Another was to Watson Elementary Art, with the amount left blank. It was explained to Gretchen by Mr. Stothers that the check was for the customary dealer's commission, which was expected to be not less than fifteen percent of the sale price.

Here Gretchen allowed herself to have some fun. "Fifteen percent dealer's fee, Mr. Stothers? Are you sure?"

"Quite sure, madame."

"Isn't it Mr. Watson who brought us together? And he who will also pay your fees? And he who will take care of the shipping and insurance and customs necessities, as he just told my dealer in Santa Barbara?" She did not wait for an answer. "Mr. Watson, I feel inclined to recognize your contributions to my happiness a little more generously. Shall we say twenty percent?"

Watson's face broke out in a huge grin. "Yes! So be it. You're most discerning, Mrs. Goodridge." He took her hand and bowed over it. "Thank you!"

Gretchen said, "I shall remain in Hong Kong till the weekend, ample time for you to give me a report on how we are proceeding." With that, she rose.

Geoffrey Watson saw her out. "It's a good deal, you know," he whispered to her. "The painting's worth much more than that."

"I trust you to see to it that I get it, Mr. Watson. Mr. Lamb expects it by air express before I get home." When she saw a flicker of worry cross his face, she added, "I'll return via Europe, where I'll spend some time. A month or so. Surely it'll beat me home?"

"Oh, yes. But we must reckon in weeks, not days. Chinese authorities are a bit too formal at times. Fortunately, it's not one of *their* pieces of art. It should go smoothly."

When Gretchen gained the street and made her way down to Central, she had the feeling, for the first time, that she had achieved what she had been sent out to do. Along with that, she felt free. A month in Europe, did she say? Why not two? What did she need to hurry home for?

Pat Riley had a similar impression when he observed Gretchen being escorted out by Watson: Mission accomplished. Return to base.

He had done very well by himself with expenses so far. He could afford to consider a holiday. Perhaps in London, even. See Fiona, stay with her for a little while. Be rather inexpensive, come to that.

One thing was bothering him in the back of his mind: He had been rather impressed with this American woman, the way she conducted herself, and her utter disregard of sham or coyness in dealing with those men. She was the one character who stood out in all the proceedings. He felt a bit ashamed that he had to spy on her. How could he make that right?

She'd still be here for a week. He, too, would not wind up his mission until the weekend. If there were a chance, should he seize it and speak to her?

He'd have to give that some thought.

"What does Mrs. Tait actually have wrong with her?" Terry said under her breath to Gretchen when they had boarded the water taxi. Anthea had been placed on a seat in the back row, and Gretchen had come forward to talk to the driver. Terry sat next to him. They rode in a hydrofoil speedboat designed for eight passengers. It was theirs alone for the trip to Macau.

"Lou Gehrig's Disease," Gretchen answered.

"I thought so," Terry nodded. "What does she think the Macau doctor can do for her?"

"Relief. Hope. Something." Gretchen shrugged. "Anything is better than nothing."

"She may be disappointed."

"I don't think so. She's realistic. You and I, we are helping her."

"I'm just a hired guide," Terry said and turned away.

They reached Macau harbor within the hour. It had been a smooth ride. Except for the noise of the waves slapping under the raised hull, they were as comfortable as if they were in a land-based limousine. At times the water sprayed up to the cabin windows, washing out the view of the many small green islands that dotted the sea. There was boat traffic coming and going; the shipping lane was as busy as any highway, Gretchen noted with surprise.

They pulled into a berth at the ferry building and climbed from the boat onto terra firma without mishap. Anthea could actually walk, even unassisted if need be, were it not for the unsteadiness that made itself felt without warning. As she had told Gretchen, she was not paralyzed. It was her muscles that were wasting away. Other than that, she said with grim humor, there was nothing wrong with her.

A private car, ordered from their Macau sister hotel by the Mandarin Oriental, met them at curbside. It was a roomy Mercedes, into which Anthea and Gretchen reclined, with Terry again in the front seat.

The driver was given the address: Rua de Sao Paulo. The "Main Street" of the old town. Terry explained that they would have to walk because the doctor's house was on a hillside near the ruins of the St. Paul's Cathedral.

They made it there through hair-raising traffic, until Colonial Portugal embraced them with its cobblestone pavement, open storefronts, colorful old buildings that defied any safety code, latticed balconies crisscrossed by the wash drying on lines, and people, people everywhere.

Terry had been given Doctor Shi Chen's address, and she now told Anthea that they would have to climb a narrow lane to the doctor's house. The walkway, up worn stone steps, was so narrow that Gretchen held Anthea by the waist like an oversized puppet. But there they were at last. A door, a name plaque, a pull bell, a speaker phone, and a buzzer. They were admitted.

The office surprised them. It was a modern office with a waiting room, a lady at the desk who was in Western dress—all in gray, with a white cap on her straight black hair. Terry spoke Mandarin to her, and she replied in kind. It was a loud conversation that resulted in an order: Wait until you are called. There was nobody else in the waiting room. Gretchen wanted to know if the doctor was in, how long the wait would be, and if Terry had told the lady they had an appointment.

The questions were moot. The doctor appeared, a small man in a dark three-piece suit with a tie and stickpin. He had a goatee and wore glasses. He looked more like the Japanese emperor than a modern Chinese doctor. His English was surprisingly good, if accented. The patient was soon identified. Terry's services were not needed. Gretchen was asked to leave and come back in two hours.

Anthea offered no objection. She followed the doctor into his office, and the door closed behind them.

Back out on the street Gretchen said, "What now?" She felt hot. It was the height of the day.

"Sightseeing," Terry suggested. "We'll use the car. I'll show you everything. Macau is not big. Or do you want to gamble?"

"I want a bathroom and lunch," Gretchen said grimly, "in that order. And air conditioning. I'm not going to walk around in this heat."

They ended up in Hotel Lisboa, near the waterfront. It looked like one of the older hotels on the Las Vegas strip, only more opulent and with less glitter.

Terry recommended a restaurant that served Portuguese food in an open-air setting inside the vast hotel lobby. They had a table facing outward. The food was good. Gretchen observed about a dozen young women walking by on high heels, pretty and sexy as red-hot peppers, chatting in high, chirping voices.

Terry noticed her looking at them. "Pros," she said, smiling. "Very busy here. More in the evening."

They were back at the doctor's office on time. Anthea was laid out on a cushioned examination table, fully clothed, seemingly asleep. Or was she?

"My friend—" Gretchen turned to the doctor "—is she all right?"

"Mrs. Tait is resting," was the reply.

From what? Gretchen wondered when Anthea opened her eyes. "A taste of what's to come. And I can take it with me."

"Mrs. Tait has a prescription. I gave her a month's supply. It can be refilled by mail." The doctor pointed to a plastic container: in it were teabag-like packets of white powder. "*Yunna paivao*: very rare. Must be brewed fresh for use. Then drink it in one swallow before it is cold. Very important. One swallow. Then rest."

It sounded to Gretchen like a scene from a Woody Allen movie where a young New York matron visits a herbal medicine man who gives her a powder that makes her invisible.

"I did it in one swallow, can you imagine," Anthea said. It wasn't clear whether she was being proud or sarcastic about it. "The doctor also hypnotized me. Didn't you, Doctor Shi?"

"Mrs. Tait needs to rest her mind," he replied.

"For how long?" Gretchen looked at her watch.

"Mrs. Tait may leave now," the doctor said.

Mrs. Tait did leave having paid a very satisfactory fee at the beginning of the consultation, as she told Gretchen when they were back in the car.

"I know you don't want me to ask if you feel any better," Gretchen said, "but I'd like to know if this has made any difference."

"To the extent that anything can. It calms my mind."

"It's not another form of ginseng, is it?"

"Sanchi ginseng, yes. But it's what they do with it that matters. The making of the powder is secret, passed down to the enlightened since the Ming Dynasty." Anthea closed her eyes. "Just let me be, Gretchen."

Looking at her, again overcome with pity, Gretchen just held her hand, which lay limp on the leather seat.

The confirmation of the closing of the art deal came on Thursday morning when a waiter brought a phone to Gretchen at the breakfast table. Watson was clearly elated. The painting would pass Chinese inspection, "and, I might add, without greasing any palms. That would not be the Hong Kong way." Official assent from Beijing was expected within a week. Then the shipping would be taken care of. "It will beat you home, as you so charmingly put it, my dear Mrs. Goodridge. Not to worry." Then he added, "Mr. Lamb says hello."

Gretchen thanked him, and her joy was genuine. She rushed upstairs to her room and went to the safe in the clothes closet to get her airline ticket. The carrier was Lufthansa. She'd take it to their office—

where would that be, in Central probably—and exchange her return ticket for one that went via Frankfurt. If the price was reasonable, she would stop off in London and New York. At last, she'd be on her own!

On the ferry across Victoria Harbor Gretchen remembered that she had promised Anthea to stay with her over the weekend. She took that to mean that as of Monday she would be free to go on her own way. Better check that with Anthea before she committed herself to a new ticket.

She hadn't been to see that wretched woman all day Wednesday. Instead, she took a tour of the New Territories with Terry, for she had learned that her guide had been born there in a small village to a traditional Chinese family. Terry's birthplace was the reason she had adopted as her "English" name, "Terry." The day was delightful and interesting, and Gretchen enjoyed true Chinese hospitality. Seeing Anthea again the next day was a promise she had made before she went with Terry.

Anthea was in her accustomed chair by the window. Even though the sun was on her—or perhaps because of it—she seemed to Gretchen to look even more wan than usual. They greeted one another with a hug and a kiss.

The tea cart stood nearby. Connie was nowhere to be seen.

"Help yourself," Anthea said. "For me, the usual. Except the cup. See that baby cup? With the snout? It's come to that."

Gretchen busied herself, adopting a cheerful mien. Anthea's cup would need to be lifted to her lips. Where was the nurse?

"I have given Connie notice, as of Saturday," Anthea said.

"Do you have someone else?" Gretchen asked.

"No. I won't need another."

"Really? How will you manage?"

"I'm leaving." Anthea pushed the cup away with her lips.

"Are you? Going home?"

Anthea closed her eyes. It was a while before she spoke again. With a dark look at Gretchen she said, "I must ask you for a final big favor."

Shock mixed with dismay made Gretchen blurt out, "No, Anthea! You can't ask that of me! I won't do it. Do you hear me? I won't!"

"Don't be such a ninny. Of course I wouldn't ask you to do anything you couldn't do." She took a deep breath. "You said you're going back via Europe?"

"Yes," Gretchen replied, relieved. "Frankfurt. My son George is working there."

"Would you mind making a small detour? I need to go to Bali, and I need someone to get me on and off the plane. Before you answer, know that you can fly from Bali to Jakarta to anywhere you want. I insist that I buy that detour ticket for you. First class. From Jakarta you're on your own."

Gretchen had to overcome some annoyance before she could answer. What if she had exchanged her ticket already? And why Bali, for God's sake?

"Why Bali?" she asked.

"Have you been there?"

"No."

"It's paradise. The highlands of Ubud, especially. I've been there many times. It's so peaceful. You've come this far; you must see it."

"This is not about me, Anthea, it's about you. Why do you want to go to Bali?"

"Doctor Shi, the Macau doctor, agrees I should go there. The healers there have something I can't get here."

"Anthea! You're off on another tangent, the way I see it."

"Perhaps. All I'm asking is that you help me to get there."

"Is that really all? I'm anxious to see my son."

"You will. We leave Saturday night. You bring me to Ubud, and you can be on your merry way. But I'll bet you'll want to stay a day or two. Up to you."

"You have a place there?"

"A hotel. There's a brochure on the table."

Gretchen got up and looked for it. What she saw was a color brochure with a picture of a young blond woman clad only in bikini briefs, leaning on a railing from a poolside deck, looking out over a verdant tropical valley. Other pictures were of the place itself, Indonesian-style open-sided buildings grouped together in a lush and luxurious setting. Yet another picture of the same blond, this time in a diaphanous gown, reclining and reading. The name of the place was Kupu Kupu Barong. Whatever that meant.

"This looks expensive, Anthea!"

"We won't be there long. I thought you might enjoy the quiet and the rest for a day or two before you journey on."

Gretchen found it impossible to refuse her. "I have to have my airline ticket rewritten for the trip to Frankfurt. Let me do that first." She picked up her handbag. "Then I'll come back and tell you."

"I've already ordered two tickets on Garuda Airlines for Saturday night. One ticket—yours—on to Jakarta on Wednesday. Tell your ticket agent that you'll need to go on from there."

"Anthea, you're a wicked woman. How could you be sure I'd go with you?"

"Because I know you, Gretchen. We're sisters."

Gretchen had surprisingly little difficulty effecting the changes in her itinerary. September was still the off-season, business was slack, and Lufthansa had a business-class seat. And there was a chance of an upgrade to first class for her non-stop flight from Bangkok to Frankfurt Sunday night—or rather Monday morning, as it would leave at fifteen minutes after midnight, arriving in Frankfurt at six-thirty in the morning. That would be September 29. The agent suggested that, upon arrival in Jakarta, she spend a day of rest or sightseeing and then catch the Garuda flight on Friday morning to Bangkok, where she should again take a day, two actually, counting Sunday, to sightsee. Did she want to book the tickets now? Gretchen declined, saying that was already taken care of. She was given a full refund of her Hong Kong-Los Angeles ticket, which was applied to the airfare to Frankfurt. There was a balance in her favor, which she accepted in Hong Kong dollars.

Gretchen left delighted. While walking back to Anthea's hotel room she thought it wasn't such a bad idea to make that detour to Bali; it would also give her a glimpse at Jakarta and Bangkok. Who knew when she'd ever get back to these parts again?

Anthea was glad to hear that things were turning out all right for Gretchen. The flight to Bali would leave at six in the evening on that coming Saturday. Anthea would have a limo from her hotel come by Gretchen's hotel at four in the afternoon. Gretchen said Friday would give her a chance to call her family about her change in itinerary and to do some shopping. Wonderful.

On Sunday morning Pat Riley decided that he would have to make an effort to see that Goodridge woman; it was high time he did so. Off he went to the Regent Hotel in Kowloon.

The last he had heard was that she was slated to leave Hong Kong on Monday, according to what Watson had told him when he spoke to her on Thursday. Riley's own affairs had been taken care of; he had informed London of the completed sale of the painting for half a million U.S. dollars to that American art collector Mrs. Goodridge. From his end, there was no evidence of a connection to Russian interests, although the antecedents of the two Balts, one of whom was of Swedish nationality, were possibly fungible (he threw that word back at London with glee), but not proven so. There would be sixteen days, including travel days, for credit on the job, ten of them actual working days requiring double credits for work in China, Hong Kong now being in China.

With that money coming into his bank in Sydney, and with plenty of cash left over that was already his, plus his passage home chargeable to the credit card, he felt that he had some leeway in deciding when to return home. Old Winnie was fine, Miss Adelaide had assured him only yesterday, and besides, those border collies had an amazing sense of independence. He'd be all right, Pat reckoned; another week or so wouldn't make his absence any worse for the dog.

To his utter amazement he learned from the Regent's desk that Mrs. Goodridge had checked out. Not to let his disappointment show, he backed away and caught his breath. Checked out? To where? America?

The answer to that question would lie with the concierge; surely he must have ordered her a car to the airport. Walking over to that desk, he rapidly developed a credible story as to why he was inquiring about that American woman. Pulling out his wallet he produced a calling card that Watson had had printed for him, showing him as an "associate" of the Watson Elementary Art Gallery, Hong Kong. It was needed for all that to and fro with that painting.

"I say," he said, pushing his card forward and addressing the man who, by the gold key on his uniform collar, was probably the chief concierge, an assumption verified when he came closer and Riley could read the name and title on his badge. "A word, please, Mr. Gomes, regarding Mrs. Goodridge."

The concierge took Riley's card with his fingertips and held it away from him in a gesture of studied disinterest. "We do not give out information on our guests, mister…ah…Riley."

Riley guessed that the concierge was probably Portuguese-Chinese;

some delicacy was required here. "Of course you don't violate the privacy of your clients. My apologies if I did not express myself correctly. The lady in question is also a client of ours. We made a business transaction with her for which we require an urgent bit of information regarding the shipment of the object involved. We presume she has not gone directly home to America—to Los Angeles, California to be exact. We thought we could catch her by telephone on her next stop. Rather important. To Mrs. Goodridge, you understand."

"Your client—she didn't tell you where she was going?"

"Alas, not. It didn't seem relevant to ask."

"Then why should I tell you?"

"Indeed. Your point is well taken. However, if Mrs. Goodridge were party to this conversation, considering the importance of the matter to her, she would be grateful if you gave out her forwarding address, I shouldn't wonder." Pat considered, and then immediately rejected, the notion of offering a bribe; it would be a bribe, no matter how unobtrusively it was passed.

"She went to Bali." The concierge pocketed Riley's calling card.

"Bali. I see. Quite. Where on Bali, Mr. Gomes?"

"I don't know. She didn't tell us. The hotel—it is not one of ours. We did not book anything for her. It seems she had a friend here with whom she went. She was picked up by that friend's limousine." The concierge sounded very much annoyed, in general and at Riley. "That is all I can tell you, sir."

"Thank you, Mr. Gomes. You have been very courteous. We shall not fail to mention that to Mrs. Goodridge. No doubt she will be pleased."

— CHAPTER SEVEN —
Flight

The plane lifted off from Denpasar at three in the afternoon. Gretchen looked down on the verdant hills and terraced valleys of Bali, the sense of the unreal, the other-worldly, that had possessed her ever since she arrived here on Saturday evening would not leave her. She adjusted her seat to recline somewhat, hoping that she could read or sleep and let Bali recede from memory as rapidly as the island was now disappearing from view, the plane breaking through the clouds on its rapid climb.

In less than two hours she would arrive in Jakarta, which reminded her: She would have to set her watch back an hour. Gretchen sighed as she did that; such a normal thing to do, taking care of time. Reality.

It had been quite otherwise, these past few days. With Anthea in Ubud, nothing had been as before. True, the place, the setting, the surroundings—all were beautiful, as Anthea had promised they would be. Under ordinary circumstances, Gretchen would have enjoyed it. But this had been different. They had shared a bungalow that had two rooms separated by a swimming pool and sundeck. During the day, Anthea's room had been empty. Local people would pick her up in the morning and bring her back at night. Gretchen had been on her own. To what end? What was her role? And what was Anthea's?

She had the eerie feeling that she had been chosen to be an escort to the portals of Anthea's "Paradise." Was she the one rowing the boat across to the "Island of the Dead," as in that painting by Böcklin, with Anthea standing upright, shrouded, her head bowed, and she, the helmswoman, allowed to return to the land of the living? This past summer, when she was immersed in the study of nineteenth-century Germanic art, she had felt uneasy with that deep dark, mysticism that was evident in their literature too. Because it had been fresh on her mind, she had mentioned that to Duncan one Wednesday during their weekly golf game. He knew. "*Island of the Dead*, huh? Twentieth-century Rachmaninoff wrote a tone poem by the same name. Do you want to have the CD?"

Duncan. What a nice boy. Like one of her own.

Gretchen shook her head, dispelling the mental cobwebs. It was time to deal with the present. Now, where was that envelope Anthea had given her, which would contain the Jakarta hotel reservation?

Ah, yes, here it was: the Mandarin Oriental, located "in the heart of Jakarta's financial and diplomatic district," as the brochure said. Anthea had had it taken care of by her hotel in Hong Kong. Gretchen was relieved. There, at last, she could relax, be herself again, and put Bali behind her. The way she had already put Hong Kong and that painting purchase behind her.

Jakarta was everything that Bali had not been—busy, noisy, smelly, a metropolis thronging with people, cars, motorized rickshaws, buses, and bicycles seemingly in total disregard for death and destruction as they jostled with one another for space. It had Gretchen on edge just watching it all as the taxi took her from the airport to her hotel. The driver rolled his eyes and grinned broadly when she had told him "Mandarin Oriental." He sped down a divided road until, only minutes later, he turned into city traffic and joined the very skillful game of chicken with everyone else headed in the same direction. At a roundabout the taxi made a sharp left at full throttle, coming to a G-force halt underneath a porticoed entrance to a tall white skyscraper: her hotel. A doorman motioned the taxi to coast to the entrance.

From that point on Gretchen was merely the object of efficient attention that deposited her, as on a conveyor belt, at the reception desk, her bags behind her, the driver paid off. Yes, madame had a suite reserved. Gretchen handed over her personal credit card. Madame will stay how long? She said she needed a reservation on a flight to Bangkok. First class. Friday morning, if possible? Madame should not worry: The concierge would take care of it.

It was with utter relief that Gretchen stretched out on her bed. The room was so quiet that the muted hum of the air conditioner was barely audible, a white noise that lulled her to sleep.

When she awoke it was dark outside. The red message light was blinking on the telephone by her bed. It was the concierge; Mrs. Goodridge had a reservation on Garuda flight 938 to Bangkok, leaving at eight A.M. Friday morning, September twenty-sixth. One first-class seat. Madame would have to go to the airline office in person to show her passport and pay for the ticket. Tomorrow morning, the hotel van would take her there, although it was not far, just across the other side of the plaza around the Welcome Statue. Thank you for allowing us to be of service. Perhaps madame would want to do an escorted sightseeing tour of Jakarta tomorrow? Please call by touching "tours." Thank you, madame. Good night.

Gretchen felt elated. The mystic cobwebs of Ubud had vanished. Yes, she would take that city tour tomorrow. And not to forget—call Georgie.

Next morning Gretchen opted to walk to the Garuda Airlines office. It was really not far—she could see the sign from her room window—and she welcomed the chance to stretch her legs.

The air was warm and sticky, with a haze like the cloudy overcast sky she was used to from her California home. Only this was not moist sea air but smoke drifting over from the vast forest fires on neighboring Sumatra. The T.V. was full of stories about it, with people wearing masks over their mouths and noses like doctors and nurses, escapees from the operating room.

She had to take a number at the airline office, and when it was her turn she learned that she had a seat because a cancellation had occurred; the plane was full otherwise. Also, there would be a two-hour layover at Medan, in northern Sumatra, about halfway to Bangkok. Her arrival time there was five P.M.

When it came time to examine her charge slip, Gretchen was astonished at the large number of rupiahs she was signing for. Later in her hotel room she did the conversion. The ticket came to the price, almost, of a first-class trip from Los Angeles to New York. She grimaced; the envelope Anthea had left for her at the hotel in Ubud was rather slim. If it was Hong Kong dollars, it would not cover her cost. Never mind. She would do all the math at the end, when she was in Frankfurt.

And—oh, yes: Call Georgie. She went to her notebook for the number. The telephone in her room allowed direct dialing, thank the lord and hang the expense. She drummed her fingers on the night table, listening for the dial tone and the ring—once, twice—. After the fourth ring a message came on. George's familiar deep voice. First in English, then in German. Please leave a number.

Rats. Not in. Gretchen wondered what time it would be in Germany now. Was it forward or backward? She'd have to check that.

At the message tone she started talking: "George? It's me, Mum. I'm so sorry I got the time difference mixed up. Anyway, I'm calling you from Jakarta. I've made a detour via Bali. It's Thursday here. Tomorrow morning I'm on my way to Bangkok to catch the Lufthansa flight to Frankfurt. From there I'll leave on Sunday. I'll be in Frankfurt at the ghastly hour of six or so on Monday morning. I'll call you again from Bangkok tomorrow, hope to catch you in this time. If for any reason you can't meet me, please leave word for me with Lufthansa. And, Georgie, I really look forward to seeing you again. Perhaps meet your girlfriend? Talk to you soon. Love you, Georgie."

Gretchen was ready and packed early on Friday. Morning had not yet dawned over the city when she got up. She called down for her baggage to be carried; two bags. Her handbag, worn on a strap across her chest, was her flightbag now. All her important papers and her money were tucked away in a hidden body belt that was large enough to be a corset.

She had laid out her clothes the night before: lightweight khaki pants, a flowery silk blouse, and a sea-green windbreaker. She decided not to wear pantyhose, but knee-high stockings and flat, sensible shoes. The jewelry from Anthea was a problem: Gretchen was meant to convey it, along with a letter, to Anthea's husband. Anthea had given her a large diamond solitaire ring and a brooch set with emeralds and diamonds, both so impressive that Gretchen decided to wear them instead of put them into her handbag. Much as she loved Anthea, this was a bit of a nuisance she had to get rid of soon. Perhaps in Germany. Georgie would know a good attorney who could be in touch with Mr.

Tait in Townsville, Australia, and arrange the safe conveyance of the pieces.

Downstairs, Gretchen settled her account at the desk. Again, large numbers of rupiah that by the magic of international currency conversion would turn up a month later in sensible U.S. dollars on her American Express statement. She didn't care, she told herself, how much this excursion cost her; the whole trip to Hong Kong had been a free ride, thanks to Getty.

Dawn was just breaking dimly through the haze when she entered the van the hotel had provided to take her to Soekarno International Airport. Despite the early hour, the traffic was heavy. It had been the same yesterday: On her city tour, Gretchen had been appalled at the magnitude of the people-crunch everywhere—not just in vehicles on the road, but on the streets, in narrow alleys, on large plazas, even in the harbor area, where crowds seemed to be thronging the docks to the water's edge. She was glad to leave, although she admitted to herself that all the people she had met had been kind and friendly to her.

There were more crowds at the airport, queuing up to check in, lining up at passport control, at customs. Gretchen was asked to open her two suitcases for a hand-and-eye search before they received a seal and were checked through to her flight. Then there was the airport tax—more rupiah. It was unnerving.

At last the call for her flight came over the public address system: Passengers to report to the check-in desk. Warily, Gretchen approached it, joining a cluster of people. They were told that their flight would not start boarding until nine-thirty. A man next to her—a European, she guessed from his accent—grumbled: This was typical of the airline: they combine two half-full planeloads into one full one to save money, and to hell with schedules.

Gretchen nodded but said nothing. What was the use?

When at long last she was on the plane she collapsed in her seat, the last row of first class, on the aisle. She was thoroughly exhausted. She had been up since four-thirty after a restless night. It was now five hours later, but she felt as if she had been through a whole day. Her clothes stuck to her body, but she dared not take her jacket off because of that damn brooch; and, besides, it would get cold once they were airborne. So she sat clutching her purse, thinking she ought to read something, but she saw nothing within reach that tempted her. Only fifteen more minutes until the doors closed.

Her next-seat neighbor was an elderly Chinese man who sat sleeping, his bony fingers clasped and resting on his lap. His seatbelt was on. Gretchen was glad; she did not feel like making small talk, either.

The captain's voice came on, apologizing for a slight delay, but they would soon get clearance for takeoff, he said. No air hostess was nearby whom Gretchen could ask what this delay was about.

After what seemed like an eternity, when the doors of the plane had still not closed, Gretchen became suffused with a sense of restlessness that would not leave her. She closed her eyes, tried to think of the fresh air blowing in from the ocean into her open windows at home. It did not work. A nauseous feeling crept up in her guts, but she ignored it resolutely, her eyes still shut.

Then she saw it. An apparition that at first was like a glowing fireball. As it grew nearer she heard a voice, distant, unintelligible, until she could make out a figure and the voice became clear.

Gretchen thought her heart would stand still.

It was her mother's. She was sure of it because she recognized her face, her features, and the presence that was strangely soothing. Gretchen had tears in her eyes. "Mother!" she mouthed.

The figure responded. Not in words, but from soul to soul: My daughter my love, you must leave this plane. Now. Without delay. Do it, daughter of mine. Do it…get out…get out….

Gradually the figure receded, the apparition vanished. Gretchen opened her eyes. The cabin was as before.

Her heart pounding against her chest, Gretchen unfastened her seatbelt. She knew what she must do. Nothing would stop her.

She looked around and saw that the curtain separating first class from the rest of the plane had not been pulled closed, and the exit just beyond it was still wide open. She got up, and in a few large steps found herself outside the plane on the boarding ramp. Nobody called after her; in fact, to her surprise, no one seemed to have noticed her at all.

A few more strides and the ramp turned. Now Gretchen was out of sight of the passengers and attendants on the plane, and it suddenly occurred to her that she might be stopped at the boarding gate, or by a security guard in the departure lounge. But there was no time to worry about any of that, and Gretchen was propelled by the inner force of the resolution she had already made. She hurried out of the boarding ramp and into the departure lounge; it was deserted except for a janitor in a dirty uniform desultorily dragging a garbage can behind him. He looked up at her briefly, then quickly averted his gaze. Looking neither left nor right, Gretchen strode toward the escalator and rode to the lower level, where the restaurants and duty-free shops were, and lost herself in the stream of people coming and going, the din of their voices mingled with public address system announcements in various languages. For Gretchen, a returning sense of reality was paired with the urgency of her mother's plea: The ominous "Get out…get out" still rang in her ears.

She felt nausea coming on, with such urgency that her eyes darted for a place of relief—there, the Lufthansa Senator Lounge. She pushed through the door, grabbing her Lufthansa ticket from her purse and waving it at the entry desk, where people were again queuing up. "Toilet?" she pleaded, a handkerchief before her mouth. With her need so apparent, she was directed down a hallway and to the left.

She found a modern facility with individual stalls, some of them open. She ran for one, locked the door, and pulled down her pants and panties. On the seat, urinating, she waited for worse.

Nothing. Only an unexpected calmness. No nausea anymore.

Gretchen checked her pulse with her wristwatch: eighteen beats in fifteen seconds. Seventy-two per minute. She had done this hundreds of times with her boys. She touched her forehead with the back of her hand: no temperature.

She was all right. The Garuda flight had left by now, from what she thought she had heard over the loudspeakers. And she was in the toilet of Lufthansa's frequent-flyer lounge at Soekarno Hatta Airport in Jakarta. Her flight to Bangkok gone. Now what?

If anything, this was a time for rational assessment of her situation. But reason was not to come to her aid. Realization did. She had left her seat on the airplane that was to take her to Bangkok. She had acted in a moment of panic when she had imagined her mother's appearance. Was this the same old fear that she thought she had overcome—the Fateful Fifth? What had made her believe she was seeing her mother? Was she going mad?

Grimly, she chided herself. This wasn't helping any. Fear or not, she needed to come to grips with the present. What should she do next?

Obviously, she needed to find another flight to Bangkok. Her luggage would be waiting for her there. But she knew there was only one daily flight, the one she had been on. So, shall she go back to the hotel and rebook a flight? Was that reasonable?

Maybe there was a simpler way: Let Lufthansa take her to Frankfurt any which way it went, and let Garuda forward her luggage. When was the next Lufthansa departure? Time to get off the pot and find out.

At the wash basin Gretchen looked at herself in the mirror. She didn't like what she saw: sallow cheeks and deep shadows under red-rimmed eyes, as if after a night of debauchery. She wished now that she had had a night like that. It would be more credible.

And whatever had made her think that this flowery blouse was attractive? She must have been out of her mind at that Ubud shop. Back she went into the stall to take it off. Her windbreaker was reversible; it had an inner lining of peachy-pink that gave her back some color, and when she zipped it up close to her neck the blouse would not be missed. She stuffed the blouse into her pocket.

Now Anthea's pin—far too gaudy. Take it off and put it away, she commanded herself. Wrapped in soft toilet paper, it went into the inner pouch of her handbag. The ring—turn the stone palmwards. That's better.

A Gretchen quite different from the one who had entered the washroom earlier emerged at last, one who felt ravenously hungry and thirsty. Lufthansa wouldn't mind if she lingered a while, partaking of the sweetrolls and coffee so temptingly displayed at the self-serve counters. And lo, there was a deep-cushioned easy chair behind a partition. She ensconced herself in it, putting on sunglasses. All she needed was a moment's rest. Respite from Bali, from Anthea, and this.

She must have fallen asleep, for some noise and commotion awakened her, distant at first, then closer. She checked her watch; it was near two o'clock. She heard exclamations of dismay, a woman's wail. What was all that? Gretchen decided to get up and check it out.

She saw people gathered around the T.V. set by the bar. She approached. A man in suit and tie turned away, shaking his head. "What happened?" she asked him.

"A plane crashed. A Garuda flight." He had a German accent. "Near Medan. All that burning in Sumatra. No wonder." He shook his head again as he left.

Medan? Garuda? Crashed!

Slowly, Gretchen focused on the T.V. screen. There it was, being repeated over and over again by an excited voice speaking in Indonesian, with a running band of figures at the bottom of the screen: Garuda flight 938...Airbus A-300...Medan, Sumatra...234 passengers....

Gretchen stood ashen-faced. That was her flight.

"Any survivors?" she whispered to an Indonesian steward next to her.

"Look." He jabbed his finger at the disaster on the screen, his voice mournful. "It says 234 dead! Nobody lived! This is a national calamity!"

"Oh my God...." Her head was spinning as the reality of the crash sank in, and she considered her own situation. Slowly, she backed away and pushed through the crowd. With weak knees she sank into the nearest seat, her head back against the cushion, staring without seeing.

So this is what it was all about. She would be dead now if she hadn't gotten off that plane, torn into unrecognizable pieces, strewn over a jungle landscape. Dead. Dead, dead, dead.

Mother you saved me, Gretchen said in her soul. You came to me and you saved me from your own fate. I will pray to God to thank him. I have never stopped praying for you, Mother. I have been blessed. I thank God...Mother....

Afterwards, Gretchen did not care that she had sat in that chair for nearly an hour. A great serenity had come over her. She had been spared. Now she must show that she had been worthy.

Getting up, she felt strong and clearheaded. However, she also felt saddened, deeply moved by the phantasmagoric pictures that were still on the T.V. screen. Now the minister of transportation was delivering a message from President Suharto: A full investigation into the cause of the crash would commence.

Gretchen was regaining her rational sense. Hadn't the T.V. said over and over again that the crash was caused by poor visibility from smoke on the ground, causing the plane to hit a tree during its approach to Medan? What other causes were there to investigate? Bombs in a suitcase, perhaps?

In one flash of insight Gretchen realized that she was in imminent danger. All along in the back of her mind she had naturally assumed that she would go to the airline office and identify herself as the one passenger who had not been on that fateful flight. Help would be given to her, and she would reciprocate by being helpful in turn. She would join in the sorrow and mourn for the dead. Miraculously, she had left the plane at the last minute.

But her suitcases had not, had they?

Gretchen knew from many a trip to England that passengers at Heathrow were asked to identify their baggage before it was loaded onto the plane. Then the passengers, one by one and under close supervision, were permitted to board. The assumption was that a mad bomber would not want to be his own victim.

Where had she come from, they would ask her. From Bali. Ah, so. There she had left behind a friend, a sick woman she had only recently met in Hong Kong, yes? Gretchen had an idea that Anthea was no longer among the living, that she had chosen to die there in Ubud. Mercy-killed was the better term, was it not? And what about this jewelry? The emerald brooch, the diamond ring—they were from the dead woman, yes? And Mrs. Goodridge herself, she was divorced, yes? And not a wealthy lady, it would soon be revealed. So what was she doing buying an expensive painting, pretending to be rich?

An icy clear realization set in: Gretchen Goodridge, the patsy, was a walking case of opportune scapegoating for the Indonesian authorities, from the airline on up to a government that could ill afford the drop in tourism that would surely follow from this disaster.

No! Gretchen stepped away from the T.V. area as she thought this and hastened out the door of the lounge into the maelstrom of people outside. No! She would not expose herself to this kind of risk. Not now, not when she had just been given her life back.

What to do? Clearheadedness was needed, and rational thinking that began with the fact that as of now, and soon officially, she, Gretchen Goodridge, would be counted among the victims of the crash.

Gretchen Goodridge was dead.

Until it was established otherwise, that pseudo-fact remained. The situation could only be righted when she returned to American soil, to law and justice. Only then could she begin to regain her real self.

Ergo, as her mother used to say when she reasoned things out with her, *hear this*: The first order of business was to leave Indonesia.

Leave? How? As Gretchen Goodridge? Soon the passenger manifest of the crashed plane would be made public. The few Western names would stand out. She would be questioned and detained.

Back to square one.

Then she remembered: She had that new passport in one of her corset compartments! For a certain Margaret Cosima Herter. Fresh. Unused.

Unused! What she needed to get out of here was an arrival stamp in those pristine pages. She could not leave the country without an arrival stamp.

Thinking quickly as she stood in the arrival hall, she knew exactly how to proceed. From the monitors in the hall she could tell that a Garuda flight was arriving from Honolulu within minutes. She would manage to join the throng passing through customs and get her stamp. Then she would go to a Jakarta hotel (not the one she had come from!) and plot her escape from Indonesia.

Not to Bangkok anymore—that was out. Rather, she would flee to an English-speaking country where she could turn to the American embassy for help.

Singapore! A law-and-order country. And it was close by.

Gretchen disappeared into a restroom again, locked herself into a stall, and opened her corset. She exchanged passports and took out U.S. dollars. Reemerging, she checked the arrivals board. The Honolulu flight was in.

The entire airport was in an uproar. T.V. crews were showing up by the vanload, and reporters were swarming the waiting areas, interviewing anyone who would stand still for them. Swarms of other personnel—police, airline officials, medical crews—were appearing in growing numbers. Clutching her Lufthansa ticket book for show, and snatching up a discarded Garuda flight envelope, Gretchen pushed her way through the crowds and approached the arrival gate for the flight from Honolulu. There, on the other side of a makeshift barricade, arriving passengers were entering the building and were being directed toward immigration to have their passports stamped. She needed to get into that line.

But how? Uniformed guards were everywhere. She couldn't just duck under one of the cordons, although that's exactly what a T.V. crew was trying to do at that very moment. Gretchen watched in fascination as a crew of four sweaty men with heavy camera equipment tried to muscle their way past the barricade in order to interview the arriving Honolulu passengers. All the guards in that area rushed to stop them, shouting and waving their arms and weapons.

In a split second, Gretchen acted.

She gracefully ducked under a cordon stretched between two wire gates and found herself in the arrival area. Wasting no time she strode across the floor. She was halfway to the stream of arriving passengers when she heard a shout from behind her. She froze and turned slowly.

The guard approached her angrily. "American?" he demanded.

Too frightened to speak, Gretchen nodded.

The guard lifted his baton. She felt adrenalin pulse through her heart. Then the guard used the baton to point. "Go there!" he shouted, pointing in the direction of the immigration control. Gretchen smiled and nodded, then meekly scurried to join her fellow Americans from Hawaii. She was the last one in the line, the last to receive her stamp verifying that she had just arrived in Jakarta.

She was then directed to the baggage claim area, but of course she had no baggage. She proceeded directly to customs, told the customs official she had nothing to claim and no baggage. The official gave her a quizzical frown.

"I'm here on business," she told him. "My company took care of all that."

The customs official waved her through, and she walked out into the main lobby of the Jakarta airport.

The next thing she knew she had to take care of was her lack of luggage; she was carrying nothing. An unlikely situation for a tourist.

The obvious answer was to create new luggage. The international airport had shops for nearly everything, including a choice of suitcases in every size and at every price. Gretchen found one that had wheels and a pull-out handle. In order to make it look full and to add weight, she went on a shopping spree that included native attire, T-shirts, sweatsuit, running shoes, and basic toiletry and cosmetic items. For good measure, she also bought a sun hat and sunglasses, as well as a folding umbrella. To add weight she picked up newspapers.

So outfitted, she marched to the exit and hailed a cab.

"Holiday Inn, please," she told the driver. It was the only hotel she knew would be everywhere, including Jakarta. It was, as a Crown Plaza. And there Mrs. Herter from Honolulu, Hawaii, U.S.A. registered and got a suite.

When evening fell she was in a hotel room again, as she had thought she would be when she had set out in the morning. Except this was not Bangkok. It was still Jakarta, a city seething with insecurity and layer upon layer of emotions that could erupt at any time, for any reason, against anyone. The T.V. was full of pictures from the crash site. Four of the passengers were American, it said. No names yet. Vast smoldering wreckage, rescuers mostly standing around helplessly. The horror was palpable. There was her would-be grave!

She grabbed the phone, dialed George's number with a shaking hand and heard the ring, then his recorded voice and the beep!

"George…uuhhh…oh…" A sob drowned her words. What words? She let the receiver fall.

Fear and deep visceral dread began to grow in her, threatening her rational self. She had to summon all her natural resistance not to succumb to panic.

There were things she could do and things she must not, under any circumstances, allow to happen. She needed to tell herself what these were, the do's and don't's. Feverishly grabbing a sheet of hotel stationery and taking a pen in hand, she drew a quivering line down the middle of the page. To the left of the line she would make the plusses, and to the right the minuses.

On the plus side: She could leave Jakarta. Tomorrow. She still had money from the Getty in U.S. hundreds amounting to several thousand dollars, right here in her corset. And she had plenty of Hong Kong dollars left.

A plus. Two plusses. She had a new, valid passport. Another big plus.

Leave? How? By air? She discarded that idea. Too much scrutiny at airports. She'd been lucky once. The dice don't come up that way twice in a row.

Then she remembered from her tour around Jakarta the great number of ships in the harbor. There had to be a way to go to Singapore by ship!

So it would be. Also, Americans needed no visas for Singapore.

So much for the plusses. What about the minuses?

Now it dawned on her with searing pain that she could not call Georgie to let him know of her change in plans. Worse, she could not call anybod*y*. Not today, nor tomorrow. Not until she was in safe haven, in American hands. But in the meantime, everyone would think she was dead! Dear God!

She sank to her knees beside the bed and prayed.

Pat Riley saw Gretchen march into the lobby of the Crown Plaza Holiday Inn, pulling a suitcase, a sun hat askew over her full hair and sunglasses darkening her eyes. It was unmistakably her, though.

It was sheer luck. And he was due some, too.

Fascinated, he watched from an armchair in the lobby as she dealt with the desk clerk. She was checking in! More luck. This was his hotel as well. It was in his price range. He had arrived yesterday from Bali after having missed her by a hair the day before at Denpasar, where he had watched her board the daily flight to Jakarta. As he had done on Bali, he was planning to check out the hotels, beginning with the priciest ones. Except he hadn't gotten very far; an Indonesian airliner had crashed that day on Sumatra with some two hundred people dead, most of them from Jakarta. The disaster was causing huge traffic jams everywhere, as well as a scarcity of taxis. He would have to hire a pedicab of sorts; not a fun thing to do, considering the heavy smog outside.

This whole business of following her from Hong Kong was beginning to look ludicrous, stupid even. He was doubting his own sanity. Why was he doing this, and what would he say if he actually spoke to her? Hello, how are you?

He might as well go home.

Well, this could change things somewhat. From his room he could call the hotel operator and ask to be connected to Mrs. Goodridge's room. Ask her down for a drink. Explain himself to her. Apologize. See what happened next.

He would give her until late afternoon, early evening. He would stay in the lobby watching in case she came down.

At six-thirty he made the call. To his stunned consternation, he was told, repeatedly and firmly, that there was no guest by the name of Mrs. Goodridge.

What in hell did this mean? Had she insisted on anonymity? If so, why?

Riley hung around the dining room for a couple of hours, feeling more and more foolish. By nine o'clock he gave up.

She would have to come down for breakfast. Tomorrow was another day.

Much against her own rules of healthy living, Gretchen had raided the minibar in her hotel room in order to knock herself out and get some sleep. Two little bottles of whiskey and one of cognac did the trick; she was out like a light and actually slept through until morning. A throbbing headache was a small price to pay for this much-needed break.

For breakfast, she ordered room service. Sitting down with another blank sheet in front of her, she put aspirin on the top of the list she was making of what else she needed to buy, along with Band-aids and sanitary napkins. More importantly, her wardrobe was lacking in some basic things, such as a nightgown or pajamas—she had slept naked under the covers last night—as well as an acceptable dress, some shoes, and pantyhose. The hotel would have shops. She would also need some reading material, a book, a novel to get lost in.

Before she would do any of that, she would need to inquire about sea connections to Singapore. She pulled the phone onto her lap and dialed the hotel travel agency.

Yes, there was an overnight ferry to Singapore, leaving at noon and arriving mid-morning the next day. Perfect. She booked it on the spot.

By the time she checked out of her hotel, Gretchen had acquired everything on her list and more, including a linen jacket, a skirt, a dressing gown, sandals, and swimsuit. The items fit easily into her rolling suitcase. The old newspapers had been discarded. The book she bought was a paperback reprint of *Wuthering Heights*; she had always wanted to read that. She wore the new jacket and skirt because she would be in staid, conservative Singapore.

For all of her charges, she paid the hotel with Hong Kong dollars, which were eagerly accepted at a rate of exchange that was no doubt favorable to the cashier. The ferry ticket was part of the bill.

She asked for a taxi, and when it came she was escorted through the lobby by the porter and an eager bellboy. The American lady tipped well, better than most other tourists.

Once again, Pat Riley was a silent witness to the goings on, unable to find a suitable moment to make his presence known to Mrs. Goodridge. When he saw her check out, he cursed himself for not having done so himself; he should have been ready-set-go at this point. Instead, he rushed after her, saw her things being loaded into a taxi, and saw her bestowing largesse upon the hotel staff. He edged close enough to hear the fellow in the braided-uniform wish madame a good trip to Singapore. He heard that word twice: "Singapore."

No mistake about that. She was going to Singapore.

How? By air, probably.

Hastily, Riley corralled another taxi and did that ridiculous thing seen in so many movies. "Follow that cab!" he commanded the driver.

But the route taken was not to the airport. It went in the opposite direction, to the harbor. It ended at the ferry building, an edifice the size of a railway station, which in fact it resembled, including crowds, loading berths, check-in counters, and customs.

When Riley saw her pass through customs, he decided he would stop following Mrs. Goodridge. He would beat her to it by taking a plane to Singapore. Besides, his luggage was still at the hotel. He would have to go back and check out. Before he left the ferry building, he helped himself to some timetables. Mrs. Goodridge would arrive in Singapore by nine-thirty A.M. the next day.

He, Pat Riley, sleuth extraordinaire, would be dockside.

"Hello! Mrs. Goodridge, I presume?"

Except, by the time he had left the hotel, gone to the airport, and scanned the departures, he had missed the day's only flight to Singapore. The next one was on SilkAir at eight the next morning.

What rotten luck. Now he would have to start all over again looking for that elusive Madame Pimpernel.

Dejected but not defeated, Riley bought a ticket on the SilkAir flight. He checked his bag and hung around the airport, sneaking into the Quantas and Singapore Air lounges, to eat, drink, and snooze. It was a long night.

The ferry to Singapore had a stopover in the early morning at Bintan Island, where half the passengers disembarked. Gretchen had a cabin and a reasonably good night. Tea and biscuits were served by a steward before she was out of bed. It revived her spirits. She dressed carefully and put on her makeup. Civilization awaited.

The ferry docked at the Tanah Merah terminal, on the Changi side of the island that was the sovereign state of Singapore. It was close to the international airport. Customs and immigration officers served both sites. Gretchen found herself among a horde of Western and Japanese women and children who had been sent by their embassies and their husbands' companies to a safe haven away from the haze and smoke that were choking Jakarta, and not least from the increasing unrest there.

The line-up was long and had many checkpoints. Luggage and baby carriages were piling up, and unruly children were constantly underfoot.

Gretchen must have been thought of as a nanny for her passport check was speedy and routine. In the back of her mind she had feared that there might be a problem. The U.S. State Department could possibly have discovered the existence of her old passport and cancelled one or the other. Singapore's state-of-the-art computer equipment would catch any error or irregularity. But she was okay. No questions were asked. Relief.

On the taxi ride into town she was astounded by how very clean and modern everything looked. It reminded her of nothing so much as Southern California, especially Orange County, where new developments and connecting parkways were changing the landscape by the month, it seemed. Well, if this was what awaited her, Singapore was just what she needed. Was she at the end of her ordeal?

She had told the driver to take her to the Regent Hotel, based on the good experience she had had in Hong Kong. As they approached the city center and turned onto Orchard Road, she was glad she had made that choice: the whole town was clean and green, hustling and bustling, a truly modern metropolis. The hotel was in a park-like setting that made her feel even more glad. Yes, this would be the turning point for her.

Pat Riley's experience was not dissimilar. He had arrived shortly after Gretchen did, had taken the same road from the airport, and had also chosen a hotel familiar to him, a Holiday Inn. According to a city map he had found in the airplane seat pocket, Orchard Road was in an area of hotels and shops where tourists would most likely prefer to stay, and this hotel was at the very beginning of it. Plenty of opportunity to walk up one way and back the other, checking out all the Orchard Road hotels. Of course, there were other hotels elsewhere in the city, but this part of town held a good chance, a likely start.

Cheap, though, it would not be. Not for him, with the Singapore dollar nearly on par with the Australian dollar. He'd give himself three days, max, to find his quarry or put the whole thing behind him. This being Monday, Thursday would be the day he'd take off for Sydney.

One thing he would do, come to think of it, was pay a visit to the Australian High Commission. A man he had known in London and who had been his relay on his Myanmar mission was stationed here. Andy Selvidge. About his age. Married, kids grown. Be fun to see him again, after all this time. And Joanie, too, if need be, although she had struck him as a boring twit. So if the Goodridge saga were to come to naught, at least he'd bend an elbow with an old chum. Small consolation, that, though.

He took a taxi to the commission office. It was on Napier Road, the other end of Orchard, and a plush area it was, too; just right for embassies that represent rich and important countries. He found three of them in a row: the British, the American, and the Australian. The Brits' building looked the most simple and commonplace, the Yanks' the most modern and the most secure, set back as it was from the road and with defense barriers cleverly blended in with the architecture. The Aussies' was set back, too, but more open and friendly. When he paid off the cabbie he could just walk up the driveway, report to the gatehouse, and wait for Andy to show up.

Bad luck: Andy ("Mr. Selvidge, the trade consul") wasn't in. Pat left word he had called.

The euphoric feeling of the previous evening carried over into a good night's sleep, making Gretchen feel well when she awoke. She tore back the curtain and stood at the window, enjoying the view of the park across from it. All was lush green, the lawns tended, the apartment buildings in the distance well spaced and well appointed, quite unlike the monolithic high-rises of Hong Kong. A light rain falling just then seemed to her most agreeable, like the sprinklers going off at her former home to douse her lawns in gentle mists. This was a wonderful place. And yes, this was her turning point.

In her bath she thought about Anthea. She needed to gain a distance from the experience of being with her; it had been a greater emotional strain than she had allowed herself to recognize.

This would be a good time to open that other envelope contained in the one Anthea had left for her at the hotel in Ubud. If it held money, as she suspected, it would probably also have a note with it. In Anthea's words? A final farewell? Oh, God. Might as well get to it. Clear the decks, as they say.

Wrapping herself in the thick cotton bathrobe the hotel had so graciously provided, she went to her corset and extracted the envelope. It was tightly sealed so that she had to use her nail file to open it.

A thin packet plopped out. It was twice wrapped in Japanese silk paper. Gretchen fingered it and held it to the light, but the paper was too opaque to read through.

There was also a sheet of Madarin Hotel stationery. Gretchen unfolded it. Anthea's hand—unmistakably; no one else would write in such an uneven, jerky manner—it began "Dearest Gretchen..." which made her groan and put the sheet down. But then she picked it up again and read on. "You are in my thoughts now as I come to the end of my journey. Do you believe in angels? I do. I believe you were sent to me to guide me across." Here Gretchen gulped; this was hitting too close to home. Her own airplane experience! Again she put the letter down, again she continued. "I pray for you, who remain behind. I thank you with all my heart. You are blessed. Love, Anthea."

As Gretchen stared at the letter, reading it again, tears welled up in her eyes. She sensed that there was a truth in Anthea's words; not a rational, knowable one, but a deeper verity that defied being explained: Anthea's acceptance of her fate, her belief in angels.

But it was not Gretchen who deserved to be so called. Was she herself not the receiver of such strange grace? How else was she to come to terms with the events that had brought her here, to this place, at this time? When under any "foreseeable" circumstances she would long ago have arrived in Frankfurt and been with Georgie, living her life?

Her *old* life. Not *this*, this new beginning she had just entered.

Wherever that would take her.

As Gretchen went about her morning routine of getting dressed, doing her hair, and applying makeup, her mind was on Anthea and what meeting her had portended for her own life. She believed deeply that what had happened was far from random and meaningless, and while she could not control the outside forces buffeting her about, she could react by applying her own judgment. In each instance there were moral dues to be paid along the way; nobody got a free ride.

The more she thought about it, the clearer it became to her that she owed Anthea one last duty: to be the bearer of the news of her fate to her husband, to deliver that letter, bring home her jewelry. Home being Townsville, Australia.

It hit her with sudden clarity that that was precisely what she had to do. And concurrent with that realization she knew that the place where she should make her own case with the American authorities was Australia, not Singapore. Australia was more like America, she had read. More congenial. Less likely to extradite her to Indonesia. Yes, Australia was her destination, or destiny, putting it that way.

She dropped her lipstick and went looking for the letter that had been brought to her along with the jewelry by that mysterious nighttime visitor to her room in Ubud. There it was. In Anthea's handwriting, it bore just the name Jerome Tait. The thought of having it mailed to him from some third party, perhaps in Germany, now struck her as uncaring, even mean-spirited.

No. She herself would do the honor to Anthea's memory. She felt relieved by the utter rightness of her decision.

Going down to breakfast, she snatched up the small packet from Anthea's letter to her; it had defied her nails in opening it, so she would use a table knife to cut through the silken envelope.

She suspected it would be money. Left-over Hong Kong dollars, most likely. Well, she would apply it to her expenses for that trip to Australia. No doubt Anthea would approve.

Before her breakfast order was brought to her table, she took the serrated knife and pried the envelope open.

It was money, as she thought. Ten bills of it. And another note from Anthea: "Gretchen—my iron reserve. It's yours now. Love, Anthea."

Gretchen looked up to see if anyone was watching her. She mustn't cry now.

Pulling out one bill, she looked at it. It was unfamiliar. The queen of England was on it. The denomination was 500 Pounds sterling.

With a searing sense of alarm, she fingered the other bills. They were all the same. Ten 500 notes, British money. Not Hong Kong at all. At the moment she had no idea how much it was worth, except that it was a lot. Enough to see a person out of a jam and off on her way, in an emergency. An "iron reserve," as Anthea had put it.

Quickly, she stuffed the notes into her handbag and snapped it shut. When her plate was put before her she tried to act normally, putting jam on her toast, forking some omelette into her mouth, sipping from her coffee cup.

What was she to do? Keep it? Anthea obviously wanted her to have it. And under the circumstances, she could certainly use the extra cash. In the future she would consider repaying it, perhaps donating money to a charity.

Yes, that was it. And she resolved as well not to be a "ninny," as Anthea called it, but to be rational and determined. After all, her own life was in a certain jeopardy. She needed to keep her wits about her.

A change in plans was called for. No longer was a visit to the American embassy an option. Instead, she must find a way to leave Singapore and go to Australia.

Books. She had to have information, tourist books, on Townsville, and thereafter on Canberra, which she knew was the capital of Australia, where her own embassy would be located.

She would have to find a travel agency. They would be listed in the telephone book in her room. Likewise, bookstores would be listed. If she compared the addresses with her hotel's location, she could design a pattern of visits that had a convenient sequence.

Lightly dressed against the tropical heat and humidity, and without the corset, which she locked into her room safe, but with plenty of her American money, Gretchen went down and had a taxi take her to Raffles City. In the late afternoon she returned, feeling a bit worn and clammy but very satisfied with the results of her excursion.

She had found a way to get to Australia that would not involve international airports; with all their scrutiny at immigration and customs, she felt she had best avoid them as much as possible. Instead, she would go by ship. One of the agencies she visited put her onto the idea. She had said she was a writer, and as such interested in the more uncommon ways to travel.

What about by sea, the agent suggested, an Indian she guessed, very bright and eager to make a deal. To Darwin, or to Perth, if she liked?

Gretchen, who had a guidebook of Australia in her shopping bag and knew that Darwin, in the north, was the closest Australian port as well as presumably the least traveled, said quickly, "Darwin, yes. That'd be just fine."

"Very well, madame!" the Indian beamed. "So it is. Yes, indeed."

"It's not a cruise ship you're suggesting, is it? I don't like cruises."

"Not at all! It's a very modern ship of Japanese registry, a container ship, but with a number of deluxe passenger cabins."

"A freighter?"

"Ah, yes, madame, a freighter!" The Indian took that as an inspired joke. "The most exclusive way to travel these days, for those who can afford it."

The idea was instantly appealing. "How much?" Gretchen asked.

The fare was about what she would have paid for a first-class air ticket. She said yes, go ahead, book it.

The agent scurried off to his computers to make the booking. In between he came back to have Gretchen fill out several forms and to collect her passport. In due course he returned, nodding and smiling. "We have a booking for you, madame. Thursday, three days from now, at eight in the morning. Your cabin is a single, deluxe. The ship's name is the *Palembang*." He handed her the passport back, and an envelope containing her ticket.

"Thank you," Gretchen said. "What do I owe you?"

He gladly took her American greenbacks, his own commission included. Then he said, "You require an Australian visa. Have you applied for it?"

"No!" Gretchen was taken aback. "How long will that take?"

"Not long at all. The Australians do it electronically. You may wish to present yourself to the Australian embassy for it. It is just a formality. Shall I call for an appointment for you?" Gretchen nodded. "Please." And so it was done. The next morning at eleven o'clock, at the Australian High Commission, 15 Napier Road. He wrote it down for her.

On the same morning Pat Riley had a meeting with Andy Selvidge at the High Commission. Andy personally escorted him in from the guard house, crossing the corridor that on one end led to the common waiting room. The consular section was adjacent to it.

Just at that moment a woman passed them, coming from the waiting room, clutching some papers and entering the office marked "Visitors & Immigrants."

Riley stood stunned, gaping, motionless.

Andy Selvidge stopped also. Looking quizzically at his friend, he asked what was the matter.

"That woman who just went in there—can you find out what it is she wants here? Please. Don't make yourself obvious. Find out from the officer in charge there, discreetly. Don't question her. Okay?" Then he added, "I'll explain later, Andy."

His friend, who had been in the business long enough to tell a query from a quest, nodded. "I'll come in from the back," he said. "You go to my office, one flight up, room 210, and wait in the anteroom."

Selvidge came back an agonizing twenty minutes later. Ushering Pat into his office and closing the door, he said, "Charming woman, that! How do you know her? Not necessarily in the biblical sense, I take it, old trout?" He winked.

"Quite right. She doesn't even know I exist."

"Surveillance, is it?"

"A bit more complicated than that. What did you find out, Andy old chum?"

"Well, your Mrs. Herter, Margaret C., U.S. citizen with a valid passport, from Los Angeles, California, currently at the Regent Hotel, has applied for a visitor's visa."

Riley did not let his surprise show at the apparent name change; nor did the last name of Herter faze him. He remembered well one of the background faxes he had received from London in Hong Kong mentioning her father's name as "Ian Frazer Herter." There it was: Herter. So why was Mrs. Goodridge a Mrs. Herter now? For that she was his former Mrs. Goodridge he had no doubt. He had seen her and recognized her instantly, downstairs.

"Where to, in Australia?"

"Darwin, apparently. The lady is a writer. A romantic, no doubt. Loves crocs. Eh?"

"Why Darwin? Did they ask, downstairs?"

"No need to. That's where her ship docks. She's embarking on the MS *Palembang* on Thursday. One of the Jap container ships, with some passenger cabins. If you ask why we allow people to enter at our backside, it's for the trade, old boy. Anytime, anyplace, anywho."

"She got a booking? Where?"

"Motwani Travel, Ltd., in Raffles City. Indian chaps. All on the up and up." Andy went to his desk and sat down. He knew better than to ask why Riley was interested. Or why he had turned up in Singapore, for that matter.

Riley let the subject drop, too. He had what he needed to know.

Later, when Andy asked him to go to lunch, he excused himself. Busy.

Right, Andy said. Not on holiday, eh? How about dinner tomorrow? Joanie would love to see him again, too.

That'd be lovely, Riley said. Providing nothing came up.

Right, Selvidge said again.

Riley took a cab straight to Raffles City and went into Motwani, Ltd. An Australian businessman looking for some respite from his labors while going home. His friends told him the MS *Palembang* was embarking for Darwin on Thursday. Lovely seven-day trip. Any cabins left, by any chance?

Yes sir, yes, indeed, Mr. Motwani assured him. And how had the gentleman heard of the firm, and of the *Palembang*? One advertises, but seldom receives feedback.

From friends at the Australian consulate. Word gets around.

Indeed it does, sir, Mr. Motwani beamed. He made another cash sale.

From his hotel room, Riley made a call to the Regent Hotel. He asked for Mrs. Herter, and when told she was out, he said he'd call back and hung up.

Proof positive.

That evening he made two more calls. One was to Fiona in London. When he told her that he would take a ship to Darwin, she said "u'hu," but was too polite to question his sanity. He said he'd go straight home from there, but not to worry if he didn't call for the next fortnight. Love you, Fi.

He also talked to Miss Adelaide. When she heard it would be another ten days or so before he was back, she said Winnie was fine. She might just keep him.

PART THREE

In Australia

― CHAPTER EIGHT ―

Passage to Darwin

The *Palambang* loomed large above her—too large, thought Gretchen, who had never sailed on a big ship before. She had to crane her neck to see the top of the bridge—if the massive superstructure had a "bridge." She counted several rows of portholes below; one of those holes would be hers, where she would look out from for the next five days. The bridge of the ship was almost at the end of the whole length of the massive hull, that back end being called the "stern," she knew. Her cabin was supposed to be air conditioned and "very comfortable and modern, indeed," if the shipping agent was to be believed.

On with it. She picked up her suitcase.

At the gangway she showed her ticket and passport to the customs agent, a very British-looking gent except for his height, which was several inches below hers. She affected a distant, rather bored look to avoid causing a dislike. Small men tended to react peculiarly to her, either being extra macho or silently irked at this Brunhilde type who towered over them. The agent was resplendent in his tight-fitting uniform. He banged a stamp into her passport and handed her papers back to her. With a sudden grin he wished her a pleasant journey, saluting. Her lone bag he waved through. Gretchen said thank you and gave him a quick smile. Goodbye, Singapore. It's been nice to know you.

The gangway had only wire ropes on either side. She could see the brownish murk of the harbor water below as she ascended steeply toward the open door of the deckhouse. Aboard at last, she put down her suitcase and looked around for a steward or somebody to tell her where to find her cabin. Several people passed her, stepping out of an elevator, hurrying across the entrance lobby, if a lobby it was, and disappearing through doors, here and there. All crew, it seemed. Nobody paid any attention to her.

Gretchen nodded to herself, picked up her bag, and walked to the elevator door. "Lift," it said outside, "to be operated by key holders only," a warning that was repeated in what she thought were Japanese characters. She was still contemplating what to do when someone approached who had a key, pressed a button and, as the lift descended, asked, "You are a passenger, madame?"

Yes, Gretchen nodded, relieved.

"I shall let you off at reception," the man said. He spoke with an English accent, clipped and overly precise, and wore a white shirt with epaulets. He was Chinese, she guessed, having met many such Britishers in Hong Kong.

"That'll be lovely, thank you," she said.

It was a short ride up, three floors for her, with three more on the button panel. The officer held the door open as she stepped out.

Reception was directly opposite, hard to miss, in an open area not unlike a hotel's or pension's, complete with a bell on the desk and pigeonholes in a rack against the wall. Gretchen rang once, twice. Presently a woman appeared, gliding in silently from somewhere and placing herself behind the desk. She wore a red-and-gold sari draped over one shoulder and had a caste mark on her forehead.

"Yes?" She looked at Gretchen expectantly, as if she had been patiently waiting for Gretchen to say something.

"Namaste," Gretchen said, putting her hands flat together. She had seen that greeting often, mostly in the movies, and had always wished she could use it sometime. This was it.

"Namaste," the woman replied, smiling. "Your name, please, madame?"

"Herter," Gretchen said, producing her passport and ticket again.

"Ah yes, Madame Herter." The woman turned to the pigeonholes and pulled out an envelope. From it she took a set of keys, one of which was a small gold one Gretchen guessed was for the "lift," and two more, the larger having a tag dangling from it. The cabin key?

The receptionist opened Gretchen's passport and entered the number and Gretchen's name into a ledger. From the ticket book she tore out a page, and she put a stamp on the remaining portion, which she gave back to Gretchen with the keys.

"You must show your ticket at mealtimes, madame, for the steward to see it, please," she said.

"Thank you, I will."

"In your cabin you will find a set of rules pertaining to which parts of the ship are allowable to use and which are not. Please read it?"

Gretchen again said, "I will."

"Very good, then." The receptionist opened a drawer to put the ledger away. "Do you require help with your baggage, madame?"

There was no bellboy in sight, and Gretchen wondered momentarily if the woman, plump and smallish as she was, would offer to carry her bag. "No, of course not. It's just one piece, not heavy at all. Thank you."

The desk clerk shrugged and busied herself with paperwork. When Gretchen had not moved away, she looked up again. "Is there anything else?"

"Yes," Gretchen said. "My passport. I'm sorry, but I think you haven't given it back to me yet." It was still lying right there, plain to see.

"Ah, quite right. The passport remains here—" she pointed to her desk drawer. "You shall have it back upon debarkation."

"I'm sorry, but I must ask that you return my passport now." She felt her color rising in her cheek. "I never leave it behind. Not ever. Not anywhere."

"It is kept safe here, madame. It is nothing to worry about!"

"Well, if that is so, you can tell me when you need to see it again. Meantime, I shall take it back." With a swift move Gretchen snatched her passport away from the clerk's right hand. The lift door opened at that moment and a man in a white suit stepped out, and Gretchen hurried over to get in. She saw the receptionist shaking her head as the door closed.

The small key was indeed the lift key, and Gretchen looked at the tag of the other: C21. C deck was two floors up. She pressed the button.

The man who had stepped out was probably not crew, not a steward as had briefly flashed through her mind as she hastened past him.

The cabin was a pleasant surprise, bright with the last rays of the sun slanting through two portholes. It was not large, but it was roomy enough to be comfortable for a single person. The bed along one wall was already opened, and a wrapped candy lay on the pillow. Neat.

A small sofa was in a corner to the left, and the coffeetable in front of it held a fruit basket with a linen table napkin and a dish with knife and fork. The corned beef lunch she had stashed away in her bag would go well with the mango and bananas. Dinner! Alone, but with her book.

She had no desire to dress and go down—up?—to dinner; night would descend rapidly within the hour, and it would be dark when the ship weighed anchor and gained the open sea, if that's what they call it here. God, she felt tired, and sticky from the humidity. She'd want to take a bath and stretch out in the air conditioned comfort promised her. Quick check: Did the bathroom have a tub or a shower stall? Yes! A tub. Not large, but round and deep, with a wooden bucket. Japanese style. The ship had Japanese owners.

There was a knock on the door. It was the chambermaid, who said her name was Dali—Dali? Like the painter?—with an envelope of shipboard activities, menus, and do's and don't's. She also brought in a cooler with bottled water on ice. Gretchen decided to give her an advance tip. That delighted the girl, who was Filipino—"From Manila. I like America. I have relatives in California!" Gretchen was delighted too. She'd need her, for her privacy. There would be nothing wrong with spending a lot of time in her cabin, reading, writing in her diary, maybe going out for an early-morning walk; the shipping line agent had told her that it was permissible at certain times to walk the length of the ship. It was in that glossy brochure he was going through with her: the dining room, the veranda, the bar. Well, she'd certainly not frequent the bar, heaven forbid, nor that "library" to play games or watch video movies. The five days to Darwin would pass quickly enough. Go out for meals? Breakfast, yes; pick and choose from the "lavish buffet." She'd show up for lunch as well. Dinner, perhaps once. Otherwise, a fruit snack and tea in her cabin. The weight she had lost in the past few weeks had made her feel better.

When Dali had left, Gretchen unpacked, a quick job. The picture frame she had bought in Singapore was a delight, with all those family faces looking at her as she put it on the coffeetable, next to her alarm clock. Peace.

It would work, this self-enforced isolation. But still Gretchen felt some apprehension: Would there still be bouts of anxiety? Once the ship had sailed, would she feel claustrophobic, want to bolt, to flee? There was no way to change her mind now. The ship was destined for Darwin, northern Australia. There she'd get off, do that thing in Townsville, then go on to Canberra and present herself to the American embassy. That was the plan. She told herself again that that was the only way. With some luck she would be home by Christmas. Did she dare think that far ahead? Was it realistic to ask for her old life back?

Not now, not tomorrow. But surely sometime in the future. She folded her hands in prayer. Please the Lord it be so....

Amen.

Later, as she prepared for bed, she looked out the porthole. The sea was calm, the sky star-studded and clear, with none of that layer of smokey haze that hung over Singapore. A good omen? She pulled the curtain.

Of the few books she had bought in Singapore she selected *Shooting Star*, by Wallace Stegner. It was a Penguin edition, she grabbed it immediately when she saw it. Stegner was a link to her past, to her days in college when she first encountered him.

Ahh. She plumped up her pillow and adjusted the lamp.

Read. Another world....

The steady throbbing of the engine lulled her to sleep.

Pat Riley was the man in the white suit Gretchen had passed when she hurried to the elevator at check-in time. He recognized her instantly and as quickly averted his gaze. This was not the moment to rendezvous. At the desk he looked back furtively, and as the elevator door closed he caught a glimpse of her examining the keys she'd been given. She had not looked at him.

Riley had already checked in. His reason for appearing again at the desk was to find out if Mrs. Herter had registered yet. No need to ask that question anymore. So what was he doing at the desk? He noticed that the clerk seemed angry, flushed in her face. Had there been a problem?

He decided to ask in his Australian voice. "Madame having it her way again?" With his thumb pointing over his shoulder and a knowing smile.

"I don't know what to do with her," the woman shook her head. "It is regulations that passengers leave their passports here."

"Of course. You're so right. I shall speak to her about that."

"You know Mrs. Herter, sir?"

He thought about that quickly. "She has checked in properly, has she? Let me see the register." Without waiting for her answer, he turned the book around. The last entry: M.C. Herter, Los Angeles, USA. "She has, indeed." He smiled at the clerk. "No worries. Let me see what I can do." He winked at her and left.

"Thank you, sir," the clerk called after him.

Riley went up to the bar and sat down on a stool. He was the only customer. The ship was still dockside. He ordered a whiskey and paid five Singapore dollars for it. "All Drinks Cash & Carry!" a hand-printed sign said, in English only. He chuckled. What might have prompted the barman to put it up?

The bar was adjacent to the pleasantly furnished dining room. There were sliding glass doors leading to a patio facing astern, with tables under a retractable awning. On warm tropical nights, this would make for pleasant dining. He made of note of that.

The whiskey came out of a Johnny Walker Black Label bottle, but it didn't taste like it to Riley. Wouldn't put it beyond the buggers to mix it with hooch, he mused. Be better off to buy a full bottle, still sealed, and take it to the cabin. They were having a trade in duty-free stuff; it said so in one of the brochures he was given. Bugger the barman.

So, here we are now with our Mrs. Herter. What had caused her to change her name, he wondered. So out of character. He couldn't figure it out. Well, she wouldn't be getting off anywhere until Darwin. Plenty of time to solve the puzzle. There were only twenty-two passengers aboard, at least half of them not the kind a single Aussie bloke would care to chat up, being men or married couples. But an attractive single American woman—now that was a natural to approach to make an even number around the dinner table. He stroked his chin. Perhaps not right away, though. Observe, first. Give it a day. Or two.

He left the rest of his drink and went down to his cabin. C level.

By morning, when Gretchen awoke from a deep sleep and threw back the curtain from her porthole, she felt curiously refreshed. The ship was plying the Java Sea, steady as a train, the water unrippled, mirror-flat. The sun was in her face, and despite the air-conditioned cabin she could feel that it would be hot outside.

A shower, that's what she needed. And to wash her hair. Start the day right. Better than that: This wasn't just the beginning of a new day, but quite possibly of her new life! By Tuesday she'd be in Darwin, the week after that in Canberra, in the friendly, English-speaking country of Australia. There she could get everything straightened out with the U.S. embassy. A mere two months after she left California she would be on her way back home.

But what a six weeks, she thought as she worked the shampoo into her hair. Enough adventures for a lifetime. None, though, that she'd want to repeat.

When she stepped out of the tiny cubicle bathroom she found a tray with coffee and a croissant on her table. Dali must have been in to bring it. Nice girl. Gretchen took sips from the scalding brew as she dressed in the silk sarong-like dress she had bought in Singapore and the Chinese open-heel slippers would be just the ticket for a hot day. Lipstick, and a dash of her favorite perfume, bought in Singapore at half U.S. prices, and the earrings from Anthea.

She looked at herself in the mirror and smiled. Not bad! She liked feeling good about herself again.

When she stepped out of the elevator on the passenger deck level and went into the dining room, one look told her that she was vastly overdressed. A motley group of men and women clad in T-shirts, jeans, and shorts, some of them barefoot, sat at half a dozen tables or were at the buffet counter, and all of them took notice of her in that sly, half-averted glance of people pretending indifference.

"Good morning!" Gretchen said, wishing she had stayed in her room. That croissant would have done nicely.

There was a murmur of a reply, and people looked away again as quickly as they had stared at her. Gretchen walked over to the buffet and took a plate. A Japanese man bowed and murmured "please," allowing her to go ahead of him. She gave him a courteous nod and picked her way along the buffet, taking a rice cake, an egg, some sushi, an orange. From a hot water dispenser she brewed up a cup of tea. Now, where to sit?

A man in a white shirt, his jacket over the back of his chair, stood up. "Won't you join me?" he asked, pulling up a chair. "Please!" He was alone at his table. He seemed to be English. She walked over and put her tray down.

"Martin Riley," He held out his hand. "How do you do?"

She shook it. "Gretchen Herter. Hi. Thank you," she said as he pushed in her chair for her. She smiled at him. He looked vaguely familiar, but in a sea of Asian faces certain kinds of Englishmen tended to look alike.

"It's going to be a hot day," he said.

"Yes," she grimaced. "And humid."

"Hmm," he said, and went back to his breakfast. Eggs, toast, and bacon. She now saw that against the other wall was another buffet table with Western food. Well, tomorrow. She bit into the rice cake, found it dry and hard, and decided to dunk a piece of it into her tea with her spoon. It didn't help much, so she began to peel her orange.

"May I presume that you're an American?" the man said.

"Yes. And you are English?"

"It's the mustache, isn't it?" He put a finger across it. "It's either being English, or to cover a scar. Either way, it's that stiff upper lip." There was a twinkle in his eye. "Sorry, didn't mean to tease you. I'm Australian, actually, born in Sydney. But I've lived in England for so long, people think of me as one of them."

"It fooled me, all right." Gretchen took her knife and whacked the tip of her egg. A white-and-yellow mess came spurting out, all the way to the man's left shirt sleeve. "Oh my gosh!" Gretchen exclaimed, dropping the shell on her plate. "I'm so sorry!"

The man laughed. "Raw egg, from the Japanese table. I was wondering what you'd do with it." He dabbed his paper napkin over the egg spots on his sleeve and said, "Think nothing of it. It'll come out in the wash."

"I'm so sorry," Gretchen stammered. "I'll see to the shirt—"

"Not at all, ah—*Mrs.* Herter, is it? Or *Miss*?"

"No 'Miss,' at my age. I'm no spinster. We use 'Ms.' in America, which I find rather stupid." She found her smile again. "Mrs. Herter is fine."

He smiled back. "Indeed it is. Would you like to have my untouched, perfectly cooked scrambled eggs and some crisp bacon?" He lifted his plate.

"Thank you, very kind of you, but I will get my own, from where you got yours." She went and filled a fresh plate. He followed her with his eyes. When she came back and sat down, he said, "Lovely dress. I'm glad the egg didn't go the other way."

"Overdressed is what I am. After fashionable Hong Kong and Singapore, I've been spoiled." She made a wry face and laughed.

"Hong Kong, Singapore—and now Australia. Where to, in my country? If you don't mind my asking."

"Townsville. Queensland. Do you know it?"

Riley barely hid his surprise. "Do I! The Great Barrier Reef. Great in every respect. Worth doing." *Townsville*? He had half expected her to say *Perth* in western Australia, the final stop of this ship. He would have booked his continuance in Darwin. His brother lived in Perth; hadn't seen him in a while.

"I'm glad." She paid attention to her plate, buttered her toast.

After a while he said, "I have a suggestion to make, and I hope you won't take this the wrong way. We seem to be the only two...ah, what's the word...native English-speakers on this ship. For the next five days, could we sit together occasionally at mealtimes, and walk together perhaps? If you wouldn't mind, and like walking? It's the only exercise we can have, the length of the ship and back. Four times makes a kilometer. You saw the brochure?"

She looked up, but said nothing in reply. She just searched his face. Then she nodded slowly. "Sometimes, as you say. I may want to take some meals in my cabin."

"Splendid!" He hit the edge of the table with his hand. "I'm pleased. Very pleased. Rest assured you'll be perfectly safe in my company."

She raised her brows. "Why wouldn't I be?"

To her surprise, he hesitated with his answer. "I admit that I feel gratified, buoyed at the prospect of talking and walking with you. If you don't mind my putting it that way, awkward though it may sound."

"I'll let it pass. I, too, like good conversation. As well as my privacy. As I said, I may not wish to come out all the time."

"Understood. We'll meet at your say-so. And we'll walk and talk. That brings up another point: Could we use first names, eventually? I can see it becoming very contrived if we don't. Entirely up to you, of course."

She looked at him broadly. "I don't want it to be misunderstood if I agree. Shipboard romances are not my cup of tea. I may agree—eventually, as you put it. If I find myself out on a limb, the deal is off."

He held out his hand: "Fair enough. I'm Martin, when it comes to it."

They both smiled. As she withdrew her hand, which he let slip from his without the slightest resistance, she said, "I have this strange feeling you look familiar. As if we have met before. Although we couldn't have. I'd remember."

"Perhaps it's because we have," he replied somberly. Then he smiled.

A joke. She smiled back.

Gretchen did not come up for lunch. Instead, she asked Dali to bring her some bananas and melon, which she ate with the croissant in her cabin. Then she got lost in her book and fell asleep.

She was awakened by a persistent buzz, like an alarm clock. Groping for the source, she found it was a telephone she hadn't known she had because it was in her table drawer. A neat, flat Japanese model with numbered buttons.

She lifted the receiver. "Hello?"

It was her new friend, Martin. "Care to go for a walk? If you didn't pack running shoes, it's all right. Use your slippers from this morning, and we'll stroll."

"I've got canvas shoes!"

"Perfect. There's a breeze up, quite refreshing."

"I'll be there."

"Meet you at the starboard companionway off D-deck. One floor down." He hung up before she could ask which side was starboard. No matter, it had to be one or the other. She'd try the right side first.

Mindful of her dress disaster that morning, Gretchen chose khaki shorts and a yellow knit shirt with an embroidered collar she had bought at the gift shop in her Singapore hotel. The canvas shoes allowed for not wearing any hose, but to prevent blisters she pulled on a pair of short athletic socks with those silly pink pompoms in the back. To shade her face she put on a visor that said "Raffles," also bought at the gift shop.

The mirror gave a favorable reflection as she turned this way and that. Tennis, anyone? Ah, never mind.

Starboard was right, facing forward. He was standing there, in shorts and T-shirt, wearing running shoes. His eyes lit up when he saw her. "Hello!"

"Martin!" she said. "I wasn't sure which side is starboard."

"Posh," he said. "Portside out, starboard home. Ask any Pommy. Reverse here: We walk starboard up, portside back. Ten minutes per. Easy."

She laughed: "P-o-s-h, posh! I remember that. What's a Pommy?"

"Your first lesson in Australian: An Englishman. Not an honorific. Take it from me. I'm often mistaken for one."

They started out. The breeze was actually more like a strong wind coming from the southwest. The air it brought was full of fragrant smells.

"Take a lungful," he said. "We are out of the smokepot of Sumatra."

"It's great!" she said, and she felt great. She had the distinct feeling that things were turning for the better. Bit by bit.

They were on their second lap when Riley stopped in the shade of a lifeboat. Gretchen stopped too and looked at him expectantly. His eyes were downcast, his right foot scraping the plank.

"Martin?" she asked. "Is something wrong?"

He nodded and looked up. "Yes. A whole lot. I've wrestled with this since this morning. You may have been wondering why I didn't show for lunch."

"Actually, I didn't go up, either. Ate in my room. Read and slept."

"Well..." his gaze wandered to the horizon "...there isn't going to be an easy way to tell you."

"Tell me what? Martin!"

"*Martin*. Okay. Let's start with the little stuff." He looked at her. "My first name *is* Martin, but only my mother has ever called me that. Because my middle name is O'Patterson, I'm Pat, Pat Riley. A *Pat* goes with the *Riley*. Properly Irish. Actually, I like being called Martin."

She gave an amused smile. "Okay, Martin it stays."

He heaved a sigh. "That's not the half of it. By the time I'm through, you may not want to call me Martin or Pat. You may want to use stronger language, if you address me at all."

"Oh? Why's that?"

Again he avoided her eyes, this time looking into the distance.

"Right." He sighed, and brought his eyes back to her. "The point is, Gretchen, I have known you since we both stepped into Geoffrey Watson's art shop in Hong Kong. Not that we have actually met, mind you; I was careful not to be introduced to you because I was on a *mission*. You'll think, 'what mission?'"

"I'm thinking. I must say you have me intrigued. A mission!" She sounded amused.

"Yeah." He gave a short laugh. "You were that elegant, rich California divorcée trying to buy that Friedrich painting from those clumsy Balts. I was the guy trailing the Balts to see who they really were, why they were selling that painting, how much they were getting for it, and whether they were the good guys or the bad guys. Follow me so far?"

"Go on." Her eyes narrowed. She was amused no longer.

"Watson made me act as if I were one of his flunkies. He made me drive his car and bring the painting over from the bank vault. Good cover. Fooled you?"

"Did I need to be fooled? Okay, I'm asking why. Were you sleuthing for somebody in the art world?"

"Not the art world. That would be easy. No, the British Secret Service, my former employer, knows about you. They fed me all this stuff on you while I was on the job."

"Fed you all what stuff on me?" Gretchen asked with a knitted brow.

"Your name, Gretchen Goodridge. Divorced. Right? Check. Daughter of Ian Frazer, well-known to the Service. Right? Check. Not rich enough to buy a million-dollar painting. Right? Check. So who's she working for? The cousins? The good Balts? The bad Balts? Who is chasing whom? Not that I care, personally. I'm out of it. To me it's just a job. A gumshoe with a per diem." He looked away, giving that short laugh again.

"You had better tell me more," she said. Her heart began pounding.

"More? I got interested in you. You had made the deal, and Watson was about to ship the painting to New York. I told the Service it was all legit and said I'd need permission to change my airline ticket because I was tacking on a holiday, and they had approved and added another week's per diem. Job well done."

"What do you mean—you got interested in me?"

"Something about you—dammit, Gretchen, this is going to sound weird—rang a bell with me. Don't ask me why or what, because I don't know. The fact is, I just couldn't let go. I kept skulking around after you. No peeping Tom, mind you, nothing of the sort. Just curiosity? No, not that either. I had observed you so many times, with that other American lady you were always with, that you became almost like a friend, a distant friend, that I didn't want to give up. Like being a fan of a movie star. I like old movies, and Ingrid Bergman is my favorite. Not that I've ever met her, mind you. She's long dead. No, it was more like...." He was searching for the right word.

"Infatuation?"

"No, no, I'm far too realistic for that kind of foolishness." He shook his head. "It's...as if we had been friends long ago, and we were running into each other again. That's not the case, of course, and frankly it causes me concern that such an idea should even pop into my head. This is not a movie. It doesn't work like that in real life."

"Is there more? How did you know I would be on this ship?"

"Yeah, there's more. I decided I'd find a way to talk to you. I went to the Regent on Sunday, but you had checked out. And if it weren't for that desk chap at the Peninsula—my hotel too, by the way—who told me that you had reservations to fly to Bali, that would have been the end of it. He also told me that you were with that sick American lady, who had booked the air tickets to Bali. Except, he didn't know where you were going on Bali. Not a big deal, though. The tourism on Bali is all at the south end of the island. The next day I took a plane to Bali. I looked everywhere, in every hotel from Nusa Dua Beach to Kuta Beach, and on and on, but no Mrs. Goodridge. Now I know. You had changed your name."

"I hadn't. Besides, the rooms were in the name of Mrs. Tait, and we were never at the beach, we were in the highlands at Ubud." She shook her head.

He looked at her, surprised. "Ubud, huh?" Then he went on. "By Wednesday, I had given up. It was not to be. I went to the airport, dejected. Damned if I didn't catch sight of you just then, as you were boarding a flight to Jakarta! Coincidence? I didn't think so. Anyway, that was all the encouragement I needed. I took the very next flight which—bad luck again—was the next day. The odds of finding you in Jakarta were minimal, I realized. But I had run into you on Bali, hadn't I, against all expectations? So I used my old routine and went from hotel to hotel. Then on Friday night I saw you walking into the Crown Plaza Hotel. Taking that as another good sign, I planted myself in the lobby, determined to wait until you came out. Nobody cared about me. Everybody was going bananas because of that Garuda flight that had crashed that day. I saw you come out the next morning and get into a taxi. I jumped into the next one with that old routine 'follow that cab,' and ended up at the harbor. You were boarding a hydrofoil to Singapore. At that point I went you one better: I took a Silk Air flight to Singapore, and there I learned that the Jakarta ferry arrived at Changi, the airport area, customs and so on. Well, here comes my hotel routine one more time. You had to be somewhere in Singapore. Where, most likely? At a place that would sound familiar, reassuring. At the Regent, where else, if you please? But I checked, and no Mrs. Goodridge." He shook his head.

"You still haven't told me why we are on the same ship now."

"You went to the Australian embassy, didn't you? Well, I happened to be there myself that day. Another coincidence? I was there because I know the bloke in security. I saw you in the corridor. It hit me like a bolt of lightning. I had my friend check you out. You were getting a visa—as Mrs. Herter! The name didn't throw me; I remembered your father's file. Herter, right, originally? One more bonus: You were going by ship, to Australia of all places! That's when I decided this was it. Fate had spoken. I booked the same trip. I was going to Australia anyway."

"My God, Martin! I can't believe all this!" Grechen had become visibly upset. "But you never spoke to me! Why?"

"I'm speaking to you now. This is the first opportunity I've had to lay it all out."

Gretchen nodded. She put her hands on her hips, walking in place for a moment. Finally she nodded "Okay. Suppose I buy your story. Somehow it rings true to me. We'll talk some more." She began jogging away from him. Half turning, she called, "I'll talk to you soon, Martin, but not today. I need some time for all this to sink in. See you." With a wave of her hand, she ran on.

She went to breakfast late the next morning. The steward informed her that the "English gentleman" had been up early but had said if the "American lady" wanted to walk again, he would "be glad of her company." The steward was very polite. She thanked him. So Martin, or Pat, would like to walk with her again? She didn't think she would oblige him. On a walk they would be side by side with no opportunity to see the other's face, eyes, and gestures. For what she had on her mind to discuss with him would require a face-to-face situation.

She pulled out some Singapore dollars and turned to the steward.

"Can you give a message to the English gentleman—Mister Riley, is it not?—from me?"

"Oh, yes, madame. Quite certainly."

"Good. Tell him I would prefer to see him at dinner tonight, around eight o'clock. And say that there is no need for him to reply unless eight o'clock is inconvenient." The steward bowed slightly. Had she not tipped enough, she wondered? Well, there would be another tip at the receiving end.

After their walk the previous day, Gretchen had returned to her cabin with Riley's revelations heavy on her mind. She felt the news needed to sink in more before she could judge what she had heard. There was also a fear that he would ask her why she had changed her name. What was she to say? Would it be foolish to tell the truth to a stranger? After she had seen the American authorities it wouldn't matter anymore, but now it still did.

After a hot and cold shower and clad only in her underwear and a cotton wrap, she summoned Dali to ask her to bring dinner. Dali brought a sampling of spicy tastes from the rijstaffel that was being served that night. The food tasted so good Gretchen decided she would tip Dali again, which she did after the girl removed the dishes and turned down her bed. By that time the desire to read more, rather than think and worry, made Gretchen cozy and contented. She soon fell asleep.

Back in her cabin after breakfast, she felt ready to assess the import of the news Riley had given her. By writing in her diary—which she kept as loose pages in a crossword puzzle magazine to hide it from prying eyes—she began to document what she thought she had heard. She wrote in a small hand, with so many of her own shorthand words and symbols that a stranger would have a hard time deciphering her scribbles. That was what she hoped, anyway.

Keeping a diary was what Gretchen had always done for special occasions, and she'd been writing daily ever since George Natalian gave her the Friedrich painting mission. Initially her entries were brief, in the form of memory joggers. But since Bali, and especially since that Jakarta debacle, she had become obsessed with recording in detail what was happening to her. She imagined being called to task on all that one day, and she became filled with fear that she would forget, or not recall exactly, the sequence of events and thus be unable to account for herself.

It took her all morning to think through and put down the gist of what Riley had told her. She also made mental notes of questions she would have to put to him. As well, she would have to come up with some revelations of her own, carefully parsed and sparingly presented. She arrived at the conclusion that meeting Riley—or rather, Riley succeeding in meeting her—could be turned to her advantage. Riley was Australian, and she could use some advice about Townsville and how to deal with Anthea's Australian husband.

At last she put the pages back into her magazine and the magazine into her suitcase. Then she went upstairs to get some fruit and coffee for her lunch. If Riley was there too, he could confirm their dinner date.

Riley was not there, but the steward saw her and hurried over. "Ah, Mrs. Herter, yes? Very good. Mister Riley said he is delighted. Eight o'clock, yes? I shall have a very good table for you. You shall sit on the veranda. Very good view of Bali, as we shall pass through the Selat Lombok, with Bali on the one side and Lombok on the other." He smiled broadly with gleaming teeth.

"Thank you, steward. Well done. We shall see you tonight?" Tip included.

"Yes, madame. A very good table, madame." Tip expected.

Gretchen decided to dress carefully for this dinner. That very idea slightly irked her—whom was she dressing for? Surely not for that motley crowd of passengers, and most certainly not for that so-called "English gentleman," who was actually an Australian gumshoe. Well then, she would dress to please herself. High time, too, considering what she had gone through.

She had several outfits, four, exactly, that she had bought in Singapore when she was replacing her wardrobe. She had inner layers and outer layers from daytime to nighttime and from casual to—just in case—cocktail. Her outfits were suitable for the tropical heat of Malaysia and environs—light cottons and silks were all she needed, and they all fit well into her one suitcase.

The seagreen pants with matching, embroidered overblouse was her final choice. They looked just as she had hoped they would, especially after she had combed her hair down evenly on all sides, snipping off some tips that needed clipping. With a center part dividing her hair, which was fading from blond to grayish, she thought she looked demurely low-country and middle aged. She sighed; perhaps her Chinese slippers would provide a local accent. For a purse she took that silly little plastic bag, all gold, that had come with the cosmetics she had bought at the parfumerie. Dabs of scent, a last look in the mirror—and Dali came in and put down the tea tray.

"What do you think, Dali?" Gretchen asked, turning.

"Oh, beautiful, so beautiful!" The girl clasped her hands to her tiny bosom. "You go to dinner, yes? With the English gentleman?"

"Who told you?"

Dali giggled. "Jeemee the steward talks…" she made her hands chatter like loose lips "…like old woman. He thinks he knows everything."

"Apparently he does," Gretchen said drily.

"Madame should have this." Dali pulled open a drawer in the closet and took out a fan and opened it up. "See? Japanese. Like so." She fanned herself, with coquettish eyes.

Gretchen laughed. "All right, thank you, Dali. Now I can hide my lips." She took the fan, looked over its rim, then folded it. "Tomorrow you must tell me what else he has told you."

When she came upstairs there was a boisterous crowd in the dining room. Karaoke was in full swing. The veranda, outside the noise, had only a few tables occupied. The steward led her to the one in the right corner, where sat Riley. He caught sight of her and rose expectantly. The steward bowed, pulled Gretchen's chair, and withdrew. Riley was dressed in a white suit and a colorful shirt with a tropical motif. He grinned broadly.

"I suppose it's okay to say that you look absolutely fabulous?"

"You may say it once. I'm allergic to flattery." She sat down.

He did also. He kept looking at her, his smile still there, then busied himself with the menu, which was a hand-printed sheet inserted into a cardboard holder. "I recommend fish," he said. "They catch it fresh daily."

Gretchen nodded. "You order for both of us." She noticed that they were both avoiding each other's first name.

The steward came over with a tray of appetizers and rice bread. Riley did all the talking, selected the fish, and ordered a wine. That done, he said, "I hope you'll like the sauterne. It's Australian. Very good, actually."

"I'm sure I will," Gretchen said.

"We'll be passing the busy part of Bali soon," Martin said. "We should be able to see the lights of Nusa Dua."

A waiter came, a smallish man, almost a boy, to bring the wine bottle, two glasses, and a corkscrew. He bowed and withdrew.

Martin took the corkscrew and began working on the bottle. "He's probably a Muslim. Can't touch the stuff, not even a few spilled drops." He smelled the cork, nodded, and poured the wine for both of them.

"Probably doesn't touch pork, either. Can you imagine Chinese food without pork?" Gretchen tried to make conversation.

"Hah!" Riley gave his dry laugh. "The Duke of York does not touch pork. The Duchess touches."

Gretchen had to laugh too. "Let's enjoy this, Martin." She raised her glass. He touched his to hers, and they both drank.

It was a good wine, and Gretchen said so. He seemed pleased. "I'm glad. And that's not just the Aussie in me speaking. It is the man lucky enough to be in the company of a beautiful woman whom he wishes to please. Whoa—hold it. I'm sorry, Gretchen. I'm veering off course here."

"Are you?" She looked at him squarely.

"Am I not? I spent the past twenty-four hours wondering what I had done to you, how you must feel having been shadowed by me wherever you went. In the beginning I could say it was all part of my job, and it was. But then the job was over, and I still kept you in my sights, so to speak. Why?"

"Well, why, Martin?"

"I don't know. I had some kind of feeling that I should, as I said yesterday, as if we had met before. Which we have not. And then there was the challenge of not letting you get out of my sight, even though I came damn close, twice." He shook his head at his own dilemma.

The fish came, a silvery specimen the size of a bass, cooked whole in its own juices, surrounded by what looked like ginger, peppers, and pineapple. Ceremoniously, the steward began to loosen two large filets from the bones, putting them on Gretchen's and Riley's plates. Then he placed small bowls on the table, containing a variety of side dishes. Martin thanked him and let him withdraw.

The pungent, mouthwatering aroma that rose from the dishes made them sample each of them, and when they began to eat the fish they both exclaimed that it was the best they had ever tasted. Martin refilled their glasses, and as they sipped, the cool liquid ran soothingly over their spice-rent tongues and gullets. They spoke little, passing the bowls back and forth, pointing with their chopsticks and making clucking noises of approval.

It was a great meal. Gretchen said she hadn't realized how hungry she had been. Martin said, same here. They finished off the wine.

"No," said Gretchen when Martin wanted to order another bottle, "not for me. But you go ahead, please."

"I'm all right too," he said. "I'm not much of a drinker."

Gretchen smiled. "That's the first personal thing I've learned about you, Martin. 'Not much of a drinker.' What else are you, or are you not?"

"I take it that you are really asking," he said. When she nodded, he sat back, went to his jacket pocket, and pulled out a thin flat tin that he opened up. "Dutch cigarillos. Do you mind?" He took one out after she declined. He smiled. "Only occasionally. I am not much of a smoker, either." He lit up.

"I'm really asking," she said. "I think it's only fair. Tell me about yourself the equivalent of what you know about me. Start anywhere."

"Yes." He blew out the first smoke. "Fair dinkum. I'm fifty years old. I have a grown daughter, Fiona, who lives in London. Lovely girl. Apple of my eye. In Neutral Bay—that's in North Sydney—I live in a small house, with Winnie." He drew from his cheroot, which made a glowing red point against the dark night sky.

"Winnie—she's your wife?"

"My dog. My wife died three years ago."

"Oh, I'm sorry."

"Thank you. You're divorced, aren't you?"

"Yes, your Service had that right. And I'll be fifty next January."

He exhaled. "Sorry about that Service thing. They weren't interested in you as a person, actually, only in whom you represented as a buyer. I told them you were fronting for a New York art dealer. That's the case, isn't it?"

"Sort of. Yes."

"Sort of?"

"Forget it. It's still your turn."

"So it is. I was born in Sydney. My father was serving with an Aussie contingent in England during the war when he met my mother, who was with a women's auxiliary, a sort of WAC, as you Yanks call it. She is the one authentic Irish in the family, born in Dublin. She came down to Sydney as a warbride. Both of my parents are dead now. My father was a bit older than my mother, by about ten years. He worked for the port authority in Sydney. We always thought that he would go first, but it was Mother who did, back in eighty-five. I have two younger brothers, Seb, a lawyer in Adelaide, and Alton, a wool brokerage manager in Perth. That's in Western Australia."

"Perth. Yes. Well. Both of my parents are dead too, sorry to say. And my mother also went first."

He inclined his head. "It's sad, isn't it? You expect it, once you get older yourself, but it's a jolt when it happens."

After some silence, she asked, "What made you go to England?"

He gave his short laugh. "All Aussies go to England. To better appreciate what they've got back home. When I mustered out of the navy I had that itch to travel. Young lad, early twenties, never been to Europe. In the navy I took a Russian language course, it was the easiest one to get into; the hardest was electronics, everyone's choice. So I took Russian. I wanted to learn something, anything. In London I met a bloke who said he could get me a job. Might even land me in some embassy post overseas. I took it. It turned out to be MI6. The Service. I had assignments abroad, one in Saigon during the Vietnam War, and during the eighties a tour at our Paris embassy. The British embassy, that is. I met my wife, Ellen, whose father was of the landed gentry, which made her an 'honorable,' you know what I mean. When she married me, the lowly colonial, it was a great act of courage on her part."

"Or love?"

"Quite right." He blew out a cloud of smoke and watched it get caught in the wind. "Feels like rain coming up. Haven't seen much of the Bali coastline, have we? Probably all clouded over. By tomorrow morning we'll be in the Indian Ocean, making a sharp portside turn and heading straight for Darwin. We could have stayed on the lee side of Indonesia, but they are always afraid something might happen near Timor. Hah. In the end we are in the Timor Sea, anyhow."

Gretchen looked at his profile as he spoke. His high forehead was partly due to his receding hairline, but his cranium was such that it took up half his head, with his face balancing the whole. She liked that ratio, had seen it in many of the portraits that hung in museums; it seemed classical to her, pleasing, harmonious. That moustache, full above his upper lip, was a nice, manly accent. She noticed that it was trimmed carefully, and that its color, dark-brown, matched that of his hair.

"I wonder if I could draw on your knowledge of Australia when we reach Darwin," she said, "I mean in terms of what's the right thing and the wrong thing to do and say."

"Of course you may," he replied smiling. "Bear in mind, though, that Darwin is quite unlike the rest of the country. It's very tropical, and frontier-like. Boisterous. Per capita, they drink more beer in Darwin than anywhere else. And people get eaten by crocs, or bitten by snakes."

Gretchen laughed. "I can see I'll need you to protect me."

"Aye. First thing you need is some bush clothes. Also, you're off to Townsville, I recall. Queensland. Similar climate there."

"Yes. Just a brief stopover. Doing a favor for a friend."

"Would that friend be that American lady you were with? Just curious."

"Well, yes, as a matter of fact. Her husband is Australian. Jerome Tait. They own the Tait Gallery in Townsville. Tait, with A-I."

"Ah. A gallery. Of course. You're both in the same line of the art business, I imagine. How long do you plan on staying there?"

Gretchen leaned back. Their chairs faced astern. The moon was partly obscured by clouds, its light when it broke through casting an eery illumination on the ship's roiling wake.

"Not very long. A couple of days. Then I expect to fly to Canberra."

"Canberra? That's not far from Sydney. Could I persuade you to stop over so I can introduce you to my dog? Easier than telling him about you." It sounded like a joke, and if she declined they could both laugh it off.

To her own surprise, she said, "Maybe...."

"Good! Tell you what: I give you my card..." he pulled one from the batch he had printed for this job. "I'll write down my private telephone and address. Call me anytime, for any reason." He handed it to her.

"Thank you." She looked at it, then put it in her plastic purse. "I can't promise, Martin. Don't count on it."

"I understand. It'd be great, though, if you could fit it into your schedule somehow. Sydney is worth a look."

"Not to mention the chance to meet Winnie," she smiled.

"Definitely. You like dogs?"

"Love 'em. My old dog died a year ago. I'm planning to get a new one as soon as I get home. What kind of dog is yours?"

"Border collie. Very intelligent, and faithful."

"Oh, I know what they are like. I wouldn't mind having one myself, but I can't. I live in a condo. It'd be cruel to coop up a dog like that. Besides, the condo bylaws state that we can't have a pet weighing more than twenty-five pounds. Ridiculous. I've been thinking of a Russell terrier."

"Good choice, under the circumstances," he said cautiously.

"Hmm," she said. "Where'd you put Winnie while you are away? That's a problem, isn't it?"

"Not in my case, thank goodness. I have an old friend next door, old in the age sense, too. She looks after him, giving him the run of my house and property. Adelaide Moore. A painter. Quite well known, actually. Perhaps you have heard of her?"

"I'm afraid not."

"You'd enjoy meeting her. With your own art background—"

Gretchen had to laugh. "So there are two good reasons to meet with you in Sydney, Winnie the dog and Adelaide the painter."

"Three. Sydney the city. Breathtaking."

"With you thrown in as a bonus!"

"You're so right." Spontaneously he reached for her hand and kissed it. "We'd all thank you for it." He let go and gave his dry laugh.

By unspoken consent, they broke up the evening. Gretchen left a good tip, and Riley said he'd take care of the bill, figuring carefully which part of it was in the prepaid fare. They did not say they'd meet for breakfast, or lunch. It was unnecessary. They were parting as friends. They'd talk again.

It wasn't breakfast that brought them together the next day. It was a violent, retching sickness that had overtaken Gretchen during the night.

She awoke from deepest slumber with a sense of alarm. All her senses were on alert, her heart was beating double time, her innards hot and churning. When she opened her eyes, in the dim shine of her night light the ceiling seemed to be spinning—or was she turning counterclockwise?

She roused herself from bed, groping for support, stumbling, making her way the short distance to the bathroom. Groaning, she sat on the low stainless steel toilet with narrow seat that had annoyed her from the first, only to rise up fast, turning around to deliver herself of a regurgitated mess that didn't seem to want to stop. In between she fought for breath, braying with each intake, finally collapsing on the floor when it was over.

She lay motionless, aware that she was covered with sweat and that her mouth was foul and burning. The bathroom, too, seemed to her to be moving when she raised her head and looked up. What was the matter with her?

Fear now entered her mind. She was ill, not just sick. An infection from all the tropical food and drink she had been exposed to. Remembering that she had been given a hepatitis-A shot by that doctor the Getty had recommended was small comfort for the moment.

Was it last night's dinner? Suppose it was? Had Martin—dear, caring Martin—got it, too? Or worse: suppose he did not get it? What would that tell her?

She began to feel cold from the sweat that was making her nightgown cling to her skin. It was important to get back to bed. So ordered, but the flesh was not so willing. Risen just halfway from the floor, she had to vomit once again, and the only good thing about that was that it wasn't quite as bad as the first time. She moaned as she lifted herself onto the sink, rinsing her mouth, splashing water over her face. Stumbling back to bed was another ordeal, but she made it. She covered herself, pulling the blanket up to her chin, and closed her eyes.

Peace. Let there be peace.

She must have fallen asleep, for the next thing she became aware of was a voice. An outside-of-her-head voice, human and real. Dare she open her eyes?

It was Dali, holding a tray from which steam was rising.

"Madame?" The voice spoke again. "You wish some tea?"

"Oh, Dali—" Gretchen reached for the girl's hand. "You are so kind, so really-really kind...." Tears came to her eyes. She wasn't dead. She was so grateful to be alive. "I am not well, Dali. Quite sick, in fact."

Dali seemed to be swaying somewhat as she put the tray on the table and poured tea into a wide-bottom mug. "Yes, madame. It will be better now." She put the mug down. "Tea too hot to drink. Wait a few minutes."

Gretchen closed her eyes again. A few minutes would be fine....

A voice. Another voice, not Dali's. "How're we doing here?" A knock on the door, vaguely familiar.

"Madame has been sick," Gretchen heard Dali say. Who's she talking to? The ship's doctor? You bet madame has been sick. Hellishly—she couldn't find the proper word to describe how she had felt—devilishly sick.

She raised one eyelid, carefully, and closed it again quickly.

Martin. The last person in the world she wanted to see right now. Or rather, the last person she wanted to be seen by. And to hell with his cheerfulness.

"Gretchen...." Now he was holding her hand. "If you can hear me, please open your eyes."

She did not feel inclined to do so. Not just yet. Let him go away first, come back later. Where was Dali, anyway? How come she let him in?

He spoke again. "Look here—actually, if you don't wish to look just yet, that's fine too. I know how you feel. That was quite a commotion last night. But it's over now, isn't it? I suggest you let the stewardess help you get dressed. Do you know what time it is?"

"No!" she said, and it came out like a croak.

"Past eleven o'clock. Too late for breakfast, too early for lunch."

"Please—" she moaned and withdrew her hand to put it over her mouth.

"Ah, yes. Sorry. I'll be back in a half an hour. We're going up on deck. Fresh air. Will do you a world of good."

She heard him say "chop-chop" in a jocular manner, presumably to Dali, and the door closed. Dali replied "yessir," giggling. It all made her angry. What's the matter with everybody? Couldn't they see she was ill?

Or maybe just sick? She raised herself up on one elbow. The room had stopped spinning, and her stomach was not revolting. She felt very thirsty. With trembling hands she reached for the cup and began drinking, one hot slurp after another. Dali stood watching her.

"All right," she said with some determination, "let's do what the gentleman said. Help me to the shower, Dali."

When Riley returned, exactly half an hour later, she was in slacks and a light jacket, sitting on the bed, putting on her canvas shoes. "We had a storm last night, Dali tells me?" She looked up and tried a smile.

"We had the last tentacles of an Indian Ocean typhoon that was swirling around like a dancing dervish. Yes, we had a storm last night."

"I like your metaphors," she stood up, smiling. "How bad was it?"

"Bad enough to put you down, I suppose. Feeling better now?"

"I couldn't have been just seasick. It was awful! I thought I was going to die. I still feel queasy."

"Well, it could have been the wine, too. A bit hung over, perhaps?"

"We shared only one bottle, Martin! One half bottle can't do that!"

"I rather think you may have had the greater half. Be that as it may, I'm glad you're restored to life."

"And you? You didn't feel anything?"

"Hah. I got my sea legs a long time ago. It's true, you know, about legs in a storm at sea. The first thing to remember is to not lie down. Stand up, go with the sway. Look at the horizon. Something to do with your inner ear."

"Well, I'm standing now, Martin. Take me to the horizon."

She stumbled a bit as they came out of the elevator on the wheelhouse deck. He caught her by the waist and did not let go as they walked aft along the portside lifeboats. There was a strong wind coming from the right, blowing away the remnants of storm clouds and the moist and fragrant air that had been with them since Singapore.

Martin pointed to a tarpaulin-covered something. "Inflatable life rafts. Care to sit down?"

Gretchen said yes: she still felt a bit weak in the knees. He punched a back rest into the soft pile and sat down next to her.

"Indonesia is thataway." Arm outstretched, he pointed through the space between the lifeboats. "And straight on—" his arm turned right "—lies Australia. We lost a bit of headway dodging the storm last night. Still, Darwin should heave into view in about three days. Wednesday morning, I should think."

Gretchen leaned back and closed her eyes. Darwin—that's where they'd part company. The thought of not having him around anymore made her uneasy.

"You're going straight back to Sydney?" she asked.

"Yes. Unless you want me to come with you to Townsville?" He smiled and looked at her.

"Oh, no, thank you. No need for that," she replied quickly. "I'll only be there a day or so. Then I'm off again."

"To Canberra, right?"

"Right. Of course, I could stop off in Sydney, as you suggested. In fact, I should do that. Who knows when the opportunity will come again?"

"I'd be very happy to show you around town. You'll like it."

"I don't want to impose on your busy schedule."

"Nonsense. I'm not busy at all. Didn't I tell you? I'm retired."

"You did. Rather young for that, though, aren't you? Why?"

He leaned back, his hands clasped behind his head. "You really want to know? Or are we just making conversation?"

"Martin! Of course I want to know. I want you to tell me because I care. It's not just idle chitchat we're having here. You understand?" For emphasis she shook him with her hand on his chest.

He brought his arms down and sat up. He took her hand in his and pressed it before she withdrew it. "Thank you. You're right. We've met not for idle chitchat. There's more to it than I can figure out at this time." Abruptly he got up, walked a few steps towards the lifeboats, then turned and looked at her. "It's very hard for me to talk about it. When your whole world comes crashing down on you from all sides, out of the blue, you become a bit unhinged. You need to work through it, but you've got to do it alone. The moment you start unburdening yourself, there is self-pity hovering about. And that's the last thing you want, being pitied."

"Tell me about it," she said. "And when it comes to it, the pity is all mine to give. You're not alone, Martin."

He kept staring at her. "All right. I'll give you the raw data, the basic stuff. No details. Ellen and I risked all our money in a very good, safe scheme. Blow number one: Ellen was diagnosed with a brain tumor, it was malignant, she underwent therapy. Blow number two: We lost all our money in what turned out to be a very bad scheme. Blow number three: Ellen died. In consequence of all that, I'm forcefully retired; and with blow number three, I don't care anymore."

Gretchen nodded. Then she got up and went to him. Putting her arms around his neck, she said, seeking his eyes, "Thank you, Martin.

One day you will hear my story. And you're right; there's a reason why we've met. And yes, I will visit you in Sydney." She put a kiss on his lips.

He did not return the kiss, nor did he speak. He drew her closer to him and nodded, once, twice. They stood that way for a moment, before they turned and started walking again.

He held her hand the whole time. She did not withdraw hers.

— CHAPTER NINE —
Magnetic Island

The ship came into port at Darwin at seven in the morning, aligning itself against the dock with a sudden, final lurch. Gretchen was roused by it from deep slumber, and when she peered at her clock she realized that she had been "out," as she termed it, for over twelve hours.

She also realized as she stretched and yawned that she was feeling well. And that it was Wednesday...and she was in Australia....

Or rather—more reality seeping in—she was on a Japanese ship that had docked in Darwin, Australia. She still had to go ashore to be truly "in," "saved" as she called in her own mind. And that walk down the gangway was predicated on the Australians letting her enter their country.

Riley had a talk with her about that very subject when they sat in the shade of the veranda having afternoon tea the day before. It had become customary for them to get together these last two days, ever since her "throwup," as he put it less than delicately. They would sit or walk and talk about all kinds of things, none of them touching on his or her traumatic past. It was utterly relaxing for Gretchen to be free from all the stress and turmoil that had been chasing her across Southeast Asia ever since she met Anthea in that hotel coffee shop. Riley, too, had remarked how it was reviving his spirits to be in the company of a bright and interesting...ah, person. ("What person?" Gretchen exclaimed in mock rebuke. "You talkin' to me? A person?" "Well," he hastened to correct himself, "a *woman* person. You, Gretchen. A lady. A friend. How's that?" "Better," she said. "Much better.")

The point Martin raised about her passport concerned a feature that, he said, was incorporated in his own. Because of his service in a certain government agency, there was a notation, so to speak, on his identity that could be accessed by British and certain other friendly authorities on their computers if the need arose, for instance, for an emergency visa for quick entry or exit, or other assistance that he may need or want. It was in some ways similar to a diplomatic passport, except of course that it lacked the outward appearance of one.

"I don't understand," Gretchen said. "What notation would that be?"

"That your travel is somehow government-connected."

"Lordy, no! Whatever gave you that idea?"

"Well, your wanting to go to Canberra, to the U.S. Embassy. It's not exactly a tourist attraction."

"And I'm not exactly a tourist. I need my government's help, is why I want to go there. Don't ask, Martin. Not now. Not yet."

"Fair enough," he nodded. "I wasn't curious, Gretchen. I was trying to be helpful." Then he added, "You must have used a different passport to enter Hong Kong. Perhaps a pre-divorce one, under the name Goodridge. Am I right?"

"You are," she said.

"I must tell you, in this context, that you'd be well advised not to mention your stay in Hong Kong or Bali to the immigration people here. There are no corresponding stamps in your passport to verify them. And if you ask how I could know that, I have it from my chum at the Australian High Commission in Singapore, who blithely declared that you had just arrived there from Jakarta. He said nothing about Hong Kong, et cetera, and I decided to leave him in his ignorance."

"Oh, God," Gretchen groaned. "I sound like an international smuggler or something. There's actually a very simple explanation for it all. Someday I hope to tell you. Meantime, will you cut me some slack here, Martin?"

"Not to worry," he patted her on the hand. "I'm on your side. It's the immigration people at Darwin we need to keep an eye on. Will you let me handle this? Just follow me? Cling to me if need be? The little woman to her man?"

Gretchen pressed his hand. "I will, Martin. I will!"

The Australian authorities came on board, setting up shop in the community room. Most of the passengers were ready to debark; those who were going on to Perth opted to stay on board until the ship left again in the late afternoon.

There were three officers, two men and one woman, smartly uniformed, the men in shorts and knee socks, the woman in a skirt and a kepi over her blond locks. A line was forming, and Riley waved his passport from the back of it to catch the officers' attention. The woman officer came over. "Australian, are you, sir?" And when Riley said yes, she led the way to another table.

Riley put his arm around Gretchen's waist and pushed her along with him. At the table he presented both his passports and hers. The officer looked at them and at the passports, one American, the other Australian, and at them again. "Are you traveling together?"

Martin put an arm over Gretchen's shoulder, pulling her closer, and replied, "Yes, we are." Gretchen looked up at him—adoringly, she hoped.

The officer nodded and spoke to Gretchen. "As a U.S. citizen, you have a tourist authorization to visit Australia. However, for prolonged stays, you need a regular visa. How long do you intend to be in our country?"

Riley answered, "We are visiting my family in Sydney. If, or should I say *when*, the need arises for a change in her visa status, we shall take the appropriate steps." Now he smiled adoringly back at Gretchen.

The woman was unmoved by it all. She consulted a portable computer that was set up in front of her. Now and again she would refer back to the U.S. passport. Gretchen became increasingly worried but tried hard not to let it show.

Addressing both of them, the officer said, "I need to see your baggage. Please bring it to this table. When you have done so, and you are passed, you cannot return to the ship, but must debark."

"We understand," Riley said and hurried back to pick up their bags, lining them up at the officer's table. Three pieces, one of them Gretchen's. The order to open them up was unnecessary. Riley was all casual compliance. The officer rose to look at Gretchen's first, lifting every item, opening each cosmetic container, shaking the crossword puzzle magazine until the loose pages fell out. Satisfied, she put everything back together.

"You are traveling light, madame," she said.

"My main suitcase was stolen en route, in Jakarta. I intend to replace my wardrobe here." Gretchen did not flinch, holding the woman's gaze.

"Do you carry any valuables, cash in large amounts?"

"Yes," Gretchen replied and unbuttoned her shirt. "Here, in my secret compartments." A money belt became visible across her stomach. She opened it up. "In this compartment, Singapore dollars. There should be about seven thousand left, plus U.S. dollars in twenties and fifties, I guess another thousand or so. Also in my pocket, a bunch of U.S. singles, for tipping."

The officer had a look. "Please open this little pouch."

"Some jewelry." Gretchen did, and showed Anthea's diamond ring and her brooch set with emeralds and rubies. "Not something I wear every day!" She tried a smile.

"I should think not," the officer said. She banged a stamp into Gretchen's passport and filled in some blanks. At last she gave it back. "You can go now, madame. Welcome to Australia." She pointed to the exit door. There was no mistaking her order to leave the ship.

"I'll wait for you at dockside, Martin," Gretchen said as she went, picking up her suitcase.

Martin came trotting down the gangway a few minutes later. He grinned. "A tough bird, she was, wasn't she?"

"How come your two pieces came through so much quicker than my single one? What was she looking for?"

"Drugs, most likely. In my case, I have that code number on my record that indicates security clearance." He laughed. "I told her we were engaged, that we met in Singapore and came here together on a romantic cruise. That did it. She seemed relieved. She had been suspicious about you."

"Are we really such believable liars? Doesn't it bother you?"

"Sort of, yes. It's a ruse, actually, that we used, not a lie. That business of being engaged is a white lie, perhaps. Nothing more."

"And that romantic cruise?"

"Actually, that hewed pretty close to the truth, for me," he smiled.

"Oh, Martin. I'm still asking you to cut me some slack."

"I do, Gretchen, I do. Now let's get going. The sun is up, and it's going to be a bastard of a hot day. See if we can find a cab."

There were several, all with signs advertising hotels and the casino. When Martin said they were headed for the Quantas office, the driver refused to take them. "Five minutes walk, mate, right across Esplanade toward the mall."

Riley said "Ta!" and started walking. He gestured Gretchen to follow him. "Do you have a credit card, or how do you want to pay for your airfare?" he asked.

"Cash is all I have."

"Those Singapore dollars? They are almost equal to the Australian dollar, but you'll get a very bad exchange rate here in this frontier town. May I make a suggestion?"

"Shoot!"

"Let's exchange your Singapores for my Aussies. A thousand, say. I'll get a better trade for it down in Sydney, and you can deal with the rest in Townsville." When Gretchen stopped and started to undo her blouse, he stayed her hand. "No, no, not here on the street." He laughed. "That can wait until we are at the airport. For the moment, let me take care of the airline."

Gretchen made a half-serious grimace. "I'm always eager to do what I am told. Remember—the little woman?"

"In your dealings with me in real life there is no reason why you should ever feel that way."

"Oh, I know, Martin. I didn't mean to imply that I'm ungrateful. Sorry."

"Don't be. Just be yourself. You're stronger than you think."

The daily flight to Sydney would leave at two P.M. That was suitable for Riley. For Gretchen, there was nothing to Townsville until the next morning, but the Quantas people phoned Ansett Airlines and found an afternoon flight to Townsville with a stopover at Alice Springs. Riley booked both flights and charged them on his credit card, ignoring Gretchen's whispered objection that she had the money. "Shh," he signaled her. "Later."

There they were, all set now, as Riley put it when they stepped outside to look for a cab. "Tell you what; let's not go out to the airport yet. We have a couple of hours. That Holiday Inn we walked by looked pretty decent to me. Let's stop off, have some tea, and see to a bush outfit for you." With raised eyebrows he made a mock appraisal of her clothes. "Not quite suitable for Alice Springs, is it?"

Gretchen, who was wearing pants with a silk overblouse and those red-and-gold Chinese slippers, smiled broadly. "You don't think so?"

"I know my mates," he laughed.

In the back of her mind Gretchen wondered what Riley would do at the Holiday Inn. Suggest they get a room to change, to—what would he say—Have a brief rest, relax? What would she do if he did?

Not to worry: Riley was all kindness and consideration. The hotel was brand new, and as he had surmised there was a gift shop and a fashion boutique on the premises. There were also public toilets where Gretchen could effect the exchange of money. When they sat down for an early lunch she was a different Gretchen, in khaki shorts and shirt, bush hat and shoes, and a very clever canvas bag doubling as a carry-on. Her suitcase was left with the sales lady at the shop. Martin also made her buy a plastic raincoat and a folding umbrella, as well as insect repellant and—Martin's extra idea—a multipurpose pocket knife with all kinds of gadgets on it, including a tiny saw. Gretchen protested laughingly, but he said, "Take it. These things are fundamental." So she took it. All her flimsy clothes fit in the new bag, with room to spare.

There was no time to go to a room even if they had wanted to. The lunch menu was plentiful, a buffet board groaning with goodies she hadn't seen since her family's summer vacation at a Wyoming dude ranch. She was going to mention that to Riley, but then stopped herself; it wouldn't do any good to have the inevitable questions raised about her family, her boys, her life.

Fortunately, Riley found another interesting story to tell, as he had on their walks these past few days. It was fascinating to her to listen to him in his British voice with those occasional Aussie intonations. What he had to say was always interesting to her; he also had a way of drawing her in that made it a two-way conversation, which she liked.

She remarked how new and modern everything looked in Darwin. He picked up on that. That was, he said, because the original town had been totally destroyed in a Christmas 1974 typhoon that had veered in from across the sea with almost supernatural force, with winds of over 170 miles per hour, flattening everything in its path. The town, which had been rebuilt after bomb damage suffered in World War II, was truly in rubble. "I was in England at the time," he said, "and I couldn't get away. But all Australia was here, helping. About a hundred people died, but the rest of the population of 30,000 were all evacuated and placed in private homes and in camps. Then the place was bulldozed flat, and as people came back, more in fact than had left, the city was rebuilt, street for street, stone for stone." He made a sweeping gesture. "So here we are. Better than ever."

"You're proud to be an Aussie, aren't you?" Gretchen said.

"Beats being a Limey." He smiled when he said that, but there was a bite to his voice. Gretchen took note of that.

They finally hailed a cab to the airport. Riley was full of advice even then. He reminded her that the eastern third of Australia was a half-hour ahead. She'd be arriving in Townsville at eight in the evening. It would be dark. He remembered a tall, round hotel near the Flinders Mall. Have a taxi take you there, he said; it shouldn't cost more than twenty dollars, tip included. And at the hotel, don't let them sell you a double room. They have singles, and they're cheaper.

It almost moved her to tears, especially when she realized that he would leave her, ahead of her; she'd be alone in this strange, huge country.

"Thank you, Martin. I don't know what I'd do without you."

"Ta," he grunted. "It doesn't have to be forever. Do you still have my card with my number?"

"Oh, yes. Right here in my wallet."

"Call me when you can."

"I will. I promise."

There was a sudden squall of heavy tropical rain, which washed red mud over the paved roadway. The taxi's wipers barely kept up. The cabbie had to strain to see where they were going, but that didn't make him slow down. By the time he deposited them in front of the terminal building, the rain had stopped and the sun was out again. The building was open on all four sides, the gates spread from it like roofed tentacles.

Martin pointed to where her gate would be, and then they walked to his gate and stood around till boarding was called and people began to line up to pass the electronic baggage check. They made small talk, Riley finishing one of his cigarillos. He had offered her one, and to his surprise she took one from the tin and put it in her newly acquired bag.

Then it was time. "Bye, Gretchen. Take care," he said, holding out his hand. She ignored that and put her arms around his neck. She kissed him on the cheek, turned, and walked away quickly.

Riley waited for her to look back. She didn't, but strode away fast, her shoulders hunched. She wasn't crying, was she? Damn.

He stepped up to the gate. As he sat in his seat on the plane and saw the city of Darwin become smaller and more insignificant in the vastness of the tropical landscape below, he realized that he had made a mistake. A godawful mistake. He shouldn't have let her go alone. He could have routed himself to Sydney via Townsville.

Aye. A mistake. Was there any doubt about that?

Gretchen didn't enjoy her flight at all. The shock of suddenly being alone again would not subside. She spent the one-hour stopover in Alice Springs in the airport building, buying some postcards with "stations" (ranches, in American) and "Old Alice" and camel-ride themes. They'd go into her diary later. She briefly thought of buying a camera (her old one was down in the Sumatra jungle somewhere, horrible to think about), then decided not to, at least not until Townsville, or maybe even Sydney. She saw T-shirts that had Ayres Rock on them and bought two, extra large, for the boys.

There wasn't enough time for a ride into town and back; her connecting flight would be boarding in half an hour. But she thought she should at least step outside the terminal building so that she could say, yes, she'd been in Alice Springs. A couple of steps were enough to make her scurry back into the relative coolness of the building. The air was dry and very hot on this mid-afternoon in October, springtime hereabouts. Imagine being here in summer!

She wished Martin were here; he'd tell her....

Townsville was a considerably larger city than Darwin, and the international airport had a modern look. She took a cab, whose driver knew exactly where "that big round hotel" was at Flinders Mall. The fare came to seventeen dollars, and she gave him twenty as Martin had suggested. At the hotel she got a single room, albeit one on the fifth floor with hardly any view. It didn't matter to her. She prepaid the room charge, which included continental breakfast delivered to the room. She'd only be staying the one night, she told the desk clerk, and all her luggage was at the airport for her flight home to Hawaii the next morning. The clerk took her money and gave her a receipt. For a Mrs. M.C. Herter, citizenship USA, address Halekulani, Honolulu, Hawaii.

She looked at her watch and wondered if she should call Georgie now. He had been on her mind constantly. But was this the time, the place? Not yet.

The next morning she awoke surprisingly refreshed. She had fretted and feared the worst about a sleepless night; but despite herself, fatigue had overtaken her. She bathed, then dressed the way she had in Singapore: lightly.

The breakfast tray was brought in at eight, as she had asked. The coffee was good and strong, the croissant warm and flaky. Munching, she consulted the telephone book. There was a street map of Townsville in the front, which she tore out. Under "Art, retail" she found the Tait Gallery listed on Flinders Street, not far from the hotel, according to the map. She would wait until after nine o'clock to make that call.

Gretchen had thought about this moment for a long time, since Singapore and on the crossing to Darwin. In her diary she had forced herself to weigh the consequences of going to Anthea's husband and telling him the news of his wife's fate. *Presumed* death, for she brought no proof one way or the other. Inevitably it would lead to questions about her own recent past, which she was not prepared to answer. Therefore she had to take every precaution not to harm herself, while at the same time doing right by Anthea. A moral debt, is what she called it from the beginning; there was no doubt in her mind that she had been saved from a horrible death in that plane crash for a reason. A debt that needed repaying here and now, as well as elsewhere as her conscience compelled her.

That's why she knew she had to speak to Anthea's husband face to face. It would be a necessary act of closure, after which it would be proper to turn her back on it and move on. She sighed with anxiety when she reviewed in her mind all the precautions she had to take to keep herself out of harm's way.

Step number one would be to not reveal her current particulars. The Mrs. Herter who was staying at this hotel would not be the person who called on Mr. Tait; it would be Mrs. Goodridge, the friend of his wife's who was undoubtedly mentioned as such in the letter she carried from Anthea. That letter, and the pieces of jewelry Anthea had wanted her to bring back, she put into her plastic purse. Then, having packed her few things, she took her bag down to the lobby desk. Could she leave it here for an hour or so? She would want to do some shopping. Of course she could. Flinders Mall was a famous shopping place.

Outside, at a pay phone, Gretchen made her call to the Tait Gallery. A woman's voice answered, a secretary she presumed. Mr. Tait wasn't in yet, so sorry. Was there a message?

Yes, Gretchen said, from Mrs. Tait. She had an important message from Mrs. Tait, for Mr. Tait. When would he be in?

The secretary perked up. Who was calling, please? Gretchen gave her the Goodridge name. She was, she told the girl, in transit and had only a short time before she'd have to return to the airport. When would Mr. Tait be in?

They settled on "in about half an hour." Gretchen said she'd be there, and then hung up. The girl hadn't asked where she was calling from.

It was a cool but sunny morning, not unlike the nascent spring days in Southern California. The shops in the mall were just being opened, and Gretchen lingered in front of a department store. After the Tait delivery, she'd come back here to buy a real purse.

The Tait Gallery was not hard to find. It was in a Victorian-style house with gingerbread curlicues and a covered porch, just like one would see in England, and New England as well, for that matter. A sign over the entrance said, "Fine Art & Antiques." Gretchen stepped in.

What she saw surprised her. The lower floor she was on had been made into one large exhibition space, with spotlights trained onto pieces of art on the walls and onto freestanding sculptures that were placed cleverly to either match or contrast with the artwork nearby. Only the staircase to the upper floor had been left untouched, although it looked improved, gleamingly polished to a fault. An electric buzzer had gone off when she opened the door; now she noticed an annex in the back wall, where a desk was visible. A young woman rose from the desk and came forward.

"I am Mrs. Goodridge," Gretchen said. "We spoke on the phone earlier this morning.

"Yes," the young woman replied, with the Aussie inflection of the *e* that Gretchen had begun to like. "Thank you for coming. Mr. Tait is expecting you." She gestured for Gretchen to follow her.

The annex was a rather large office, with an anteroom where the secretary's desk was. The inner office had a floor-to-ceiling windowed partition with blinds hanging down. The blinds were open. A man could be seen sitting behind a desk. He waved for them to come in. The secretary opened the door and let Gretchen step through. "Mrs. Goodridge," she said, and withdrew.

"Mrs. Goodridge." The man stood up. "I'm Jerome Tait. How do you do?" It was a plummy, very English voice.

"Mr. Tait." Gretchen held out her hand, which forced him to lean over to accept her handshake. The desk was large, boomerang-shaped, of highly polished, probably exotic wood. He had to place one hand on the desktop to shake her hand with the other. It was an awkward gesture that put him off balance for the moment. As the self-assured, self-made entrepreneur that she knew him to be from Anthea's talks, he could not be pleased with that.

"You have news from my wife, you say." He had righted himself. They both remained standing. He was taller than Gretchen had thought, and slimmer. A well-conditioned, tough, no-nonsense type in the prime of life, full head of dark hair, sharp penetrating eyes. She knew he was almost ten years younger than Anthea, but in her mind she had placed him in his mid-fifties. But Tait looked younger than that; mid-forties was more like it.

"Yes, but I'm not a bearer of good news, I'm afraid."

"Indeed? How so?"

"Mr. Tait, your wife and I spent about two weeks together, not every moment of the day, of course, but frequently enough to become friends. You know Anthea went to Hong Kong?"

"Yes, of course." There was an air of impatience about him as he made a courteous gesture. "Why don't we sit down over there," he pointed to a seating corner, "and you tell me what you have to say." Without waiting for her answer, he went and pulled out a chair for her. "May I offer you some coffee, or tea?"

"No, thank you." Gretchen sat down. "I've just had breakfast, and I'm in a bit of a hurry." She added, "I have a plane to catch."

"Ah." Jerome Tait sat down. "We had better get down to the nub of things then, hadn't we? Not good news, you say?" There was not a trace of anxiety in his demeanor.

"Well, yes. It's not easy for me to talk about, Mr. Tait. I have come to respect and like Anthea very much, and I was horrified at her terrible fate. You know she was quite ill. She told me that you knew."

"ALS. Amyotrophic Lateral Sclerosis. Incurable. Yes, I know." He leaned back with an appearance of sadness that did not seem entirely genuine to Gretchen. "Thea went to Hong Kong—against the best medical advice available here, I might say—to consult with some Chinese healer of sorts. Are you telling me she was not successful?"

Gretchen nodded. "But she knew of a Buddhist sage in Bali. It was her last hope, she said. Because she was quite unsteady and often lost her ability to speak properly, she asked me to accompany her on the trip. I was glad to help."

"Bali! That's news." He did seem surprised. "You are American, Mrs. Goodridge, may I assume that? Yes. What was it that brought you together in Hong Kong, Mrs. Goodridge? Were you consulting the same healer?"

"No. I was in Hong Kong on vacation. I happened to be in the same hotel. She had an incident, and I came to her rescue. We talked, and Anthea also being American, we naturally saw more of one another as time went on. I was overwhelmed, frankly, by her terrible illness and her ability to bear her burden with such courage." Gretchen had tears in her eyes.

Jerome Tait placed a box of tissues in front of her. "Yes. Now, Mrs. Goodridge, the news, please. The details can wait."

"Thank you." Gretchen dabbed her eyes. "When we arrived in Bali we went straight up to the highlands area of Ubud. Anthea said it was truly beautiful, almost like the Garden of Eden. Have you been there?"

"I haven't, but Thea has been, on buying trips for primitive art objects. Two or three times, as I recall, and alone. She often travels alone. I tend to stay here and mind the business. Someone has to."

Gretchen noted that he spoke of his wife in the present tense. Did he really not suspect that the news she was bringing was that she had died? Had he really not heard from his wife in three weeks and had not worried?

She fumbled in her purse and brought out the letter. It was on the stationery of their hotel in Ubud and bore just the scribbled name of Jerome Tait. "We left Hong Kong late on Sunday September 20. The first day we were in Ubud she was visited by a number of people from what I thought was a local artists' colony. We were in a bungalow kind of setting, two bedrooms with a lot of open space between them, and a private pool, very quiet, very exclusive. It was up on a lush hillside, with a river below of crystal pure water."

"Kupu Kupu Barong, was that it?"

Gretchen did not hide her surprise. "You know it?"

He made a dismissive gesture. "Thea stayed there on her past trips to Bali. Go on, please."

"On the morning of the second day, Tuesday, when I came to check on her, I found her room empty, the bed not slept in. I was concerned that she might have met with an accident, and I ran out to the pool, but I saw nothing there. Nor any sign of her in the rest of the bungalow. I contacted the front desk and asked if they had seen her. I was told that she had been picked up before midnight by two people, a man and a woman, both Balinese, and I was told I should wait until I heard from her. By nightfall a man came by, again a native. He just showed up in front of my room, unannounced and on silent feet. It really scared me."

Gretchen had to stop. The memory of that apparition was still vivid in her mind. She forced herself to go on. "He brought a letter and a palm-leaf box. He also had a cellular telephone, which he used to dial a number. He then handed the phone to me. It was Anthea. It was not easy to understand her, as her ability to speak had deteriorated markedly. What I gathered was that she would not return, that at a time when certain stellar conditions were auspicious she would join the spiritual world. I'm not quite sure I've got it right—it was a bit of a shock—but the indications were clear to me that she had chosen the time of her death. She spoke of you lovingly, and asked me to see to it that you received this letter and these two pieces of jewelry, both of which you gave her." She went to her pocket again and produced the tissue-wrapped pieces. "I had to wear these on certain occasions, such as when passing through customs. They are safe now with you."

She unwrapped the diamond ring and the brooch and tenderly put them and the letter on the table. "Anthea specifically asked that I hand them to you personally, from her to you."

Tait cast hardly a glance at them. He looked through the glass partition and summoned his secretary. "Suzanne, have you been watching us as I have instructed you to?"

"Yes, Mr. Tait."

"Mrs. Goodridge has put these three items on the table. Observing us, have you seen me touch them in any way?"

"No, I did not see you touch them."

"Good. For the record, I have not touched them. Now, carefully, please, get an evidence envelope and put these three items into it. Use art gloves. Then call Mr. Morton and make an appointment for tomorrow morning."

"Yes, Mr. Tait." The young woman busied herself going to a drawer, taking out a plastic envelope, putting on white gloves, and placing the letter and the jewelry into the envelope, which she sealed, signed, and dated.

Gretchen watched the strange goings-on in uncomprehending silence.

Tait now resumed talking to her. "Do I understand correctly, madame, that it is your assumption that my wife has died?"

"I must assume so, yes."

"When, do you *assume*, did that happen?"

"I have no idea. It could have happened the same night she left, or later. I wouldn't know." She added, "The answer would most likely be in that letter, Mr. Tait. The one you have just sealed away."

Her sharp tone was lost on him. "Assumptions are all we have. Isn't that so, Mrs. Goodridge? We are dealing with a case of premeditated death here, are we not? Do we have any proof, one way or the other, of what happened?"

Gretchen began to feel increasingly irritated. "Mr. Tait, these are matters for you to decide. I am just a messenger, not unlike the man who brought me your wife's things."

He kept a fixed glare on her. "Your assumptions, madame, are not doing any of us any favors. If my wife has died, she may not have died of her own free will. Tut-tut!" He raised his hands. "Say nothing. I make no accusations. She could have chosen to be euthanized. Helped along toward her death. Which is against the law in certain civilized jurisdictions, as you well know. Was it really a suicide? Or was it manslaughter? These are important questions which must be answered by *facts*. My solicitor, Mr. Morton, will have to deal with these legal questions. In his investigation he will represent me, the aggrieved party. You, madame, will be—nay *are*—a key witness."

"I believe not, Mr. Tait. I was your wife's travel companion. If she intended to be 'euthanized,' as you put it, she certainly did not share those intentions with me. Again I tell you, my role here is that of a messenger, carrying back to you those three items which you have just had put away by your secretary. With that, my duty to Anthea, and to you, Mr. Tait, has been fulfilled."

"Not quite. I beg to differ. No doubt my solicitor will want your complete statement under oath, recorded and submitted to the court for the purpose of obtaining a declaration of death. Without which, I might add, our dear Thea will remain in limbo, materially and legally. Don't you see?"

All of a sudden anxiety replaced irritation in Gretchen's mind. She knew enough of Wilfred's law practice to know that a sworn deposition was a legal instrument, full of all kinds of data pertaining to the person deposed, not just to the subject matter in question. If there was one thing she could not under any circumstances afford at this time, it was a probing into her recent past. At the very least she needed counsel of her own, in the protection of her own country's laws. She feared now that she had been very foolish to stop here in Townsville; she should have flown straight down to Canberra.

Outwardly composed, she replied, "Sorry, I have a plane to catch today, Mr. Tait, as I told you when I came in here. I find it impossible to be of any further help to you at this time."

With that, she rose and made for the door.

Quickly he waylaid her, barring her exit with his arm. "Surely one day more cannot be such a discomfort to you, Mrs. Goodridge. Please reconsider. Of course, any expenses you may incur by prolonging your stay, as well as those you have incurred in coming here, for which I am very grateful, will be gladly reimbursed to you." He was so close she could smell his warm, fetid breath.

"Are you physically preventing me from leaving your office, Mr. Tait?"

"Of course not." His arm came down. "You are free to go. You would be well advised, however, to consider your position if you do leave town now. You would force me to have my solicitor issue a warrant to detain you, which our customs people would be enjoined to honor." A small, cold smile played around his lips. "None of us would want that kind of trouble. Would we, Mrs. Goodridge?"

Gretchen pushed past him. "Goodbye, Mr. Tait." At the secretary's desk she took a business card from its holder, and waved it. "I shall have my own lawyer get in touch with you, sir."

Tait caught up with her again in the showroom. "Please, Mrs.

Goodridge, at least allow me to drive you back to the airport. We can talk some more."

"About what, Mr. Tait? Are you anxious to know what your wife's condition was in her last days? Are you wondering what took me so long—two weeks, Mr. Tait!—to come here in person? Are you at all interested in the letter she wrote you, except for putting it in an evidence envelope? Really, Mr. Tait. These questions are too late now, I'm afraid. I'm on my way, and you had better not stop me."

He stood mute, anger in his eyes. As she closed the door behind her she heard him shout, "Just don't you leave town, you hear? We'll find you!"

Gretchen walked away in long strides. Her heart was pounding. Fear of what could happen, of being "detained" after all, began crowding her thinking. She was almost certain that she had not succeeded in cowing Tait. If he had her arrested, would the real truth about her not come cascading out in a torrent of disclosures, revelations, and confessions?

There was only one way out. She had to disappear, immediately. Become invisible. But where, in a small town like this where neighbors knew one another and where tourists were like gaggles of geese descending from the clouds, like flocks of sheep herded across roadways? Not like her, a single goose, a single ewe.

She had reached the mall again. Those gaggles of Europeans, Americans, and Japanese, were everywhere, disgorged by the busload dispersing into the entrances of shops and stores.

Gretchen had a sudden idea: She would hang out with them for a while, see where they were going, perhaps go with them. She hurried to her hotel, picked up her bag, tipped the busboy for it, and ran out to the mall again.

The department store was her first stop. A man in front of her had just reached the door; when he saw her, he held it open, bowed, and said politely, "After you, please." In German!

Surprised, Gretchen replied, also in German, "Thank you. Very nice of you." The man wore a porkpie hat, a colorful sportshirt, shorts, and brown socks in black sandals. He seemed middle aged, and married, for his wife came through the door now, pushing him. "On you go, Hans. Don't dawdle."

The man rolled his eyes comically and said to his wife, "We have a *landsmännin* here, Inge. We should greet one another." He made a quick, boyish bow and said, "*Wir sind die Nagels.* Boom-boom" he made a nail-hammering gesture, *Nagel* meaning nail in German. "Without us things just don't hold together."

It occurred to Gretchen that the Nagels might be her ticket out of town. She introduced herself. "Grete Herter." They all shook hands. "And where are you from?" She tried to look pleased at meeting people so far from home.

"From Duderstadt. Near the Harz mountains. We have an inn and pub there. And you, Frau Herter?"

"From Bremen." Not true, but her mother was from there.

"I knew it. You look like a North German. Doesn't she, Inge?"

Frau Nagel was clearly anxious to do her shopping. "Yes. We don't have much time, Hans. The group meets again at eleven, and the ferry goes at eleven-thirty."

"The ferry?" Gretchen asked. "To where?"

"Magnetic Island." Hans Nagel was highly amused. "*Magnetische Insel!* One cannot pass that up, can one?"

"Magnetic Island!" Gretchen feigned astonishment. "Where is that?" She knew very well where it was; she found it on the map she tore out of the telephone book. It was one of a chain of islands stretching along the coast of Queensland, the Great Barrier Reef, just offshore from Townsville.

Hans said, "About ten kilometers off the coast here. Twenty minutes by ferry. Plenty of beaches. Highly recommended."

"Oh, what a great idea!" Gretchen clapped her hands. "Could I join you, do you think?"

Frau Nagel was not so sure. "We are with a tour group...."

Herr Nagel felt otherwise. "But remember old Dr. Lehmann? He checked himself into hospital yesterday. We have one place open!" To Gretchen he said, "You are alone, Frau Herter?"

"For the next day, yes. Then I shall be joined by someone to drive to Alice Springs."

"Then all is in order! I shall speak to our guide. Of course, you would have to pay a proportional share, Frau Herter!"

"Of course," Gretchen said immediately. "Thank you so much, Herr Nagel, Frau Nagel!" She shook hands with both of them. "Where do we meet?"

Herr Nagel looked at his watch. "In thirty-five minutes, out at the fountain in the mall. Plenty of time."

"Not if we stand around here chatting much longer," Frau Nagel said dryly, and finally succeeded in pushing her husband into the aisles.

Gretchen agreed. She, too, had some sudden shopping to do, to look as touristy as possible. She grabbed things as she went from aisle to aisle, selecting first a bathing suit, then some beach shorts, a T-shirt, a sun hat, suntan lotion, and a light jacket. Once she had paid for the items she changed into them, except for the bathing suit. Her Chinese slippers she shoved under a chair—good riddance!—in favor of her canvas shoes. She put some lotion on her arms and neck, and bought a pair of oversized sunglasses from a rack and hurried out. Her one bag would soon be full; on Magnetic Island she would have to buy another.

Her new-found friends were already waiting for her at the fountain. They hardly recognized her at first, but then Herr Nagel made complimentary noises, cut short by his wife's admonition that it was a good fifteen minutes' walk to the ferry landing site. She pointed to some of the group who were already ambling along.

The tour group eventually assembled at dockside, some two dozen people, Gretchen guessed. The guide, a perky young woman with a clipboard, counted them all as they boarded the boat. The Nagels brought up the rear. Hans Nagel had a brief conversation with the guide, who kept shaking her head, finally turning to Gretchen and asking her in German, "What is your name? Please spell it for me." She wrote it on her clipboard. She said, "You need to prepay two nights in advance, plus the ferry coming and going."

"How much?" Gretchen asked.

The guide had a quick answer. "Thirty-eight dollars, Australian."

"Ja." Gretchen smiled and gave her two twenty-dollar bills. She waved away the change and followed the Nagels, who were already aboard.

"You are not covered by the group insurance plan, Frau Herter!" the guide called after her. Gretchen gave a sign that that was okay. She was glad the deal had worked; Nagel had hammered it together, all right.

The members of the travel group were congregating at the bow of the ship, chatting loudly and taking videos as the ferry began chugging up Ross Creek channel toward the open sea. The Nagels were there, among their own kind. Except for Hans once giving her a wink, Gretchen was left to her own devices. It suited her fine. The less she had to mingle, the safer it was for her. Not to be remembered by most was a plus.

Gretchen selected a place on a bench that had some shade from the bridge. As the boat left the placid waters of the channel, the waves became a bit rougher; it was not likely she'd become seasick on this short crossing, but one never knew. Satisfied, she pulled the hat over her eyes and tried to rest, or at least pretend she was sleeping. Her mind, though, was still on that encounter with Jerome Tait.

In real terms, her situation was fraught with potential danger. The worst-case scenario looked like this: She may have evaded Tait's searchers, which he could have assembled by now, but such respite would be short-lived. In a small town like Townsville it would not be too difficult to find an odd-looking stranger, unless....

Unless the stranger was amorphous, part of a group of strangers in which one was not discernible from the other and all were being herded by a guide. That was her present case. Carefully considered, she felt safe for the moment. But only for today, until Tait, his leads in Townsville not panning out, turned his attention to the obvious alternative, which was where she was headed now: Magnetic Island. By tomorrow his gaze might well be directed there. By tomorrow, therefore, she would have to be out of here, out of the whole Townsville area.

Out of here—to where, in God's name?

And how? By train, by bus, by plane, by rental car?

She discounted the last two immediately. Both would require personal identification.

By train then, or by bus. Yes. Either one was feasible.

Where to? Still to Canberra?

She was sure of the obvious answer, the one and only choice she had that would not compromise her but would help her regain her footing: She would go to Sydney first, to Martin Riley. Her knight in a white suit. He would have the answers. She'd be safe. At the very least she could stop running for a while.

She pushed her hat back and looked for her plastic purse—she still hadn't bought a replacement!—and rummaged in it for the card he had given her. Ah, yes, here it was. With relief she pressed it to her breast.

Tonight. She would call him from the hotel she was lodged in with the tour group. Surely he'd be home in the evening.

She carefully put the card back, this time into her zippered pouch under her T-shirt.

Martin O'Patterson Riley. Officer and gentleman. Albeit of a secret service, but certainly an Australian gentleman.

Gretchen smiled as she thought of him. He came across as such a nice, honest guy and had seemed sincere when he urged her to come to Sydney to visit with him before she went on to Canberra. She had been a fool not to take him up on it right away, twice the fool not to ask for his experience, his counsel, before taking another step, any step. There was nothing she could do about the former, but the latter foolishness was still open to remedy.

She looked at her watch: Only a few hours to evening, to hearing his voice. To not being alone anymore.

The ferry docked at Picnic Bay, a pleasant, tree-shaded locale that was like any other of its kind, from Hawaii to the Caribbean, where tourists are loaded off and on; a place where transport was available and souvenirs would be bought, along with some basic food and drink. As the ferry emptied its load onto the wharf, the German group was led by its clipboard-waving leader to a waiting bus to which their luggage was already being carried from the ship. The bus was open on all sides, its canvas tarps currently rolled up.

Gretchen caught up with the Nagels again. "Is that bag all you have?" wondered Frau Nagel. Gretchen's reply, that her real luggage was still at the airport, seemed to satisfy her. "I hope you brought a bikini," leered Herr Nagel, "so you can go topless." Inge boxed him for that. Hans rubbed his arm. "It's true! It's in the travel brochures: 'Swim with the fishes, in the natural state.' What else could that mean?" His wife rolled her eyes. Gretchen tried to look amused.

Presently the bus lurched around onto the roadway. They passed a parking lot where beach buggies were lined up under a sign that gave the dollar figures for daily and weekly rentals. Hans, who had read his brochures, said, "They're called 'mokes' here. You can go anywhere on the island with them. Inge and I will rent one. They seat only two," he added, regretfully.

The bus stopped at the halfway point, and everyone got off and meandered single-file down a footpath to a cafe where lunch was to be served. Gretchen stayed close to the Nagels; she didn't want to take up with any of her other temporary companions. The less said, the less lied. Besides, some in the group were elderly, had difficulty walking, or were obese, sweating profusely in the heat.

The lunch was a full meal, buffet style, with meats and fish aplenty. Gretchen, who realized that she was hungry, loaded her plate with rice and freshly baked fish, papaya, and pineapple. Drinks came out of an open icebox, beer and cola. She took a beer. Seeing the Nagels in conversation at a table for four, she bypassed them and sat down on a chair under a palm tree.

Suddenly, seemingly out of nowhere, a huge clattering cloud descended upon the outdoor dining area and alighted upon every branch of every tree with a raucous clamor of deafening volume. Parrots. With green bodies and red heads, both colors in brilliant extremes, they came by the dozens, flocks and flocks of them, taking possession of the place. Some of the women shrieked; the men laughed and clapped their hands to shoo the pesky birds off—to no avail. The parrots—or were they parakeets?—were there to stay. Gretchen found them fascinating. She observed them as they picked at some fruits and leaves, heads bobbing, jumping, fluttering, leaving droppings that produced more shrieks. She heard the proprietress explain that the budgerigars were protected, and that they would leave when they were done. That, at last, they did, flock by flock, until quiet returned.

The group moved on after everyone had eaten and used the "facilities." The road became more hilly, vegetation brushing the top of the bus. On occasion Gretchen, who had an outside seat, caught a glimpse of a sandy beach below, the blue waters beyond. They were on Horseshoe Bay Road. Hans was saying that that's where they were headed, Horseshoe Bay, at the north end of the island. The beach, according to his brochures, was the largest and most beautiful. It was the one Captain Cook saw when he sailed by, but a problem with his compass had prevented him from putting ashore. Something to do with his magnets not working. Hence the name he gave it, Magnetic Island. Hans said it in such a humorous way, gesturing, his eyes going from his wife to Gretchen, that both women had to laugh.

He wasn't such a bad sort, that Hans. Gretchen decided she liked him. Too bad she had to lie to him.

They arrived at their final destination, a hotel and campground complex a few hundred yards up from the beach. It was called Geoff's Place. Everyone filed out, the luggage was unloaded, and the group gathered around their guide, now joined by a man from the hotel. The deal was this: The elderly people all had cabins for eight, each with two bathrooms and a common room. The younger crowd was dispersed over communal huts sleeping twelve or more. Owing to the fact that the summer season had not yet started, singles were available in the four-bedroom cabins for eight. Hans and Inge, although certainly not elderly but more in Gretchen's age group, opted for the upgrade, and so did Gretchen, who would want a single. Room assignments were dealt out at last.

Gretchen thought of summer camp as she followed the Nagels into their abode. Even the interior was like that, rustic and simple, but clean. She entered her assigned room and closed the door. The first thing she noticed, besides bold warning signs about poisonous snakes in the woods and equally poisonous jellyfish in the water, was the absence of a bathroom. Consulting the guest directory, she learned that "facilities" were available in the main lodge. The lodge also had showers and saunas and telephones.

She sighed. That was not a place she could use to call Martin in the evening. Not within earshot of passersby. She'd have to find another phone.

Meantime, it was mid-afternoon. She'd want to go to the beach— except where would she leave her money, her papers? The guest directory said that valuables should be deposited with the hotel, to be kept in a safe. Not for her!

Gretchen decided she needed to organize herself better. She unpacked all the items she carried in the bag, then locked the door and undressed down to her bare skin, laying everything out on the bed.

It was a relief to take off the money belt she had been wearing all day. Sweat formed so easily underneath it in this weather that she felt rivulets of it forming on her skin. Still, this was by far the most important part of her "wardrobe," for it held all her cash as well as her Goodridge passport and the photos of her family. It was clear to her that she would have to keep wearing it until she reached the safety of Sydney.

In one pocket of her shorts was the money purse with about eight hundred Australian dollars left from the amount she had exchanged with Martin for her Singapore dollars. Enough to get her to Sydney, she reckoned. The other pocket was for her Herter passport, wrapped in wads of tissue. There was a bunch of smaller bills in that plastic purse of hers that she still hadn't replaced. Okay.

Now, having put the money belt back on, she tried on her bathing suit. Ouch. After some pulling and tugging, the suit stayed up. Putting the shorts back on and wearing a Townsville cotton T-shirt resulted in disguising the ungainly bulge of the money belt. Good. With her sun hat she'd look touristy enough as she strolled about looking for a telephone she could use.

Gretchen stuffed all her clothes back into her little suitcase and put it away. If somehow she had to abandon it, there would not be a great loss. Clothes could always be replaced. Money and passports could not, and those things she was carrying at all times. Her fear was beginning to ebb.

At five o'clock, almost on the hour, she declared herself ready to call Martin Riley. She had found a phone, right on the beach in front of a snack bar and store. Inside, before she saw the phone on a pole that was stuck, not quite upright, into the sand near the entrance, she had looked for a purse and found one of "pure croc leather," although it felt soft and pliable. Good riddance, plastic. Now, with her hand that held Martin's business card trembling slightly, she dialed the number, area code 02, followed by seven digits.

"Hullo." A male voice.

"Martin?" Oh, God, let it be him. "Uh...Mister Riley?"

"Gretchen? That you?" He sounded upbeat, surprised.

She laughed. "How'd you guess?"

"Easy. There isn't a woman in the world who calls me Martin."

"There's one now."

"So right. How goes it? Okay?"

She giggled with relief. "I'm on the lam, Martin."

"Lam? Nothing to do with baby sheep? An American expression, no doubt."

"Yes. I'm on the run, is what it means. From Jerome Tait. A nasty shock. I'll tell you about it later. I need to get away from here. Is that offer still open to meet Winnie and that painter lady of yours?"

"Too right. Winnie loves company, especially when it is needed. As for Adelaide, funny you should ask. I just talked to her about you possible staying at her house for a bit. I described you as an art enthusiast and connoisseur. You can have her guest room."

"Oh, Martin, that's so wonderful to hear."

"Yeah. Where are you calling from? What's the background noise?"

"Kids. People. I'm on the beach. On Magnetic Island."

"Magnetic Island! Really? Having fun?"

"I had to run from that ghastly Tait man. I joined a German tourist group. They were headed for here. Now I need to get out again, and down to Sydney. I can't take a plane, because Tait surely has the airport covered. Rental car, ditto. That leaves train or bus. I need your advice."

"Well." His voice was serious now. "If I hear you correctly, you need to get down here without being intercepted, or questioned by authority. That so?"

"Yes." She nodded vigorously.

"I don't suppose it can wait for me to come up there and get you."

"I don't think so. No." Then she added, "I need to get out of Townsville, Martin. It's not my fault everything is so screwed up."

"I know. You'll tell me later. Two questions: Are you safe for the night? I mean, will tomorrow morning be soon enough?"

"Yes, I think so."

"Good. Do you have enough Australian dollars left?"

"About eight hundred."

"Good again. Now, here's what you do. When's the earliest ferry in the morning? Six-thirty? Seven o'clock? That reminds me. Where are you staying?"

"Horseshoe Bay. Geoff's Place."

"Geoff's Place? Good old Geoff again? All right, I can find his telephone number from here, in case I need to call you back."

"They don't have phones in the cabins, Martin. That's why I'm calling from the beach. But that doesn't matter, I'll call you. So I'll take the seven o'clock ferry, say. Then what?"

"Walk to the bus terminal. Here in Australia we have transit centers. It can't be too far away from the ferry wharf in Townsville. Take one of two bus lines, Greyhound—sound familiar?—or McCafferty. Buy a ticket, not to Sydney, but to Brisbane. In case someone checks it out later."

"Yes."

"It'll take you twenty hours or more to get there. Practically one day. Now, Brisbane is a big city, like San Francisco, only larger. You will arrive at the transit center on Roma Street. Don't leave the center. Walk over to the train section. There are major trains running south every day. Call me from Brisbane when you've arrived. I'll have a reservation for you."

"Oh, Martin, I'm so grateful."

"It's not O'Martin where the Irish in me lurks, but O'Patterson. That aside, let me say I'm awfully glad you called, dear girl."

"I'm glad I called, too."

"There we are, then. I shall be at the house from now on until I hear from you on Wednesday morning from Brisbane. You call me anytime, though. If you are in any kind of trouble, you call me first. Then keep your mouth shut. Understand?"

"Yes. And thank you."

"Ta-ta." He hung up.

Gretchen put the receiver back and sat down on the wooden bench near the entrance to the store. People were walking by her, in and out of the store. She was numb with new-found joy. How could she have been so lucky, just when she was nearly down and out, to run into someone like Martin O'Patterson Riley? She tried to picture his face, an open, honest face, with those blue-gray eyes that seemed always to have a twinkle at the corners when he looked at her; and that silly moustache that tickled her when she kissed him, that one time.

Yes, she had found a good man.

— CHAPTER TEN —
Neutral Bay

That evening at Geoff's Place, Gretchen made it a point to sit with the Nagels. It was a barbeque, very beachy, and it didn't matter where anyone sat when they came from the open pits carrying their trays. There were long tables that defied creating cliques as people came and went, plopping down to eat and drink, getting up for more food and beer. The talk was loud and raucous, the German group being sprinkled into the motley crowd of Australian vacationers.

The Nagels were in a good mood. Hans had succeeded in renting a moke. Tomorrow's group schedule called for a trip to the rain forest section of the island, with a visit to the famous koala farm.

"Not for us," he said, chewing on a piece of steak. "Inge and I, we came here for the beaches. Radical Bay and Balding Bay. *FKK—Freikörperkultur.*"

"Nude bathing is what he means." Inge thought she had to explain. "We belong to the FKK. Every year we go to Sylt or to Rügen with the children."

"It's good for body and mind. *Mens sana in corpore sana*, you know?"

Yes, Gretchen nodded, she knew. High ideals, although not for her, and she didn't mind others doing it. The thought of both Nagels cavorting in the nude did not invite further speculation.

She changed the subject. "I have talked to my friend this afternoon. We will continue on, so I am leaving here tomorrow morning."

Murmurs of regret from both Nagels. Gretchen nodded. "Please don't bother to inform the group leader about it until she asks you about me. I don't mind losing the extra night. It was very nice meeting you both, though."

"You are American, aren't you? Inge and I were talking. Your German is very good, but one can hear an accent." Hans gave her a knowing smile.

Gretchen looked at both of them. "Yes. I am sorry I said I was German. I am not, but my mother was. She was born near Bremen, in Oyten."

"Oyten?" Hans put down his fork and knife in astonishment. "That's where we buy our carp! You know, for our restaurant, for New Year? Big, wonderful carp. The best!"

Gretchen smiled and nodded. She had no idea why one needed carp, or any other moss-backed, lazy fish, for New Year. "I'm glad," she said.

"So, what time are you leaving?" Hans wanted to know.

"Early. I'd like to catch the first ferry. Seven o'clock, I think."

"I'll take you in the moke," Hans said immediately.

"Oh, no, thank you. I'm sure I can get a taxi or a bus."

"You should let Hans take you," Inge said. "You'll save time. You are glad to see your friend again, no? Life is for living. We think you have a problem. We don't need to know what it is, but if your problem is solved now, you should run back quickly. We will give you some help, because we all need help sometime."

"Absolutely," Hans grinned. "Inge is right." He patted his wife on the back. "So, shall we say six-thirty. Would that be early enough? That's about daybreak. I don't know if the moke has headlights."

"You are so, so wonderful!" Gretchen reached across the table to embrace them both. "I don't know how to thank you!"

"Come stay with us," Hans fished a calling card out of his wallet "when you are in Germany. We are close to Hannover. Hotel Harzer Post. See?" He pointed to the postman's horn on his calling card. "We're open year-round."

Next morning, when Hans knocked at her cabin door, Gretchen

was packed and ready, even though it was not yet six-thirty. The drive to the ferry wharf at Picnic Bay went faster than she thought, with Hans talking a blue streak about his hotel and his children—his oldest son was seventeen and already learning the hotel business—and how they had been busier before reunification because Duderstadt was just this side of the East German border and they would get sightseers and foreign journalists doing stories on the Death Strip. All Gretchen had to do was to make small exclamations to keep him going.

Hans insisted on carrying her bag to the landing. She gave him a hug and thanked him, saying again how sorry she was she had lied to him and Inge about where she was from. Hans said "*Auf Wiedersehen in Duderstadt*" and ambled back to the moke. She waved goodbye as he gunned up the noisy little motor.

On the trip across to the mainland Gretchen stayed inside, balancing a large paper cup of hot coffee against those sharp bounces the ferry made in the waves. Except for her customary vitamin pill and a glass of bottled water, she hadn't had any breakfast. Now the crumpet she had saved from last night's barbeque was welcome nourishment. The morning sun was out, slanting through the cabin windows. A new day. She was imbued with confidence. She was going someplace of her own choosing, the first steps in the long journey ahead.

The bus terminal was a short walk from the ferry landing. With her sunglasses on and her hat pulled down, Gretchen marched briskly, looking over her shoulder furtively now and again. The early morning crowds were thin, mostly people hurrying to work. She reached the transit center at Plummer and Plume, as her map indicated with an arrow, at just before eight o'clock. Inside the terminal she scanned the departure board and saw that the Brisbane-Sydney-Canberra-Melbourne express bus was leaving in twenty minutes. She rushed to the ticket window and queued for an interminable time, made worse by an urgent need to pee, until she reached the cashier.

"One, to Canberra, please," she blurted out. She peeled off three hundred dollars and got some bills back in change. Platform three. Consulting her watch, she raced to the washroom. Ten minutes to spare. Please, let there be an empty stall.

There was. Her bus still idled several more minutes after she had found her window seat in the midsection and put her bag up in the rack. An elderly lady had the aisle seat. The midsection is best because you don't feel the bounding of the wheels, she explained to Gretchen with a confidential air.

"Too right," Gretchen responded, Aussie-like, and put on her eyeshades, nestling into the corner and pretending to sleep.

Finally the driver announced departure. Gretchen heard the door hiss closed, and the deep rumbling idle of the diesel engine changed to an even purr.

The bus, although called an "express," stopped several times along the way to deliver and accept bags of mail and to refuel. At each stop passengers had a chance to get off to stretch their legs and buy refreshments. Gretchen bought a roadmap, and when they stopped at Rockhampton for "tea," she realized that they were only halfway to Brisbane, and it was already nearing evening. Well, she would try to sleep the night hours away, in air-conditioned comfort. Her seat neighbor had gotten off. No new passenger had claimed the aisle seat.

The bus reached the outskirts of Brisbane in the early morning. It took another half-hour to reach the transit center on Roma Street. Gretchen looked out in amazement at a beautiful, modern city with such greenery and stretches of water.

At last the bus pulled to a stop. She took her bag and climbed down the steps onto the platform. She would not have the same bus going on to Sydney and Canberra; the bus driver had announced the departure points and various platforms during the drive through the city.

She'd phone Riley first. He had asked her to call from Brisbane.

He must have been sitting by the phone, because his husky-voiced "hulloh!" came on right after the first ring.

"Martin, good morning. It's Gretchen!"

"I'd recognize your voice any time, Gretchen. And a jolly good morning to you, too. Where're you calling from, Brisbane?"

"Yes. All went well. No sign of the Tait gang."

"Good. And good riddance, too. Now, may I make a suggestion?"

"Of course!"

"You've bought a bus ticket to where?"

"Canberra."

"Splendid. Let them look there for you, if they still do. Now you take the train. Use first class, not because you're a snob, but for the greater privacy it will afford. Fewer passengers, less chance of a nosy seat neighbor."

"Okay, I will." She scanned the big departures screen in the hall. "I see one leaving at 10:10, an XTP to Sydney-Melbourne."

"Perfect. Take that one if you can. Should get you here by six or so."

"Six-thirty-five."

"Yeah. Call me back when you have your ticket. If you don't have an opportunity, call me from the train; failing that, from the Sydney station."

"I will."

"I'll give you directions to Neutral Bay. Here's what you do: From Central Station, you take a taxi to—get this—Circular Quay Station, three words." He spelled it for her—needlessly, she thought. "That's for the ferries across the bay. Go to quay number four, that's the one for Neutral Bay. In any case, call me from there before you get on. By the time you've crossed, I'll be at the dock to pick you up."

"Martin, you're wonderful. I'm so glad, so relieved to have you there."

"You're very welcome." She heard a cough. Then "Ta-ta," and he hung up.

Gretchen had every intention of calling Riley back after she bought her ticket, but it wasn't possible. The whole business of getting herself over to the train station and lining up first at the wrong window and then at the right one to buy her ticket (yes, there was a first-class seat available for her) took too much of her time and attention in this strange and bewildering city. There was another chance, though, when she sat in the dining car and found that she could use a phone at her table.

She dialed Martin's number. "Guess who?" she said when he picked up at his end.

"Gretchen!"

"Guess where!"

He chuckled. "It better be on the train; right?"

"Too right, to use your language. The dining car, yet. I just ordered lunch. Stuffed trout. Did you know meals come with the ticket?"

"That's first class. In Australia we mean what we say."

"You do, indeed. Martin, I keep thinking what I would do without you. I tell you, these past two weeks have been a nightmare for me. If it hadn't been for you stepping in, as it were, I don't know that I could have brought it off."

"'Stepping in' is a kind way of putting it. We old spys don't like to be thought of as 'stalking' or 'skulking.' Not when it comes to the likes of you. So you forgive me, Gretchen?"

"Martin, I'm in your debt! Whatever it is you did, I'm glad you did it."

"And whatever it is that you needed to bring off, I'm glad you could."

"Yes." She hesitated for a moment. "Martin, there's a lot I have to tell you, but not right away. Give me some breathing space?"

"For as long as you wish, Gretchen, that's understood. Now, you needn't call again unless something's gone awry. I'll be at the dock when your ferry comes in." Again he ended the conversation abruptly.

Gretchen stared at the phone suddenly gone silent. Was he being rude? Thinking about it, she decided that he wasn't. On the contrary, by avoiding the customary goodbye which, at least in her native land, seemed to have to end with 'love you,' he prevented false sentiments from creeping in.

Martin was being true and honest, and she appreciated that. After all, those were real sentiments.

Arriving in Sydney on time, Gretchen had no trouble reaching the Circular Quay ferry wharfs, and no difficulty boarding the Neutral Bay ferry. She found herself in the company of a Saturday night crowd of commuters and tourists who were loud and boisterous as the boat gained open water against the blood-red sky of the sinking sun. Observing the people, she wondered when she could again be as carefree and joyful as they.

Stepping off the gangplank and walking slowly lugging her suitcase, she craned her neck to make out Martin. The ferry passengers were streaming by her on foot, some on bicycles, and as the crowd thinned she stood, looking.

Up aways, the door of a dark van opened and a man came out, followed by a dog. The man was dressed in jeans and a polo shirt; the dog was a shaggy sheep dog of some kind. In the dusk, Gretchen wasn't sure: Martin and Winnie?

When they came closer, she knew: Yes.

"Hello!" Riley opened his arms and smiled broadly.

Gretchen put down her suitcase and came toward him, smiling back. "Hi!"

They embraced. "Welcome," he said. Their hug lasted a tad longer than normal. "Welcome to our shores."

"Thank you." She felt her eyes moistening and directed her glance at the dog who was sitting, watching close-mouthed, ears perked. "You must be Winnie," Gretchen said, and bending down, she patted him on the head and ruffled his pelt. "Hello, Winnie!"

Riley spoke to his dog. "Good boy. This is Gret." He bent down and praised him, using Gretchen's hand with his to pat his side. Then he let both their hands slide off the dog's snout, letting him smell them. "Good boy." With a command gesture he ordered the dog to run back into the van.

Riley took her suitcase. "Right on time," he said. "How was the trip?"

"As you said, first class. I don't know why I haven't come to Australia before."

"Now's the time. Good as any."

"Better," she nodded. She climbed into the passenger side when he held the door open for her. Winnie was sitting on the back seat on a blanket.

As he got into his seat and started the engine, Riley said, "It's just a short ride." He turned the car around. "We live close to the water. Don't we, Winnie?"

"I'm glad," Gretchen said, and stroked Winnie behind the ears.

They entered a tree-lined side street. There were small, one-story houses on either side. Martin pulled up into the driveway of one of them. "Here we are, Riley's cottage." He opened the door, and the dog jumped over the seat and out, then stood waiting.

"It looks lovely," Gretchen said as she got out of the car. "It's a cottage all right. Very English, rose bushes and all." There were rose beds on either side of the walkway to the front door. She followed him and the dog.

As Riley unlocked the door, the dog leaped ahead of them into the house. It was a small one, all right. Gretchen followed Riley who carried her suitcase, then stood and turned on the lights. "Living and dining," he said, pointing to his left and his right. There was no entry hall.

"Lovely," she said, and it was, at first sight. Small rooms, but simply furnished; and paintings on the walls.

"Follow me," he said, leaving the suitcase standing.

"You left the door open," she reminded him.

"On purpose. Miss Adelaide—I told you about her, didn't I?"

"The painter neighbor?"

"Yes. She will have seen us, and she's coming over." He walked on. "She will give us tea."

Gretchen walked on behind him. They were in a short hallway with doors to either side and at the end of it. Riley entered the one at left. "My office, such as it is." Winnie was already there, on his haunches, tilting his head attentively. "The next room is my bedroom. Up ahead, the loo."

Gretchen followed him through an opening on the right: the kitchen, again small but with a clever use of the limited space, and modern appliances—stove, microwave, fridge. "Nice," she said, nodding.

"You may want to freshen up," he suggested. "I'll fix drinks. What would you like?"

"Oh, uh, scotch, I guess. Water and ice?" Gretchen made for the "loo." There were fresh towels, new soap, and even a toothbrush still sealed in a plastic case. She washed up. Her soapy face looked back at her in the mirror: Where am I? What am I doing here?

When she returned to the living room, a woman was sitting next to Riley on the sofa. Miss Adelaide, no doubt, except that she didn't match the mental image Gretchen had made of her. Was she old? Yes, but not adorned with the gray-haired bun that should go with an aging artist. Nor did she wear sensible shoes, nor did she have a wrinkled face without make-up.

Instead, Gretchen came over to shake the hand of a stylish, modern woman of a certain age who gave the impression of being well born, well brought up, and well preserved. No silver hair, but brunette curls—tinted?—in a short coif. Moreover, she was dressed in silk, a mauve shift that hung over her midriff flapper-style and ended above her ankles. The suede pumps were of matching color, and she wore silk hose. Pearls, three long strands of them, gave the finishing touch of bygone days. Better days, no doubt.

"How do you do?" she said. "Will you let me call you Gretchen? Yes? Of course, I am Miss Adelaide to all and sundry." There was an inflection in her voice that defied immediate identification.

"Yes, please, Miss Adelaide. Martin has told me so much about you."

"*Martin*, is it?" She looked at him with raised eyebrow.

'Queen Alexandra,' Gretchen thought. 'That's what she looks like.' All that was missing was a lorgnette.

Riley answered. "Well, yes. Martin is my given Christian name, actually, and Pat is what I'm called." He smiled. "Convenience. Just as your full name does not lend itself to common use." To Gretchen he added, "Miss Adelaide descends from the royal Danish house, she tells me."

"Well, then, I was right," Gretchen said, chancing a laugh. "To me, at first sight, you look like Queen Alexandra."

"She was my great-great-aunt," was the matter-of-fact reply. "I am of the house of Glücksburg-Sonderburg. The beastly Germans made us give it up."

"Really," Gretchen said. Riley was handing out drinks. She caught his eye, but he just shrugged.

"Welcome." He raised his glass. "Cheers."

They all drank.

The tea, as Martin called it, was two plates of cold cuts, cheeses, and breads. The actual tea was steeping in the kitchen.

When they had helped themselves to platefuls, they sat down again in the living room. Gretchen now sat next to "the royal," as she dubbed Miss Adelaide in her mind. Riley was in a chair opposite.

"That painting over the fireplace—Miss Adelaide did it." He nodded in her direction.

Gretchen rose to look at it close up. It was quite simple in theme: An armchair to the side of a fireplace, an ormulu clock and a floral arrangement on the mantle above. The colors were what attracted the eye; there were flowers, flowers everywhere, on the chair's upholstery, in large pots and vases on the floor, and even in the motifs of the striped wallpaper. As in an English country house drawing room. Gretchen liked it.

"It's signed 'A. Moore!'" she said.

"It's me. From my Paris period. My husband's dead now. I came to Australia. It seemed far enough away. Do you like it? The painting."

"Very much. It speaks to me."

"To me, too," Martin got up and went to touch it, lightly, with his fingertips. "I inherited it from my mother. Imagine. Living next door to the painter now!"

"Sold it for a quid then. It was giving it away, but it found a home."

Gretchen watched the two during that brief exchange. There was genuine fondness between them. Like mother and son. She spoke earnestly. "You are a true artist, I can see that, Miss Adelaide, from this one piece alone."

"Nonsense. What do you really mean? No flattery, please. Speak truthfully to me, girl, or not at all."

"All right. Truthfully, I've recently begun to learn something about art. Your work, judging by this one, is post-Impressionist, I would say."

"Right you are. I studied in Paris with Constantin Kluge, during the wild sixties. He was the only artist I could find who was not wild."

Gretchen did not say anything to that. She had seen some of Kluge's work in the catalogues that George Natalian had given her. Idly leafing through them, appalled by the mediocre and often incomprehensibly ugly nature of most of the modern works for sale, she had found refuge in the lightness and bold-colored beauty in the work of one artist whose name she remembered for just that reason: Kluge, and it helped that in German "klug" meant "gifted, talented." Should she now say, yes, I know of Kluge, and risk being thought a weisenheimer, as her father used to term it? Better let it go for now. Identifying Alexandra was weisenheimery enough. And besides, Miss Adelaide could have been putting her on. Although that would appear out of character. Queen Alexandra, indeed.

They returned to their food and made small talk. There were tales to be told about what had gone on while Riley had been away. And how smart Winnie was, really. Miss Adelaide gave him a saucer of steak tartare.

"It's a good thing Fiona didn't see that," Riley remarked. "Feeding him from the table."

Miss Adelaide was unperturbed. "She'll be here at Christmastime. Then we'll see. I know a thing about dogs, too."

"Fiona is my daughter," Riley said to Gretchen. "She lives in London."

"How lovely for you," Gretchen said. "You mentioned your daughter to me before, Martin. How clever she is, working for an international bank and all."

"You'll like her," Miss Adelaide said. "And she'll like you, I'm sure."

"Oh, I'm sure, too, but I'm afraid I won't be here then. As soon as my affairs are straightened out, I'll be on my way home to California."

"Well, however long that may be, you are welcome to stay with me. Pat and I talked about it. Unless you feel inconvenienced. Do you?" Those blue eyes bore in on her, brooking no dissent.

"No, of course not. I mean, yes, I'd be glad to stay with you, Miss Adelaide. Very glad. Of course, you must let me help with some things, groceries and so on."

"My guests are not paying guests, young lady. What should I call you, Gretchen? Dreadful German name, if you don't mind my saying so. Have you another?"

Gretchen smiled, unoffended. "Cosima, after my mother."

"Ah, better. Much better. Cosima! I like it."

"I like it too," said Riley laughing. "Let's all drop our common names. From Pat to Martin, Gretchen to Cosima. What can you drop, Miss Adelaide?"

"Don't be impertinent, young man. You remain Pat, to me. It'll be a cold day in Woolloomooloo before you'll hear me call you anything else."

Riley, still laughing, said to Gretchen: "Woolloomooloo—eight o's, three l's. It's where Miss Adelaide has her gallery."

"Yes. You must come and see it, Cosima. Ah. It caresses, that name."

Gretchen, who had followed the exchange quietly, now nodded. "I like it, too. It's my mother's, and I loved her very much. Nobody else has claimed it. I always thought I'd give it to my daughter. But I have two sons."

"Then it's settled. Cosima and Pat. What *you* call each other is your business." Miss Adelaide looked at her tiny gold wristwatch. "It's getting on. Time, for me! You must be tired, too, my dear. How long have you been up?"

"Oh…I don't really know. I've slept on the bus, and on the train."

"Quite right." Martin got up. "It's time you got some sleep."

The party broke up soon after. Martin said he'd do the dishes later. He picked up the suitcase and the procession wound itself out of the house, down one driveway and up the next, Miss Adelaide in the lead and Winnie bringing up the rear, and into a house that appeared much the same as Martin's but had a more lived-in look, more old-fashioned, perhaps, if that's what it was that made a first impression on Gretchen as she was led through the length of it and out again in the back, across a lawn that ended in front of an annex. Through an open door they stepped into a barn of a structure that was obviously Miss Adelaide's studio. The turned-on light revealed canvas leaning against the wall, two easels with a long, low table between them that was full of paint tubes, and tubs with brushes and other paraphernalia. Gretchen wondered briefly if she was expected to make her bed on the battered couch nearby, but Miss Adelaide opened yet another door and turned a light switch: A smaller room, tastefully furnished with a canopied bed, desk, chairs, wardrobe, and a dresser.

Gretchen was delighted, and said so when Miss Adelaide told her that this and an adjoining bathroom were hers to use.

"You're a bit away from the house, but quite safe, I assure you," Miss Adelaide said.

"It's nice of you to give her the studio," said Martin. "I thought you said Gretchen would be in your guest room."

"I changed my mind when she turned out to be a Cosima," was the curt reply. "And now, I suggest we give our guest her privacy and some rest."

Gretchen, saying "thank you, thank you, thank you," hugged her and Riley and kissed Winnie on the top of his head.

When all three of them had left and the door had closed behind them, Gretchen sat on the bed, hands folded in her lap, and contemplated where she was, to what waystation this day had brought her. A respite?

Yes. For the first time since leaving Hong Kong she felt that she had arrived somewhere. Not home—not yet—but at the far end of her journey; a long, often perilous journey, and this would be the halfway point. The worst was behind her, that much was certain. Thank God. For a while now she would rest, catch her breath, think clearly without being rushed. Do it right. Yes.

As she began to turn down the bed, undressed, opened her suitcase to put her money belt into it, as she took her kit into the bathroom, tested the shower and found it working, one thought, one name kept popping into her mind over and over again: Martin.

Martin—who had appeared just at the right time in her life. Why?

Martin—who was so helpful to her, and whom she could trust. Who would be there to see things through, of that she had no doubt.

And now this strange woman, this Queen Alexandra figure, who preferred calling her Cosima—was this the doing of her mother's ghost again?

It made her shiver under the hot water.

These were all coincidences, weren't they? Perfectly explainable? Of course. What else was she to think?

— CHAPTER ELEVEN —
Road's End

The first days of her "respite" went well for Gretchen. She slept past breakfast time, waking to the noise that came from the studio, where Miss Adelaide was busy setting herself up for another day's work. The first time it happened she poked her head through the door, sheepishly saying good morning and that she'd be out very soon.

"Not to worry." The old lady waved at her cheerfully and told her that she would find the coffee still hot in the kitchen and the porridge just needing to be warmed up a bit. And there was toast and juice.

Gretchen thanked her and withdrew. The next couple of times she simply got herself ready and came back into the studio holding a mug of coffee and munching on a muffin. She walked around examining the artwork that hung on the wall or was stacked, two and three deep, in the slots of storage bins. Miss Adelaide carried on undisturbed, busy at work with her paraphernalia like a cook in a gourmet kitchen.

Soon Gretchen would leave her and walk over to Riley's house, where he would get the dog and they would set out on a long morning walk that would be interrupted only by a brief stop at a roadside diner for a Coke or ice cream. Yes, Riley had a sweet tooth, he admitted. Off they went, on a path that skirted the bay, now and again encountering views that were breathtakingly beautiful. By noon they would be back, and Miss Adelaide would have lunch ready, a salad or sandwiches, beer, and tea. As for who was footing the bill for the repasts, it appeared that Riley stuffed dollar bills into a tin in the kitchen for Miss Adelaide to take to the food market. Neither of them worried whether it came out even. Meal times at no set hour; Miss Adelaide would fix lunch at noon and Riley would come in to join her or drop in later when work held him up. Gretchen soon got the hang of it and put in her share.

As the first weekend neared, the routine became different: Miss Adelaide had to travel across to Sydney to attend her booth at the Woolloomooloo Art Cooperative. She asked Gretchen if she wanted to come along and got an enthusiastic "yes." Art and the business end of it, Gretchen told her, were increasingly becoming interests of hers. Yes, she wanted to go Saturday *and* Sunday. Nine to six. Absolutely. It would be fun.

Riley drove them to the ferry. When he came in the evening to pick them up again, he noticed that Gretchen was uncommonly quiet. He looked at Miss Adelaide next to him in the front seat, but she just arched her eyebrows and shook her head a bit.

Riley took Gretchen out to the pub that evening. Over a pint he asked her what was wrong. She looked around, saw people, men and women standing or sitting at the bar, talking loudly, quaffing beer, laughing, and then turned to Riley.

"It was awful. Not the art show, not that at all. That was great. But the crowd. So many of them were American tourists." She stopped and shook her head. "When I heard an American voice I had to turn away, hide my face, bend down, and pretend I was doing something...."

"Why?" Martin asked in a calm manner. "Why would you want to hide?"

She traced a crack in the wooden tabletop with her finger. Then she looked at him. "Because...I might be recognized...."

"Recognized? What do you mean by that?"

"Well, you know, someone who knew me from home, a neighbor, or a club member, anyone...." She shrugged.

"What would be so...so frightful about that?"

She waited to answer, poking with her fingernail along the crack in the table. Then she said, "I don't know if I should tell you."

"Let me see if I can help. Does it have anything to do with that sick woman from Hong Kong?"

"No. Oh, no. Except that if I hadn't met her I would be in Germany with my son now." She gave him a shy smile. "And of course, we would never have met, Martin."

He smiled back. "I'm not so sure about the latter. I might have followed you to Germany."

She held his hand: "Oh Martin, how different everything would be!"

Gently, he said, "Not that different from the here and now. But let's go on. Does it have anything to do with your name change?"

"It's not a name change so much as a passport change. I had the name legally changed a year ago, after my divorce, and took back my maiden name. My new passport didn't come through until just before my departure, and all my reservations and tickets were still under my married name. And the government never asked for my old passport back."

"So, let me get this straight. You were Mrs. Goodridge for the trip from the U.S., for your stay in Hong Kong, and in Bali and Jakarta?" When she nodded, he continued. "And Mrs. Herter from Singapore on? Why the sudden change? What happened?"

She gave a low moan. "The plane crash…on that Friday.…"

He looked puzzled for a moment. Then he said, "You mean—the Garuda flight that crashed on Sumatra? Is that the one?"

"Yes."

"Can you explain that a bit more?"

"I was on it."

He was taken aback. "But…you couldn't have! The news said there were no survivors!"

"I know! God knows I know that. What happened is that I got off at the last moment, while the doors were still open and we were waiting for the okay to pull away from the gate."

Riley now leaned forward and gripped her arms with both hands. In a low voice, he said, "Gretchen, listen to me. I'm beginning to understand, but you've got to give me more details if I am going to help you. And help you I will—unless you absolutely forbid me not to, in which case the conversation ends here and no more questions will be asked."

Tears were welling up in her eyes. "I need you," she whispered.

"All right. Okay." He sat back and signaled the waitress. "Let's get out of here. Let's go back to my van, sit down, and talk where no one can observe us or hear us."

At the car, Winnie was glad to see them. "Now there's one happy fellow," Riley said, roughing up the dog's coat and slapping him on the side. "There's a lesson here for us humans. Take each day as it comes and enjoy one another's company." He found a dog chew in his pocket and gave it to Winnie, who retreated with it to the back seat.

"I wish it were that easy for us," Gretchen said as she climbed in.

He came in from his side and closed the door. "It could be," he said, looking at her, "if we trust each other as much."

"Oh, I trust you, Martin."

"And I you. There we are, then. Let's see what develops. Want to drive somewhere? Have a bite to eat?"

"I'm not hungry."

"Want a drink?" He reached into the glove compartment. "I still have some of those little bottles from the airplane." He took out two and gave her one. "Scotch. Single malt. Eminently sippable."

They touched bottles, the plastic making no noise. "Cheers."

"Okay." He had taken a good swig and was wiping his mouth with his sleeve. "How do we do this? I ask questions, and you fill in the details, or vice versa?"

She had only sipped at her drink, letting the liquid run hot down her gullet. "You start."

"Fair dinkum. Where were we? You were running off the plane just before take-off, right? Why?"

She took another sip. "This is going to sound crazy." She saw him nod. "I felt...I had this eerie feeling.... No. It started earlier. My departure day from Los Angeles was the fifth of September. That was the day, the exact day, that my mother died in a plane crash twenty-two years ago. She was on an airliner coming in from San Francisco, and over Santa Barbara a small plane hit the big one. They both crashed. No survivors. A terrible thing. It's been with me ever since. Unforgettable."

He put an arm around her shoulder and gave her a squeeze. "I'm so sorry."

"So, on the day I was to leave—the days before—I had this, uh, this thing in the pit of my stomach: 'What if my plane crashes, too? On

Friday, the fifth of *September*?' But it was silly, of course. And I got talked out of it."

"And nothing happened. The odds are hugely against it."

"Exactly what Duncan said." She took another sip. "Duncan is my half-brother, but he is younger than my sons. After my mother's death, my father remarried."

"Ah. Go on."

"I put it out of my mind. But then, sitting in that airplane—again on a *Friday* in *September*, mind you—I suddenly had a vision. Nothing figurative, no angel or anything like that, but an apparition, like the light that keeps burning your eyes after a flash has gone off. You understand?" She hesitated.

He nodded. "Yes, I think I do."

"It was so intense that if I close my eyes now I can still see it. It spoke to me in my head, that vision did—in my mother's voice, I'm sure. It urged me to get up, leave the plane, and do it now. *Now!*" She shook her head in disbelief. "You read about people who've had near-death experiences, how they felt disembodied and how, for some reason, they come back to life and have difficulty putting into words what they experienced. That's how it is with me."

Riley observed her closely. "How did you get off? Didn't anyone see you or stop you? The plane must have been full."

"I was sitting in first class, last row, left, in an aisle seat. At the window seat was an elderly Chinese man who had his eyes closed. The partition curtain was directly behind my row. It had not been pulled yet, and the exit door was behind that, still open. I just got up and turned right and right again out of the plane, entered the gangway that snaked to the right, and ran into the waiting area that was crowded with people around the various check-in desks. Nobody saw me. Nobody called after me. I ran on, feeling very sick to my stomach. I was sure I had to throw up, so I looked frantically for a bathroom and found it further down in the Lufthansa lounge. Waving my Lufthansa ticket, I rushed in, my handkerchief covering my mouth so that the woman at the counter knew I was a passenger who was going to be sick. I ran into the ladies' room and closed the stall door. All along, my heart had been beating in my throat. I sat there for a while until my heart calmed down and wasn't beating like crazy anymore. I took my pulse: normal. Also, I was no longer nauseous. And reason had returned. I knew then that

I had missed my flight to Bangkok. My luggage had been checked through. All I had on me were the valuables hidden on my person and my handbag with my ticket and passport."

Riley sat silently, his arm still across the back of her seat. He did not touch her, reassuringly or otherwise, but kept his eyes on her. They were parked near a lamppost, and there was enough illumination for him to make out her features. He did not get the impression that she was lying or fabricating her story. On the contrary, she sounded honest.

Gretchen took another swig, and then the little bottle was empty. "Wow," she said, "I can't believe I finished this."

Riley reached for the glove compartment, but she stopped him. "Not for me, please. But you go ahead and have another." He didn't.

"Telling you this is almost like a reenactment." She grimaced. "I was so thirsty then, in that flight lounge, that I had a drink, a sherry, I believe, and some crackers. I sat down with it in an easychair. Eventually I fell asleep. Deeply. A solid two hours. I was awakened by some commotion, people close by, and a T.V. voice, but not in English. I perked up and went to see what was going on. They had the plane crash on T.V. That Garuda flight I had been on had crashed on Sumatra. Not immediately, but slowly, the enormity of that event began to sink in. I was stunned."

Riley asked, "What did you do then?"

She looked at him. "You tell me, what would you have done?"

"Good question. Let me see.... Go to the Garuda counter, say, 'Ahem, about that Garuda flight—I wasn't on it.' Something like that."

"Yes. That occurred to me. Then what do you think would follow?"

"Questions. Incredulity that I hadn't been on that plane. Was it just luck? Why had I left that plane, and how had I managed to do so unobserved?" He looked at her. "How'm I doin'?"

"Just fine. Keep going."

"You mentioned you had your luggage checked through, right? Yes. I suppose they would want to know more about me. Who was I? Where did I come from? Why had I made a detour from Hong Kong to Bali? Who was that woman I was with, and what happened to her? Lots of questions."

"Exactly. My thoughts ran along those lines too. This can all be explained, and I need to rebook a flight to Bangkok. Just then a government official appeared on T.V. The bartender had switched the T.V.

to CNN. It was in English now. The man promised a thorough investigation into the cause of the crash. Pilot error? Poor visibility due to smoke at the landing site? Sabotage?"

Riley whistled through his teeth. "Sabotage! A mad bomber. The only person whose luggage was on board but who had escaped at the last moment, and who had just come from Bali, where a friend had been left behind—what, dead? Is there a connection? Is there a motive? Money, valuables, the person's life in disarray? What had that person been doing in Hong Kong—buying art? For half a million dollars, U.S.? My goodness, the possibilities for spinning this story are endless."

"Yes! You got it. And the Indonesian authorities would be crazy not to go after it. And the press—don't forget them!"

"Indeed. I can see your predicament. What did you do?"

"I almost froze with fear. Then I told myself two things: One, I was alive; I was not among that debris on the ground. I have my mother to thank for that. There is no rational explanation for my running off that plane at the last moment before takeoff. Two, nobody would believe my story, at least not in Indonesia, which was hit hard by the tragedy." She looked at him: "Do *you* believe my story?"

"Yes. I do." His answer came quickly. He added, "I have watched you long enough to know that you are a genuine, decent person."

She leaned back and heaved a sigh of relief. "That's good. Thank you for that. I haven't been able to share this with anyone until now."

"You were tempted to talk to me on that ship, though, weren't you? I wish you had. We could have made things a little easier for you. Still, you did very well on your own. I suppose using your other passport was your ticket out of that disaster. All of your peculiar moves that I saw make sense now. In fact, as an old and seasoned spook, I'm impressed. You acted with admirable logic and skill." He put his arm over her shoulder and gave her a pat. "And with courage."

Gretchen sought his hand. "Thank you, Martin."

"Right," he said, pulling his arm away and starting the car.

"Where are we going?" she asked.

"Home, if you wish."

"Not particularly. I could use some food just about now."

"Right," he said again as he pulled out into the road.

Riley knew of a place on the Spit that he would frequent "now and again" as he put it. "Good seafood," and "They're licensed," he said. On the ride there they hardly spoke. Winnie put his head on the armrest between the front seats and let himself be petted by Gretchen.

The restaurant was a good place, very nautical, with a view of Pearl Bay. They agreed they should have some champagne, and that Riley would be allowed to order "yabbies"—he promised to explain later—for both of them.

Gretchen felt wonderfully relaxed. The idea, she told him, that she could be free to talk with someone and discuss her situation was overwhelming. She hoped he didn't mind her sharing it with him.

"Why should I mind?" he asked.

"Well," she laughed, "you're now my co-conspirator!"

"I suggest we not make light of it, Gret. Your troubles are not yet over. In fact, it could be argued that they are only now beginning."

"Martin! What do you mean by that?"

"The plane crash occurred a month ago. Officially, you're dead."

"Oh, I know! That's why I have to go to the American embassy, present myself, and explain things. Don't you see?"

The food came. Yabbies turned out to be crawfish served with a buttery dip and a salad. Gretchen tried a bit and pronounced it delicious. Dealing with the crustaceans without making too much of a mess required Riley's expert advice. It was fun.

Over coffee, with Martin smoking one of his cigarillos, the talk came back to the main theme, which had never been far from their minds.

"I think you'll agree we must consider your next steps very carefully," he said. Gretchen, thankful for the plural "we," nodded eagerly. "There's always a possibility that you'll meet not with sympathy, but with suspicion, even from your countrymen. You need a fall-back position."

"Fall-back? To what? I'm telling the truth! I did nothing wrong!"

"Yes, but the truth is based on people accepting your 'ghost' story, if you'll let me call it that for simplicity's sake. The reality is that you left a plane that two hours later would crash with no survivors. There's no getting around that point. It will arouse suspicion."

"But, Martin, that's why I didn't stay in Jakarta! Why I came all the way here!"

"Here may not be all that different, is what I'm trying to warn you about. Hence the fall-back."

"Such as?"

"You need a lawyer who can accompany you to the embassy after you have given a sworn statement to him. He could also get you to a higher-level official than you would get just walking in off the street. Alone, you would have to deal with underlings who would probably spill your story to the press the first chance they have."

She thought about that and said, "I can see the need for a lawyer, yes. Is there someone you can recommend?"

"Let me work on that. It would have to be a firm in Canberra that has connections to the U.S. Embassy. No point in using the consulate general here. Your position is too precarious."

"Precarious? How?"

"Vulnerable is perhaps a better word. You leave a trail that, when unraveled, may put nearly everything you have done into a different light. From the Getty Museum to the Hong Kong deal, to Bali with your dying friend, to the Garuda flight to Townsville: All can be made to look bad. Not to mention the fact that your brother is a politician married to one of England's greatest fortunes. All tabloid-press fodder."

"Good lord." Gretchen bit her lip. "Maybe it would have been better if I'd stayed on that plane." She fought back tears."

Riley took her hand in both of his. "Never! Never, ever, say that again. There's a purpose in your being here. Perhaps you cannot discern it yet, but it's true. Believe it. Don't despair. We'll work it out."

"Will we? Martin I so wish we could!"

"Believe it," he said again.

It took nearly a week for Riley to find a law firm that fit the requirements, based on what he could learn about them: Uphagen, Rice, and Tonti, barristers and solicitors. Donald Uphagen, the senior partner, had a reputation for plying the diplomatic trade in Canberra. Riley got an appointment with him, but not without some difficulty. After all, it had to be made clear that he himself was not the client, but that he was acting for a friend, a lady who needed help in gaining admission to the United States. Uphagen's father and Riley's father had been chums in their early years in Sydney and belonged to the same Masonic lodge; it was the one argument that won the day. And that day, so to speak, would be a Tuesday morning in mid-November.

It put Gretchen into an apprehensive frenzy. This would be her "defining moment," she kept repeating to Riley, her first step on her journey to regain her former life. Riley was very supportive. On their walks with Winnie they discussed what she should say and how she should say it. He told her she should act entirely natural, but that she should beware of spilling all the beans right away.

"Hah!" Gretchen exclaimed. What beans, then, should she spill first?

He said, "Never mind, just be yourself. Speak from the heart. Just be aware that Uphagen needed to be convinced that he should take your case, so you should concentrate on the plane crash and nothing else." No Hong Kong, no Bali, no Townsville; those could come later, when she had become a client. There was also the matter of the retainer. If she was short, Riley would be glad to loan her some money.

It was at that point that Gretchen mentioned her pounds sterling. British money he wondered? Where did she get that?

From Anthea Tait, she said; she had left it for her in an envelope, on Bali. In fact, she still had that same envelope, untouched.

Riley was concerned by that news. He felt she should not mention this to anyone, this monetary connection to a helpless, dying woman. How much was it? Five thousand pounds? He whistled. Over ten thousand Australian dollars—more like twelve thousand. She had better put it in a bank.

Off they went to a local branch of Commonwealth Bank, where an American artist named Gret Cosima Herter opened a checking account, the new checkbook to be mailed to her at her local address, which happened to be the same as Miss Adelaide's. Done.

On the way back, Gretchen said, "You mustn't mind my asking, Martin, and you certainly needn't answer if you don't want to—"

"Cut the twaddle," he said. "What do you want to know?"

"How do you make your living? I never see you working. I mean—"

"I know what you mean. We'll get into that one day. First we'll solve your problem."

"Yeah."

On the Monday before she left for Canberra, Gretchen packed all her belongings; it was best, she said, if she stayed on in Canberra for the duration of her time there with the law firm and the embassy. Of course, she'd be back afterward, no matter what.

Of course, Riley agreed. He offered to drive her down. Only a couple of hours. No, no, it'd be a pleasure.

"Thank you," said Gretchen. "Can Winnie come too?"

"Yeah. Be ready to leave at the crack of dawn," he said.

That night they took Miss Adelaide out to dinner. In the end they all had a wee bit too much to drink. The women hugged each other tearily.

It was still dark when Martin came to pick up Gretchen. She was packed and ready, waiting in the kitchen, where Miss Adelaide, in her housecoat, was busy fixing a snack to take along—sandwiches, fruit, and a thermos of coffee. Gretchen didn't feel like eating, but accepted a glass of orange juice.

Riley, impatient, said "let's go" and picked up Gretchen's new suitcase, which was bulging. Gretchen embraced Miss Adelaide and said, "I may be back this evening, for all we know." She fought back a lump in her throat. "You're so wonderful. This is not goodbye; we'll do that later, sometime."

It was a cool morning. There had been rain overnight, and Gretchen shivered even through the lining of her Burberry. It, too, was new, as were the cashmere outfit she was wearing underneath and the sensible half-heel pumps. It was necessary to dress well, Riley had suggested, to make a favorable first impression at the solicitors'. Gretchen agreed.

Riley put the car into gear and rumbled out onto Military Road. He knew how best to use the various motorways to connect to the South Western Freeway, which would take them straight down to Canberra. He estimated that they would get a good head start by leaving early, but even so it would take close to four hours in normal traffic to reach Canberra. The car had a full tank of gas; there would be no need to stop anywhere, except to give Winnie a pee break. And others feeling so inclined.

Gretchen leaned back against her seat. Dawn had not yet broken. The engine purred assuringly, the dashboard lights glowed dimly. On the back seat Winnie was curled up, sleeping.

"Do what he does, why don't you?" Riley suggested. "Let the back down, close your eyes. We'll be a while yet."

"Uh-uh, thank you. I'm too keyed up." She hadn't slept much during the night, either. The small world of Miss Adelaide and Martin

Riley, especially Martin, had been the first secure harbor she had known since that fateful day in Jakarta. Sleep would not come to her for thinking about them and about what she was about to embark upon.

Riley shrugged his shoulders. Gretchen watched him: eyes on the road, turning this way and that, speeding up and slowing down. A careful man. A good man. A trusted friend.

They had gained the motorway by the time the sun was up. Riley said, "Time to have some coffee. Would you mind?" He pointed to the picnic basket. Gretchen said "glad to" and put two cups into the holder and poured the coffee. It was hot and strong, creamy and sweet. Miss Adelaide's. Gretchen sipped. The rays of the sun slanted through her side window, making her feel warm enough to loosen her seatbelt and wriggle out of her coat, which she stowed on the floor behind her seat. "Ah," she said, "that's better."

"Right-o."

They drove in silence for a good while. Then she asked:

"Martin? May I ask you something personal?"

"Try me."

"About you not working and all. I'm not prying, okay? It's just that I want to know because I really care. You don't mind my asking?"

He kept his eye on the road. "It's personal. But I said I'd tell you someday. Maybe this is the day."

It took him a moment to begin. "It's a tale of woe entirely of my own making." He shook his head. "Pride, greed, and bad decisions based on both." He shook his head again, seemingly lost in his folly.

"In what way, pride?"

"Class. Upper versus middle. Middle wanting to be upper." He cast her a quick glance. "Have you ever heard of Names, capital N?"

"Names? As in what: Aristocratic family names?"

"That's what it's derived from, I'm sure. In this case, though, it's Lloyd's. Lloyd's of London."

"The insurance company?"

"The underwriters, yes. Gathered around by people who have money in their pockets and are greedy for more, betting on the outcome of faraway events—floods, earthquakes, oil spills, Betty Grable's legs, anything that if it doesn't come about makes them money when they close the books on it. Easy money. Lots of it, and often. They're called syndicates."

"Yes? You were betting on syndicates?"

"I was *in* one. In fact, more than one. Several. Some good ones. It's like Las Vegas: Why walk away from the table when you're winning, eh?"

"That's exactly when one should walk away. Not that I'd know."

"Yeah. I didn't know either. Besides, it was such an *honor*, just to be asked to join Lloyd's. Not everyone is, you know. They won't accept you walking in off the street. You have to have connections. They check you out—your family, your holdings, your clubs, the colors of your school tie. After all, Lloyd's is the preferred investment house for Tory M.P.s, Labour lordships, dowager duchesses, and movie stars. It's an honor for a chap like me just to be asked to be in their presence."

"That doesn't sound like you, Martin."

"Yeah. It looks like it in retrospect, though. How could I possibly have thought we'd get something for nothing, Ellen and I? Ellen had just inherited her father's country estate in Wiltshire. We could keep it and run it marginally to pay the estate tax, or we could sell it and pay off and have very little, if anything, left. But there was a third choice: Keep it, pay off Inland Revenue, and make money on top of it."

"Have your cake and eat it to."

"You Yanks have a way with words. Yes. Money was important for our future. We've never really had much. Ellen was a teacher and I was a civil servant. There was very little left over at the end of the month. And Fiona had to be properly educated. Greed, you see."

"I don't see it as greed. It sounds more like normal ambition to me." She shook her head. "A lot of people lose money investing."

"In my case it should read, people lose a lot of money investing with Lloyd's. I knew what was at stake. Yes, of course, you are liable for all you own, if the ship goes down and the syndicate pays off the contract. But they calculate that into the premiums they charge, don't they? And all that the insureds have to know is that the Lloyd's contract is underwritten by members who have such good *names* that even excess losses, improbably though they may seem, would be covered. Simple enough, eh?"

"So what went wrong?"

"Failure to consider the improbable is what went wrong. The Names, capital-N, had unlimited liability in case of loss. Unlimited! When you sign with a syndicate, you put up all your assets as collateral. A pledge, more's the pity, because you never sign them over to Lloyd's, you see; you just pledge them. In the meantime, while the syndicate is running, you still collect the income from your assets—rents, royalties, dividends, interest, what have you. Now, if your syndicate makes money, then every year you receive a handsome return on your pledge. In addition to what your assets may have brought in."

"Sounds like you get what you pay for."

"Yankee wisdom again. Quite right. Trouble is, Ellen and I hadn't really started getting it when the dam broke. I don't mean that literally: it just felt like it. First demands for payment came in, and not small ones, either. There went the nest egg. Then more demands, and we were hard put to meet them. Mortgage the Wiltshire place; it's just temporary. Right? Wrong." He stopped.

"Martin! How horrible."

"Horrible? Not yet. That was just beginning. Ellen developed fainting spells—dropping things like teacups, bumping into doors. We thought it was the strain of it all. Wrong again. A brain tumor was what the doctors told us eventually. Curable, though, they said, modern medicine being so advanced. We fought it—bravely, Ellen did: less bravely I, who was hiding my fear. In the end it was all for naught." He hurrumphed. "It didn't end there. Lloyd's has a right to pursue any funds that belong to the Names. Salaries, dividends, trusts, anything that the Names has legal title to. And that right extends in perpetuity. I took early retirement because pensions are not attachable. Fiona, thank God, was safe, as she had a trust fund in her own name from her grandfather. But even now I cannot earn an income, as it would go to Lloyd's."

Gretchen had followed his sparse recital of horror with a surging sense of empathy and alarm. This man, her friend, was baring his own wounds, still raw, still hurting. She could hear that in his voice, see it in his demeanor. She wondered if she was selfish in accepting his help, his many kindnesses, and as if they were her due. She told him warmly, "Martin, I'm glad you're sharing your past with me. More than glad, thankful. I wish I had known before."

"What difference would it have made?"

"Oh, a lot. I would have thought more about you, about your own troubles, instead of concentrating selfishly on my own. I'm sorry."

"You're nice to say that, but don't be sorry. My own troubles, as you call them, are past, done, irreversible. Yours are more acute, present, still developing, and they require a great deal of careful attention."

As if to avoid further discussion, Riley pulled into a roadside service area and parked under some trees. "Gotta give Winnie a chance, eh?" Martin reached over and put a leash on the dog. "Us humans, too, I think."

When they drove off again they found that their conversation was a little easier, less strained, as if they had removed an obstacle that had been there and that they had labored to overcome.

Gretchen raised a question that had been on her mind during the sleepless hours of the night: What did he think she should expect from the American authorities?

"How do you mean that?" Riley asked.

"Well, will they be anxious to help me, or will they view me with suspicion? I mean, here I am, alive and well but officially dead."

"That's the key point of it all, Gret. That's why you need someone standing by you to negotiate away your weak points and stress your strong points, your basic rights as a citizen. It may not be all smooth sailing. And it may take time. That's why you are taking a room in Canberra, isn't it? To be ready at a moment's notice."

His answer did not satisfy her. "Suppose," she said, "they don't believe me. Then what?"

"Belief is not the issue; proof is. Facts are. The U.S. consuls will surely want to investigate and verify whatever you tell them. They'll check to make sure you haven't broken any laws, of Indonesia or of Australia. Again, this is where your lawyers will come in handy."

"Suppose Mr. Uphagen won't take my case?"

"Oh, he will, he will all right. Yours is an interesting case, a challenging case. Not to mention that it is also connected to deep pockets, American pockets. Donald Uphagen is the least of your worries."

She mulled this over. She asked, "Your frank opinion, Martin: What are the chances of this all coming out right?"

"I take it you mean your approach to the American authorities and the assistance of the Australian law firm?"

"You make it sound as if there is another choice."

"There may be."

"Like what? Tell me, Martin. We're not playing a guessing game here!"

"I'd rather not. It has to occur to you, thinking of it independently, for it to be viable. Sorry, but that's where we are."

"If that's where we are, why is it that you won't tell me what's on your mind? I have the feeling you're holding something back! I need to know what that is, I'm in the middle of a high-stakes game here!"

He reached over and took her right hand, which had been gesticulating in the air. "Calm down. You'll be all right. Trust your instincts. That's what has pulled you through so far."

"You!" Furious, she withdrew her hand. She didn't want to appear to be sulking, but she felt too angry to talk anymore. She looked out her window and saw a green and hilly countryside flitting by, quite lovely, actually, bathed in sunshine.

After a while she lowered her seat back, reclined, and closed her eyes. Instinct, indeed. If she had it, why didn't she see the other option?

She must have dozed off, for when she heard Riley say "Canberra, now!" and sat up to look, they were entering the city's suburbs.

"Canberra? Already?"

"Too right. Welcome to the Australian Capital Territory." Martin put on his Aussie accent, which she had noticed he would do at times, like wearing a bush hat.

A little later he said, "Now we're on Northbourne Avenue. Like the Champs in Paris, it's as straight an avenue as there is. See that body of water ahead? It's a lake, man-made—*man* being a generic term, but actually it was designed by a man, one of your chaps, Burley Griffin, nearly a hundred years ago. We were so grateful we named it after him."

"I see." Gretchen did not like his sarcastic undertone.

"Beyond the water, you see a slight rise, do you, and a low-slung building with a kind of steeple in the middle? That's Parliament House, on Capital Hill. We'll drive by, if you like."

"Sure, let's." Gretchen looked at her watch. "We've made good time. There's well over an hour until my appointment."

"Yes. The straightaway is now called Commonwealth Avenue, for obvious reasons. To our right, as we cross over the lake, we'll have the suburb of Yarralumla, which is the posh diplomatic district. The U.S. embassy is there, near Stirling Park, with a lovely view of the lake."

"Let's drive by there first, please, Martin? And speak normally to me, not like a tour guide. We're friends."

He looked at her as he wheeled to an exit. A smile played on his lips. "We are that, aren't we?"

"Is that a question, or a statement, Martin?"

"A statement, now that you mention it."

The American embassy was every bit as attractive as the one she had seen in Singapore, Gretchen thought, except that here it was not set behind elaborate security barriers. In fact, it resembled a Virginia estate of Monticello vintage. She liked it and said so to Riley.

"Want to go in, have a look around?" he asked her.

"Now now," she said, "thank you."

The road curved, following the shoreline. The freshness of spring was everywhere—green lawns, blue water, azure sky. They cruised slowly.

Suddenly Gretchen said, "Stop the car. Please, Martin, stop!"

"Why? What's wrong?" Martin pulled into a turnout. "You all right?"

"I just want to get out." She sounded strained, serious. "Alone. Please?"

He brought the car to a halt. Gretchen jumped out on her side and began walking toward the water's edge. Trees threw mottled shade over the grassy slope. Riley watched her through the open car door. The car's motor was still running. Winnie had come forward, his head between the seats. What was this about? Riley turned off the engine. "Down, boy!" he said.

A few yards from the lake, Gretchen stopped. She stood still, gazing across the waters.

Riley decided to get out of the car, Winnie following him in one leap. Riley kept his eyes on Gretchen, who hadn't moved. He was uncertain what to do. Should he approach her? He turned to Winnie. "Go!" he said. "Go get!" The dog trotted off, turning his head once, and when he saw his master's gesture urging him forward, he continued until he was about ten feet from Gretchen. Then he hunkered down, head resting on his front paws, the tip of his tail twitching.

Gretchen remained unaware, her hands clasped to her chest now, her posture almost as if in meditation. Riley moved slowly forward, keeping a constant eye on her. He wondered what she was doing. Praying? He dared not call her name. The dog, too, inched forward a bit, eyes and ears keen. Now Gretchen dropped her arms, bowed her head, and brought her hands to her face. Her shoulders began to heave.

At that point Riley rushed forward. The dog reached her ahead of him, nuzzling her legs, sitting back, looking up. Gretchen bent down and patted the dog on the head. Riley, now at her side, caught her by the shoulder. "Gret, for heaven's sake, what's the matter?"

"Martin!" Her face was tear-stained when she turned around. Throwing her arms around him, she buried her head in his neck and sobbed quietly. No words came out of her, just deep, lowing moans. Still holding her, stroking her back, he murmured "Now, now, easy now," his own feelings stirred.

They stood in their embrace, swaying slightly, until the emotional onrush began to ebb. Riley spoke into her ear. "You all right?" She nodded, but held tight. He said, "You'll want a drink. Put things to right?"

Now she broke off and half laughed as she wiped away her tears with her fingers. "From your glove compartment? Oh Martin!"

"I dunno what else to say."

"You poor dear. Say nothing. I'll speak, you listen." She reached down to pat the dog. "That goes for you, too, Winnie." The dog cocked his head and reset himself attentively.

Gretchen now turned to Martin and said, "Here it is, listen carefully. I may be an emotional wreck, and you may think me silly, but...I simply cannot bear the thought of leaving you. There. I've said it." She nodded vigorously. "That's the nub and the truth of it, Martin. God, it doesn't come easy for me to say outloud what has been in the back of my mind all through that sleepless night and the drive down here. Just now, as we drove by the embassy, it occurred to me that if I walk through that entrance I might be shutting a door behind me, and you would be on the outside, forever. If there is a third way, any alternative, Martin, you must tell me. And even then, if it involves leaving you I won't do it. I won't go away unless you send me away. See? That is what I know in my heart to be true."

His eyes were locked on hers as he replied. "I hear what you're saying. I can't quite comprehend the turn of events, but you must know that you are utterly, unreservedly, totally welcome to stay. Dammit, Gretchen, I might as well be just as frank: I love you. Yes, the thought of you leaving me has been hard to bear at times. No, no, please," she was sniffling again, "get this straight. There is an element of wish-fulfillment in this, because I yearned for you in my foolish heart even before you knew I existed, and before there was ever any chance that we would meet. Now, with what you've just said, there may be something here, a good thing, for both of us to hang on to."

She took his face in her hands and kissed him spontaneously. When he tried to kiss her back she put a finger over his lips. "Uh-uh. Not yet, please, Martin."

He agreed immediately. "You're right. There's a lot to do, some of it right now. Come on." He took her by the waist and walked her back to the car. Winnie loped ahead and waited at the open car door. From the dashboard Riley took the telephone and, pulling a card from his wallet, dialed the number of the solicitors' office. He asked for Donald Uphagen, and when he came on told him that the client in question had an apparent change of mind and would not be able to keep the appointment. He, Riley, was sorry, but he would keep an eye on the situation and be in touch later.

"There," he said. "Done."

"Thank you, Martin. Oh, I'm so relieved. Glad, actually."

"So am I." He helped her into the car. "Time to go home, eh?"

"In time for Miss Adelaide's tea?"

"I suppose so; or how do you mean that?"

"I mean, let's not go home just yet. We need to have time for ourselves. Start over again! Don't you think?"

"I do indeed." He gunned the engine. "Well then, let's get out of Canberra before you change your mind."

"No chance of that!"

"Here's a suggestion. Let's head back up north where we came from. But instead of going east to Sydney, we make a sharp left and enter the Blue Mountains National Park. I've been meaning to take you there, but I haven't had the chance."

"Great! I've heard of that! Where exactly in the Blue Mountains?"

"A place I've passed through several times and have always wanted to stay. A pretty place, a village in the old style, very elegant, quaint, artistic, what have you. It's called Leura." He spelled it for her.

"We'd be staying overnight?"

"If we can get a room. We may; it's still early in the season."

"You mean, one room?"

"Yes." He shot her a bemused glance. "Okay with you?"

"It depends. Would we make love?"

He chuckled. "If we're very lucky. As you say, it depends."

She said, "Luck may have nothing to do with it. I'm totally out of practice. It's been years."

"No matter."

"I mean it, Martin. I may disappoint you."

"At our age, the emphasis is on love, not on making it. We'll be all right." He patted her right leg. "Relax."

"What about Winnie?"

"Worry about him, too, do you?" He nodded. "He can stay in the car. He's used to sleeping in here on fishing trips and so on. He'd watch your luggage, too. We won't need the half of it."

Relax is what Gretchen finally did, after Riley had coaxed her into opening Miss Adelaide's picnic basket and serving them sandwiches and the rest of the coffee as they drove on. They ate with a hearty appetite that had been absent during the tense early-morning drive; and Riley gave a running commentary on Australian politics and social customs that was of great interest to Gretchen, who asked more and more questions.

They turned west at Parametta towards Katoomba, where they entered Blue Mountains National Park and spectacular scenery that reminded Gretchen of the American southwest. Riley said it was only a few more kilometers to Leura. The afternoon sun was still high over the mountains. It was a glorious day, after all.

When they came to Leura with its quaint mansions and pretty gardens on treelined streets, Gretchen had another flashback, this time to Santa Barbara where she had visited the Lambs. My God, was it only three months ago? She shut off the thought at once.

"What do you say? How does it strike you, this town?" Riley looked at her inquiringly.

"I was just thinking it's like a small artsy town in California called Santa Barbara. Except Santa Barbara is very Spanish-Colonial."

"This is more English-Colonial. But it's artsy, too. Think we should stay here?"

"Oh, yes. Find us a place, Martin, one we'll want to come back to."

"Right."

It was early in a work week, and they had a choice of several nice places. In the end they chose a small inn at the edge of town with the mountain ranges beyond. They were given a spacious room that had a balcony from which they had a panoramic view of hill and dale. Gretchen was enchanted. "We can be happy here, Martin!" she exclaimed.

"I can be happy with you anywhere," he replied, folding her into his arms. This time she let him kiss her, a tentative, searching kiss, to which she responded cautiously.

They unpacked and went down to take Winnie for a long walk through town, stopping at a licensed shop for a bottle of good wine from Hunter Valley, a St. Semillon that Riley favored. They drank it with their dinner at the inn, and the talk that went back and forth between them was as lively and easy as if they were old friends.

When they got back to their room it was an animated Gretchen who stopped Riley from switching on the lights and whispered in his ear, daring him that this was it, now or never. It did not occur to him to argue. Within minutes they were in bed, under the covers, kissing and caressing and clinging to each other until, when they let go, they realized they had been making love.

Gretchen, relaxed with her arms under her head, looked up at Riley. "This is soooh good! I feel wonderful. Young! You, too, Martin!"

He laughed, turning to lie beside her. "Who said we're not young? We have a whole new life ahead of us!" He stroked her cheek.

She turned to her side also. "Oh, Martin, let's think that! Do you really believe there's a new life ahead for us? A good life?"

He pulled her close. "Believe it," he said, and kissed her.

They left early the next morning, heading straight back to Sydney. Gretchen was restive. She felt she had to say something that was important, but she didn't quite know how to begin or how to phrase it.

It was Riley who broke the silence. "Gret, we went to Canberra to solve a major problem for you. We haven't done it, have we? Never mind why not. The point is, it's become *our* problem. So what now?"

"Yes," she agreed fervently. "You're so right, Martin. Our problem, as you call it, is still there. I can't live a happy life with you here without ever seeing my children or my family again. You mentioned a third alternative; this is the time to tell me. Don't wait until I stumble upon it on my own."

He nodded. "It's been very much on my mind, not just today, but for some time. There's a service station up ahead. Why don't we stop there? We need petrol anyhow. Then take a walk. Winnie will be grateful too."

The stop ahead off the Western Motorway had a picnic area and footpaths meandering off into the countryside. They kept the dog on its leash and started walking.

Riley spoke first. "We have to step back and view the situation more calmly. The shock of what happened to you in Jakarta will reverberate for some time yet, but it shouldn't cause us to remain tied to it emotionally forever. Let me ask you a question: What would you have done if the plane were an American plane, and it crashed in America?"

"Well, of course I would have run to the airline and the phones and called everybody to say 'Hey, I wasn't on that flight. I'm alive!'"

"Right. So the problem is not the crash itself, but where and how it happened, isn't it? It was that place and the circumstance you found yourself in that made you run instinctively. Were you afraid?"

"Oh, yes! I don't think anybody there would have believed me. Not with that whole business of Anthea and the Hong Kong episode behind me. We've been over that before, Martin!"

"Yes, we have. Do you still think you made the right decision?"

"Absolutely!"

"I agree. Your instinct served you well. So we have nothing to blame ourselves for on that score, do we?"

She shook her head.

"Then the next point is how you deal with your family about this. Remember, you've done nothing wrong; you were in a terrible fix, and you came through alive. Before we go on, can't we be grateful for that? Can't we believe you were saved for something?"

"I do. I was." She took his hand and pressed it. "You know that."

"Good. Now, to your family. The stark reality of it is that they had no reason to think that you didn't die in that crash. They've mourned you already and begun taking care of your affairs. Suppose that just about now they heard from the U.S. embassy in Australia that you showed up there, alive and well, that for some lucky reason you ran off that fated plane at the last moment before take-off. What would they feel?"

"Relief, I hope. No, I know. They'd be happy."

"Of course. Overwhelmingly so. But would it remain just a tight little family secret, do you think? Or, given the public persona of your brother, for instance, would the press get wind of it?"

"The press! It'd be all over the papers!" she groaned. "I've been aware of that all along. They'd hound us! And the Indonesians would get into the act! And I couldn't prove my innocence! That's just the point, Martin. I might as well have reported myself alive in *Jakarta*!"

"Precisely. We're back to square one. And once again I applaud you for your instinctively correct action yesterday. It is important that we deal with the reality of the situation. Things are as they are, not as we wish them to be." He put his arm around her shoulder. "That's the way I've been seeing it ever since I heard your full story. You can't undo what's done. Now, please listen carefully. You can still see your family, you can still live a full life, but you'd do that as a new you." He stopped walking and looked at her squarely.

"But how, Martin?" she wailed. "How can I be *new*? I am who I am!"

"You are not who you *were*. You must realize that. Your new life begins there. That kind of change is not as complicated as you might think. In my business I've had some experience in helping create new lives for people who came over to our side."

"Defectors and such? But they *gave up* their families for it, didn't they? I couldn't do that, don't you see?"

"I see what you mean, but it doesn't follow that you can't see your sons or your brothers ever again. You can and you shall. As the new you."

"You keep saying 'the new you.' How, Martin?"

"How, indeed. By your own doing! You're already halfway there! You're Cosima Herter, remember? You thought of that yourself. And you are ideally situated here in Australia, where people speak your language and you can live in a huge metropolis where people mind their own business. Nobody will give you a second look. You're safe in your anonymity. That's the base we work from to achieve the same end as if you had barged in at the American embassy, spilled your guts to them, and taken the consequences."

Gretchen's gaze wandered to the distant hills. She was still holding Riley's hand. At last she looked at him and nodded gravely. "Yes. I see it now." She leaned over and kissed him. "Thank you, Martin."

"All right." He kissed her back. "This is the first step, then. It's going to be a long journey, but maybe there'll be some shortcuts."

"*Shortcuts?* Such as?"

"Fiona. She'll be here at Christmas. She's the one we have to confide in. She'll have ideas. You'll see."

── CHAPTER TWELVE ──
Fiona

It became apparent very soon after they arrived home that they would have to take Miss Adelaide into their confidence, at least to some degree; and while it didn't have to be the whole story in every detail, the salient parts of it would have to be disclosed to her. Not only was it the right thing to do, as they agreed even before they pulled into the driveway, but it was distasteful to think they would have to deceive this trusting old friend day in and day out for heaven knows how long.

They asked her over for tea at Riley's house. Miss Adelaide, who had heard the car pull in next door but assumed it was only Riley returning, was dumbstruck to see Gretchen there too.

Joyfully, she embraced her. When she heard that "Canberra wouldn't work; I'm back for good," she told Riley that that's exactly what she'd been hoping, that he would see reason and keep this woman here. To Gretchen she said, "And that's true for you, too, my dear. You're right for each other."

Martin raided the fridge, and with the two women helping they had a cold supper of roast beef and salad. Miss Adelaide rushed over to her house and came back with a bottle of French champagne that had been lying in her fridge "waiting for an occasion," and this was it. They toasted love and friendship and life, each with clinking of glasses and hearty draughts that in the end brought color to the women's cheeks.

Miss Adelaide seemed to assume that Gretchen would move in with Riley; and she agreed to call him Martin from now on.

"Actually," Gretchen said, "we'd rather we kept the current arrangement going for a while yet, if you wouldn't mind?"

"Right," Riley cut in. "It's Fiona, you see. She'll be coming at Christmas again, and we thought it best to wait until she's here before we...well, sort of formalize things, you see."

"I don't see at all. They way I know Fiona, she'll be delighted to see you two wanting to make a go of it!"

"There's more to it than that," Gretchen said. "Miss Adelaide, you need to know that I'm in a bit of trouble with my...recent background, so to speak. That's why I thought visiting the American embassy would help. I was quite unsure, and at the last moment didn't go in to see them." She sighed. "Martin, do you want to tell her?"

"Yes. Gretchen's situation is very confidential, Miss Adelaide, as you will realize as soon as I have told you. And you must promise to keep it that way."

"Spy stuff, is it? You can trust me. Mum's the word."

"Wish it were that simple. The long and the short of it is that, officially, Gretchen is dead. Died in that Indonesian plane crash back in September, except that she ran off the plane just before take-off because she was feeling ill. That simple act meant life for her. Naturally, the Indonesians would be suspicious, thinking she had a bomb in her suitcase and ran to save her own skin. Poor girl, she's been running away from that trouble ever since." Riley took Gretchen's hand.

"My God!" Miss Adelaide clutched her hands to her chest.

"Yes. Once on the run, she couldn't stop, of course. The die had been cast. She fled to Singapore, and from there to Australia. I was with her from that point on, even though we had run into each other a few times along the way, starting in Hong Kong. The rest you know."

"My God," Miss Adelaide said again, her hands sinking into her lap. "What are you going to do?" She turned to Gretchen.

"My first thought was to make a clean breast of it to my own people at the embassy. On the way down yesterday, it occurred to me that that might not solve anything at all. I might not even be believed." She looked at Miss Adelaide. "What would you have done in my position?"

Miss Adelaide had caught herself now. "My dear girl, I've been on the run myself once or twice. It never pays to look back, you know. Lot's wife, pillar of salt." She took Gretchen's hand. "Steady on now, is my advice. Time is on your side. Solutions will offer themselves."

"Exactly my point," Riley agreed. "Time is what she needs. Steady, as you say. A certain sameness, routine, familiarity, blending in. What that means in detail is what we should discuss now."

He left the rest of the bubbly to the women and poured himself a stiff scotch. Sipping from it, he discoursed on what he saw as the most suitable way to bridge the time until Fiona's arrival, a mere five weeks or so away. Would Miss Adelaide be willing to keep Gretchen as her boarder? The answer was such a heartfelt yes, as if that were the most natural thing in the world, and Gretchen nearly burst into tears. Miss Adelaide then suggested that if she let it drop here and there that the "young lady" was a niece of hers, in Australia for an extended stay, it might even be better all around. Gretchen threw her arms around her neck and said, "I wish it were really so!" Whereupon Miss Adelaide declared her to be her "honorary niece" and said that she wished to be called "Auntie."

Riley saw the discussion slip away from him into some emotional quagmire. He felt it necessary, he said, to consider the practical side of it. Steps needed to be taken soon, although not before Christmas, to change Gretchen's legal status in Australia from tourist to legal resident. As luck would have it, he could call upon a mate who worked in the immigration department to help them cross that bridge when they came to it. Also, it might not be a bad idea to have Gretchen join the art community in some fashion, as a volunteer, perhaps, until she could get a work permit, that too to be obtained with the help of the aforementioned mate. Miss Adelaide said nonsense, she often hired help now and again for short periods; fetch and carry though it mostly was, she could envision Gretchen being a real help in displaying and selling her art, at the Sydney collective, for instance, and also here at home. There was much work. Would that do? she asked.

Perfectly! Gretchen exclaimed.

Riley said perhaps they could find a way to offset Gretchen's lodging costs with what she would earn for her work, arriving at a zero equation that would not run afoul of immigration and tax laws. If there was one thing they needed to avoid, it was the mere appearance of skirting the law.

There was agreement all around. Clinking of glasses for the final dregs. And so to bed. In different quarters.

In the days following, Riley had telephone conversations with his daughter in London. At first it seemed that Fiona had plans for the Christmas and New Year holidays, seeing that both began on Thursdays this year, thus creating two successive long weekends. Roger, that wicked vet from Truro, had dangled the joys of an Austrian skiing holiday in front of her impressionable eyes. Riley let it go unchallenged for the time being.

When he called back a couple of days later, he asked if there were any way that the skiing holiday could be put off until January. There was a rather important matter for which her presence in Sydney was...uh...very nearly indispensable.

"What kind of matter, Father? Don't be cryptic with me. Are you all right? Is it your health?"

"My health couldn't be better, Fi. It's more than that. Good news, actually."

"Out with it!"

"I've met a woman...."

"You've what?"

"A woman, Fi. Let me finish. I've been around her since Hong Kong, in a way. She's my age. We're serious about one another, but there are some difficulties, not to say complications, for which we need your presence. It can't be done over the phone, if you're wondering."

"I'm wondering all right! Is it her health, then?"

"In a manner of speaking; although not physical, mind you."

"I'm minding! If not physical, is it mental? Is she a bit off?"

Now he had to laugh. "Nothing of the sort. She's got a very keen mind. She's tall, blond, and beautiful. You'll see."

"What's her name?"

"Uh...Margaret."

"Uh Margaret? You're not sure?"

"I don't call her that, is why the *uh*, Fiona."

"What *do* you call her, Father?"

"Look here, can we leave it for the time being?"

"Certainly. I'll tell Roger *he's* off, skiing over Christmas. I'll be topless on Manly Beach, instead. Should I bring Roger?"

"I can't tell you not to, but it would complicate matters."

"Not to worry. Roger hates Australia. For what you're doing to the dingoes. Not to mention your crocs. I'll come alone."

"There's a good girl."

"Father? Is there a picture I can have, of you and her?"

"I think I can oblige, yes."

"Good. She better look like a fiftyish woman who is tall and blond and beautiful, and not off." She sent him a kiss and hung up.

The next night she called back to apologize for not being "nice." "Of course it's good news, as you said, Father. It just came as such a surprise. It's a load off my shoulders, too, having somebody close by looking after you. Have you thought of her name yet?"

"Gretchen."

"Ah! Margaret-Gretchen. Got it. German, is she?"

"American."

"American is better. Much."

"Fiona! You just got through apologizing for not being nice."

"You're right. I'm sorry. It's the education you and Mum gave me. St. Trinian's. Beastly. Roger feels much the same way."

"About what? And you didn't go to any St. Trinian's. Council school and London University, that's what you are. Look what it made you! Be proud! And, say, does it really hurt that much that I might get hitched?"

A moment's silence. Then, "I'm so used to looking after you...."

"There'll be plenty more for you to look after. We're in a bit of a muddle. When can you be here?"

"Oh, Father." She sighed. "I've been looking at my schedule. I can be there by twenty-one December. A Sunday. I'd leave Saturday."

"Perfect. Thank you, Fi."

"How's Winnie? With her, I mean?"

"Great chums, both ways. Now, sweet Fi, relax. Be good."

"Right. And if I can't be good, I'll be careful."

"I love you, Fi. Always will. Okay? Okay."

To her own great surprise the ensuing weeks flew by for Gretchen. Summer was coming, and with it the Christmas season. Everything and everyone was busy. She forgot about Thanksgiving until Riley showed her some ads in the paper about several restaurants advertising "real turkey dinners" for American ex-patriots.

She grimaced. "No, thank you. I'm no glutton for punishment. This is one holiday I'd rather not focus on, if you don't mind."

Riley didn't mind. Instead he suggested they take the weekend for a trip north to one of the beach resorts, while they were not yet touristy; and the water would be just perfect now. They could rent a cabin. Winnie would love to come along.

"Well," Gretchen laughed, "if Winnie would love to come along then we mustn't disappoint him, must we?"

They looked at the map, and Riley moved his finger along Highway 1 past Newcastle and Taree until it came to rest at the south end of a national park. "Hat Head," he said, "at the point where the scenic drive meets the water; Crescent Head. Small place, but safe beaches and lots of nature. They have cabins for rent. Do you think you'd like that?"

Gretchen knew what he meant by that. "We'd be private, wouldn't we?"

"Very."

"Let's make it a long weekend?" The unmentionable Thanksgiving Thursday was on her mind. "Could we leave Wednesday?"

Wednesday it was. Martin called and reserved a room at a small beachside retreat by name of "Head's Rest." "Is this where you rest your weary?" Gretchen chuckled. Martin just smiled back.

The place turned out to be a pleasant surprise: Low-slung thatched-roof bungalows spreading out finger-like from a main lodge. Nice. Because they had a dog, they were given an outside location on one of the fingers just this side of where gentle dunes led to the sea.

There was not much unpacking to do. It was hours yet until dinner, so they decided to explore the beach. Barefoot and in shorts, T-shirts, and sun hats, they set out, Winnie running ahead excitedly. It was a glorious afternoon, the sun still quite warm. They walked holding hands.

The beach they were on was crescent-shaped, the water so clear that their toes stirred flurries of sand, and so shallow they could wade in for yards off shore and not have it go above their knees. The whole bay seemed part of a lagoon, with outcroppings of rocks standing like sentinels here and there.

"Wonderful." Gretchen stood breathing in deeply. "I'm so happy!"

"Really!" Riley put his arm around her waist, looking with her at the horizon. "Tell me what you are happy about."

She smiled. "You." She turned and made the tips of their noses touch. "Me. Us. The place here."

He pulled her closer. "The here and now. Our being together."

"Yes," she agreed, and she let him kiss her.

"I love you. Do you love me?"

"Yes."

"Just like that—yes?" He snapped his fingers. "You sure?"

She nodded. "I've been sure about it for some time."

"Have you!" He seemed genuinely astonished at her quick answer.

She took his face in her hands and said, "Martin, I can't imagine my future without you. I simply can't imagine it. That was the one real reason I pulled back from going ahead with my plan in Canberra."

"I know you said that back in Canberra," he said. "No second thoughts since?"

"None. Only first thoughts, stronger by the day."

Martin picked up a piece of driftwood and threw it for Winnie, who splashed after it like a dolphin rising in and out of the water. "We've got some decisions to make, you know. I'd like us to be very clear how we're going to handle the future."

"What kind of decisions? Marriage? If I dare say the word."

"Ideally and ultimately, yes. There maybe some formidable hindrances to overcome. That's why I want Fiona here."

"Your daughter is, what, twenty-six? With all due respect, what wisdom can she impart to us, her elders?"

"Not wisdom so much as insight. She is wiser than her years, and she has a grasp of reality, of today, that may put things in a different perspective for us. At any rate, we can use all the help we can get."

"We would have to tell her everything, wouldn't we? More than we've told Auntie Adelaide. It's like concentric circles. Where does it go from there? Who else has to be included?"

"Eventually, members of your family. A select few at first, more as the circles widen. Our aim must be to return you to the bosom of your family, in a manner of speaking."

She took his arm and looked him squarely in the eyes. "Martin! Do you know what you are saying? Deliver me to the bosom of my family, to use your quaint expression? Where would that leave you? 'Mission accomplished?'" She threw a mock salute.

"It leaves me with a woman who is free, not a fugitive who is sheltered by me and therefore dependent on me. A woman who can marry me if she wants to hitch her wagon to mine. A woman who chooses me freely."

Gretchen threw her arms around his neck. "I *am* the woman who chooses you freely. It's just a matter of getting our two wagons hitched!" She managed a smile as tears welled up.

"Right." He kissed her wet cheek. "That's the job ahead, isn't it? Shall we?" He led her out of the water.

Back in their room they fed the dog and let him find a curling-up place. Then they had a shower and went to bed to make love. Afterwards they were too comfortable to dress and go out to eat. The usual picnic basket from Miss Adelaide was still plentiful, and Martin had bought a Hunter Valley wine at the last petrol station. They toasted their good fortune in having three full days ahead of them.

Thanksgiving was not mentioned once.

In mid-December Fiona had some bad news as she was talking to her father: Peter Allard had died. Lisa, his daughter, had called, and Fiona felt more or less obliged to attend the services, which would take place the following Sunday in Thame, near Oxford. That was the weekend she would have arrived in Sydney. Fortunately, the airline ticket was open-ended and could be changed without trouble.

When he had digested the news, Riley said he understood. Yes, Fiona should be there and attend the services. After all, Peter had been an old and trusted friend of his mother's; during her years with the Service in London, Peter had been her landlord at that row house on Nemo Lane where he had rooms to let after his own wife died. Meg and Peter had become close confidants and companions, but never lovers, Riley was sure.

"You're quite right, Fi. One of us should do the honors. You, in this instance."

"Yes. I think Gram would have wanted us to."

They realized as they continued talking about it that Fiona's trip would have to be postponed, because the bad news was two-pronged: Her boss at the bank had looked with displeasure at her two-week absence just at the time when the bank was in the middle of preparations for the Euro conversion a year hence, with the pound sterling not yet joining in. As Fiona explained it, they had to plan two contingencies, pound in and pound out, with all that that entailed; not to mention the enormous bother of the "Y2K" problem looming just ahead.

"What are you saying, that you can't come at all?"

"No, Father, that's not what I'm saying. I will come, but very likely not before the second half of January. By that time I'll have some unused holidays due me from this year, so they'll have to let me use them. Also, all the people who are taking Christmas and New Year holidays now will be back by then."

"I see. So we'll put your visit off by a month, is what it means."

"Hope you don't mind. It'll go quickly. How's your ladyfriend?"

"Anxious to meet you."

Fiona laughed. "Anxious? So now she'll be relieved; it'll be another month before she'll need to be anxious again!"

Her father laughed too and said they'd talk again Christmas Day.

Fiona was right: The time did go quickly, so much so that neither Christmas nor New Year were sentimental downers. For Gretchen the beginning of the antipodean summer was such a novelty and so different from her Christmas past that she threw herself with carefree abandon into the activities Riley had lined up.

First, though, the religious part: The three of them, Miss Adelaide included, went to High Mass on Christmas Eve at St. Mary's Cathedral. The service was a grand, joyful, uplifting event, with much familiar music and pageantry, making Gretchen misty-eyed remembering the many happy Christmas holidays she'd had as a child and as a mother. Riley, ever sensitive, sought her hand and pressed it.

Miss Adelaide cooked for them on Christmas Day, a true Scandinavian feast, with roast goose and smorgasbord. Riley made a punchbowl, and afterwards they all played poker at Riley's place, with Miss Adelaide winning outrageously. Late in the evening Fiona called. They each shouted, wishing her a merry Christmas, then Martin took the call into his room.

Fiona reported on the Allard funeral. The service had been at the old Norman church, before a large congregation of mourners. It had been a moving sermon. Lisa and her husband and their children were very composed, very beautiful. Afterwards came the interment into the frosty ground of the churchyard, and Peter's body was laid to rest next to that of Marjorie, his wife. There was a catch in Fiona's voice as she related the story. She said people were asking about him, "old Pat." Was he ever coming back to pay a visit to his old friends? "When, indeed, Father?" Fiona asked. "This whole Lloyd's business is getting very tiresome. What can they still do to you?"

"About a hundred thousand pounds worth, is what, Fi. You know that. It's cheaper living here."

"With your ladyfriend?"

"Good heavens, Fi, her name is Gretchen. Do you mind?"

"*Gretchen*." Her voice gave away the face she must be making. "Of course. Sorry. No offense."

"Practice it. When will you be coming? A firm date yet?"

"Aye. Saturday, the twenty-fourth. Be there Sunday. Mark it down."

"Aye-aye here, too. What're you doing New Year's eve?"

"Taking a quick trip to Chamonix, skiing. With Roger."

"Roger. Will I ever meet him?"

"I don't know. I'll know better after Chamonix."

Martin whistled. "That crucial, huh? Troubles?"

"Some. Not to worry. Happy New Year, Father. Same to Gretchen."

New Year for Gretchen and Riley was a long beachgoing weekend: Manly, Bondi, Coogee, daytrips with snorkeling and catching waves, and long walks along the water. They talked a blue streak, about everything. Sometimes, in the small hours of the night when thoughts were crowding in on her, she wondered about her past. Was it sinful to enjoy the present? She asked Riley that once; he took her in his arms, holding her.

On Monday, the fifth of January, it was back to work for Gretchen, mostly at the art cooperative. A couple of women running a sculpting workshop needed her, setting things up, fetching this and that. It was interesting, absorbing work, and Gretchen loved it. "Another day, another dollar," she laughed when Martin asked how things were going.

"Good for you," he replied.

"Thanks to you!" She gave him a kiss.

In the last week of January they set out to drive to Sydney's Kingsford-Smith Airport on Botany Bay. Fiona's arrival was slated for noon on

Sunday the twenty-fifth, no doubt about that, as she had called from her stopover in New Delhi the night before. Riley suggested they leave for the airport with plenty of time to spare; this Sunday was part of a holiday, Monday being National Day, with lots of people on the road taking advantage of the long summer weekend. Traffic would be heavy, he said, and so it was. Even so, they still had half an hour to wait before Fiona cleared customs and emerged from the crowd, waving, breaking into a trot when she spotted her father. Riley met her halfway.

She dropped the bag she had slung over her shoulder and embraced him, letting herself be hugged and bussed on the cheek by her father.

"Fiona," he said when they had let go, "I want you to meet my ladyfriend, as you called her: Gretchen Herter."

"Hello!" Fiona stepped forward, smiling, eyes bright. "So nice to meet you at last. How do you do?" She held out a hand.

Gretchen took it. "I'm glad to meet you too, Miss Riley. How was your flight?"

"Fine, thank you. I slept through most of it," she laughed, "even the movies." It was a warm, throaty laugh that drew back her generous mouth and revealed even white teeth. Gretchen liked her instantly.

Riley picked up her bag, a long, round canvas thing stuffed like a sausage. "This all?" he wondered aloud as he hefted it up. Then he followed the women, who had already started toward the exit, already making small talk, smiling, nodding. In the din of airport noise he couldn't hear what they said, but his eyes were on them. How similar they are, he mused. Same height, same body build, same dark-blond hair. Gretchen's hair was cut short, with nary a gray streak, thanks to some clever tinting. Fiona's long and wavy mane was held at the nape by a butterfly clasp. They even walked in similar long-legged strides, arms swinging, and when their heads turned to each other as they talked, it struck him that one could imagine they were mother and daughter. Absurd, laughable. They were of quite different temperaments, as he well knew. Still, it would be nice if they could get along as if they were alike. After all, if he married Gretchen, then Fi would become Gretchen's stepdaughter, wouldn't she? Was that so absurd, so laughable?

They arrived home to a waiting Miss Adelaide, who, inevitably, had tea ready at her house. If Fiona was surprised that Gretchen was lodging there, she didn't show it. She had gone first to her father's house and seen the sofa bed made up for her, as on previous occasions. Returning, freshened up and bearing gifts, she sat down at Miss Adelaide's table.

"These you should have had for Christmas," she said, handing the gifts to her father, to the hostess, and to the "ladyfriend." So labeled on the package sticker. "Go ahead, open them up!"

They all had fun with that. "'Ladyfriend'? How do I know it's for me?" Gretchen chuckled. "Couldn't there be another?"

"Not at all," declared Miss Adelaide. "The only other lady here is I, the old lady. It's you, all right, dearie."

"It says here…" Riley peered as if deciphering the label "… 'for the Old Bugger'.… Can't mean me?"

"Is there any other?" Miss Adelaide said.

"Father, you will be if you don't take that 'bugger' back and open your parcel!" said Fiona.

"Well," he said and went to his pocket, "I have one here that says 'For my darling.' Do I hear any bids?"

"Here!" shouted Miss Adelaide.

Gretchen laughed. "Et tu, Auntie?"

"'Auntie'?" Fiona snatched the parcel from her father's hand and kissed him on the forehead. "What's going on here?"

"That's what we want to discuss with you." Martin said. "Sit down, take some nourishment. You'll need your strength." He poured the wine.

It was a very merry post-Christmas, and instead of "Silent Night" they sang "Waltzing Matilda." Fiona admired her gift, an opal ring that now graced her left ring finger. "Huge! Beautiful! Must have cost you a fortune!"

"It did. Gretchen here chipped in with some of her wages."

"Wages?" She turned to Gretchen. "Is this true? Who are you working for? Not poor Father?"

"For me," said Miss Adelaide. "I'm overpaying her. But she's my niece. What can I do?" she shrugged.

Fiona groaned. "Will you people please tell me what's going on?"

Telling Fiona what was going on took more than that one evening. It took a father-daughter walk the next morning, a Gretchen-Fiona chat over lunch, just the two of them at a Neutral Bay tea room, and the next day an evening drive for the three of them, four counting Winnie, looking for a place to have dinner. They ended up sitting on a stone wall at Kirribilli Point, with a view across Port Jackson toward the scalloped roofs of the opera house, eating fish and chips out of paper bags, drinking beer from the bottle. By that time they were talked out; everything had been gently revealed, thoroughly explained, and somberly rationalized to a largely mute Fiona, who took it all in just as gently and somberly. Now they just sat there, munching, pulling from their bottles, even Gretchen, who didn't much care for beer, let alone without a glass.

A ship was coming in, an ocean liner by the size of it, heading toward the docks by Harbour Bridge. The three of them stared at it, slowly moving their heads as it passed by.

"Bollocks." Fiona spat out the word like something stuck in her craw.

Her father turned his head, eyebrows raised.

"Bollocks, bollocks, bollocks." She didn't take her eyes off the ship. For good measure she said it once more: "bollocks."

"Perhaps you'd care to explain yourself," Riley said. Gretchen looked at her too.

"Perhaps I'd better." Fiona jumped off the wall, facing the two of them. "This is one big, glorious, royal, imperial cockup." She swung her beer bottle in an all-inclusive arc.

"Ah." Riley threw back his head as if everything had become perfectly clear now. "How good of you, Fi, to give us the benefit of your wisdom."

"Wisdom?" His daughter glared at him. "There has been pitifully little of that!" She stood there in her shorts and a cotton shirt that was open to a hint of a cleavage, bare legs defiantly apart, her hair teased by the gentle breeze coming off the water. "What a mess!"

"Mess," Riley deadpanned to Gretchen, "is the same as cockup."

Gretchen heaved herself off the wall and went over to Fiona, put her arm around her neck, and drew the young woman toward her. She placed a kiss on her cheek. "I know, Fiona. You're right. I understand how you feel." When Fiona let her head sink to Gretchen's shoulder, she patted her back. "There, there. We're burdening you with so much. And you care so much."

"I do," came a moan, "I really do." When she lifted her head to glare at her father, she said in a thick voice, "What did you expect from me, Father? That I would have the answers for you? Huh?" Two big tears were rolling down her cheeks.

"Of course not," Gretchen answered for him. "It's not fair to unload this on you all at once, and so much of it. But we had to tell you, don't you agree? Or would you rather not have known?"

Fiona shook her head. She put her beer bottle in the sand and took a tissue out of her pocket, dabbing off her tears and blowing her nose.

Riley jumped off the wall, making Winnie take the same jump, since he was on a leash. "Look," Riley said, and took his daughter's face in his hands. "Learning about what has happened to Gretchen and how I got involved with her, and she and I with one another, is essential for you. Cockup or not, that's where we are. The three of us together. Because you are part of us." Stroking her cheek, he let go of her face.

Gretchen came closer and embraced the two of them. Both she and Fiona were smiling now, holding back tears. The dog was dancing around the three of them, tying them together with his leash.

Fiona had to laugh. "It's four of us, Father! Look at Winnie!" She bent down to unhook Winnie, who raced off toward the water.

Riley commanded him back instantly and, tying him up again, said, "So, what's the general consensus? Should we leave it for tonight, and reconvene tomorrow?"

"No!" Fiona shook her head resolutely. "We're having it out now, tonight, no matter how long it takes."

"I agree," said Gretchen.

"Aye. Motion carried." Riley started walking. "Let's go home and put the kettle on."

"What about Auntie?" Gretchen asked.

"We shan't invite her in, this time. This is strictly family."

They sat around the dining room table with strong coffee that they knew would keep them awake. Gretchen found the torte she had bought at the French bakery the day before, still in its wrapping, and in the course of the night they finished it off between the three of them.

Earlier, while they were still setting the table, Fiona asked her father, "What was in the envelope I brought you from Lisa?"

"It came from Peter Allard's estate, didn't it? What did Lisa say it was?"

"She had no idea. It has Gram's return address on it, and was addressed to Peter. Peter, in turn, left it with his personal papers."

"Did she open it, do you think?"

"I asked her that. She said she hadn't, and wouldn't. She guessed it was personal, between your mother and her father. That's why you'd be the obvious recipient, she told me. The two original parties are dead."

"So they are." Martin shook his head. "I've only peeked into the envelope once. It contains papers. I recognized my mother's handwriting." He shook his head again. "I'd rather deal with it another time, if you don't mind."

"Before I go back to London?"

"I can't promise. I'm not keen on rummaging in the past. I'll let you know eventually. You're curious, of course?"

"It's more than curiosity. I loved Gram too."

"I know you did, sweets." He squeezed her shoulder. "I know."

The conversation around the coffee table grew livelier by the cupful. When the last crumb of cake had been devoured, they wondered how hungry they must have been and how their stomachs would have to pay for their sins. Riley said there was a natural remedy for that, and produced a bottle of cognac. He insisted they each take a good dram for penance.

"Well," he said putting his glass down, "where did we leave off?"

"Fiona was telling us about the mess we're in," said Gretchen.

Fiona looked down at her hands; her fingers were twirling the glass. "It's not my place to tell you, actually. You're my elders." She looked up. "If you can't see it, what am I to do?"

"Can't see what, Fi? Be specific." Her father met her gaze. "And never mind that 'elders' business. That's just a cop-out. Tell us what you think. You have all the facts."

Fiona glared at him. It was apparent that she strained to contain her emotions. "Is that what you want, what I think about the *facts*? Is that because without my telling you, you wouldn't know how to deal with them? What is that, some kind of obtuseness that gags you when you get old?" She didn't wait for an answer. "Here you are, living the hermit life in this fairytale cottage in faraway Sydney! You,

Father, still hiding from the wrath of those bleeding sods at Lloyd's, and you, Gretchen, in denial about what really happened to you! Troubled now, are you, you poor blighters? Cor blimey, you jolly well should be!" She blew away a strand of hair that hung over her nose.

Gretchen kept quiet. Riley said evenly, "It would help, Fi, if you could be more specific, as I asked earlier."

"All right! All right! More specific. Let's take you first, Father. You still have friends over there in England who ask about you, who care. How many friends have you made here, huh? Give me a number."

"Well, I have mates...."

"Who? The publican? The vet? The postman? Not mates, Father; it's chums I'm asking for. People who knew you and Mum. Before you grew that silly mustache. People you'd go to Burgundy with, or to the test matches, and to each other's birthdays. They are still there. Where are you, pray tell?"

Riley pinched the bridge of his nose. "You're a bit unfair there, Fi. That was when your Mum was alive. And before Lloyd's."

"Unfair? How old are you now? Fifty. What are you going to do for the next fifty years, go into perpetual mourning? Live off your meager pension? How long do you suppose that detective work is going to last that your erstwhile employers are throwing your way like a bone to an aging dog? Two years? Three? And then what? The dole?"

"Your father is a fine man, Fiona. You shouldn't talk to him like that!" Gretchen was red in the face.

"You keep out of it, Gret. I'm coming to you next. So then, what's your answer, Father?"

Martin heaved a sigh. "I don't have one. I've thought about it, God knows I have, but I don't know how to get out of it. The spot I'm in. You're right there, Fi."

"But you expect me to show you an easy out!" Shaking her head, she turned to Gretchen. "And you. What in the world do you think you're doing, running away from your problem? And you keep running and running...."

Riley interjected, "Hold it! I won't have you using that tone of voice with her. Gretchen's running away is the smartest thing she did, beginning with that airplane. All the other running follows from that!"

"That was then, Father, and this is now. Do you want to keep running, Gretchen? Or is this the end of the line, you and Martin, cozy together, letting the world pass you by?"

Gretchen was a big flustered. "You know I tried to take my case to the American authorities—"

"Hah! The government! Bureaucrats are going to solve your problem! Is that it?"

"Now, see here, Fi. You're out of line now!"

"Out of line, Father? You keep calling her *her*, this woman, mother of two grown sons! You say it's love, but what do you call *each other*? Honey? Sweetheart? I hear you oh-so-properly using your Christian names, but I'm still waiting for you to use a pet name or an endearment, either of you! Isn't that what lovers are supposed to do?"

Gretchen spoke. "We are very private about our feelings, Fiona. Your father is the man I've come to love. You might as well know that. And Martin," she held up a hand when she saw him starting to speak, "please, no matching public confessions. *We* know, and that is enough." She turned to Fiona. "Yes, I am the mother of grown sons. As Martin loves you, his daughter, so I love my sons. That love is a two-way street. There are times when we, your *elders*, need to hear from you. We seek your opinion, your assessment of our situation. That's why we're talking here. We value what you have to offer, good or bad."

Gretchen's motherly tone had an effect on the young woman. "I'm sorry. I'm a bit of a beast, sometimes. Particularly when I'm frustrated by something I care deeply about. It's just that you can't see...."

"Can't see what? Tell us! For heaven's sake, Fiona, speak up!"

"All right! I will!" She puffed away at that hair again. "You are sitting here on Cloud Nine, two happy lovebirds, but those clouds are made of air, when they vanish you'll have to come down to earth! Don't you see! Here it is: I think you're fooling yourselves. Your problem is not solved, is it! And neither is my father's. He should be back in England making a new life for himself, and Lloyd's be damned. And you, Gretchen, should go to England with him. You have a son in Frankfurt with General Motors? You should get into a car and drive to the continent and show up on your son's doorstep and say, 'Here I am. I'm not dead. Let me tell you all about it.'" She slapped her hand on the table and leaned back, looking from her father to Gretchen and back. "That's what I would expect if you were my mum."

Martin caught himself first. "Well. I daresay you may be right. The thought's crossed my mind, too. Way back in my mind, however. There are too many pressing things up front to deal with first. All those little steps that make up a journey. Perhaps this is the time to look at the intended arrival. What do you think, Gret?"

"I don't know." She was clearly stunned. "Just get on the plane and fly to England? Then drive to Germany, just like that?" She snapped her fingers. "My passport! What if I find at immigration that my passport's been canceled? And everything comes unraveled?"

"That's a question you need to address, then, isn't it?" Fiona said. "I suppose leaving Australia is not the problem. Arriving in England may be. Still, you'd be on British soil, and British law would apply. You have done nothing wrong, have you, Gretchen? That'll come out in the end, and you can live your life again."

"Oh, God...." Gretchen buried her face in her hands.

Riley reached over and gently took her hands away, making her see his earnest face. "I believe she's right, Gret. On both counts."

"Do you?" Her eyes were rimmed with red. "Will you go to England with me, Martin?"

"You know I will. All the way." He groped in his jacket pocket for the leather pouch that held his cigars. The woman watched and exchanged glances as he cut the tip, wet the end, snapped the match flame, and drew the first blue smoke. "It may be madness, but at least we can apply some method to it. We can't just pick up and go to Europe, can we?" He looked for consent and got nods. "Well, then, I compliment you, Fi, for being the catalyst that brings about change. And I agree with you, Gret, that it can't be done just like that." He snapped his fingers. "It needs some preparation, some thinking through, for the scheme to work. Fiona, see here: You're employed in a responsible position in your bank, you're doing Euro work, whatever that is, and quite possibly you could wrangle a trip to Brussels, say. Couldn't you?"

Fiona said, "I've done that before. Yes. I see what you're getting at."

"Do you? Gretchen has the address and telephone number of her son—George, is it?—yes, George Goodridge. In care of Opel, Germany, easy to find on the map."

"It's in Rüsselsheim, near Mainz, just south of Frankfurt," said Gretchen. "I can show it to you on a map."

"Here's how I see it. You call the chap first, of course. From London, from your bank. That's always impressive. Is he an impressionable young man, Gret?"

"Oh, yes. I can show you a picture, Fiona. Perhaps we can have it duplicated and you can take it with you!"

"There you are. Tell him whatever you can think of that will sound plausible and tell him that on your next trip to the continent you'd like to speak to him. Of course, at that point no hint of your true intentions."

"Hmm." Fiona smiled. "Some scheme. Sounds dishy."

"I think George is engaged," said Gretchen.

"So is Fiona," said Riley. "No problem there."

"Roger may be the problem," Fiona grimaced.

"Can we leave the Roger problem off the table, please?" Riley had been told by Fiona that it hadn't gone all that well in Chamonix, and she'd asked him to keep it under his hat for the time being. "We're talking about a simple, cautious first contact where you act as a go-between for Gretchen and her son. Do you think you're up to it?"

"Certain. But it's not the contact per se that's difficult, it's what I tell the son about his not-so-dead mother. What if he wants to dash off to London to see her, and you're not there yet? Point one. And point two, how do I prove to him that she's alive? With a photograph of her holding up a copy of *The Australian* with today's date?"

"Nothing quite so crass," her father said. "That sounds like a ransom note is forthcoming. No, we have to be a little bit more subtle, and quite as believable. How about having him call here and talk to her?"

Gretchen cut in. "The way I know Georgie, he'll get on the next plane to Sydney and show up here in person. No, no. Nothing gets done until we are in London. I'll have to insist on that."

"All right." Riley nodded. "I agree."

"Perhaps I could soften it up a bit. The idea of going to Brussels, which we at the bank do quite often and for which I could wrangle an invitation to come along, that seems to present the possibility of taking a half-day off to drive down to—what's that place called, again?"

"Rüsselsheim, with an umlaut. I'll write it down for you. His home and business addresses."

"Right. Just exploring, as it were." Fiona rubbed her hands gleefully. "I love it. I may have inherited your spy bug, Father."

"There's no such thing, Fi. At any rate, you wouldn't be spying."

She looked at him mischievously out of the corners of her eyes. "If you say so."

"I do. And I thank you—I mean we thank you, don't we Gret, for the great help you've been after all, Fiona!"

"And for the help you've promised to come! I'm touched. I truly am. Thank you, dear Fiona."

Soon after that they decided it was time to retire. They hugged each other, and Gretchen stole across quietly to her lair at Aunt Adelaide's.

Tucked in and pulling the duvet up to her chin, Gretchen felt for the first time that she was nearing the end of the dark tunnel that had been her life since Jakarta. A ray of hope. Pray that it be so! Dear Martin! What had Fiona said, that they didn't have terms of endearment for one another? Oh, yes they did. I love you, Martin. I love you, I love you....

She woke from a deep and restful sleep. Her clock showed it was near ten o'clock. She pulled the curtain. Riley's car was not there. When she went to Aunt Adelaide's kitchen, the breakfast table was set for her, with a note: Fiona, it said in the old lady's spidery handwriting, had wanted to see Melbourne, and Pat—crossed out—Martin was taking her to the station. Adelaide was riding along to be dropped off at the market, where P—crossed out again—Martin could pick her up on the way home. Gretchen was to help herself. Sorry there was no bacon.

Gretchen smiled. She'd have some quick juice and coffee and then take a luxurious bath. It occurred to her as she lay in the bubbles that this day was the last one of her "forties;" tomorrow she'd turn fifty. Many a time in Los Angeles during the months after she turned forty-nine she had imagined what she would want to do on her "Big Five-O." Ignore it? Or have a party? She had felt like ignoring it.

What a change! Look at her now! What would Martin say?

— CHAPTER THIRTEEN —
The Birthday

It was after their midnight gabfest, when Gretchen had left to go back to her room in the house next door, that Fiona, coming out of the bathroom, spoke to her father. "Would you mind awfully if I went to Melbourne tomorrow?"

"Melbourne?" Riley, astonished, looked at his daughter.

"Well," she stood before him in her pajamas, a towel still on her arm, "I've been to Perth, and to Adelaide, but never to Melbourne. It seems a shame, Melbourne being so close and all, and such a cultural center, or so one hears. I thought I'd go tomorrow, stay overnight, and return Friday night."

"You're leaving for home Saturday," Riley said. It was true, had it not been for his brothers inviting their niece to their cities of Perth, way over in western Australia, and to Adelaide, in southern Australia, chances were that Fiona would not have seen much of Australia at all on her previous visits, even though he had taken her to Brisbane once and of course to the Blue Mountains and the beaches. It seemed reasonable to give her a couple of days for herself, away from the old people she was stuck with here. He said, "I suppose that wouldn't be a problem. As long as you're back on time. Do you have any ideas about what to do or see? I'm afraid I don't know anyone in Melbourne who could advise you."

"Father!" She put an arm around him and kissed his cheek. "Not to worry. I'll find my way around. I'm a grown woman."

"So you are." He patted her hand. "Let's see where I have my train schedules. Early morning departure?"

They left shortly after eight o'clock. Miss Adelaide, who had seen them climb into the van, ran out and said that Gretchen was still asleep; should she wake her? When they told her what was going on, she asked for a lift across to Sydney, as she had some shopping to do. Perhaps Riley could pick her up on the way back from the station?

So it went. They told the dog to watch the house and mind the sleeping guest.

The van returned to a radiant and soapy-fresh Gretchen, who rushed out to greet Riley and Adelaide, each with a kiss on the cheek, except in Martin's case where the kiss slipped close to the corner of his mouth.

"Hi ya, girl!" Riley quickly wiped his lips with the back of his hand. Gretchen smiled at him.

They helped carry the groceries into Miss Adelaide's kitchen. Then, back in Riley's house, they talked.

"That was quite a surprise, that note of Auntie's saying that Fiona went to Melbourne. When is she coming back?" Gretchen asked.

"Saturday morning, actually," Riley answered. "I suggest she take the overnight tomorrow and arrive in Sydney with plenty of time to spare to catch her afternoon flight back to England." He added, "Of course, we'll be at the station to take her to the airport and see her off."

"Hmm." Gretchen nodded. "Did you know she was going to go off by herself? Not that I mind."

"No. She sprang it on me last night before she went to bed. Of course, I could see her point. She's done yeoman work here with us old fogies. She's entitled to have some time to herself. Don't you agree?"

"Certainly. It's just that I've grown rather fond of her, and I would have liked more of her company. Selfish of me, I suppose."

"Not at all, dear. I'm glad you two got on so well." He came over and held her by the waist. "It's your birthday, tomorrow, isn't it?"

"My fiftieth! But don't you dare make a fuss over it!"

He smiled. "I shan't. Just a quiet, wonderful excursion of our own." He let go of her hand and got out the leather notebook he carried in his jacket pocket. Pulling out out an envelope, he said, "Here we are. A private weekend all by ourselves."

She took it. It was an envelope with a hotel imprint on the outside. She turned it this way and that.

"Go ahead, open it," he said.

Gretchen smiled at him, shook her head, and took out a letter. It was a reservation form, made out to Mr. and Mrs. Martin O'Patterson Riley of Neutral Bay, NSW. One harbor view suite, arrival 29 January, departure 31 January.

Gretchen gasped. "My goodness, that starts today!"

"Correct. We check in this afternoon and leave early Saturday to pick up Fiona. Not quite two days, but two full nights."

"And now I see—it's the Regent! They have one here, too?"

"I thought it only fair. You said you enjoyed the Hong Kong one."

Gretchen shook her head in disbelief. "Martin! When did you dream all this up?"

Somewhat anxiously, he said, "Of course, we can cancel. But I thought we should do something special, and when Fiona sprang her surprise on me I saw an opportunity for us. I rang them up last night, and this morning on the way back I picked up the confirmation. Do you think it's all right?"

"Of course it is, you knucklehead! It's terrific!" She put her arms around his neck and kissed him. "'Mr. and Mrs. Martin O'Patterson Riley.' How impressive. Did you tell them I'm your mistress?"

"Lucky fellow I am, aren't I?" He laughed and kissed her back.

They had lunch with Miss Adelaide, who quite agreed when they told her of their plans, and said she would be glad to have Winnie to herself again, even if only for two days. Did they know that the dog loved being in her studio? He'd curl up at her feet when she was working, his eyes alert, ears perking up at every sound. Such a trusted companion, he was. Back in her younger days she'd had three dogs, an Airedale, a spaniel, and a setter. All males. When the females around were in heat—watch out, here came the rutters of the neighborhood!

Riley, who had heard all this before, said he hoped Winnie would live up to her expectations and asked if he and Gretchen could now be excused. They still had a little packing to do.

"Go! Go, you two, and have a good time. Shoo!" She waved them off.

On the way across to Sydney, Gretchen, sitting in the van next to Riley, who was driving, became aware of a curious sensation that seemed to spread throughout her body like some kind of low-voltage current that kept her atingle. She looked at Riley. They would make love today, and tomorrow, and she would be very happy....

Correction: *They* would be very happy, because *she* would make *him* happy, and she could not be happy without him being happy.

Riley began to notice. "You're staring at me. Something wrong?"

"On the contrary!" She moved closer to him and put her arm around his neck. "Everything's so right! We'll be happy together."

"Is that a promise, or a prediction?"

"Both," she laughed.

His hand moved to pat her thigh. She gently pushed it away. "Wait. First get us there. Then," she kissed his smiling face, "happiness!"

For happiness it was, plain and pure, to be with him, in every sense of the word, in his presence, in his arms, and she would receive him body and soul. What she felt—she stole a glance at him again, at her man, who was minding the road—was joyful anticipation.

She couldn't remember when—if ever—she had felt that way about Wilfred, her husband of so many years.

She shook her head, half in shame—was it her fault?—and then in acknowledgment of fact: She had not loved Wilfred, not truly, not wholly. She had been a faithful wife to him and a devoted mother to their children, but that was all, and it was not enough. She knew that now.

Yes, she had been happy at the birth of George, and then of Fred, and she had been—still was!—a good mother to the boys.

And yes, also, to the many times she had considered herself fulfilled, content, secure, rewarded—all true. Her life had not been a vale of misery. On the contrary; often, in prayer, she had thought herself blessed and been humbly thankful.

But *happy*? Just dumb-plumb, deep-down *happy*?

The last time she had been so elated was before she became a woman, and it had nothing to do with a man or a boy. It was on the occasion of her tenth birthday. Her family was already living in California. Her father was in his teaching position (not yet tenured), and her other was doing her residency at the UCLA Medical Center. Every free moment, or so it seemed, she had asked to be driven to Will Rogers Park, the place in the hills off Sunset Boulevard where the great cowboy sage and comic had left his ranch, his polo fields, and his stables to the good people of Los Angeles. There, a lanky girl tall for her age, she had fallen in love with horses and learned to ride them and brush them and help saddle them. She had gone on trail rides under towering eucalyptus trees and up through low underbrush on the stony hillsides. There was nothing more exhilarating to her than being on the back of a horse, patting its mane down with her hand, hearing the animal's blustery snorts, and inhaling the dusty smell of its sweat when they returned.

A fervent wish: Would that she had her own horse! Could she?

It was not possible, she was told. Having a horse to look after was too much for a little girl, and besides, they would have to rent or buy a horse trailer to carry it whenever there was a horse show she wanted to enter.

But she didn't care about horse shows! And never, never would she take it anywhere, except here, where its home stables were, and just on these trails and hills! Oh, she would *so* love a horse of her own!

Her birthday had still been weeks away when she began to notice certain signs that something was underfoot. Her parents would both come out to the stables to talk with the trainer, the manager, and the woman who was in charge of the girls' riding classes. When Gretchen slyly chanced upon them in the great rotunda of the stables, the conversation would suddenly stop. Smiles—knowing smiles among the adults, silent smiles to her—would be exchanged, and she was told to go wait outside. Eventually she was taken to see a particular horse, a bay-brown mare with docile eyes and a white star on her forehead, not tall, twelve or thirteen hands maybe, with a smooth, round behind and a sagging belly and the unexciting name of "Maidy."

Then, on her tenth birthday, her parents came to her room early in the morning. They hugged her and kissed her. She was told to put on her riding breeches and boots, not to forget her helmet. Then, after her little brother, Jim, had been picked up for school by his carpool, she was driven to the Will Rogers stables. A cold morning sun was rising over the Santa Monica Mountains as they wound their way along Sunset Boulevard.

"This is your first two-digit birthday, Gretchen," her father said, smiling at her through the rearview mirror. All tense anticipation, she sat in the back of the car, or rather leaned forward, poised to jump out as soon as they arrived. "You won't add another digit until you're a hundred!"

What a joker, her father! A hundred years! She could hardly imagine being twenty. "Yes, Daddy," she smiled back at him.

Her mother, her beautiful mother, reached back and patted her cheek and stroked her hair lightly. "I hope you'll be very happy today, Gretel. You remember *Maidy*, that horse we showed you and talked about? We are giving it to you for your birthday."

Gretchen thought her heart would stand still. A moment later she leaped up and over the seat put her arms around her mother's neck, kissing her wildly. "Oh, thank you, Mummy, thank you, thank you, thank you!" And to her father, "Thank you, Daddy, so-so-so-much!" She kissed him too, and he warded her off, laughing, saying, "I've got to mind the road, sweetheart!"

Now halfway towards those Daddy-promised hundred years, Gretchen shook her head. That scene, that intense feeling of joy, was as fresh now as it had been in those far-gone days, as was the kind of inner glow that she was feeling towards Martin and their coming time together.

If only they could both find happiness…now and always.

It started out as a dream come true, a wish fulfilled. They had a sun-filled room—a "suite" with a step-down section that separated the bedroom from the sitting room. The suite had a view down to the Rocks and the Harbor Bridge on one side, and across to the Opera House on the other. A cruise liner was docked right there at the quay, and yachts and ferries went criss-cross over the waters, leaving wakes that bounced cockleshell sailboats and skiffs like so much flotsam.

It was like Hong Kong's Victoria Harbor all over again. Gretchen was enchanted. "How wonderful! Come look, Martin!"

He stood behind her, his arms around her waist. "Like it?" He kissed her neck.

The door buzzer rang loudly. Riley went to answer it. It was a waiter pushing a cart. Prominently on it was a wine bucket, its contents shielded by a serviette.

Riley directed the waiter to leave it for them at the sitting room table, then signed the chit and sent him off.

"Voilà, madame!" With a flourish he lifted the linen off the bottle. "Champagne, a *vôtre service*!"

Another flourish and the linen came off a centerpiece, revealing a tiered tray with sandwiches, pastries, nuts, and chocolates. Also on the cart were scones and clotted cream, strawberries, jams, and toast.

Gretchen stood speechless, her hand over her mouth.

Riley beamed. "This is not, mind you, a devious attempt to trick you into a birthday party. Not at all. For one thing, your birthday's tomorrow in your country. For another, I have something for you." He turned and scurried off to his suitcase, and came back with a small parcel, wrapped, but not elaborately. "Here you are. I hope you'll find it acceptable."

Gretchen took it, cupping it in her hands, looking at it for a moment before opening it. It was an opal brooch with many golden-flecked stones arranged like a sunflower. Gretchen was visibly moved, her thank-you thick in her throat as she came over and embraced him. "Beautiful, it really is, Martin, my dearest. I'll treasure it." Her face was at his neck, and she knew that she was shedding tears.

"Now, now," he patted her on the back, "it's all right. No tears. There." He lifted her head and kissed her. "Shall we have a toast?" He went to the bottle.

"Oh, yes." She half laughed, dabbing at her tears with the back of her hand. "I'm such a nutcase when it comes to things like this."

He had the cork out of the champagne, and poured the golden liquid into two flutes. He ignored the foam that spilled over the rims, and handed her a glass, clinking it with his. "To us?"

"Yes, to us," Gretchen responded, nodding vigorously.

They sipped. The glasses had been less than half full, so Riley quickly poured some more, this time watching the froth.

"It was a *question*, actually, that you said yes to. Did you notice?"

"Yes, I noticed. And 'yes' is my answer."

"Hmm." He handed her a full glass. "It makes me very happy. As a matter of fact, unexpected as it is when I look back on my recent years, it's almost unbelievable that I should be so lucky." He sought her eyes. "You sure?"

"Yes."

"Unequivocally?"

"Truly and solemnly. Yes."

He raised his glass. "Then, in the light of this—what is the word—affirmation, I pledge to you my love," his hand began to tremble, and his voice had a catch in it as he continued, "now and forever."

"Oh, Martin, put the glass down, you're spilling it!" She put hers down too. "And come to me, you dear old bear!" They kissed.

It became an embrace, so passionate that they scurried off, shedding their clothes in haste, and very nearly bumped heads as they tore the covers off the bed. That made them laugh, and they did all the silly things lovers do, which Gretchen, at lucid in-between moments, registered with mild astonishment before plunging back into the jolly fray.

It was early evening when they returned to the table to devour every last crumb of the edibles, not minding that the champagne had gone stale. They exchanged stupid grins as they did so.

Oh love! Oh life!

Far into the night Gretchen woke from deepest sleep and felt for Riley's presence. She found his place empty.

She sat bolt upright, wide awake now.

Her eyes adapted quickly to the dim illumination that came through the window from the glitter of the city twenty-some stories below.

Riley was not in the room!

Then she noticed a line of light coming from beneath the door to the bathroom.

Relieved but still anxious, she jumped out of bed and ran to the bathroom. "Martin?" She knocked. "Martin, are you all right?"

She heard a muffled reply. "Martin? May I come in?"

The door opened. Riley, with only a towel around his waist, motioned her to come in. His expression was serious, his voice somber.

"Look," he said, pointing to the counter.

Gretchen looked. All she saw were some papers on top of a brown envelope. "Look at what, Martin? Are you all right?"

He nodded and made a resigned motion with his hand.

Gretchen thought he looked pale. "Is it that letter...?"

He nodded again: "I've been a fool. A damn fool. Couldn't leave well enough alone."

"Martin!" Gretchen, standing there naked before him, said sternly. "You have to explain yourself. But not here. Come to bed."

He gave a short, derisive laugh. "You may not want me in bed. Not after you hear what I have to tell you."

"Nonsense. Now you really are being silly." She pointed to the papers. "Whatever it is that upset you, a fool you are for bringing that old business to this occasion. It is *not* going to come between us. You might as well know that now."

He gave a resigned shrug as she turned on her heels and, taking his hand, dragged him back into the bedroom.

Gretchen made sure they were tucked in close to one another, and as she put her hand over his chest she caressed the spot where his heart lay. He was breathing easier now.,

"Tell me what upset you so. Is it that the letter from your mother to her friend?"

"Peter Allard. Yes."

"A confession?"

"Of sorts, yes, but not what you think." He swore under his breath, "I'd promised Fiona I'd read the stuff and tell her what's in it before she flies home. Damn fool idea. I thought that when I woke up I'd take it to the bathroom, go over it in all that quiet, then put it away. I didn't want to spoil our precious time together, you know?"

"Tell me. Start from the beginning."

"I might be well advised not to. Let sleeping dogs lie."

"Come on."

He heaved a heavy sigh. "I ought to burn that letter. Nobody would be any the wiser."

"You're forgetting that you already know. If it's that upsetting to you, then you need to tell me. We're in this together."

There was a long silence from him. Then he spoke in a low voice. "You're quite right. We're in this together." He kissed her forehead. "My mother wrote the letter and attached some papers to it in the months before she died in 1985. She addressed it to Peter, begging him to safeguard it until he decided who to give it to. Peter immediately realized that I was the only logical recipient. In those days I was happily married, Fiona was at school, life was nice and easy. But he didn't pass it on to me then. He may well have forgotten that he still had it as the years went by. He died last December, and it fell into Lisa's hands as she went through his papers. She may have glanced at it, seen that it was not her father's affair but my mother's, and she probably would have given it to me had I been at the funeral. Instead she gave it to Fiona to pass on. And here we are."

"Do you think Lisa read it?"

"I doubt it. It's old mush to her, and she had other, more serious matters to attend to. Fiona was the next best choice."

"Well then, do you think *she* read it?"

"I rather think not. She's a very proper girl, you know. She's loathe to pry into other people's private lives. That's how we brought her up. One spy in the family is enough." He sighed. "On the other hand, she's keen enough to put two and two together, or at least to want to. She'd love to know what's in it."

"I imagine so. Tell me first, then we'll decide what, if anything, to tell her."

"If I do, you may well decide that I'd have been smart to burn the whole damn thing. But by then it'll be too late."

Gretchen said, "Put your feet in the crook of my knees. You're ice cold."

Riley gave a short laugh, and they rearranged themselves so that they were lying face to face now.

In a low voice, barely above a whisper, he began to talk. She let him find his pace, catching his hand in hers, pressing it now and again to let him know she was with him.

It was an extraordinary tale, going back nearly half a century to early April 1946, when a woman subaltern was dispatched to Croydon Airfield near London to receive a young man, a British subject sent there from the British Army Security Branch in the British zone of occupation of defeated Germany. The subaltern's orders were to guide the young man through immigration and customs, and then take him straightaway to Paddington Station and put him on the train to Oxford, where he would be met by another officer and transported to Auldenham Manor in nearby Thame.

"The woman officer in London was my mother. Guess who the young man was." Martin nudged her, but Gretchen just said, "tell me."

"A certain Ian Frazer, born 16 March, 1923, in Pietermaritzburg, Natal, Union of South Africa."

"My father," Gretchen whispered back. She'd suspected it would be him. "I remember him saying he went to Oxford in that year."

"So he did. All arranged by British intelligence, in which my mother was a low-ranking clerk-officer. It was her duty to provide him periodically with chits and vouchers to keep up the pretense that he was a visiting fellow at the manor."

"He read history at Magdalen College," Gretchen said. "Are you saying my father and your mother met back then?"

"Would that that were all. You have to understand that my mother's letter and notes to Peter Allard are a form of confession. She knew she was dying. Peter was the only person she could trust."

"Trust with what?"

"Wait. Let's proceed chronologically. Ian Frazer's visa was for two months. He had to be out of England by the third of June. But apparently something happened during his stay at Oxford having to do with Kim Philby, and it had everybody up and bothered. Once again, FANY officer Megan O'Patterson was ordered to see your father out, the way she had seen him in. Low key. Routine clerical. Make sure he gets on the train at Victoria Station to return to the continent. I don't know the details; my mother's letter does not go into any. What it does go into, though, in more detail than I would have wished, was what took place between the time she picked him up at Oxford on June first and the time she took him to catch the train out on June third. Care to guess?"

Gretchen shook her head. They squeezed hands.

"They had a tryst. A merry old romp, making love. Next she's taking him to church on Sunday, where he met her mother. Then back to the 'safe house,' so called, for more romping. Until early morning."

"Meeting her mother at church...?"

He nodded. "Aye. Then on 18 June, Megan O'Patterson, demobed from her service, boarded a ship at Liverpool to sail to Australia, where she married Sean Riley, formerly of the Royal Australian Air Force."

"Your father."

"Her husband. The journey was a torture to her. She was seasick from the Bay of Biscay on. She got off the ship at Capetown and wired Sean Riley, who suggested she book a flight to Australia, never mind the cost—actually, she had money saved—using a service just then becoming popular to cross the Indian Ocean. Sean met her in Perth, having come over from Sydney. They married right away. On the eighth of March, 1947, their first child was born, a couple of weeks early."

"You! I must remember the date. Eighth of March."

"Yes. The date is important. Now fast-forward through the forties, the fifties, and the sixties to 1976. By now my mother was back in London working as a clerk for MI6. She was quite ill, as it would turn out, and especially photosensitive. The bright sun of Australia was literally murder for her. Besides, my father was nearing retirement. My mother, in her early fifties, still had a chance to work toward a better pension. So she went to London, where I had been living for several years already. Tell me what Ian Frazer was doing in 1976."

"Oh my God, it was a terrible time. My mother had died in the plane crash the previous fall; my brother Jim had disappeared from his post-graduate studies in Germany; my father, depressed and anxious, flew to Germany to see what had happened to Jim. We were all very worried."

"Right. In that envelope from my mother there is a magazine clipping about that plane crash, naming some of the victims. Your mother's name was mentioned as the wife of anthropologist Ian Frazer at UCLA. My mother sent him a condolence note. In the note she mentioned a word that only he would understand: farthing."

"Far—what?"

"Farthing, the smallest coin in British money. It's not used anymore. And Ian Frazer understood. He called her from Germany. There is a transcript, a word-by-word log of their conversation in the envelope. I'll show you tomorrow."

"What are you telling me?"

"That they met again. Ian went to London, hoping for help in his son's disappearance. You probably know that."

"Yes. After the fact. We would have been even more worried had we known that he hooked up with British intelligence again."

"Apparently he was successful. He and my mother met in London. Peter Allard was in the party. Ian buggered off to look for his son behind the Iron Curtain. He found him and returned showing a great deal of luck and pluck. On his way home to America, he stopped off in Paris, where he met—whom, do you guess?"

"Your mother?"

"Yes. My mother was seeing a specialist for her disease. It was lupus, the systemic kind. Slowly but inevitably fatal. She needed him by her side. There is a lot in her writing about how wonderful your father was and how much she still loved him. They spent the night in the same hotel room. They did not make love, so she stated, underlined. Nor did she—here comes the kicker—tell him the truth."

"The truth? About her disease?"

"No, he knew about the disease. He was there to buck her up, fine fellow that he was."

"The way you say that, it doesn't sound very complimentary, Martin."

"That's where you're wrong. She kept him in the dark to the end. If I sound sarcastic, it's because I'm shocked."

"About what?" Somehow Gretchen was afraid to hear the answer.

"What my mother didn't tell him, then and didn't tell anyone until her confession to Peter Allard, is that Ian Frazer was the father of her first-born son."

"Her first-born son, that's—Martin, that's you, isn't it?"

He did not reply. In the dark she heard him breathe heavily, and she took pity on him. She stroked his face with her right hand, pressing his hand with her other. "Shh," she soothed. "We'll talk about this in the morning. Come, let's be close and try to sleep. By daylight everything looks better." She kissed him. "Martin, I'm yours and you are mine. Nothing can change that."

They awoke when the maid knocked on the door. Gretchen got up first, grabbed a towel, and went to the door. She told the maid to come back later, picked up the paper, and closed the door. She peeked at the bed. Martin was on his back, his arm over his eyes, shielding them from the bright sunlight that streamed through the window. He made no effort to speak or get up. Tiptoeing to the bathroom, Gretchen decided to let him be. She drew a bath.

Later, when both had made their morning ablutions, their breakfast had been rolled in and served, and they had taken their place at the table, it was impossible to avoid the heavy subject of their midnight conversation.

Martin half smiled when he spoke, but he was half sad as well. "I suppose there's only one way to put it? We're half-brother and half-sister."

Gretchen nodded. "If your mother's letter is really a confession and not the fantasy of a dying woman."

"Oh, I'm sure she was sane and lucid when she wrote it. I've been told that I was early, by nearly a month, and was rather small. Five and a half pounds. She mentioned the wartime nutritional problems."

"Do you think your father knew?"

"Sean Riley, you mean? Well, he is and was my father. He loved me and brought me up, and I love him still. No, I'm sure he didn't know. He'd have been very unforgiving. There wouldn't have been any further Rileys. My mother knew that. She kept her secret well."

Gretchen shook her head. "This is such a pity. My father was the kind of man who was very emotional about love and marriage. When he fell in love, he'd love with all his heart and mind, and all his loyalty. I'm sure his affair with your mother was like that, not a 'tryst,' as you put it last night. Or were those your mother's words?"

"Mine. But it changes nothing. They had an affair."

"Wouldn't they have used birth control if they were serious about one another?"

"My mother was a strict Catholic. Absolutely not. That would be piling sin on sin. No, they—or certainly she—went in to it with eyes open. They trusted their luck."

"Lucky she was, having you. My father never knew, I'm sure."

"He didn't. In her letter she makes it a point in her letter of saying that she couldn't bring herself to tell him at their last meeting in Paris."

"But she did write this confession. She couldn't have known then that my father would never hear about it. Perhaps in a roundabout way she wanted him to know, but only after her death."

"I believe I am the recipient she had in mind. And now, thirteen years later, I do know. Ian Frazer is my biological father. And I am in a tryst with his daughter." He gave one of his short laughs.

"Martin, you have to stop using that word! Ours is not a *tryst*, nor was theirs. Please!"

"It's not a bad word, actually. It's what lovers do secretly."

They fell quiet, each buttering some toast and poking at their eggs.

Martin looked up. "Two questions come to mind having to do with the real world, the here and now. One: What do I tell Fiona? And two: Where does that leave us, you and me?"

"Regarding Fiona, I can only give you my opinion. You'll have to be the final judge."

He nodded. "Agreed. What is your opinion?"

"It's a question, I suppose: Why does she have to know?"

"Because I won't lie to her."

"Not telling the whole story isn't really lying. If she were my daughter, I would say that my mother's deathbed confession was very personal and somewhat embarrassing, and that to honor her memory I have decided to let it be and destroy the letter."

"Fiona would still ask why."

"And I'd still be firm, closing the subject. It's really not any of her business. She knows that. And in the end she won't mind."

"Hmm." He stroked his mustache. "Question number two: What about us? Brother and sister? How can we be man and wife?"

"There my position is much firmer." She smiled at him. "We are half-siblings, brought up worlds apart, meeting in middle age. We didn't know about one another, we did not fall in love for incestuous reasons, and we will not procreate. There. End of problem."

"I admire your inventive intelligence. It's undoubtedly what got you through all those close calls this past year. Please, this is not a compliment. No, I admire that. It's one of the reasons I love you and I want to share my life with you."

"Thank you, my darling." She was amused. "Of course, this discovery of your mother's 1985 letter changes nothing about us. Besides, how can we be sure she had her facts right? Her illness could have affected her mind, couldn't it? Here we are, taking her words as pure gospel."

"Her mind was lucid to the end. We'd besmirch her memory if we doubted her. I don't mind your skepticism, but for myself, I believe her. She loved Ian Frazer, and I'm her love child. Of course, I agree with you, I can't go around saying that to all and sundry. People would smirk and laugh, and that, too, would besmirch her memory. So, I'll go along with your suggestion that we destroy the letter and talk to no one about what it really contained."

"Good." Gretchen nodded her consent.

"There remains one question: You and I do know. How do we react?"

"It doesn't bother me. In my family I already have a half-brother, a stepsister, a stepmother. Now I have another half-brother. Welcome to the Frazer bunch."

He had to laugh now. "Fascinating. I hope to meet all of them. As in-laws. That is, we will get married, won't we?"

She laughed too. "In church? What will you tell the monsignor?"

"The same thing I'll tell Fiona if she asks."

"No problem with the Lord?"

"'Man seeth what is before the eyes. The Lord looketh upon the heart.' Samuel."

"And your heart is pure."

"I'm content to let the Lord decide that."

Gretchen got up and came around to him. He rose and met her. They embraced. "I shall walk to that alter with you, Martin, my love."

They hugged each other closely, swaying, Martin nuzzling her neck, Gretchen responding by kissing his cheek. They were both deeply moved. Martin told her he thought he'd never find love again. It made her cry when she said that was true for her, too.

Later, in the bathroom, they shredded into small pieces every bit of paper that had been in the Allard envelope and flushed it all down the toilet. The envelope itself they tore into quarters and dropped in the wastebasket. Done. Gone. They shook hands on it.

They met Fiona at the station the next morning. She had had a wonderful time in Melbourne and couldn't stop talking about it. They decided that the smart thing to do was to drive out to the airport, check her in for her flight, and then have lunch there.

It worked out well, not having to worry about traffic and such. At the airport Fiona checked her bag through and got her boarding pass plus guest passes for the frequent flyer lounge. She grinned when she came back to Riley and Gretchen. "Lookee here! Lounge admission for me, and for me mum an' dad too!"

There was more. When they were seated, in a corner quieter than others, she produced two small, nicely wrapped parcels and gave them to her father and to Gretchen. She said open them later, at home.

"Oh, aren't you nice!" Gretchen exclaimed. "Thank you so much!"

"It's her birthday today, over where she's from," said Riley.

Fiona was surprised. "Really? The thirty-first of January? How old, may one ask?" Instantly her hand flew to her lips for having said "old."

Gretchen laughed. "One may. Fifty."

"Actually," laughed Riley, always a stickler for accuracy, "Gretchen's birthday is the thirtieth, which is what it is now, over where she's from."

It called for a toast. Martin went and rounded up three drinks, which he brought back in plastic cups. "Whiskey. Single malt. Cheers!"

Cheers it was. They looked at each other, smiling quietly.

Fiona asked the question that was on her mind. "When are you coming to England, Gretchen? Any date yet?"

"Not yet," Gretchen replied. "As a matter of fact," she turned to Riley, for this would be news to him, "I've decided to stay here."

"Have you?" Fiona was astonished. "What happened to all the urge to be with your children, to be reunited with your family?"

"That hasn't changed, but my priorities have. Martin and I have decided to marry. You're the first to know."

"Really!" Fiona wrung her hands in mock exasperation. "I leave you alone for two days, and look what happens!"

Riley took Gretchen's hand. "Yes. We shall marry."

"And that means we'll tackle together whatever it is that comes at us. I couldn't just fly off to England, try to link up with my family, and expect Martin to sit here, waiting patiently for my return." When neither of the two responded to that, she added, "I mean, the genie is out of the bottle, anyway. The problem exists, whether here or there. In which case, I prefer to deal with it from here, with Martin."

"It's a wonderful, generous decision, Gretchen, my love."

Fiona shook her head. "Forgive me, but did you just cook that up? It has a kind of cuckooish ring to it. What am I to do about contacting George-boy with all the finesse of an MI6 operation?"

"Nothing has changed there," Gretchen said, "except the time element and my immediate presence."

"Let's keep it in abeyance until you're back home, Fi," Martin added. "We'll confer by telephone."

"Besides," Gretchen added, "it occurs to me that it is just as easy for my sons to visit me here. In fact, easier. Particularly as I have no intention of hurrying back to the States. My home is here now."

Martin was again taken by surprise. "Thank you for saying that!"

Fiona was still working on the first part. "So, you're getting married. Will there be a wedding? Church bells, champagne, bridesmaids, a best man?"

Gretchen and Riley looked at each other. It was clear they hadn't thought about this, either. "Details, Fi," he said. "We'll keep you posted. In any case, it won't be anything elaborate."

"Of course, we'd want you present, Fiona!" Gretchen said. "You'll be my bridesmaid, won't you?"

"Am I expected to show up here? When? A month? Two? With Georgie in tow to give you away?" She half groaned.

"That would be lovely," Gretchen smiled at her. "But with or without anyone in tow, I want you by my side. With all my heart!"

Riley said, "Fiona, we're flying by the seat of our pants here. All we know is that we want to live our life together from now on. And we want you to remain part of it."

Fiona shook her head in disbelief, but grinned at both of them. "Father, Gretchen, you're a pair, all right. Congratulations!"

Later, when Gretchen had excused herself to go to the washroom, Fiona had her father to herself. "I can't say I blame you. This woman is good for you, Father. And you for her. A good match. I can see that."

"A qualified approval. Thank you."

"Oh, come on. I'm happy for you." She pulled him over to her and gave him a kiss. "This is the break you've been waiting for."

"You might say that to Gretchen, too, Fi."

"I will." She sat back. "About Gram's letter to Peter Allard—I suppose you didn't have a chance to look at it?"

"Yes, I did." He sighed. "It was not a pleasure, I assure you."

"What's the gist of it? Can you tell me?"

"Well, it was a sort of confession. You know Gram wrote this four months before she died. Peter kept it until he died. In my opinion, he should have destroyed it. Perhaps he intended to, but forgot about it."

"What kind of confession? An *affaire d'amour*?"

"I suppose you could call it that. It would have been better all around if it had been forgotten."

"Will you let me see it some day?"

"Fiona, I did what Peter should have done: I destroyed it."

"Father! That could have waited until I had seen it!"

"No, it couldn't. Look, my mother unburdened herself of something that had clouded her conscience. She confessed—not only to Peter, I'm sure—and was forgiven. It should have gone to her grave with her. I had no choice but to do that for her now. Let her rest in peace."

Fiona sighed and looked down at her hands. Then she said, "One final question: In this affair—was Peter the object?"

"No. It was someone you don't know, someone I didn't know. It took place a long time ago. Let's leave it at that, Fiona." His tone was firm.

Fiona nodded. "Does Gretchen know?"

"She hasn't read it, but I told her everything. She agrees that it's best not to talk about it further."

A little later Gretchen returned. "What've you been talking about? You look upset, Fiona. Has it to do with me?"

Fiona grinned at her father in a conspiratorial way: "Everything, nowadays, has to do with you. But no, this one was a typical father-daughter chat. Not to worry."

"I'm so relieved," Gretchen smiled.

Fiona asked, "I do have a question, about your son George—is he a true-blue, straight-arrow sort of chap? Or a bit of a rogue? Do I have to be on my guard with him?"

"My goodness, Fi—I don't think so. He has a girl, last I heard. All he's interested in is cars, automobiles, how they're made; how they run is all the running he cares about."

"Fine fellow. I think I'll go look him up."

Martin was glad for the break. He made it a point to consult his watch. "I think it's time we took you to your gate, Fi, my dear."

They left the lounge, the women walking briskly arm in arm, with Martin trailing behind, carrying Fiona's bag and coat. At the gate it was an emotional farewell, Fiona saying more than once that she'd probably be back before year's end, wouldn't she, and Gretchen telling her how lucky she felt getting such a wonderful daughter, and never mind the "step-". Riley didn't say much, but gave his daughter a huge hug, then turned away as if to check the traffic out on the tarmac.

In the car, slowed by traffic that was inching along, Riley turned to Gretchen. "There she goes, our Fiona. Things have been set in motion. Soon you won't be an exile anymore, Gret."

"You were an exile in London, weren't you? Or are you an exile here?"

"I'm British, and I can be that in England or in Australia. Your situation is different. You can marry me, but that won't make you British, will it?"

"Would you want me to try?"

"No, frankly, I wouldn't. This episode reinforced my conviction that our goal ought to be bring you back to America, your country, if only for visits. You need to meet again with your family."

"Not without you. Definitely not without you, Martin."

"Aye. Thank you for saying that. I'll be by your side. For the immediate future, we have plenty to keep us busy arranging our own life together. But all along we'll have to think about how we can bring you back to your people. We need to close that circle."

Gretchen spontaneously leaned over and gave him a smacking kiss on the cheek. He laughed. "Thank you. I have to get used to your outbursts of affection. I've gone a long time without such wifely favors."

"So have I, believe me. Husbandly, in my case. How did Fiona put it? We're a pair, all right!"

"Let's ask Miss Adelaide for tea, what do you say?"

"When we are home, yes."

It did not occur to Gretchen to wonder how naturally that word came to her: Home.